DORIS LESSING, winner of the Nobel Prize for Literature 2007, is one of the most celebrated and distinguished writers of recent decades. A Companion of Honour and a Companion of Literature, she has been awarded the David Cohen Memorial Prize for British Literature, Spain's Prince of Asturias Prize, the International Catalunya Award and the S.T. Dupont Golden PEN Award for a Lifetime's Distinguished Service to Literature, as well as a host of other international awards. She lives in north London.

By the same author

NOVELS
The Grass is Singing
The Golden Notebook
Briefing for a Descent into Hell
The Summer Before the Dark
Memoirs of a Survivor
Diary of a Good Neighbour
If the Old Could . . .
The Good Terrorist
The Fifth Child
Playing the Game
   (illustrated by Charlie Adlard)
Love, Again
Mara and Dann
The Fifth Child
Ben, in the World
The Sweetest Dream
The Story of General Dann and Mara's
   Daughter, Griot and the Snow Dog
The Cleft

'Canopus in Argos: Archives' series
Re: Colonised Planet 5, Shikasta
The Marriages Between Zones
   Three, Four, and Five
The Sirian Experiments
The Making of the Representative for
   Planet 8
Documents Relating to the Sentimental
   Agents in the Volyen Empire

'Children of Violence' novel-sequence
Martha Quest
A Proper Marriage
A Ripple from the Storm
Landlocked
The Four-Gated City

OPERAS
The Marriages Between Zones Three,
   Four and Five (Music by Philip Glass)
The Making of the representative for
   Planet 8 (Music by Philip Glass)

SHORT STORIES
Five
The Habit of Loving
A Man and Two Women
The Story of a Non-Marrying Man
   and Other Stories
Winter in July
The Black Madonna
This Was the Old Chief's Country
   (Collected African Stories, Vol. 1)
The Sun Between Their Feet
   (Collected African Stories, Vol. 2)
To Room Nineteen
   (Collected Stories, Vol. 1)
The Temptation of Jack Orkney
   (Collected Stories, Vol. 2)
London Observed
The Old Age of El Magnifico
Particularly Cats
Rufus the Survivor
On Cats
The Grandmothers

POETRY
Fourteen Poems

DRAMA
Each His Own Wilderness
Play with a Tiger
The Singing Door

NON-FICTION
In Pursuit of the English
Going Home
A Small Personal Voice
Prisons We Choose to Live Inside
The Wind Blows Away Our Words
African Laughter
Time Bites

AUTOBIOGRAPHY
Under My Skin: Volume 1
Walking in the Shade: Volume 2

DORIS LESSING

This Was the Old Chief's Country

Collected African Stories
Volume One

Flamingo
An Imprint of HarperCollinsPublishers

Flamingo
An imprint of HarperCollins*Publishers*
77–85 Fulham Palace Road,
Hammersmith, London W6 8JB

Flamingo is a registered trade mark of
HarperCollins*Publishers* Limited

www.**fire**and**water**.com

A Flamingo Modern Classic 2003

7

Previously published in paperback by
Grafton 1979, Paladin 1992 and Flamingo 1994
First published in Great Britain by
Michael Joseph Ltd 1951

'Events in the Skies' first published in 1987 in *Granta*

Photograph of Doris Lessing © Chris Saunders 2002

ISBN 978 0 586 09113 5

Set in Times

Contents

BIOGRAPHICAL NOTE

This first volume of Doris Lessing's Collected African Stories was published in hardcover by Michael Joseph in 1973. Apart from 'A Home for the Highland Cattle', 'Eldorado' and 'The Antheap' which appeared in *Five* (Michael Joseph, 1953), and 'Events in the Skies' which was first published in *Granta* in 1987, all the other stories in this volume appeared in the first collection entitled *This Was the Old Chief's Country* (Michael Joseph, 1951). All these stories including five of those in *The Sun Between Their Feet*, the second volume of Collected African Stories, appeared in *African Stories* (Michael Joseph, 1964).

These stories have also appeared previously in paperback in the following editions: 'The Old Chief Mshlanga', 'A Sunrise on the Veld' and 'No Witchcraft for Sale' have appeared in *The Black Madonna*; the short novels 'A Home for the Highland Cattle', 'Eldorado' and 'The Antheap' are also published in *Five*; the rest of the stories in this volume appear in *Winter in July*.

Preface for the 1964 Collection

Most of these stories come from two earlier collections: *This Was the Old Chief's Country*, and *Five*. The first has been out of print for some time. Some of its stories are among my favourites, and I am happy to have them around again.

The stories an author likes are not necessarily those chosen by other people. This happens to every writer. Because I was brought up in Southern Africa (Southern Rhodesia) a part of my work has been set there, and the salience of the colour clash has made it inevitable that those aspects which reflect 'the colour problem' should have overshadowed the rest. When my first novel, *The Grass is Singing*, came out, there were few novels about Africa. That book, and my second, *This Was the Old Chief's Country*, were described by reviewers as about the colour problem . . . which is not how I see, or saw, them. But then, a decade ago, manifestations of race prejudice in Africa, terribly familiar to those of us who had to live with them, were still a surprise, apparently, to Britain. Or, to put it as cynically as some people feel it, indignation about the colour bar in Africa had not yet become part of the furniture of the progressive conscience. If people had been prepared to listen, two decades earlier, to the small, but shrill-enough, voices crying out for the world's attention, perhaps the present suffering in South Africa and Southern Rhodesia could have been prevented. Britain, who is responsible, became conscious of her responsibility too late; and now the tragedy must play itself slowly out. Meanwhile there are dozens of novels, stories, plays about what one happy reviewer called 'the colour bore'.

Writers brought up in Africa have many advantages — being at the centre of a modern battlefield; part of a society in rapid, dramatic change. But in a long run it can also be a handicap: to wake up every morning with one's eyes on a fresh evidence of inhumanity; to be reminded twenty times a day of injustice, and always the same brand of it, can be limiting. There are other things in living besides injustice, even for the victims of it. I know an African short-story writer whose gift is for satirical comedy, and he says that he has to remind himself, when he sits down to write, that 'as a human being he has the right to laugh'. Not only have white sympathizers criticized him for 'making comedy out of oppression', his compatriots do too. Yet I am sure that one day out of Africa will come a great comic novel to make the angels laugh, pressed as miraculously from the bitter savageries of the atrophy as was *Dead Souls*.

And while the cruelties of the white man towards the black man are among the heaviest counts in the indictment against humanity, colour prejudice is not our original fault, but only one aspect of the atrophy of the imagination that prevents us from seeing ourselves in every creature that breathes under the sun.

I believe that the chief gift from Africa to writers, white and black, is the continent itself, its presence which for some people is like an old fever, latent always in their blood; or like an old wound throbbing in the bones as the air changes. That is not a place to visit unless one chooses to be an exile ever afterwards from an inexplicable majestic silence lying just over the border of memory or of thought. Africa gives you the knowledge that man is a small creature, among other creatures, in a large landscape.

My favourites in *This Was the Old Chief's Country* are not necessarily those that have been most translated, which are *Little Tembi*, *The Old Chief Mshlanga*, and *No Witchcraft for Sale*. *A Sunrise on the Veld*, for instance, and *Winter in July* are both larger stories than the directly social ones.

These stories have in common that they are set in Africa, but that is all they have in common. For one thing, while the *Old Chief* was a collection of real short stories, *Five* is five long stories, almost short novels. A most enjoyable form this, to write, the long story, although of course there is no way of getting them printed out of book form. There is space in them to take one's time, to think aloud, to follow, for a paragraph or two, on a side-trail – none of which is possible in a real short story,

I hope these stories will be read with as much pleasure as I had in . . . but I mean it. I enjoy writing short stories very much, although fewer and fewer magazines print them, and for every twenty novel readers there is one who likes short stories. Some writers I know stopped writing short stories because, as they say, 'there is no market for them'. Others like myself, the addicts, go on, and I suspect would go on even if there really wasn't any home for them but a private drawer.

Preface for the 1973 Collection

The first clutch of short stories I wrote was called *This Was the Old Chief's Country*. Those stories, with three long ones from a collection called *Five*, make up Volume One of this new collection, which is again called *This Was the Old Chief's Country*. It is a title which is accommodating: after all, it can be said of all white-dominated Africa that it was – and indeed still is – the Old Chief's Country. So all the stories I write of a certain kind, I think of as belonging under that heading: tales about white people, sometimes about black people, living in a landscape that not so very long ago was settled by black tribes, living in complex societies that the white people are only just beginning to study, let alone understand. Truly to understand, we have to lose the arrogance that is the white man's burden, to stop feeling superior, and this is only just beginning to happen now.

In the last decade or two, all over the world, the aggressive, thrusting, technical societies that killed, or starved out, or infected with disease, or allowed to die out from ignorance and lack of imagination the tribal societies they supplanted, have started to understand their responsibility for what has been lost. Australia and New Zealand, Canada and the United States, Brazil, Africa – it is always the same story. The white men came, saw, coveted, conquered. The children and grand-children of these invaders condemn their parents, wish they could repudiate their own history. But that is not so easy.

I am not able to write about what has been lost, which was and still is recorded orally. As a writer that is my biggest regret, as it is of all the white writers from Africa I have known. The tribal life that was broken seems now to have had more real dignity, more responsibility for what is important in people –

their self-respect, more tolerance of individuality, than our way of living has. The breakup of that society, the time of chaos that followed it, is as dramatic a story as any; but if you are a white writer, it is a story that you are told by others.

All the stories here are set in a society which is more short-lived than most: white-dominated Africa cannot last very long. But looking around the world now, there isn't a way of living anywhere that doesn't change and dissolve like clouds as you watch.

Doris Lessing
January 1972

They were good, the years of ranging the bush over her father's farm which, like every white farm, was largely unused, broken only occasionally by small patches of cultivation. In between, nothing but trees, the long sparse grass, thorn and cactus and gully, grass and outcrop and thorn. And a jutting piece of rock which had been thrust up from the warm soil of Africa unimaginable eras of time ago, washed into hollows and whorls by sun and wind that had travelled so many thousands of miles of space and bush, would hold the weight of a small girl whose eyes were sightless for anything but a pale willowed river, a pale gleaming castle – a small girl singing: 'Out flew the web and floated wide, the mirror cracked from side to side . . .'

Pushing her way through the green aisles of the mealie stalks, the leaves arching like cathedrals veined with sunlight far overhead, with the packed red earth underfoot, a fine lace of red-starred witchweed would summon up a black bent figure croaking premonitions: the Northern witch, bred of cold Northern forests, would stand before her among the mealie fields, and it was the mealie fields that faded and fled, leaving her among the gnarled roots of an oak, snow falling thick and soft and white, the woodcutter's fire glowing red welcome through crowding tree trunks.

A white child, opening its eyes curiously on a sun-suffused landscape, a gaunt and violent landscape, might be supposed to accept it as her own, to take the msasa trees and the thorn trees as familiars, to feel her blood running free and responsive to the swing of the seasons.

This child could not see a msasa tree, or the thorn, for what they were. Her books held tales of alien fairies, her rivers ran slow and peaceful, and she knew the shape of the leaves of an ash or an oak, the names of the little creatures that lived in English streams, when the words 'the veld' meant strangeness, though she could remember nothing else.

Because of this, for many years, it was the veld that seemed unreal; the sun was a foreign sun, and the wind spoke a strange language.

The black people on the farm were as remote as the trees and the rocks. They were an amorphous black mass, mingling and thinning and massing like tadpoles, faceless, who existed merely to serve, to say 'Yes, Baas,' take their money and go. They changed season by season, moving from one farm to the next, according to their outlandish needs, which one did not have to understand, coming from perhaps hundreds of miles North or East, passing on after a few months – where? Perhaps even as far away as the fabled gold mines of Johannesburg, where the pay was so much better than the few shillings a month and the double handful of mealie meal twice a day which they earned in that part of Africa.

The child was taught to take them for granted: the servants in the house would come running a hundred yards to pick up a book if she dropped it. She was called 'Nkosikaas' – Chieftainess, even by the black children her own age.

Later, when the farm grew too small to hold her curiosity, she carried a gun in the crook of her arm and wandered miles a day, from vlei to vlei, from kopje to kopje, accompanied by two dogs: the dogs and the gun were an armour against fear. Because of them she never felt fear.

If a native came into sight along the kaffir paths half a mile away, the dogs would flush him up a tree as if he were a bird. If he expostulated (in his uncouth language which was by itself ridiculous) that was cheek. If one was in a good mood, it could be a matter for laughing. Otherwise one passed on, hardly glancing at the angry man in the tree.

On the rare occasions when white children met together they could amuse themselves by hailing a passing native in order to make a buffoon of him; they could set the dogs on him and watch him run; they could tease a small black child as if he were a puppy – save that they would not throw stones and sticks at a dog without a sense of guilt.

Later still, certain questions presented themselves in the child's mind; and because the answers were not easy to accept, they were silenced by an even greater arrogance of manner.

It was even impossible to think of the black people who worked about the house as friends, for if she talked to one of them, her mother would come running anxiously: 'Come away; you mustn't talk to natives.'

It was this instilled consciousness of danger, of something unpleasant, that made it easy to laugh out loud, crudely, if a servant made a mistake in his English or if he failed to understand an order – there is a certain kind of laughter that is fear, afraid of itself.

One evening, when I was about fourteen, I was walking down the side of a mealie field that had been newly ploughed, so that the great red clods showed fresh and tumbling to the vlei beyond, like a choppy red sea; it was that hushed and listening hour, when the birds send long sad calls from tree to tree, and all the colours of earth and sky and leaf are deep and golden. I had my rifle in the curve of my arm, and the dogs were at my heels.

In front of me, perhaps a couple of hundred yards away, a group of three Africans came into sight around the side of a big antheap. I whistled the dogs close in to my skirts and let the gun swing in my hand, and advanced, waiting for them to move aside, off the path, in respect for my passing. But they came on steadily, and the dogs looked up at me for the command to chase. I was angry. It was 'cheek' for a native not to stand off a path, the moment he caught sight of you.

In front walked an old man, stooping his weight on to a stick, his hair grizzled white, a dark red blanket slung over his shoulders like a cloak. Behind him came two young men, carrying bundles of pots, assegais, hatchets.

The group was not a usual one. They were not natives seeking work. These had an air of dignity, of quietly following their own purpose. It was the dignity that checked my tongue. I walked quietly on, talking softly to the growling dogs, till I was ten paces away. Then the old man stopped, drawing his blanket close.

"Morning, Nkosikaas,' he said, using the customary greeting for any time of the day.

'Good morning,' I said. 'Where are you going?' My voice was a little truculent.

The old man spoke in his own language, then one of the young men stepped forward politely and said in careful English: 'My Chief travels to see his brothers beyond the river.'

A Chief! I thought, understanding the pride that made the old man stand before me like an equal – more than an equal, for he showed courtesy, and I showed none.

The old man spoke again, wearing dignity like an inherited garment, still standing ten paces off, flanked by his entourage, not looking at me (that would have been rude) but directing his eyes somewhere over my head at the trees.

'You are the little Nkosikaas from the farm of Baas Jordan?'

'That's right,' I said.

'Perhaps your father does not remember,' said the interpreter for the old man, 'but there was an affair with some goats. I remember seeing you when you were . . .' The young man held his hand at knee level and smiled.

We all smiled.

'What is your name?' I asked.

'This is Chief Mshlanga,' said the young man.

'I will tell my father that I met you,' I said.

The old man said: 'My greetings to your father, little Nkosikaas.'

'Good morning,' I said politely, finding the politeness difficult, from lack of use.

"Morning, little Nkosikaas,' said the old man, and stood aside to let me pass.

I went by, my gun hanging awkwardly, the dogs sniffing and growling, cheated of their favourite game of chasing natives like animals.

Not long afterwards I read in an old explorer's book the phrase: 'Chief Mshlanga's country'. It went like this: 'Our destination was Chief Mshlanga's country, to the north of the river; and it was our desire to ask his permission to prospect for gold in his territory.'

The phrase 'ask his permission' was so extraordinary to a

white child, brought up to consider all natives as things to use, that it revived those questions, which could not be suppressed: they fermented slowly in my mind.

On another occasion one of those old prospectors who still move over Africa looking for neglected reefs, with their hammers and tents, and pans for sifting gold from crushed rock, came to the farm and, in talking of the old days, used that phrase again: 'This was the Old Chief's country.' 'It stretched from those mountains over there way back to the river, hundreds of miles of country.' That was his name for our district: 'The Old Chief's Country'; he did not use our name for it – a new phrase which held no implication of usurped ownership.

As I read more books about the time when this part of Africa was opened up, not much more than fifty years before, I found Old Chief Mshlanga had been a famous man, known to all the explorers and prospectors. But then he had been young; or maybe it was his father or uncle they spoke of – I never found out.

During that year I met him several times in the part of the farm that was traversed by natives moving over the country. I learned that the path up the side of the big red field where the birds sang was the recognized highway for migrants. Perhaps I even haunted it in the hope of meeting him: being greeted by him, the exchange of courtesies, seemed to answer the questions that troubled me.

Soon I carried a gun in a different spirit; I used it for shooting food and not to give me confidence. And now the dogs learned better manners. When I saw a native approaching, we offered and took greetings; and slowly that other landscape in my mind faded, and my feet struck directly on the African soil, and I saw the shapes of tree and hill clearly, and the black people moved back, as it were, out of my life: it was as if I stood aside to watch a slow intimate dance of landscape and men, a very old dance, whose steps I could not learn.

But I thought: this is my heritage, too; I was bred here; it is my country as well as the black man's country; and there is plenty of room for all of us, without elbowing each other off the pavements and roads.

It seemed it was only necessary to let free that respect I felt when I was talking with old Chief Mshlanga, to let both black and white people meet gently, with tolerance for each other's differences: it seemed quite easy.

Then, one day, something new happened. Working in our house as servants were always three natives: cook, houseboy, garden boy. They used to change as the farm natives changed: staying for a few months, then moving on to a new job, or back home to their kraals. They were thought of as 'good' or 'bad' natives; which meant: how did they behave as servants? Were they lazy, efficient, obedient, or disrespectful? If the family felt good-humoured, the phrase was: 'What can you expect from raw black savages?' If we were angry, we said: 'These damned niggers, we would be much better off without them.'

One day, a white policeman was on his rounds of the district, and he said laughingly: 'Did you know you have an important man in your kitchen?'

'What!' exclaimed my mother sharply. 'What do you mean?'

'A Chief's son.' The policeman seemed amused. 'He'll boss the tribe when the old man dies.'

'He'd better not put on a Chief's son act with me,' said my mother.

When the policeman left, we looked with different eyes at our cook: he was a good worker, but he drank too much at week-ends – that was how we knew him.

He was a tall youth, with very black skin, like black polished metal, his tightly-growing black hair parted white man's fashion at one side, with a metal comb from the store stuck into it; very polite, very distant, very quick to obey an order. Now it had been pointed out, we said: 'Of course, you can see. Blood always tells.'

My mother became strict with him now she knew about his birth and prospects. Sometimes, when she lost her temper, she would say: 'You aren't the Chief yet, you know.' And he would answer her very quietly, his eyes on the ground: 'Yes, Nkosikaas.'

One afternoon he asked for a whole day off, instead of the customary half-day, to go home next Sunday.

'How can you go home in one day?'

'It will take me half an hour on my bicycle,' he explained.

I watched the direction he took; and the next day I went off to look for this kraal; I understood he must be Chief Mshlanga's successor: there was no other kraal near enough our farm.

Beyond our boundaries on that side the country was new to me. I followed unfamiliar paths past kopjes that till now had been part of the jagged horizon, hazed with distance. This was Government land, which had never been cultivated by white men; at first I could not understand why it was that it appeared, in merely crossing the boundary, I had entered a completely fresh type of landscape. It was a wide green valley, where a small river sparkled, and vivid water-birds darted over the rushes. The grass was thick and soft to my calves, the trees stood tall and shapely.

I was used to our farm, whose hundreds of acres of harsh eroded soil bore trees that had been cut for the mine furnaces and had grown thin and twisted, where the cattle had dragged the grass flat, leaving innumerable criss-crossing trails that deepened each season into gullies, under the force of the rains. This country had been left untouched, save for prospectors whose picks had struck a few sparks from the surface of the rocks as they wandered by; and for migrant natives whose passing had left, perhaps, a charred patch on the trunk of a tree where their evening fire had nestled.

It was very silent: a hot morning with pigeons cooing throatily, the midday shadows lying dense and thick with clear yellow spaces of sunlight between and in all that wide green park-like valley, not a human soul but myself.

I was listening to the quick regular tapping of a woodpecker when slowly a chill feeling seemed to grow up from the small of my back to my shoulders, in a constricting spasm like a shudder, and at the roots of my hair a tingling sensation began and ran down over the surface of my flesh, leaving me goose-fleshed and cold, though I was damp with sweat. Fever? I thought; then uneasily, turned to look over my shoulder; and realized suddenly that this was fear. It was extraordinary, even humiliating. It was a new fear. For all the years I had walked by myself over this country I had never known a moment's uneasiness; in the beginning because I had been supported by a gun and the dogs, then because I had learnt an easy friendliness for the Africans I might encounter.

I had read of this feeling, how the bigness and silence of Africa, under the ancient sun, grows dense and takes shape in the mind, till even the birds seem to call menacingly, and a deadly spirit comes out of the trees and the rocks. You move warily, as if your very passing disturbs something old and evil, something dark and big and angry that might suddenly rear and strike from behind. You look at groves of entwined trees, and picture the animals that might be lurking there; you look at the river running slowly, dropping from level to level through the vlei, spreading into pools where at night the buck come to drink, and the crocodiles rise and drag them by their soft noses into underwater caves. Fear possessed me. I found I was turning round and round, because of that shapeless menace behind me that might reach out and take me; I kept glancing at the files of kopjes which, seen from a different angle, seemed to change with every step so that even known landmarks, like a big mountain that had sentinelled my world since I first became conscious of it, showed an unfamiliar sunlit valley among its foothills. I did not know where I was. I was lost. Panic seized me. I found I was spinning round and round, staring anxiously at this tree and that, peering up at the sun which appeared to have moved into an eastern slant, shedding the sad yellow light of sunset. Hours must have passed! I looked at my watch and found that this state of meaningless terror had lasted perhaps ten minutes.

The point was that it was meaningless. I was not ten miles from home: I had only to take my way back along the valley to find myself at the fence; away among the foothills of the kopjes gleamed the roof of a neighbour's house, and a couple of hours walking would reach it. This was the sort of fear that contracts the flesh of a dog at night and sets him howling at the full moon. It had nothing to do with what I thought or felt; and I was more disturbed by the fact that I could become its victim than of the physical sensation itself: I walked steadily on, quietened, in a divided mind, watching my own pricking nerves and apprehensive glances from side to side with a disgusted amusement. Deliberately I set myself to think of this village I was seeking, and what I should do when I entered it – if I could find it, which was doubtful, since I was walking aimlessly and it might be anywhere in the hundreds of thousands of acres of bush that stretched about me. With my mind on that village, I realized that a new sensation was added to the fear: loneliness. Now such a terror of isolation invaded me that I could hardly walk; and if it were not that I came over the crest of a small rise and saw a village below me, I should have turned and gone home. It was a cluster of thatched huts in a clearing among trees. There were neat patches of mealies and pumpkins and millet, and cattle grazed under some trees at a distance. Fowls scratched among the huts, dogs lay sleeping on the grass, and goats frisked a kopje that jutted up beyond a tributary of the river lying like an enclosing arm round the village.

As I came close I saw the huts were lovingly decorated with patterns of yellow and red and ochre mud on the walls; and the thatch was tied in place with plaits of straw.

This was not at all like our farm compound, a dirty and neglected place, a temporary home for migrants who had no roots in it.

And now I did not know what to do next. I called a small black boy, who was sitting on a log playing a stringed gourd, quite naked except for the strings of blue beads round his neck, and said: 'Tell the Chief I am here.' The child stuck his thumb in his mouth and stared shyly back at me.

For minutes I shifted my feet on the edge of what seemed a deserted village, till at last the child scuttled off, and then some women came. They were draped in bright cloths, with brass glinting in their ears and on their arms. They also stared, silently; then turned to chatter among themselves.

I said again: 'Can I see Chief Mshlanga?' I saw they caught the name; they did not understand what I wanted. I did not understand myself.

At last I walked through them and came past the huts and saw a clearing under a big shady tree, where a dozen old men sat cross-legged on the ground, talking. Chief Mshlanga was leaning back against the tree, holding a gourd in his hand, from which he had been drinking. When he saw me, not a muscle of his face moved, and I could see he was not pleased: perhaps he was afflicted with my own shyness, due to being unable to find the right forms of courtesy for the occasion. To meet me, on our own farm, was one thing; but I should not have come here. What had I expected? I could not join them socially: the thing was unheard of. Bad enough that I, a white girl, should be walking the veld alone as a white man might: and in this part of the bush where only Government officials had the right to move.

Again I stood, smiling foolishly, while behind me stood the groups of brightly-clad, chattering women, their faces alert with curiosity and interest, and in front of me sat the old men, with old lined faces, their eyes guarded, aloof. It was a village of ancients and children and women. Even the two young men who knelt beside the Chief were not those I had seen with him previously: the young men were all away working on the white men's farms and mines, and the Chief must depend on relatives who were temporarily on holiday for his attendants.

'The small white Nkosikaas is far from home,' remarked the old man at last.

'Yes,' I agreed, 'it is far.' I wanted to say: 'I have come to pay you a friendly visit, Chief Mshlanga.' I could not say it. I might now be feeling an urgent helpless desire to get to know these men and women as people, to be accepted by them as a friend, but the truth was I had set out in a spirit of curiosity: I had wanted to see the village that one day our cook, the reserved and obedient young man who got drunk on Sundays, would one day rule over.

'The child of Nkosi Jordan is welcome,' said Chief Mshlanga.

'Thank you,' I said, and could think of nothing more to say. There was a silence, while the flies rose and began to buzz around my head; and the wind shook a little in the thick green tree that spread its branches over the old men.

'Good morning,' I said at last. 'I have to return now to my home.'

''Morning, little Nkosikaas,' said Chief Mshlanga.

I walked away from the indifferent village, over the rise past the staring amber-eyed goats, down through the tall stately trees into the great rich green valley where the river meandered

and the pigeons cooed tales of plenty and the woodpecker
tapped softly.

The fear had gone; the loneliness had set into stiff-necked
stoicism; there was now a queer hostility in the landscape, a
cold, hard, sullen indomitability that walked with me, as strong
as a wall, as intangible as smoke; it seemed to say to me: you
walk here as a destroyer. I went slowly homewards, with an
empty heart: I had learned that if one cannot call a country to
heel like a dog, neither can one dismiss the past with a smile in
an easy gush of feeling, saying: I could not help it, I am also a
victim.

I only saw Chief Mshlanga once again.

One night my father's big red land was trampled down by
small sharp hooves, and it was discovered that the culprits were
goats from Chief Mshlanga's kraal. This had happened once
before, years ago.

My father confiscated all the goats. Then he sent a message
to the old Chief that if he wanted them he would have to pay
for the damage.

He arrived at our house at the time of sunset one evening,
looking very old and bent now, walking stiffly under his regally-
draped blanket, leaning on a big stick. My father sat himself
down in his big chair below the steps of the house; the old man
squatted carefully on the ground before him, flanked by his two
young men.

The palaver was long and painful, because of the bad English
of the young man who interpreted, and because my father
could not speak dialect, but only kitchen kaffir.

From my father's point of view, at least two hundred pounds'
worth of damage had been done to the crop. He knew he could
get the money from the old man. He felt he was entitled to
keep the goats. As for the old Chief, he kept repeating angrily:
'Twenty goats! My people cannot lose twenty goats! We are
not rich, like the Nkosi Jordan, to lose twenty goats at once.'

My father did not think of himself as rich, but rather as very
poor. He spoke quickly and angrily in return, saying that the
damage done meant a great deal to him, and that he was
entitled to the goats.

At last it grew so heated that the cook, the Chief's son, was called from the kitchen to be interpreter, and now my father spoke fluently in English, and our cook translated rapidly so that the old man could understand how very angry my father was. The young man spoke without emotion, in a mechanical way, his eyes lowered, but showing how he felt his position by a hostile uncomfortable set of the shoulders.

It was now in the late sunset, the sky a welter of colours, the birds singing their last songs, and the cattle, lowing peacefully, moving past us towards their sheds for the night. It was the hour when Africa is most beautiful; and here was this pathetic, ugly scene, doing no one any good.

At last my father stated finally: 'I'm not going to argue about it. I am keeping the goats.'

The old Chief flashed back in his own language: 'That means that my people will go hungry when the dry season comes.'

'Go to the police, then,' said my father, and looked triumphant.

There was, of course, no more to be said.

The old man sat silent, his head bent, his hands dangling helplessly over his withered knees. Then he rose, the young men helping him, and he stood facing my father. He spoke once again, very stiffly; and turned away and went home to his village.

'What did he say?' asked my father of the young man, who laughed uncomfortably and would not meet his eyes.

'What did he say?' insisted my father.

Our cook stood straight and silent, his brows knotted together. Then he spoke. 'My father says: All this land, this land you call yours, is his land, and belongs to our people.'

Having made this statement, he walked off into the bush after his father, and we did not see him again.

Our next cook was a migrant from Nyasaland, with no expectations of greatness.

Next time the policeman came on his rounds he was told this story. He remarked: 'That kraal has no right to be there; it should have been moved long ago. I don't know why no one has done anything about it. I'll have a chat to the Native Commissioner next week. I'm going over for tennis on Sunday, anyway.'

Some time later we heard that Chief Mshlanga and his people had been moved two hundred miles east, to a proper native reserve: the Government land was going to be opened up for white settlement soon.

I went to see the village again, about a year afterwards. There was nothing there. Mounds of red mud, where the huts had been, had long swathes of rotting thatch over them, veined with the red galleries of the white ants. The pumpkin vines rioted everywhere, over the bushes, up the lower branches of trees so that the great golden balls rolled underfoot and dangled overhead: it was a festival of pumpkins. The bushes were crowding up, the new grass sprang vivid green.

The settler lucky enough to be allotted the lush warm valley (if he chose to cultivate this particular section) would find, suddenly, in the middle of a mealie field, the plants were growing fifteen feet tall, the weight of the cobs dragging at the stalks, and wonder what unsuspected vein of richness he had struck.

A Sunrise on the Veld

Every night that winter he said aloud into the dark of the pillow: Half past four! Half past four! till he felt his brain had gripped the words and held them fast. Then he fell asleep at once, as if a shutter had fallen; and lay with his face turned to the clock so that he could see it first thing when he woke.

It was half past four to the minute, every morning. Triumphantly pressing down the alarm-knob of the clock, which the dark half of his mind had outwitted, remaining vigilant all night and counting the hours as he lay relaxed in sleep, he huddled down for a last warm moment under the clothes, playing with the idea of lying abed for this once only. But he played with it for the fun of knowing that it was a weakness he could defeat without effort; just as he set the alarm each night for the delight of the moment when he woke and stretched his limbs, feeling the muscles tighten, and thought: Even my brain – even that! I can control every part of myself.

Luxury of warm rested body, with the arms and legs and fingers waiting like soldiers for a word of command! Joy of knowing that the precious hours were given to sleep voluntarily! – for he had once stayed awake three nights running, to prove that he could, and then worked all day, refusing even to admit that he was tired; and now sleep seemed to him a servant to be commanded and refused.

The boy stretched his frame full-length, touching the wall at his head with his hands, and the bedfoot with his toes; then he sprang out, like a fish leaping from water. And it was cold, cold.

He always dressed rapidly, so as to try and conserve his night-warmth till the sun rose two hours later; but by the time he had on his clothes his hands were numbed and he could scarcely hold his shoes. These he could not put on for fear of waking his parents, who never came to know how early he rose.

As soon as he stepped over the lintel, the flesh of his soles contracted on the chilled earth, and his legs began to ache with cold. It was night: the stars were glittering, the trees standing black and still. He looked for signs of day, for the greying of the edge of a stone, or a lightening in the sky where the sun would rise, but there was nothing yet. Alert as an animal he crept past the dangerous window, standing poised with his hand on the sill for one proudly fastidious moment, looking in at the stuffy blackness of the room where his parents lay.

Feeling for the grass-edge of the path with his toes, he reached inside another window farther along the wall, where his gun had been set in readiness the night before. The steel was icy, and numbed fingers slipped along it, so that he had to hold it in the crook of his arm for safety. Then he tiptoed to the room where the dogs slept, and was fearful that they might have been tempted to go before him; but they were waiting, their haunches crouched in reluctance at the cold, but ears and swinging tails greeting the gun ecstatically. His warning under-tone kept them secret and silent till the house was a hundred yards back: then they bolted off into the bush, yelping excit-edly. The boy imagined his parents turning in their beds and muttering: Those dogs again! before they were dragged back in sleep; and he smiled scornfully. He always looked back over his shoulder at the house before he passed a wall of trees that shut it from sight. It looked so low and small, crouching there under a tall and brilliant sky. Then he turned his back on it, and on the drowsing sleepers, and forgot them.

He would have to hurry. Before the light grew strong he must be four miles away; and already a tint of green stood in the hollow of a leaf, and the air smelled of morning and the stars were dimming.

He slung the shoes over his shoulder, veld skoen that were crinkled and hard with the dews of a hundred mornings. They would be necessary when the ground became too hot to bear. Now he felt the chilled dust push up between his toes, and he let the muscles of his feet spread and settle into the shapes of the earth; and he thought: I could walk a hundred miles on feet like these! I could walk all day, and never tire!

He was walking swiftly through the dark tunnel of foliage that in daytime was a road. The dogs were invisibly ranging the lower travelways of the bush, and he heard them panting. Sometimes he felt a cold muzzle on his leg before they were off again, scouting for a trail to follow. They were not trained, but free-running companions of the hunt, who often tired of the long stalk before the final shots, and went off on their own pleasure. Soon he could see them, small and wild-looking in a wild strange light, now that the bush stood trembling on the verge of colour, waiting for the sun to paint earth and grass afresh.

The grass stood to his shoulders; and the trees were showering a faint silvery rain. He was soaked; his whole body was clenched in a steady shiver.

Once he bent to the road that was newly scored with animal trails, and regretfully straightened, reminding himself that the pleasure of tracking must wait till another day.

He began to run along the edge of a field, noting jerkily how it was filmed over with fresh spiderweb, so that the long reaches of great black clods seemed netted in glistening grey. He was using the steady lope he had learned by watching the natives, the run that is a dropping of the weight of the body from one foot to the next in a slow balancing movement that never tires, nor shortens the breath; and he felt the blood pulsing down his legs and along his arms, and the exultation and pride of body mounted in him till he was shutting his teeth hard against a violent desire to shout his triumph.

Soon he had left the cultivated part of the farm. Behind him the bush was low and black. In front was a long vlei, acres of long pale grass that sent back a hollowing gleam of light to a satiny sky. Near him thick swathes of grass were bent with the weight of water, and diamond drops sparkled on each frond.

The first bird woke at his feet and at once a flock of them sprang into the air calling shrilly that day had come; and suddenly behind him, the bush woke into song, and he could hear the guinea-fowl calling far ahead of him. That meant they would not be sailing down from their trees into thick grass, and it was for them he had come: he was too late. But he did not mind. He forgot he had come to shoot. He set his legs wide, and balanced from foot to foot, and swung his gun up and down in both hands horizontally, in a kind of improvised exercise, and let his head sink back till it was pillowed in his neck muscles, and watched how above him small rosy clouds floated in a lake of gold.

Suddenly it all rose in him: it was unbearable. He leapt up into the air, shouting and yelling wild, unrecognizable noises. Then he began to run, not carefully, as he had before, but madly, like a wild thing. He was clean crazy, yelling mad with the joy of living and a superfluity of youth. He rushed down the vlei under a tumult of crimson and gold, while all the birds of the world sang about him. He ran in great leaping strides, and shouted as he ran, feeling his body rise into the crisp rushing air and fall back surely on to sure feet; and thought briefly, not believing that such a thing could happen to him, that he could break his ankle any moment, in this thick tangled grass. He cleared bushes like a duiker, leaped over rocks; and finally came to a dead stop at a place where the ground fell abruptly away below him to the river. It had been a two-mile-long dash through waist-high growth, and he was breathing hoarsely and could no longer sing. But he poised on a rock and looked down at stretches of water that gleamed through stoop-ing trees, and thought suddenly, I am fifteen! Fifteen! The words came new to him; so that he kept repeating them wonderingly, with swelling excitement; and he felt the years of his life with his hands, as if he were counting marbles, each one hard and separate and compact, each one a wonderful shining thing. That was what he was: fifteen years of this rich soil, and this slow-moving water, and air that smelt like a challenge whether it was warm and sultry at noon, or as brisk as cold water, like it was now.

There was nothing he couldn't do, nothing! A vision came to him, as he stood there, like when a child hears the word 'eternity' and tries to understand it, and time takes possession of the mind. He felt his life ahead of him as a great and wonderful thing, something that was his; and he said aloud, with the blood rising to his head: all the great men of the world have been as I am now, and there is nothing I can't become, nothing I can't do; there is no country in the world I cannot make part of myself, if I choose. I contain the world. I can make of it what I want. If I choose, I can change everything that is going to happen: it depends on me, and what I decide now.

The urgency, and the truth and the courage of what his voice was saying exulted him so that he began to sing again, at the top of his voice, and the sound went echoing down the river gorge. He stopped for the echo, and sang again: stopped and shouted. That was what he was! – he sang, if he chose; and the world had to answer him.

And for minutes he stood there, shouting and singing and waiting for the lovely eddying sound of the echo; so that his own new strong thoughts came back and washed round his head, as if someone were answering him and encouraging him: till the gorge was full of soft voices clashing back and forth from rock to rock over the river. And then it seemed as if there was a new voice. He listened, puzzled, for it was not his own. Soon he was leaning forward, all his nerves alert, quite still: somewhere close to him there was a noise that was no joyful bird, nor tinkle of falling water, nor ponderous movement of cattle.

There it was again. In the deep morning hush that held his future and his past, was a sound of pain, and repeated over and over: it was a kind of shortened scream, as if someone, something, had no breath to scream. He came to himself, looked about him, and called for the dogs. They did not appear: they had gone off on their own business, and he was alone. Now he was clean sober, all the madness gone. His heart beating fast, because of that frightened screaming, he stepped carefully off the rock and went towards a belt of trees. He was moving cautiously, for not so long ago he had seen a leopard in just this spot.

At the end of the trees he stopped and peered, holding his gun ready; he advanced, looking steadily about him, his eyes narrowed. Then, all at once, in the middle of a step, he faltered, and his face was puzzled. He shook his head impatiently, as if he doubted his own sight.

There, between two trees, against a background of gaunt black rocks, was a figure from a dream, a strange beast that was horned and drunken-legged, but like something he had never even imagined. It seemed to be ragged. It looked like a small buck that had black ragged tufts of fur standing up irregularly all over it, with patches of raw flesh beneath . . . but the patches of rawness were disappearing under moving black and came again elsewhere; and all the time the creature screamed, in small gasping screams, and leaped drunkenly from side to side, as if it were blind.

Then the boy understood: it *was* a buck. He ran closer, and again stood still, stopped by a new fear. Around him the grass was whispering and alive. He looked wildly about, and then down. The ground was black with ants, great energetic ants that took no notice of him, but hurried and scurried towards the fighting shape, like glistening black water flowing through the grass.

And, as he drew in his breath and pity and terror seized him, the beast fell and the screaming stopped. Now he could hear nothing but one bird singing, and the sound of the rustling, whispering ants.

He peered over at the writhing blackness that jerked convulsively with the jerking nerves. It grew quieter. There were small twitches from the mass that still looked vaguely like the shape of a small animal.

It came into his mind that he should shoot it and end its pain; and he raised the gun. Then he lowered it again. The buck could no longer feel; its fighting was a mechanical protest of the nerves. But it was not that which made him put down the gun. It was a swelling feeling of rage and misery and protest that expressed itself in the thought: if I had not come it would have died like this: so why should I interfere? All over the bush things like this happen; they happen all the time; this is how life goes on, by living things dying in anguish. He gripped the gun between his knees and felt in his own limbs the myriad swarming pain of the twitching animal that could no longer feel, and set his teeth, and said over and over again under his breath: I can't stop it. There is nothing I can do. He was glad the buck was unconscious and had gone past suffering so that he did not have to make a decision to kill it even when he was feeling with his whole body: this is what happens, this is how things work.

It was right – that was what he was feeling. *It was right and nothing could alter it.*

The knowledge of fatality, of what has to be, had gripped him and for the first time in his life; and he was left unable to make any movement of brain or body, except to say: 'Yes, yes. That is what living is.' It had entered his flesh and his bones and grown into the farthest corners of his brain and would never leave him. And at that moment he could not have performed the smallest action of mercy, knowing as he did, having lived on it all his life, the vast unalterable cruel veld, where at any moment one might stumble over a skull or crush the skeleton of some small creature.

Suffering, sick, and angry, but also grimly satisfied with his new stoicism, he stood there leaning on his rifle, and watched the seething black mound grow smaller. At his feet, now, were ants trickling back with pink fragments in their mouths, and there was a fresh acid smell in his nostrils. He sternly controlled the uselessly convulsing muscles of his empty stomach, and reminded himself: the ants must eat too! At the same time he found that the tears were streaming down his face, and his clothes were soaked with the sweat of that other creature's pain.

The shape had grown small. Now it looked like nothing recognizable. He did not know how long it was before he saw the blackness thin, and bits of white showed through, shining in the sun – yes, there was the sun, just up, glowing over the rocks. Why, the whole thing could not have taken longer than a few minutes.

He began to swear, as if the shortness of the time was in itself unbearable, using the words he had heard his father say. He strode forward, crushing ants with each step, and brushing them off his clothes, till he stood above the skeleton, which lay sprawled under a small bush. It was clean-picked. It might have been lying there years, save that on the white bones were pink fragments of gristle. About the bones ants were ebbing away, their pincers full of meat.

The boy looked at them, big black ugly insects. A few were standing and gazing up at him with small glittering eyes.

'Go away!' he said to the ants, very coldly, 'I am not for you – not just yet, at any rate. Go away.' And he fancied that the ants turned and went away.

He bent over the bones and touched the sockets in the skull; that was where the eyes were, he thought incredulously, remembering the liquid dark eyes of a buck. And then he bent the slim foreleg bone, swinging it horizontally in his palm.

That morning, perhaps an hour ago, this small creature had been stepping proud and free through the bush, feeling the chill on its hide even as he himself had done, exhilarated by it. Proudly stepping the earth, tossing its horns, frisking a pretty white tail, it had sniffed the cold morning air. Walking like kings and conquerors it had moved through this free-held bush, where each blade of grass grew for it alone, and where the river ran pure sparkling water for its slaking.

And then – what had happened? Such a swift surefooted thing could surely not be trapped by a swarm of ants?

The boy bent curiously to the skeleton. Then he saw that the back leg that lay uppermost and strained out in the tension of death, was snapped midway in the thigh, so that broken bones jutted over each other uselessly. So that was it! Limping into the ant-masses it could not escape, once it had sensed the danger. Yes, but how had the leg been broken? Had it fallen, perhaps? Impossible, a buck was too light and graceful. Had some jealous rival horned it?

What could possibly have happened? Perhaps some Africans had thrown stones at it, as they do, trying to kill it for meat, and had broken its leg. Yes, that must be it.

Even as he imagined the crowd of running, shouting natives, and the flying stones, and the leaping buck, another picture came into his mind. He saw himself, on any one of these bright ringing mornings, drunk with excitement, taking a snap shot at some half-seen buck. He saw himself with the gun lowered, wondering whether he had missed or not; and thinking at last that it was late, and he wanted his breakfast, and it was not worth while to track miles after an animal that would very likely get away from him in any case.

For a moment he would not face it. He was a small boy again, kicking sulkily at the skeleton, hanging his head, refusing to accept the responsibility.

Then he straightened up, and looked down at the bones with an odd expression of dismay, all the anger gone out of him. His mind went quite empty: all around him he could see trickles of ants disappearing into the grass. The whispering noise was faint and dry, like the rustling of a cast snakeskin.

At last he picked up his gun and walked homewards. He was telling himself half defiantly that he wanted his breakfast. He was telling himself that it was getting very hot, much too hot to be out roaming the bush.

Really, he was tired. He walked heavily, not looking where he put his feet. When he came within sight of his home he stopped, knitting his brows. There was something he had to think out. The death of that small animal was a thing that concerned him, and he was by no means finished with it. It lay at the back of his mind uncomfortably.

Soon, the very next morning, he would get clear of everybody and go to the bush and think about it.

The Farquars had been childless for years when little Teddy was born; and they were touched by the pleasure of their servants, who brought presents of fowls and eggs and flowers to the homestead when they came to rejoice over the baby, exclaiming with delight over his downy golden head and his blue eyes. They congratulated Mrs Farquar as if she had achieved a very great thing, and she felt that she had – her smile for the lingering, admiring natives was warm and grateful.

Later, when Teddy had his first haircut, Gideon the cook picked up the soft gold tufts from the ground, and held them reverently in his hand. Then he smiled at the little boy and said: 'Little Yellow Head'. That became the native name for the child. Gideon and Teddy were great friends from the first. When Gideon had finished his work, he would lift Teddy on his shoulders to the shade of a big tree, and play with him there, forming curious little toys from twigs and leaves and grass, or shaping animals from wetted soil. When Teddy learned to walk it was often Gideon who crouched before him, clucking encouragement, finally catching him when he fell, tossing him up in the air till they both became breathless with laughter. Mrs Farquar was fond of the old cook because of his love for the child.

There was no second baby; and one day Gideon said: 'Ah missus, missus, the Lord above sent this one; Little Yellow Head is the most good thing we have in our house.' Because of that 'we' Mrs Farquar felt a warm impulse towards her cook; and at the end of the month she raised his wages. He had been with her now for several years; he was one of the few natives who had his wife and children in the compound and never wanted to go home to his kraal, which was some hundreds of miles away. Sometimes a small piccanin who had been born the same time as Teddy, could be seen peering from the edge of the bush, staring in awe at the little white boy with his miraculous fair hair and northern blue eyes. The two little children would gaze at each other with a wide, interested gaze, and once Teddy put out his hand curiously to touch the black child's cheeks and hair.

Gideon, who was watching, shook his head wonderingly, and said: 'Ah, missus, these are both children, and one will grow up to be a Baas, and one will be a servant'; and Mrs Farquar smiled and said sadly, 'Yes, Gideon, I was thinking the same.' She sighed. 'It is God's will,' said Gideon, who was a mission boy. The Farquars were very religious people; and this shared feeling about God bound servant and masters even closer together.

Teddy was about six years old when he was given a scooter, and discovered the intoxications of speed. All day he would fly around the homestead, in and out of flowerbeds, scattering squawking chickens and irritated dogs, finishing with a wide dizzying arc into the kitchen door. There he would cry: 'Gideon, look at me!' And Gideon would laugh and say: 'Very clever, Little Yellow Head.' Gideon's youngest son, who was now a herdsboy, came especially up from the compound to see the scooter. He was afraid to come near it, but Teddy showed off in front of him. 'Piccanin,' shouted Teddy, 'get out of my way!' And he raced in circles around the black child until he was frightened, and fled back to the bush.

'Why did you frighten him?' asked Gideon, gravely reproachful.

Teddy said defiantly: 'He's only a black boy,' and laughed. Then, when Gideon turned away from him without speaking, his face fell. Very soon he slipped into the house and found an orange and brought it to Gideon, saying: 'This is for you.' He could not bring himself to say he was sorry; but he could not bear to lose Gideon's affection either. Gideon took the orange unwillingly and sighed. 'Soon you will be going away to school, Little Yellow Head,' he said wonderingly, 'and then you will be grown up.' He shook his head gently and said, 'And that is how our lives go.' He seemed to be putting a distance between himself and Teddy, not because of resentment, but in the way a person accepts something inevitable. The baby had lain in his arms and smiled up into his face: the tiny boy had swung from his shoulders, had played with him by the hour. Now Gideon would not let his flesh touch the flesh of the white child. He was kind, but there was a grave formality in his voice that made Teddy pout and sulk away. Also, it made him into a man: with Gideon he was polite, and carried himself formally, and if he came into the kitchen to ask for something, it was in the way a white man uses towards a servant, expecting to be obeyed.

But on the day that Teddy came staggering into the kitchen with his fists to his eyes, shrieking with pain, Gideon dropped the pot full of hot soup that he was holding, rushed to the child, and forced aside his fingers. 'A snake!' he exclaimed. Teddy had been on his scooter, and had come to a rest with his foot on the side of a big tub of plants. A tree-snake, hanging by its tail from the roof, had spat full into his eyes. Mrs Farquar came running when she heard the commotion. 'He'll go blind,' she sobbed, holding Teddy close against her. 'Gideon, he'll go blind!' Already the eyes, with perhaps half an hour's sight left in them, were swollen up to the size of fists: Teddy's small white face was distorted by great purple oozing protuberances. Gideon said: 'Wait a minute, missus, I'll get some medicine.' He ran off into the bush.

Mrs Farquar lifted the child into the house and bathed his eyes with permanganate. She had scarcely heard Gideon's words; but when she saw that her remedies had no effect at all, and remembered how she had seen natives with no sight in their eyes, because of the spitting of a snake, she began to look for the return of her cook, remembering what she had heard of the efficacy of native herbs. She stood by the window, holding the terrified, sobbing little boy in her arms, and peered help-lessly into the bush. It was not more than a few minutes before she saw Gideon come bounding back, and in his hand he held a plant.

'Do not be afraid, missus,' said Gideon, 'this will cure Little Yellow Head's eyes.' He stripped the leaves from the plant, leaving a small white fleshy root. Without even washing it, he put the root in his mouth, chewed it vigorously, then held the spittle there while he took the child forcibly from Mrs Farquar. He gripped Teddy down between his knees, and pressed the balls of his thumbs into the swollen eyes, so that the child screamed and Mrs Farquar cried out in protest: 'Gideon, Gideon!' But Gideon took no notice. He knelt over the writhing child, pushing back the puffy lids till chinks of eyeball showed, and then he spat hard, again and again, into first one eye, and then the other. He finally lifted Teddy gently into his mother's arms, and said: 'His eyes will get better.' But Mrs Farquar was weeping with terror, and she could hardly thank him: it was impossible to believe that Teddy could keep his sight. In a couple of hours the swellings were gone; the eyes were inflamed and tender but Teddy could see. Mr and Mrs Farquar went to Gideon in the kitchen and thanked him over and over again. They felt helpless because of their gratitude: it seemed they could do nothing to express it. They gave Gideon presents for his wife and children, and a big increase in wages, but these things could not pay for Teddy's now completely cured eyes. Mrs Farquar said: 'Gideon, God chose you as an instrument for His goodness,' and Gideon said: 'Yes, missus, God is very good.'

Now, when such a thing happens on a farm, it cannot be long before everyone hears of it. Mr and Mrs Farquar told their neighbours and the story was discussed from one end of the district to the other. The bush is full of secrets. No one can live in Africa, or at least on the veld, without learning very soon that there is an ancient wisdom of leaf and soil and season – and, too, perhaps most important of all, of the darker tracts of the human mind – which is the black man's heritage. Up and down the district people were telling anecdotes, reminding each other of things that had happened to them.

'But I saw it myself, I tell you. It was a puff-adder bite. The kaffir's arm was swollen to the elbow, like a great shiny black bladder. He was groggy after half a minute. He was dying. Then suddenly a kaffir walked out of the bush with his hands full of green stuff. He smeared something on the place, and next day my boy was back at work, and all you could see was two small punctures in the skin.'

This was the kind of tale they told. And, as always, with a certain amount of exasperation, because while all of them knew that in the bush of Africa are waiting valuable drugs locked in bark, in simple-looking leaves, in roots, it was impossible to ever get the truth about them from the natives themselves.

The story eventually reached town; and perhaps it was at a sundowner party, or some such function, that a doctor, who happened to be there, challenged it. 'Nonsense,' he said. 'These things get exaggerated in the telling. We are always checking up on this kind of story, and we draw a blank every time.'

Anyway, one morning there arrived a strange car at the homestead, and out stepped one of the workers from the laboratory in town, with cases full of test-tubes and chemicals.

Mr and Mrs Farquar were flustered and pleased and flattered. They asked the scientist to lunch, and they told the story all over again, for the hundredth time. Little Teddy was there too, his blue eyes sparkling with health, to prove the truth of it. The scientist explained how humanity might benefit if this new drug could be offered for sale; and the Farquars were even more pleased: they were kind, simple people, who liked to think of something good coming about because of them. But when the scientist began talking of the money that might result, their manner showed discomfort. Their feelings over the miracle (that was how they thought of it) were so strong and deep and religious, that it was distasteful to them to think of money. The scientist, seeing their faces, went back to his first point, which was the advancement of humanity. He was perhaps a trifle perfunctory: it was not the first time he had come salting the tail of a fabulous bush-secret.

Eventually, when the meal was over, the Farquars called Gideon into their living-room and explained to him that this baas, here, was a Big Doctor from the Big City, and he had come all that way to see Gideon. At this Gideon seemed afraid; he did not understand; and Mrs Farquar explained quickly that it was because of the wonderful thing he had done with Teddy's eyes that the Big Baas had come.

Gideon looked from Mrs Farquar to Mr Farquar, and then at the little boy, who was showing great importance because of the occasion. At last he said grudgingly: 'The Big Baas wants to know what medicine I used?' He spoke incredulously, as if he could not believe his old friends could so betray him. Mr Farquar began explaining how a useful medicine could be made out of the root, and how it could be put on sale, and how thousands of people, black and white, up and down the continent of Africa, could be saved by the medicine when that spitting snake filled their eyes with poison. Gideon listened, his eyes bent on the ground, the skin of his forehead puckering in discomfort. When Mr Farquar had finished he did not reply. The scientist, who all this time had been leaning back in a big chair, sipping his coffee and smiling with sceptical good humour, chipped in and explained all over again, in different words, about the making of drugs and the progress of science. Also, he offered Gideon a present.

There was silence after this further explanation, and then Gideon remarked indifferently that he could not remember the root. His face was sullen and hostile, even when he looked at the Farquars, whom he usually treated like old friends. They were beginning to feel annoyed; and this feeling annulled the guilt that had been sprung into life by Gideon's accusing manner. They were beginning to feel that he was unreasonable. But it was at that moment that they all realized he would never give in. The magical drug would remain where it was, unknown and useless except for the tiny scattering of Africans who had the knowledge, natives who might be digging a ditch for the municipality in a ragged shirt and a pair of patched shorts, but who were still born to healing, hereditary healers, being the nephews or sons of the old witch doctors whose ugly masks and bits of bone and all the uncouth properties of magic were the outward signs of real power and wisdom.

The Farquars might tread on that plant fifty times a day as they passed from house to garden, from cow kraal to mealie field, but they would never know it.

But they went on persuading and arguing, with all the force of their exasperation; and Gideon continued to say that he could not remember, or that there was no such root, or that it was the wrong season of the year, or that it wasn't the root itself, but the spit from his mouth that had cured Teddy's eyes. He said all these things one after another, and seemed not to care they were contradictory. He was rude and stubborn. The Farquars could hardly recognize their gentle, lovable old ser-vant in this ignorant, perversely obstinate African, standing there in front of them with lowered eyes, his hands twitching his cook's apron, repeating over and over whichever one of the stupid refusals that first entered his head.

And suddenly he appeared to give in. He lifted his head, gave a long, blank, angry look at the circle of whites, who seemed to him like a circle of yelping dogs pressing around him, and said: 'I will show you the root.'

They walked single file away from the homestead down a kaffir path. It was a blazing December afternoon, with the sky full of hot rain-clouds. Everything was hot: the sun was like a bronze tray whirling overhead, there was a heat shimmer over the fields, the soil was scorching underfoot, the dusty wind blew gritty and thick and warm in their faces. It was a terrible day, fit only for reclining on a veranda with iced drinks, which is where they would normally have been at that hour.

From time to time, remembering that on the day of the snake it had taken ten minutes to find the root, someone asked: 'Is it much farther, Gideon?' And Gideon would answer over his shoulder, with angry politeness: 'I'm looking for the root, baas.' And indeed, he would frequently bend sideways and trail his hand among the grasses with a gesture that was insulting in its perfunctoriness. He walked them through the bush along unknown paths for two hours, in that melting destroying heat, so that the sweat trickled coldly down them and their heads ached. They were all quite silent: the Farquars because they were angry, the scientist because he was being proved right again; there was no such plant. His was a tactful silence.

At last, six miles from the house, Gideon suddenly decided they had had enough; or perhaps his anger evaporated at that moment. He picked up, without an attempt at looking anything but casual, a handful of blue flowers from the grass, flowers that had been growing plentifully all down the paths they had come.

He handed them to the scientist without looking at him, and

marched off by himself on the way home, leaving them to follow him if they chose.

When they got back to the house, the scientist went to the kitchen to thank Gideon: he was being very polite, even though there was an amused look in his eyes. Gideon was not there. Throwing the flowers casually into the back of his car, the eminent visitor departed on his way back to his laboratory.

Gideon was back in his kitchen in time to prepare dinner, but he was sulking. He spoke to Mrs Farquar like an unwilling servant. It was days before they liked each other again.

The Farquars made enquiries about the root from their labourers. Sometimes they were answered with distrustful stares. Sometimes the natives said: 'We do not know. We have never heard of the root.' One, the cattle boy, who had been with them a long time, and had grown to trust them a little, said: 'Ask your boy in the kitchen. Now, there's a doctor for you. He's the son of a famous medicine man who used to be in these parts, and there's nothing he cannot cure.'

Then he added politely: 'Of course, he's not as good as the white man's doctor, we know that, but he's good for us.'

After some time, when the soreness had gone from between the Farquars and Gideon, they began to joke: 'When are you going to show us the snake-root, Gideon?' And he would laugh and shake his head, saying, a little uncomfortably: 'But I did show you, missus, have you forgotten?'

Much later, Teddy, as a schoolboy, would come into the kitchen and say: 'You old rascal, Gideon! Do you remember that time you tricked us all by making us walk miles all over the veld for nothing? It was so far my father had to carry me!'

And Gideon would double up with polite laughter. After much laughing, he would suddenly straighten himself up, wipe his old eyes, and look sadly at Teddy, who was grinning mischievously at him across the kitchen: 'Ah, Little Yellow Head, how you have grown! Soon you will be grown up with a farm of your own . . .'

The Second Hut

Before that season and his wife's illness, he had thought things could get no worse: until then, poverty had meant not to deviate further than snapping point from what he had been brought up to think of as a normal life.

Being a farmer (he had come to it late in life, in his forties) was the first test he had faced as an individual. Before he had always been supported, invisibly perhaps, but none the less strongly, by what his family expected of him. He had been a regular soldier, not an unsuccessful one, but his success had been at the cost of a continual straining against his own inclinations; and he did not know himself what his inclinations were. Something stubbornly unconforming kept him apart from his fellow officers. It was an inward difference: he did not think of himself as a soldier. Even in his appearance, square, close-bitten, disciplined, there had been a hint of softness, or of strain, showing itself in his smile, which was too quick, like the smile of a deaf person afraid of showing incomprehension, and in the anxious look of his eyes. After he left the army he quickly slackened into an almost slovenly carelessness of dress and carriage. Now, in his farm clothes there was nothing left to suggest the soldier. With a loose, stained felt hat on the back of his head, khaki shorts a little too long and too wide, sleeves flapping over spare brown arms, his wispy moustache hiding a strained, set mouth, Major Carruthers looked what he was, a gentleman going to seed.

The house had that brave, worn appearance of those struggling to keep up appearances. It was a four-roomed shack, its red roof dulling to streaky brown. It was the sort of house an apprentice farmer builds as a temporary shelter till he can afford better. Inside, good but battered furniture stood over worn places in the rugs; the piano was out of tune and the notes stuck; the silver tea things from the big narrow house in England where his brother (a lawyer) now lived were used as ornaments, and inside were bits of paper, accounts, rubber rings, old corks.

The room where his wife lay, in a greenish sun-lanced gloom, was a place of seedy misery. The doctor said it was her heart; and Major Carruthers knew this was true: she had broken down through heart-break over the conditions they lived in. She did not want to get better. The harsh light from outside was shut out with dark blinds, and she turned her face to the wall and lay there, hour after hour, inert and uncomplaining, in a stoicism of defeat nothing could penetrate. Even the children hardly moved her. It was as if she had said to herself: 'If I cannot have what I wanted for them, then I wash my hands of life.'

Sometimes Major Carruthers thought of her as she had been, and was filled with uneasy wonder and with guilt. That pleasant conventional pretty English girl had been bred to make a perfect wife for the professional soldier she had imagined him to be, but chance had wrenched her on to this isolated African farm, into a life which she submitted herself to, as if it had nothing to do with her. For the first few years she had faced the struggle humorously, courageously: it was a sprightly attitude towards life, almost flirtatious, as a woman flirts lightly with a man who means nothing to her. As the house grew shabby, and the furniture, and her clothes could not be replaced; when she looked into the mirror and saw her drying, untidy hair and roughening face, she would give a quick high laugh and say, 'Dear me, the things one comes to!' She was facing this poverty as she would have faced, in England, poverty of a narrowing, but socially accepted kind. What she could not face was a different kind of fear; and Major Carruthers understood that too well, for it was now his own fear.

The two children were pale, fine-drawn creatures, almost transparent-looking in their thin nervous fairness, with the defensive and wary manners of the young who have been brought up to expect a better way of life than they enjoy. Their anxious solicitude wore on Major Carruthers' already oversensitized nerves. Children had no right to feel the aching pity which showed on their faces whenever they looked at him. They were too polite, too careful, too scrupulous. When they went into their mother's room she grieved sorrowfully over them, and they submitted patiently to her emotion. All those weeks of the school holidays after she was taken ill, they moved about the farm like two strained and anxious ghosts, and whenever he saw them his sense of guilt throbbed like a wound. He was glad they were going back to school soon, for then – so he thought – it would be easier to manage. It was an intolerable strain, running the farm and coming back to the neglected house and the problems of food and clothing, and a sick wife who would not get better until he could offer her hope.

But when they had gone back, he found that after all, things were not much easier. He slept little, for his wife needed attention in the night; and he became afraid for his own health, worrying over what he ate and wore. He learnt to treat himself as if his health was not what he was, what made him, but something apart, a commodity like efficiency, which could be estimated in terms of money at the end of a season. His health stood between them and complete ruin; and soon there were medicine bottles beside his bed, as well as beside his wife's.

One day, while he was carefully measuring out tonics for himself in the bedroom, he glanced up and saw his wife's small reddened eyes staring incredulously but ironically at him over the bedclothes. 'What are you doing?' she asked.

'I need a tonic,' he explained awkwardly, afraid to worry her by explanations.

She laughed, for the first time in weeks; then the slack tears began welling under her lids, and she turned to the wall again. He understood that some vision of himself had been destroyed, finally, for her. Now she was left with an ageing, rather fussy gentleman, carefully measuring medicine after meals. But he did not blame her; he never had blamed her; not even though he knew her illness was a failure of will. He patted her cheek uncomfortably, and said: 'It wouldn't do for me to get run down, would it?' Then he adjusted the curtains over the windows to shut out a streak of dancing light that threatened to fall over her face, set a glass nearer to her hand, and went out to arrange for her tray of slops to be carried in.

Then he took, in one swift, painful movement, as if he were leaping over an obstacle, the decision he had known for weeks he must take sooner or later. With a straightening of his shoulders, an echo from his soldier past, he took on the strain of an extra burden: he must get an assistant, whether he liked it or not.

So much did he shrink from any self-exposure, that he did not even consider advertising. He sent a note by native bearer to his neighbour, a few miles off, asking that it should be spread abroad that he was wanting help. He knew he would not have to wait long. It was 1931, in the middle of a slump, and there was unemployment, which was a rare thing for this new, sparsely-populated country.

He wrote the following to his sons at boarding-school:

> I expect you will be surprised to hear I'm getting another man on the place. Things are getting a bit too much, and as I plan to plant a bigger acreage of maize this year, I thought it would need two of us. Your mother is better this week, on the whole, so I think things are looking up. She is looking forward to your next holidays, and asks me to say she will write soon. Between you and me, I don't think she's up to writing at the moment. It will soon be getting cold, I think, so if you need any clothes, let me know, and I'll see what I can do . . .

A week later, he sat on the little veranda, towards evening, smoking, when he saw a man coming through the trees on a bicycle. He watched him closely, already trying to form an estimate of his character by the tests he had used all his life: the width between the eyes, the shape of the skull, the way the legs were set on to the body. Although he had been taken in a dozen times, his belief in these methods never wavered. He was an easy prey for any trickster, lending money he never saw again, taken in by professional adventurers who (it seemed to him, measuring others by his own decency and the quick warmth he felt towards people) were the essence of gentlemen. He used to say that being a gentleman was a question of instinct: one could not mistake a gentleman.

As the visitor stepped off his bicycle and wheeled it to the veranda, Major Carruthers saw he was young, thirty perhaps, sturdily built, with enormous strength in the thick arms and shoulders. His skin was burnt a healthy orange-brown colour. His close hair, smooth as the fur of an animal, reflected no light. His obtuse, generous features were set in a round face, and the eyes were pale grey, nearly colourless.

Major Carruthers instinctively dropped his standards of value as he looked, for this man was an Afrikaner, and thus came into an outside category. It was not that he disliked him for it, although his father had been killed in the Boer War, but he had never had anything to do with the Afrikaans people before, and his knowledge of them was hearsay, from Englishmen who had the old prejudice. But he liked the look of the man: he liked the honest and straightforward face.

As for Van Heerden, he immediately recognized his tra-ditional enemy, and his inherited dislike was strong. For a moment he appeared obstinate and wary. But they needed each other too badly to nurse old hatreds, and Van Heerden sat down when he was asked, though awkwardly, suppressing reluctance, and began drawing patterns in the dust with a piece of straw he had held between his lips.

Major Carruthers did not need to wonder about the man's circumstances: his quick acceptance of what were poor terms spoke of a long search for work.

He said scrupulously: 'I know the salary is low and the living quarters are bad, even for a single man. I've had a patch of bad luck, and I can't afford more. I'll quite understand if you refuse.'

'What are the living quarters?' asked Van Heerden. His was the rough voice of the uneducated Afrikaner: because he was uncertain where the accent should fall in each sentence, his speech had a wavering, halting sound, though his look and manner were direct enough.

Major Carruthers pointed ahead of them. Before the house the bush sloped gently down to the fields. 'At the foot of the hill there's a hut I've been using as a storehouse. It's quite well-built. You can put up a place for a kitchen.'

Van Heerden rose. 'Can I see it?'

They set off. It was not far away. The thatched hut stood in uncleared bush. Grass grew to the walls and reached up to meet the slanting thatch. Trees mingled their branches overhead. It was round, built of poles and mud and with a stamped dung floor. Inside there was a stale musty smell because of the ants and beetles that had been at the sacks of grain. The one window was boarded over, and it was quite dark. In the confusing shafts of light from the door, a thick sheet of felted spider web showed itself, like a curtain halving the interior, as full of small flies and insects as a butcher-bird's cache. The spider crouched, vast and glittering, shaking gently, glaring at them with small red eyes, from the centre of the web. Van Heerden did what Major Carruthers would have died rather than do: he tore the web across with his bare hands, crushed the spider between his fingers, and brushed them lightly against the walls to free them from the clinging silky strands and the sticky mush of insect-body.

'It will do fine,' he announced.

He would not accept the invitation to a meal, thus making it clear this was merely a business arrangement. But he asked, politely (hating that he had to beg a favour), for a month's salary in advance. Then he set off on his bicycle to the store, ten miles off, to buy what he needed for his living.

Major Carruthers went back to his sick wife with a burdened feeling, caused by his being responsible for another human being having to suffer such conditions. He could not have the man in the house: the idea came into his head and was quickly dismissed. They had nothing in common, they would make each other uncomfortable – that was how he put it to himself. Besides, there wasn't really any room. Underneath, Major Carruthers knew that if his new assistant had been an Englishman, with the same upbringing, he would have found a corner in his house and a welcome as a friend. Major Carruthers threw off these thoughts: he had enough to worry him without taking on another man's problems.

A person who had always hated the business of organization, which meant dividing responsibility with others, he found it hard to arrange with Van Heerden how the work was to be done. But as the Dutchman was good with cattle, Major

Carruthers handed over all the stock on the farm to his care, thus relieving his mind of its most nagging care, for he was useless with beasts, and knew it. So they began, each knowing exactly where they stood. Van Heerden would make laconic reports at the end of each week, in the manner of an expert foreman reporting to a boss ignorant of technicalities – and Major Carruthers accepted this attitude, for he liked to respect people, and it was easy to respect Van Heerden's inspired instinct for animals.

For a few weeks Major Carruthers was almost happy. The fear of having to apply for another loan to his brother – worse, asking for the passage money to England and a job, thus justifying his family's belief in him as a failure, was pushed away; for while taking on a manager did not in itself improve things, it was an action, a decision, and there was nothing that he found more dismaying than decisions. The thought of his family in England, and particularly his elder brother, pricked him into slow burning passions of resentment. His brother's letters galled him so that he had grown to hate mail-days. They were crisp, affectionate letters, without condescension, but about money, bank-drafts, and insurance policies. Major Carruthers did not see life like that. He had not written to his brother for over a year. His wife, when she was well, wrote once a week, in the spirit of one propitiating fate.

Even she seemed cheered by the manager's coming; she sensed her husband's irrational lightness of spirit during that short time. She stirred herself to ask about the farm; and he began to see that her interest in living would revive quickly if her sort of life came within reach again.

But some two months after Van Heerden's coming, Major Carruthers was walking along the farm road towards his lands, when he was astonished to see, disappearing into the bushes, a small flaxen-haired boy. He called, but the child froze as an animal freezes, flattening himself against the foliage. At last, since he could get no reply, Major Carruthers approached the child, who dissolved backwards through the trees, and followed him up the path to the hut. He was very angry, for he knew what he would see.

He had not been to the hut since he handed it over to Van

Heerden. Now there was a clearing, and amongst the stumps of trees and flattened grass, were half a dozen children, each as tow-headed as the first, with that bleached sapless look common to white children in the tropics who have been subjected to too much sun.

A lean-to had been built against the hut. It was merely a roof of beaten petrol tins, patched together like cloth with wire and nails and supported on two unpeeled sticks. There, holding a cooking pot over an open fire that was dangerously close to the thatch, stood a vast slatternly woman. She reminded him of a sow among her litter, as she lifted her head, the children crowding about her, and stared at him suspiciously from pale and white-lashed eyes.

'Where is your husband?' he demanded.

She did not answer. Her suspicion deepened into a glare of hate: clearly she knew no English.

Striding furiously to the door of the hut, he saw that it was crowded with two enormous native-style beds: strips of hide stretched over wooden poles embedded in the mud of the floor. What was left of the space was heaped with stained and broken belongings of the family. Major Carruthers strode off in search of Van Heerden. His anger was now mingled with the shamed discomfort of trying to imagine what it must be to live in such squalor.

Fear rose high in him. For a few moments he inhabited the landscape of his dreams, a grey country full of sucking menace, where he suffered what he would not allow himself to think of while awake: the grim poverty that could overtake him if his luck did not turn, and if he refused to submit to his brother and return to England.

Walking through the fields, where the maize was now waving over his head, pale gold with a froth of white, the sharp dead leaves scything crisply against the wind, he could see nothing but that black foetid hut and the pathetic futureless children. That was the lowest he could bring his own children to! He felt moorless, helpless, afraid: his sweat ran cold on him. And he did not hesitate in his mind; driven by fear and anger, he told himself to be hard; he was searching in his mind for the words with which he would dismiss the Dutchman who had brought his worst nightmares to life, on his own farm, in glaring daylight, where they were inescapable.

He found him with a screaming rearing young ox that was being broken to the plough, handling it with his sure under-standing of animals. At a cautious distance stood the natives who were assisting; but Van Heerden, fearless and purposeful, was fighting the beast at close range. He saw Major Carruthers, let go the plunging horn he held, and the ox was shot away backwards, roaring with anger, into the crowd of natives, who gathered loosely about it with sticks and stones to prevent it running away altogether.

Van Heerden stood still, wiping the sweat off his face, still grinning with the satisfaction of the fight, waiting for his employer to speak.

'Van Heerden,' said Major Carruthers, without prelimi-naries, 'why didn't you tell me you had a family?'

As he spoke the Dutchman's face changed, first flushing into guilt, then setting hard and stubborn. 'Because I've been out of work for a year, and I knew you would not take me if I told you.'

The two men faced each other, Major Carruthers tall, flyaway, shambling, bent with responsibility; Van Heerden stiff and defiant. The natives remained about the ox, to prevent its escape – for them this was a brief intermission in the real work of the farm – and their shouts mingled with the incessant bellowing. It was a hot day; Van Heerden wiped the sweat from his eyes with the back of his hand.

'You can't keep a wife and all those children here – how many children?'

'Nine.'

Major Carruthers thought of his own two, and his perpetual dull ache of worry over them; and his heart became grieved for Van Heerden. Two children, with all the trouble over every-thing they ate and wore and thought, and what would become of them, were too great a burden; how did this man, with nine, manage to look so young?

'How old are you?' he asked abruptly, in a different tone.

'Thirty-four,' said Van Heerden, suspiciously, unable to understand the direction Major Carruthers followed.

The only marks on his face were sun-creases; it was impossible to think of him as the father of nine children and the husband of that terrible broken-down woman. As Major Carruthers gazed at him, he became conscious of the strained lines on his own face, and tried to loosen himself, because he took so badly what this man bore so well.

'You can't keep a wife and children in such conditions.'

'We were living in a tent in the bush on mealie meal and what I shot for nine months, and that was through the wet season,' said Van Heerden drily.

Major Carruthers knew he was beaten. 'You've put me in a false position, Van Heerden,' he said angrily. 'You know I can't afford to give you more money. I don't know where I'm going to find my own children's school fees, as it is. I told you the position when you came. I can't afford to keep a man with such a family.'

'Nobody can afford to have me either,' said Van Heerden sullenly.

'How can I have you living on my place in such a fashion? Nine children! They should be at school. Didn't you know there is a law to make them go to school? Hasn't anybody been to see you about them?'

'They haven't got me yet. They won't get me unless someone tells them.'

Against this challenge, which was also an unwilling appeal, Major Carruthers remained silent, until he said brusquely: 'Remember, I'm not responsible.' And he walked off, with all the appearance of anger.

Van Heerden looked after him, his face puzzled. He did not know whether or not he had been dismissed. After a few moments he moistened his dry lips with his tongue, wiped his hand again over his eyes, and turned back to the ox. Looking over his shoulder from the edge of the field, Major Carruthers could see his wiry, stocky figure leaping and bending about the ox whose bellowing made the whole farm ring with anger.

Major Carruthers decided, once and for all, to put the family out of his mind. But they haunted him; he even dreamed of them; and he could not determine whether it was his own or the Dutchman's children who filled his sleep with fear.

It was a very busy time of the year. Harassed, like all his fellow-farmers, by labour difficulties, apportioning out the farm tasks was a daily problem. All day his mind churned slowly over the necessities: this fencing was urgent, that field must be reaped at once. Yet, in spite of this, he decided it was his duty to build a second hut beside the first. It would do no more than take the edge off the discomfort of that miserable family, but he knew he could not rest until it was built.

Just as he had made up his mind and was wondering how the thing could be managed, the bossboy came to him, saying that unless the Dutchman went, he and his friends would leave the farm.

'Why?' asked Major Carruthers, knowing what the answer would be. Van Heerden was a hard worker, and the cattle were improving week by week under his care, but he could not handle natives. He shouted at them, lost his temper, treated them like dogs. There was continual friction.

'Dutchmen are no good,' said the bossboy simply, voicing the hatred of the black man for that section of the white people he considers his most brutal oppressors.

Now, Major Carruthers was proud that at a time when most farmers were forced to buy labour from the contractors, he was able to attract sufficient voluntary labour to run his farm. He was a good employer, proud of his reputation for fair dealing. Many of his natives had been with him for years, taking a few months off occasionally for a rest in their kraals, but always returning to him. His neighbours were complaining of the sullen attitude of their labourers: so far Major Carruthers had kept this side of that form of passive resistance which could ruin a farmer. It was walking on a knife-edge, but his simple human relationship with his workers was his greatest asset as a farmer, and he knew it.

He stood and thought, while his bossboy, who had been on this farm twelve years, waited for a reply. A great deal was at stake. For a moment Major Carruthers thought of dismissing the Dutchman; he realized he could not bring himself to do it: what would happen to all those children? He decided on a course which was repugnant to him. He was going to appeal to his employee's pity.

'I have always treated you square?' he asked. 'I've always helped you when you were in trouble?'

The bossboy immediately and warmly assented.

'You know that my wife is ill, and that I'm having a lot of trouble just now. I don't want the Dutchman to go, just now when the work is so heavy. I'll speak to him, and if there is any more trouble with the men, then come to me and I'll deal with it myself.'

It was a glittering blue day, with a chill edge on the air, that stirred Major Carruthers' thin blood as he stood, looking in appeal into the sullen face of the native. All at once, feeling the fresh air wash along his cheeks, watching the leaves shake with a ripple of gold on the trees down the slope, he felt superior to his difficulties, and able to face anything. 'Come,' he said, with his rare, diffident smile. 'After all these years, when we have been working together for so long, surely you can do this for me. It won't be for very long.'

He watched the man's face soften in response to his own; and wondered at the unconscious use of the last phrase, for there was no reason, on the face of things, why the situation should not continue as it was for a very long time.

They began laughing together; and separated cheerfully; the African shaking his head ruefully over the magnitude of the sacrifice asked of him, thus making the incident into a joke; and he dived off into the bush to explain the position to his fellow-workers.

Repressing a strong desire to go after him, to spend the lovely fresh day walking for pleasure, Major Carruthers went into his wife's bedroom, inexplicably confident and walking like a young man.

She lay as always, face to the wall, her protruding shoulders visible beneath the cheap pink bed-jacket he had bought for her illness. She seemed neither better nor worse. But as she turned her head, his buoyancy infected her a little; perhaps, too, she was conscious of the exhilarating day outside her gloomy curtains.

What kind of a miraculous release was she waiting for? he wondered, as he delicately adjusted her sheets and pillows and laid his hand gently on her head. Over the bony cage of the skull, the skin was papery and bluish. What was she thinking? He had a vision of her brain as a small frightened animal pulsating under his fingers.

With her eyes still closed, she asked in her querulous thin voice: 'Why don't you write to George?'

Involuntarily his fingers contracted on her hair, causing her to start and to open her reproachful, red-rimmed eyes. He waited for her usual appeal: the children, my health, our future. But she sighed and remained silent, still loyal to the man she had imagined she was marrying; and he could feel her thinking: *the lunatic stiff pride of men.*

Understanding that for her it was merely a question of waiting for his defeat, as her deliverance, he withdrew his hand, in dislike of her, saying: 'Things are not as bad as that yet.' The cheerfulness of his voice was genuine, holding still the courage and hope instilled into him by the bright day outside.

'Why, what has happened?' she asked swiftly, her voice suddenly strong, looking at him in hope.

'Nothing,' he said; and the depression settled down over him again. Indeed, nothing had happened; and his confidence was a trick of the nerves. Soberly he left the bedroom, thinking: I must get that well built; and when that is done, I must do the drains, and then . . . He was thinking, too, that all these things must wait for the second hut.

Oddly, the comparatively small problem of that hut occupied his mind during the next few days. A slow and careful man, he set milestones for himself and overtook them one by one.

Since Christmas the labourers had been working a seven-day week, in order to keep ahead in the race against the weeds. They resented it, of course, but that was the custom. Now that the maize was grown, they expected work to slack off, they expected their Sundays to be restored to them. To ask even half a dozen of them to sacrifice their weekly holiday for the sake of the hated Dutchman might precipitate a crisis. Major Carruthers took his time, stalking his opportunity like a hunter, until one evening he was talking with his bossboy as man to man, about farm problems; but when he broached the subject of a hut, Major Carruthers saw that it would be as he feared: the man at once turned stiff and unhelpful. Suddenly impatient, he said: 'It must be done next Sunday. Six men could finish it in a day, if they worked hard.'

The black man's glance became veiled and hostile. Responding to the authority in the voice he replied simply: 'Yes, baas.' He was accepting the order from above, and refusing responsibility: his co-operation was switched off; he had become a machine for transmitting orders. Nothing exasperated Major Carruthers more than when this happened. He said sternly: 'I'm not having any nonsense. If that hut isn't built, there'll be trouble.'

'Yes, baas,' said the bossboy again. He walked away, stopped some natives who were coming off the fields with their hoes over their shoulders, and transmitted the order in a neutral voice. Major Carruthers saw them glance at him in fierce antagonism; then they turned away their heads, and walked off, in a group towards their compound.

It would be all right, he thought, in disproportionate relief. It would be difficult to say exactly what it was he feared, for the question of the hut had loomed so huge in his mind that he was beginning to feel an almost superstitious foreboding. Driven downwards through failure after failure, fate was becoming real to him as a cold malignant force; the careful balancing of unfriendly probabilities that underlay all his planning had developed in him an acute sensitivity to the future; and he had learned to respect his dreams and omens. Now he wondered at the strength of his desire to see that hut built, and whatever danger it represented behind him.

He went to the clearing to find Van Heerden and tell him what he had planned. He found him sitting on a candle-box in the doorway of the hut, playing good-humouredly with his children, as if they had been puppies, tumbling them over, snapping his fingers in their faces, and laughing outright with boyish exuberance when one little boy squared up his fists at him in a moment of temper against this casual, almost contemptuous treatment of them. Major Carruthers heard that boyish laugh with amazement; he looked blankly at the young Dutchman, and then from him to his wife, who was standing, as usual, over a petrol tin that balanced on the small fire. A smell of meat and pumpkin filled the clearing. The woman seemed to

Major Carruthers less a human being than the expression of an elemental, irrepressible force: he saw her, in her vast sagging fleshiness, with her slow stupid face, her instinctive responses to her children, whether for affection or temper, as the symbol of fecundity, a strong, irresistible heave of matter. She fright- ened him. He turned his eyes from her and explained to Van Heerden that a second hut would be built here, beside the existing one.

Van Heerden was pleased. He softened into quick confiding friendship. He looked doubtfully behind him at the small hut that sheltered eleven human beings, and said that it was really not easy to live in such a small space with so many children. He glanced at the children, cuffing them affectionately as he spoke, smiling like a boy. He was proud of his family, of his own capacity for making children: Major Carruthers could see that. Almost, he smiled; then he glanced through the doorway at the grey squalor of the interior and hurried off, resolutely prevent- ing himself from dwelling on the repulsive facts that such close- packed living implied.

The next Saturday evening he and Van Heerden paced the clearing with tape measure and spirit level, determining the area of the new hut. It was to be a large one. Already the sheaves of thatching grass had been stacked ready for next day, shining brassily in the evening sun; and the thorn poles for the walls lay about the clearing, stripped of bark, the smooth inner wood showing white as kernels.

Major Carruthers was waiting for the natives to come up from the compound for the building before daybreak that Sunday. He was there even before the family woke, afraid that without his presence something might go wrong. He feared the Dutchman's temper because of the labourers' sulky mood.

He leaned against a tree, watching the bush come awake, while the sky flooded slowly with light, and the birds sang about him. The hut was, for a long time, silent and dark. A sack hung crookedly over the door, and he could glimpse huddled shapes within. It seemed to him horrible, a stinking kennel shrinking ashamedly to the ground away from the wide hall of fresh blue sky. Then a child came out, and another; soon they were spilling out of the doorway, in their little rags of dresses, or hitching khaki pants up over the bony jut of a hip. They smiled shyly at him, offering him friendship. Then came the woman, moving sideways to ease herself through the narrow door-frame – she was so huge it was almost a fit. She lumbered slowly, thick and stupid with sleep, over to the cold fire, raising her arms in a yawn, so that wisps of dull yellow hair fell over her shoulders and her dark slack dress lifted in creases under her neck. Then she saw Major Carruthers and smiled at him. For the first time he saw her as a human being and not as something fatally ugly. There was something shy, yet frank, in that smile; so that he could imagine the strong, laughing adolescent girl, with the frank, inviting, healthy sensuality of the young Dutchwoman – so she had been when she married Van Heerden. She stooped painfully to stir up the ashes, and soon the fire spurted up under the leaning patch of tin roof. For a while Van Heerden did not appear; neither did the natives who were supposed to be here a long while since; Major Carruthers continued to lean against a tree, smiling at the children, who nevertheless kept their distance from him, unable to play naturally because of his presence there, smiling at Mrs Van Heerden who was throwing handfuls of mealie meat into a petrol tin of boiling water, to make native-style porridge.

It was just on eight o'clock, after two hours of impatient waiting, that the labourers filed up the bushy incline, with the axes and picks over their shoulders, avoiding his eyes. He pressed down his anger: after all it was Sunday, and they had had no day off for weeks; he could not blame them.

They began by digging the circular trench that would hold the wall poles. As their picks rang out on the pebbly ground, Van Heerden came out of the hut, pushing aside the dangling sack with one hand and pulling up his trousers with the other, yawning broadly, then smiling at Major Carruthers apologetically. 'I've had my sleep out,' he said; he seemed to think his employer might be angry.

Major Carruthers stood close over the workers, wanting it to be understood by them and by Van Heerden that he was responsible. He was too conscious of their resentment, and knew that they would scamp the work if possible. If the hut was to be completed as planned, he would need all his tact and good-humour. He stood there patiently all morning, watching the thin sparks flash up as the picks swung into the flinty earth. Van Heerden lingered nearby, unwilling to be thus publicly superseded in the responsibility for his own dwelling in the eyes of the natives.

When they flung their picks and went to fetch the poles, they did so with a side glance at Major Carruthers, challenging him to say the trench was not deep enough. He called them back, laughingly, saying: 'Are you digging for a dog-kennel then, and not a hut for a man?' One smiled unwillingly in response; the others sulked. Perfunctorily they deepened the trench to the very minimum that Major Carruthers was likely to pass. By noon, the poles were leaning drunkenly in place, and the natives were stripping the binding from beneath the bark of nearby trees. Long fleshy strips of fibre, rose-coloured and apricot and yellow, lay tangled over the grass, and the wounded trees showed startling red gashes around the clearing. Swiftly the poles were laced together with this natural rope, so that when the frame was complete it showed up against green trees and sky like a slender gleaming white cage, interwoven lightly with rosy-yellow. Two natives climbed on top to bind the roof poles into their conical shape, while the others stamped a slushy mound of sand and earth to form plaster for the walls. Soon they stopped – the rest could wait until after the midday break.

Worn out by the strain of keeping the balance between the fiery Dutchman and the resentful workers, Major Carruthers went off home to eat. He had one and a half hours' break. He finished his meal in ten minutes, longing to be able to sleep for once till he woke naturally. His wife was dozing, so he lay down on the other bed and at once dropped off to sleep himself. When he woke it was long after the time he had set himself. It was after three. He rose in a panic and strode to the clearing, in the grip of one of his premonitions.

There stood the Dutchman, in a flaring temper, shouting at the natives who lounged in front of him, laughing openly. They had only just returned to work. As Major Carruthers approached, he saw Van Heerden using his open palms in a series of quick swinging slaps against their faces, knocking them sideways against each other: it was as if he were cuffing his own

children in a fit of anger. Major Carruthers broke into a run,
erupting into the group before anything else could happen. Van
Heerden fell back on seeing him. He was beef-red with fury.
The natives were bunched together, on the point of throwing
down their tools and walking off the job.

'Get back to work,' snapped Major Carruthers to the men:
and to Van Heerden: 'I'm dealing with this.' His eyes were an
appeal to recognize the need for tact, but Van Heerden stood
squarely there in front of him, on planted legs, breathing
heavily. 'But Major Carruthers . . .' he began, implying that as
a white man, with his employer not there, it was right that he
should take the command. 'Do as I say,' said Major Carruthers.
Van Heerden, with a deadly look at his opponents, swung on
his heel and marched off into the hut. The slapping swing of
the grain-bag was as if a door had been slammed. Major
Carruthers turned to the natives. 'Get on,' he ordered briefly,
in a calm decisive voice. There was a moment of uncertainty.
Then they picked up their tools and went to work.

Some laced the framework of the roof; others slapped the
mud on to the walls. This business of plastering was usually a
festival, with laughter and raillery, for there were gaps between
the poles, and a handful of mud could fly through a space into
the face of a man standing behind: the thing could become a
game, like children playing snowballs. Today there was no
pretence at good-humour. When the sun went down the men
picked up their tools and filed off into the bush without a glance
at Major Carruthers. The work had not prospered. The grass
was laid untidily over the roof-frame, still uncut and reaching
to the ground in long swatches. The first layer of mud had been
unevenly flung on. It would be a shabby building.

His own fault, thought Major Carruthers, sending his slow,
tired blue glance to the hut where the Dutchman was still
cherishing the seeds of wounded pride. Next day, when Major
Carruthers was in another part of the farm, the Dutchman got
his own back in a fine flaming scene with the ploughboys: they
came to complain to the bossboy, but not to Major Carruthers.
This made him uneasy. All that week he waited for fresh
complaints about the Dutchman's behaviour. So much was he
keyed up, waiting for the scene between himself and a grudging

bossboy, that when nothing happened his apprehensions deepened into a deep foreboding.

The building was finished the following Sunday. The floors were stamped hard with new dung, the thatch trimmed, and the walls grained smooth. Another two weeks must elapse before the family could move in, for the place smelled of damp. They were weeks of worry for Major Carruthers. It was unnatural for the Africans to remain passive and sullen under the Dutchman's handling of them, and especially when they knew he was on their side. There was something he did not like in the way they would not meet his eyes and in the over-polite attitude of the bossboy.

The beautiful clear weather that he usually loved so much, May weather, sharpened by cold, and crisp under deep clear skies, pungent with gusts of wind from the drying leaves and grasses of the veld, was spoilt for him this year: something was going to happen.

When the family eventually moved in, Major Carruthers became discouraged because the building of the hut had represented such trouble and worry, while now things seemed hardly better than before: what was the use of two small round huts for a family of eleven? But Van Heerden was very pleased, and expressed his gratitude in a way that moved Major Caruthers deeply: unable to show feeling himself, he was grateful when others did, so relieving him of the burden of his shyness. There was a ceremonial atmosphere on the evening when one of the great sagging beds was wrenched out of the floor of the first hut and its legs plastered down newly into the second hut. That very same night he was awakened towards dawn by voices calling to him from outside his window. He started up, knowing that whatever he had dreaded was here, glad that the tension was over. Outside the back door stood his bossboy, holding a hurricane lamp which momentarily blinded Major Carruthers.

'The hut is on fire.'

Blinking his eyes, he turned to look. Away in the darkness flames were lapping over the trees, outlining branches so that as a gust of wind lifted them patterns of black leaves showed clear and fine against the flowing red light of the fire. The veld was illuminated with a fitful plunging glare. The two men ran off into the bush down the rough road, towards the blaze.

The clearing was lit up, as bright as morning, when they arrived. On the roof of the first hut squatted Van Heerden, lifting tins of water from a line of natives below, working from the water-butt, soaking the thatch to prevent it catching the flames from the second hut that was only a few yards off. That was a roaring pillar of fire. Its frail skeleton was still erect, but twisting and writhing incandescently within its envelope of flame, and it collapsed slowly as he came up, subsiding in a crash of sparks.

'The children,' gasped Major Carruthers to Mrs Van Heerden, who was watching the blaze fatalistically from where she sat on a scattered bundle of bedding, the tears soaking down her face, her arms tight round a swathed child.

As she spoke she opened the cloths to display the smallest infant. A swathe of burning grass from the roof had fallen across its head and shoulders. He sickened as he looked, for there was nothing but raw charred flesh. But it was alive: the limbs still twitched a little.

'I'll get the car and we'll take it in to the doctor.'

He ran out of the clearing and fetched the car. As he tore down the slope back again he saw he was still in his pyjamas, and when he gained the clearing for the second time, Van Heerden was climbing down from the roof, which dripped water as if there had been a storm. He bent over the burnt child.

'Too late,' he said.

'But it's still alive.'

Van Heerden almost shrugged; he appeared dazed. He continually turned his head to survey the glowing heap that had so recently sheltered his children. He licked his lips with a quick unconscious movement, because of their burning dryness. His face was grimed with smoke and inflamed from the great heat, so that his young eyes showed startlingly clear against the black skin.

'Get into the car,' said Major Carruthers to the woman. She automatically moved towards the car, without looking at her husband, who said: 'But it's too late, man.'

Major Carruthers knew the child would die, but his protest against the waste and futility of the burning expressed itself in this way: that everything must be done to save this life, even against hope. He started the car and slid off down the hill. Before they had gone half a mile he felt his shoulder plucked from behind, and, turning, saw the child was now dead. He reversed the car into the dark bush off the road, and drove back to the clearing. Now the woman had begun wailing, a soft, monotonous, almost automatic sound that kept him tight in his seat, waiting for the next cry.

The fire was now a dark heap, fanning softly to a glowing red as the wind passed over it. The children were standing in a half-circle, gazing fascinated at it. Van Heerden stood near them, laying his hands gently, restlessly, on their heads and shoulders, reassuring himself of their existence here, in the flesh, and living, beside him.

Mrs Van Heerden got clumsily out of the car, still wailing, and disappeared into the hut, clutching the bundled dead child.

Feeling out of place among that bereaved family, Major Carruthers went up to his house, where he drank cup after cup of tea, holding himself tight and controlled, conscious of over-strained nerves.

Then he stooped into his wife's room, which seemed small and dark and airless. The cave of a sick animal, he thought, in disgust; then, ashamed of himself, he returned out of doors, where the sky was filling with light. He sent a message for the bossboy, and waited for him in a condition of tensed anger.

When the man came Major Carruthers asked immediately: 'Why did that hut burn?'

The bossboy looked at him straight and said: 'How should I know?' Then, after a pause, with guileful innocence: 'It was the fault of the kitchen, too close to the thatch.'

Major Carruthers glared at him, trying to wear down the straight gaze with his own accusing eyes.

'That hut must be rebuilt at once. It must be rebuilt today.'

The bossboy seemed to say that it was a matter of indifference to him whether it was rebuilt or not. 'I'll go and tell the others,' he said, moving off.

'Stop,' barked Major Carruthers. Then he paused, frightened, not so much at his rage, but his humiliation and guilt. He had foreseen it! He had foreseen it all! And yet, that thatch could so easily have caught alight from the small incautious fire that sent up sparks all day so close to it.

Almost he burst out in wild reproaches. Then he pulled himself together and said: 'Get away from me.' What was the use? He knew perfectly well that one of the Africans whom Van Heerden had kicked or slapped or shouted at had fired that hut; no one could ever prove it.

He stood quite still, watching his bossboy move off, tugging at the long wisps of his moustache in frustrated anger.

And what would happen now?

He ordered breakfast, drank a cup of tea, and spoilt a piece of toast. Then he glanced in again at his wife, who would sleep for a couple of hours yet.

Again tugging fretfully at his moustache, Major Carruthers set off for the clearing.

Everything was just as it had been, though the pile of black debris looked low and shabby now that morning had come and heightened the wild colour of sky and bush. The children were playing nearby, their hands and faces black, their rags of clothing black – everything seemed patched and smudged with black, and on one side the trees hung withered and grimy and the soil was hot underfoot.

Van Heerden leaned against the framework of the first hut. He looked subdued and tired, but otherwise normal. He greeted Major Carruthers and did not move.

'How is your wife?' asked Major Carruthers. He could hear a moaning sound from inside the hut.

'She's doing well.'

Major Carruthers imagined her weeping over the dead child; and said: 'I'll take your baby into town for you and arrange for the funeral.'

Van Heerden said: 'I've buried her already.' He jerked his thumb at the bush behind them.

'Didn't you register its birth?'

Van Heerden shook his head. His gaze challenged Major Carruthers as if to say: Who's to know if no one tells them? Major Carruthers could not speak: he was held in silence by the thought of that charred little body, huddled into a packing-case or wrapped in a piece of cloth, thrust into the ground, at the mercy of wild animals or of white ants.

'Well, one comes and another goes,' said Van Heerden at last, slowly, reaching out for philosophy as a comfort, while his eyes filled with rough tears.

Major Carruthers stared: he could not understand. At last the meaning of the words came into him, and he heard the moaning from the hut with a new understanding.

The idea had never entered his head; it had been a complete failure of the imagination. If nine children, why not ten? Why not fifteen, for that matter, or twenty? Of course there would be more children.

'It was the shock,' said Van Heerden. 'It should be next month.'

Major Carruthers leaned back against the wall of the hut and took out a cigarette clumsily. He felt weak. He felt as if Van Heerden had struck him, smiling. This was an absurd and unjust feeling, but for a moment he hated Van Heerden for standing there and saying: this grey country of poverty that you fear so much, will take on a different look when you actually enter it. You will cease to exist; there is no energy left, when one is wrestling naked with life, for your kind of fine feelings and scruples and regrets.

'We hope it will be a boy,' volunteered Van Heerden, with a tentative friendliness, as if he thought it might be considered a familiarity to offer his private emotions to Major Carruthers. 'We have five boys and four girls – three girls,' he corrected himself, his face contracting.

Major Carruthers asked stiffly: 'Will she be all right?'

'I do it,' said Van Heerden. 'The last was born in the middle of the night, when it was raining. That was when we were in the tent. It's nothing to her,' he added, with pride. He was listening, as he spoke, to the slow moaning from inside. 'I'd better be getting in to her,' he said, knocking out his pipe against the mud of the walls. Nodding to Major Carruthers, he lifted the sack and disappeared.

After a while Major Carruthers gathered himself together and forced himself to walk erect across the clearing under the curious gaze of the children. His mind was fixed and numb, but he walked as if moving to a destination. When he reached the house, he at once pulled paper and pen towards him and wrote, and each slow difficult word was a nail in the coffin of his pride as a man.

Some minutes later he went in to his wife. She was awake, turned on her side, watching the door for the relief of his coming. 'I've written for a job at Home,' he said simply, laying his hand on her thin dry wrist, and feeling the slow pulse beat up suddenly against his palm.

He watched curiously as her face crumpled and the tears of thankfulness and release ran slowly down her cheeks and soaked the pillow.

Two narrow tracks, one of them deepened to a smooth dusty groove by the incessant padding of bare feet, wound from the farm compound to the old well, through half a mile of tall blond grass that was soiled and matted because of the nearness of the clustering huts: the compound had been on that ridge for twenty years.

The native women with their children used to loiter down the track, and their shrill laughter and chattering sounded through the trees as if one might suddenly have come on a flock of brilliant noisy parrots. It seemed as if fetching water was more of a social event to them than a chore. At the well itself they would linger half the morning, standing in groups to gossip, their arms raised in that graceful, eternally moving gesture to steady glittering or rusted petrol tins balanced on head-rings woven of grass; kneeling to slap bits of bright cloth on slabs of stone blasted long ago from the depths of earth. Here they washed and scolded and dandled their children. Here they scrubbed their pots. Here they sluiced themselves and combed their hair.

Coming upon them suddenly there would be sharp exclamations; a glimpse of soft brown shoulders and thighs withdrawing to the bushes, or annoyed and resentful eyes. It was their well. And while they were there, with their laughter, and gossip and singing, their folded draperies, bright armbands, earthenware jars and metal combs, grouped in attitudes of head-slowed indolence, it seemed as if the bellowing of distant cattle, drone of tractor, all the noises of the farm, were simply lending themselves to form a background to this antique scene: Women, drawing water at the well.

When they left the ground would be scattered with the

bright-pink, fleshy skins of the native wild-plum which contracts the mouth shudderingly with its astringency, or with the shiny green fragments of the shells of kaffir oranges.

Without the women the place was ugly, paltry. The windlass, coiled with greasy rope, propped for safety with a forked stick, was sheltered by a tiny cock of thatch that threw across the track a long, intensely black shadow. For the rest, veld; the sere, flattened, sun-dried veld.

They were beautiful, these women. But she whom I thought of vaguely as 'The cross-eyed one', offended the sight. She used to lag behind the others on the road, either by herself, or in charge of the older children. Not only did she suffer from a painful squint, so that when she looked towards you it was with a confused glare of white eyeball; but her body was hideous. She wore the traditional dark-patterned blue stuff looped at the waist, and above it her breasts were loose, flat crinkling triangles.

She was a solitary figure at the well, doing her washing unaided and without laughter. She would strain at the windlass during the long slow ascent of the swinging bucket that clanged sometimes, far below, against the sides of naked rock until at that critical moment when it hung vibrating at the mouth of the well, she would set the weight of her shoulder in the crook of the handle and with a fearful snatching movement bring the water to safety. It would slop over, dissolving in a shower of great drops that fell tinkling to disturb the surface of that tiny, circular, dully-gleaming mirror which lay at the bottom of the plunging rock tunnel. She was clumsy. Because of her eyes her body lumbered.

She was the oldest wife of 'The Long One', who was our most skilful driver.

'The Long One' was not so tall as he was abnormally thin. It was the leanness of those driven by inner restlessness. He could never keep still. His hands plucked at pieces of grass, his shoulder twitched to a secret rhythm of the nerves. Set a-top of that sinewy, narrow, taut body was a narrow head, with wide-pointed ears, which gave him an appearance of alert caution. The expression of the face was always violent, whether he was angry, laughing, or – most usually – sardonically critical. He had a tongue that was feared by every labourer on the farm. Even my father would smile ruefully after an altercation with his driver and say: 'He's a man, that native. One must respect him, after all. He never lets you get away with anything.'

In his own line he was an artist – his line being cattle. He handled oxen with a delicate brutality that was fascinating and horrifying to watch. Give him a bunch of screaming, rearing three-year-olds, due to take their first taste of the yoke, and he would fight them for hours under a blistering sun with the sweat running off him, his eyes glowing with a wicked and sombre satisfaction. Then he would use his whip, grunting savagely as the lash cut down into flesh, his tongue stuck calculatingly between his teeth as he measured the exact weight of the blow. But to watch him handle a team of sixteen fat tamed oxen was a different thing. It was like watching a circus act; there was the same suspense in it: it was a matter of pride to him that he did not need to use the whip. This did not by any means imply that he wished to spare the beasts pain, not at all; he liked to feed his pride on his own skill. Alongside the double line of ponderous cattle that strained across acres of heavy clods, danced, raved and screamed the Long One, with his twelve-foot-long lash circling in black patterns over their backs; and though his threatening yells were the yells of an inspired madman, and the heavy whip could be heard clean across the farm, so that on a moonlight night when they were ploughing late it sounded like the crack and whine of a rifle, never did the dangerous metal-tipped lash so much as touch a hair of their hides. If you examined the oxen as they were outspanned, they might be exhausted, driven to staggering-point, so that my father had to remonstrate, but there was never a mark on them.

'He knows how to handle oxen, but he can't handle his women.'

We gave our natives labels such as that, since it was impossible ever to know them as their fellows knew them, in the round. That phrase summarized for us what the Long One offered in entertainment during the years he was with us. Coming back to the farm, after an absence, one would say in humorous anticipation: 'And what has the Long One been up to now, with his harem?'

There was always trouble with his three wives. He used to come up to the house to discuss with my father, man to man, how the youngest wife was flirting with the bossboy from the neighbouring compound, six miles off; or how she had thrown a big pot of smoking mealie-pap at the middle wife, who was jealous of her.

We grew accustomed to the sight of the Long One standing at the back door, at the sunset hour, when my father held audience after work. He always wore long khaki trousers that slipped down over thin bony hips and went bare-chested, and there would be a ruddy gleam on his polished black skin, and his spindly gesticulating form would be outlined against a sea of fiery colours. At the end of his tale of complaint he would relapse suddenly into a pose of resignation that was self-consciously weary. My father used to laugh until his face was wet and say: 'That man is a natural-born comedian. He would have been on the stage if he had been born another colour.'

But he was no buffoon. He would play up to my father's appreciation of the comic, but he would never play the ape, as some Africans did, for our amusement. And he was certainly no figure of fun to his fellows. That same thing in him that sat apart, watchfully critical, even of himself, gave his humour its mordancy, his tongue its sting. And he was terribly attractive to his women. I have seen him slouch down the road on his way from one team to another; his whip trailing behind in the dust, his trousers sagging in folds from hip-bone to ankle, his eyes broodingly directed in front of him, merely nodding as he passed a group of women among whom might be his wives. And it was as if he had lashed them with that whip. They would bridle and writhe; and then call provocatively after him, but with a note of real anger, to make him notice them. He would not so much as turn his head.

When the real trouble started, though, my father soon got tired of it. He liked to be amused, not seriously implicated in his labourers' problems. The Long One took to coming up not occasionally, as he had been used to do, but every evening. He was deadly serious, and very bitter. He wanted my father to persuade the old wife, the cross-eyed one, to go back home to her own people. The woman was driving him crazy. A nagging woman in your house was like having a flea on your body; you could scratch but it always moved to another place, and there was no peace till you killed it.

'But you can't send her back, just because you are tired of her.'

The Long One said his life had become insupportable. She grumbled, she sulked, she spoilt his food.

'Well, then your other wives can cook for you.'

But it seemed there were complications. The two younger women hated each other, but they were united in one thing, that the old wife should stay, for she was so useful. She looked after the children; she did the hoeing in the garden; she picked relishes from the veld. Besides, she provided endless amusement with her ungainliness. She was the eternal butt, the fool, marked by fate for the entertainment of the whole-limbed and the comely.

My father referred at this point to a certain handbook on native lore, which stated definitely that an elder wife was entitled to be waited on by a young wife, perhaps as compensation for having to give up the pleasures of her lord's favour. The Long One and his ménage cut clean across this amiable theory. And my father, being unable to find a prescribed remedy (as one might look for a cure for a disease in a pharmacopoeia) grew angry. After some weeks of incessant complaint from the Long One he was told to hold his tongue and manage his women himself. That evening the man stalked furiously down the path, muttering to himself between teeth clenched on a grass-stem, on his way home to his two giggling younger wives and the ugly sour-faced old woman, the mother of his elder children, the drudge of his household and the scourge of his life.

It was some weeks later that my father asked casually one day, 'And by the way, Long One, how are things with you? All right again?'

And the Long One answered simply: 'Yes, baas. She's gone away.'

'What do you mean, gone away?'

The Long One shrugged. She had just gone. She had left suddenly without saying anything to anyone.

Now, the woman came from Nyasaland, which was days and days of weary walking away. Surely she hadn't gone by herself? Had a brother or an uncle come to fetch her? Had she gone with a band of passing Africans on their way home?

My father wondered a little, and then forgot about it. It wasn't his affair. He was pleased to have his most useful native back at work with an unharassed mind. And he was particularly pleased that the whole business was ended before the annual trouble over the water-carrying.

For there were two wells. The new one, used by ourselves, had fresh sparkling water that was sweet in the mouth; but in July of each year it ran dry. The water of the old well had a faintly unpleasant taste and was pale brown, but there was always plenty of it. For three or four months of the year, depending on the rains, we shared that well with the compound.

Now, the Long One hated fetching water three miles, four times a week, in the water-cart. The women of the compound disliked having to arrange their visits to the well so as not to get in the way of the water-carriers. There was always grumbling.

This year we had not even begun to use the old well when complaints started that the water tasted bad. The big baas must get the well cleaned.

My father said vaguely that he would clean the well when he had time.

Next day there came a deputation from the women of the compound. Half a dozen of them stood at the back door, arguing that if the well wasn't cleaned soon, all their children would be sick.

'I'll do it next week,' he promised, with bad grace.

The following morning the Long One brought our first load of the season from the old well; and as we turned the taps on the barrels a foetid smell began to pervade the house. As for drinking it, that was out of the question.

'Why don't you keep the cover on the well?' my father said to the women, who were still loitering resentfully at the back door. He was really angry. 'Last time the well was cleaned there were fourteen dead rats and a dead snake. We never get things in our well because we remember to keep the lid on.'

But the women appeared to consider the lid being on, or off, was an act of God, and nothing to do with them.

We always went down to watch the well-emptying, which had the fascination of a ritual. Like the mealie-shelling, or the first rains, it marked a turning-point in the year. It seemed as if a besieged city were laying plans for the conservation of supplies. The sap was falling in tree and grass-root; the sun was withdrawing high, high, behind a veil of smoke and dust; the fierce dryness of the air was a new element, parching foliage as the heat cauterized it. The well-emptying was an act of faith, and of defiance. For a whole afternoon there would be no water on the farm at all. One well was completely dry. And this one would be drained, dependent on the mysterious ebbing and flowing of underground rivers. What if they should fail us? There was an anxious evening, every year; and in the morning, when the Long One stood at the back door and said, beaming, that the bucket was bringing up fine new water, it was like a festival.

But this afternoon we could not stick it out. The smell was intolerable. We saw the usual complement of bloated rats, laid out on the stones around the well, and there was even the skeleton of a small buck that must have fallen in in the dark. Then we left, along the road that was temporarily a river whose source was that apparently endless succession of buckets filled by greyish, evil water.

It was the Long One himself who came to tell us the news. Afterwards we tried to remember what that look that always expressive face wore as he told it.

It seemed that in the last bucket but one had floated a human arm, or rather the fragments of one. Piece by piece they had fetched her up, the Cross-eyed Woman, his own first wife. They recognized her by her bangles. Last of all the Long One went down to fetch up her head, which was missing.

'I thought you said your wife had gone home?' said my father.

'I thought she had. Where else could she have gone?'

'Well,' said my father at last, disgusted by the whole thing, 'if she had to kill herself, why couldn't she hang herself on a tree, instead of spoiling the well?'

'She might have slipped and fallen,' said the Long One.

My father looked up at him suddenly. He stared for a few moments. Then: 'Ye-yes,' he said, 'I suppose she might.'

Later, we talked about the thing, saying how odd it was that natives should commit suicide; it seemed almost like an impertinence, as if they were claiming to have the same delicate feelings as ours.

But later still, apropos of nothing in particular, my father was heard to remark: 'Well, I don't know, I'm damned if I know, but in any case he's a damned good driver.'

The veranda, which was lifted on stone pillars, jutted forward over the garden like a box in the theatre. Below were luxuriant masses of flowering shrubs, and creepers whose shiny leaves, like sequins, reflected light from a sky stained scarlet and purple and apple-green. This splendiferous sunset filled one half of the sky, fading gently through shades of mauve to a calm expanse of ruffling grey, blown over by tinted cloudlets; and in this still evening sky, just above a clump of darkening conifers, hung a small crystal moon.

There sat Major Gale and his wife, as they did every evening at this hour, side by side trimly in deck chairs, their sundowners on small tables at their elbows, critically watching, like connoisseurs, the pageant presented for them.

Major Gale said, with satisfaction: 'Good sunset tonight,' and they both turned their eyes to the vanquishing moon. The dusk drew veils across sky and garden; and punctually, as she did every day, Mrs Gale shook off nostalgia like a terrier shaking off water and rose, saying: 'Mosquitoes!' She drew her deck chair to the wall, where she neatly folded and stacked it.

'Here is the post,' she said, her voice quickening; and Major Gale went to the steps, waiting for the native who was hastening towards them through the tall shadowing bushes. He swung a sack from his back and handed it to Major Gale. A sour smell of raw meat rose from the sack. Major Gale said with the kindly contempt he used for his native servants: 'Did the spooks get you?' and laughed. The native who had panted the last mile of his ten-mile journey through a bush filled with unnameable phantoms, ghosts of ancestors, wraiths of tree and beast, put on a pantomime of fear and chattered and shivered for a moment like an ape, to amuse his master. Major Gale dismissed the boy. He ducked thankfully around the corner of the house to the back, where there were lights and companionship.

Mrs Gale lifted the sack and went into the front room. There she lit the oil lamp and called for the houseboy, to whom she handed the groceries and meat for removal. She took a fat bundle of letters from the very bottom of the sack and wrinkled her nose slightly: blood from the meat had stained them. She sorted the letters into two piles; and then husband and wife sat themselves down opposite each other to read their mail.

It was more than the ordinary farm living-room. There were koodoo horns branching out over the fireplace, and a bundle of knobkerries hanging on a nail; but on the floor were fine rugs, and the furniture was two hundred years old. The table was a pool of softly-reflected lights; it was polished by Mrs Gale herself every day before she set on it an earthenware crock filled with thorny red flowers. Africa and the English eighteenth century mingled in this room and were at peace.

From time to time Mrs Gale rose impatiently to attend to the lamp, which did not burn well. It was one of those terrifying paraffin things that have to be pumped with air to a whiter-hot flame from time to time, and which in any case emit a continuous soft hissing noise. Above the heads of the Gales a light cloud of flying insects wooed their fiery death and dropped one by one, plop, plop, plop to the table among the letters.

Mrs Gale took an envelope from her own heap and handed it to her husband. 'The assistant,' she remarked abstractedly, her eyes bent on what she held. She smiled tenderly as she read. The letter was from her oldest friend, a woman doctor in London, and they had written to each other every week for thirty years, ever since Mrs Gale came to exile in Southern Rhodesia. She murmured half-aloud: 'Why, Betty's brother's daughter is going to study economics,' and though she had never met Betty's brother, let alone the daughter, the news seemed to please and excite her extraordinarily. The whole of the letter was about people she had never met and was not likely ever to meet – about the weather, about English politics. Indeed, there was not a sentence in it that would not have struck an outsider as having been written out of a sense of duty; but when Mrs Gale had finished reading it, she put it aside gently and sat smiling quietly: she had gone back half a century to her childhood.

Gradually sight returned to her eyes, and she saw her husband where previously she had sat looking through him. He appeared disturbed; there was something wrong about the letter from the assistant.

Major Gale was a tall and still military figure, even in his khaki bush-shirt and shorts. He changed them twice a day. His shorts were creased sharp as folded paper, and the six pockets of his shirt were always buttoned up tight. His small head, with its polished surface of black hair, his tiny jaunty black moustache, his farmer's hands with their broken but clean nails – all these seemed to say that it was no easy matter not to let oneself go, not to let this damned disintegrating gaudy easy-going country get under one's skin. It wasn't easy, but he did it; he did it with the conscious effort that had slowed his movements and added the slightest touch of caricature to his appearance: one finds a man like Major Gale only in exile.

He rose from his chair and began pacing the room, while his wife watched him speculatively and waited for him to tell her what was the matter. When he stood up, there was something not quite right – what was it? Such a spruce and tailored man he was; but the disciplined shape of him was spoiled by a curious fatness and softness: the small rounded head was set on a thickening neck; the buttocks were fattening too, and quivered as he walked. Mrs Gale, as these facts assailed her, conscientiously excluded them: she had her own picture of her husband, and could not afford to have it destroyed.

At last he sighed, with a glance at her; and when she said: 'Well, dear?' he replied at once, 'The man has a wife.'

'Dear me!' she exclaimed, dismayed.

At once as if he had been waiting for her protest, he returned briskly: 'It will be nice for you to have another woman about the place.'

'Yes, I suppose it will,' she said humorously. At this most familiar note in her voice, he jerked his head up and said aggressively: 'You always complain I bury you alive.'

And so she did. Every so often, but not so often now, she allowed herself to overflow into a mood of gently humorous

bitterness; but it had not carried conviction for many years; it
was more, really, of an attention to him, like remembering to
kiss him good night. In fact, she had learned to love her
isolation, and she felt aggrieved that he did not know it.

'Well, but they can't come to the house. That I really couldn't
put up with.' The plan had been for the new assistant – Major
Gale's farming was becoming too successful and expanding for
him to manage any longer by himself – to have the spare room,
and share the house with his employers.

'No, I suppose not, if there's a wife.' Major Gale sounded
doubtful; it was clear he would not mind another family sharing
with them. 'Perhaps they could have the old house?' he
enquired at last.

'I'll see to it,' said Mrs Gale, removing the weight of worry
off her husband's shoulders. Things he could manage: people
bothered him. That they bothered her, too, now, was something she had become resigned to his not understanding. For
she knew he was hardly conscious of her; nothing existed for
him outside his farm. And this suited her well. During the early
years of their marriage, with the four children growing up,
there was always a little uneasiness between them, like an
unpaid debt. Now they were friends and could forget each
other. What a relief when he no longer 'loved' her! (That was
how she put it.) Ah, that 'love' – she thought of it with a small
humorous distaste. Growing old had its advantages.

When she said 'I'll see to it,' he glanced at her, suddenly,
directly; her tone had been a little too comforting and maternal.
Normally his gaze wavered over her, not seeing her. Now he
really observed her for a moment; he saw an elderly Englishwoman, as thin and dry as a stalk of maize in September, sitting
poised over her letters, one hand touching them lovingly,
gazing at him with her small flower-blue eyes. A look of guilt
in them troubled him. He crossed to her and kissed her cheek.
'There!' she said, inclining her face with a sprightly, fidgety
laugh. Overcome with embarrassment he stopped for a
moment, then said determinedly: 'I shall go and have my bath.'

After his bath, from which he emerged pink and shining like
an elderly baby, dressed in flannels and a blazer, they ate their
dinner under the wheezing oil lamp and the cloud of flying

insects. Immediately the meal was over he said 'Bed,' and moved off. He was always in bed before eight and up by five. Once Mrs Gale had adapted herself to his routine. Now, with the four boys out sailing the seven seas in the navy, and nothing really to get her out of bed (her servants were perfectly trained), she slept until eight, when she joined her husband at breakfast. She refused to have that meal in bed; nor would she have dreamed of appearing in her dressing-gown. Even as things were she was guilty enough about sleeping those three daylight hours, and found it necessary to apologize for her slackness. So, when her husband had gone to bed she remained under the lamp, re-reading her letters, sewing, reading or simply dreaming about the past, the very distant past, when she had been Caroline Morgan, living near a small country town, a country squire's daughter. That was how she liked best to think of herself.

Tonight she soon turned down the lamp and stepped on to the veranda. Now the moon was a large, soft, yellow fruit caught in the top branches of the blue-gums. The garden was filled with glamour, and she let herself succumb to it. She passed quietly down the steps and beneath the trees, with one quick solicitous glance back at the bedroom window: her husband hated her to be out of the house by herself at night. She was on her way to the old house that lay half a mile distant over the veld.

Before the Gales had come to this farm, two brothers had it, South Africans by birth and upbringing. The houses had then been separated by a stretch of untouched bush, with not so much as a fence or a road between them; and in this state of guarded independence the two men had lived, both bachelors, both quite alone. The thought of them amused Mrs Gale. She could imagine them sending polite notes to each other, invitations to meals or to spend an evening. She imagined them loaning each other books by native bearer, meeting at a neutral point between their homes. She was amused, but she respected them for a feeling she could understand. She had made up all kinds of pretty ideas about these brothers, until one day she learned from a neighbour that in fact the two men had quarrelled continually, and had eventually gone bankrupt because they could not agree how the farm was to be run. After this discovery Mrs Gale ceased to think about them; a pleasant fancy had become a distasteful reality.

The first thing she did on arriving was to change the name of the farm from Kloof Nek to Kloof Grange, making a link with home. One of the houses was denuded of furniture and used as a storage space. It was a square, bare box of a place, stuck in the middle of the bare veld, and its shut windows flashed back light to the sun all day. But her own home had been added to and extended, and surrounded with verandas and fenced; inside the fence were two acres of garden, that she had created over years of toil. And what a garden! These were what she lived for: her flowering African shrubs, her vivid English lawns, her water-garden with the goldfish and water lilies. Not many people had such a garden.

She walked through it this evening under the moon, feeling herself grow lightheaded and insubstantial with the influence of the strange greenish light, and of the perfumes from the flowers. She touched the leaves with her fingers as she passed, bending her face to the roses. At the gate, under the hanging white trumpets of the moonflower she paused, and lingered for a while, looking over the space of empty veld between her and the other house. She did not like going outside her garden at night. She was not afraid of natives, no: she had contempt for women who were afraid, for she regarded Africans as rather pathetic children, and was very kind to them. She did not know what made her afraid. Therefore she took a deep breath, compressed her lips, and stepped carefully through the gate, shutting it behind her with a sharp click. The road before her was a glimmering white ribbon, the hard-crusted sand sending up a continuous small sparkle of light as she moved. On either side were sparse stumpy trees, and their shadows were deep and black. A nightjar cut across the stars with crooked trailing wings, and she set her mouth defiantly: why, this was only the road she walked over every afternoon, for her constitutional! These were the trees she had pleaded for, when her husband was wanting to have them cut for firewood: in a sense they were her trees. Deliberately slowing her steps, as a discipline, she moved through the pits of shadow, gaining each stretch of clear moonlight with relief, until she came to the house. It looked dead, a dead thing with staring eyes, with those blank windows gleaming pallidly back at the moon. Nonsense, she told herself. Nonsense. And she walked to the front door, unlocked it, and flashed her torch over the floor. Sacks of grain were piled to the rafters, and the brick floor was scattered with loose mealies. Mice scurried invisibly to safety and flocks of cockroaches blackened the walls. Standing in a patch of moon-light on the brick, so that she would not unwittingly walk into a spiderweb or a jutting sack, she drew in deep breaths of the sweetish smell of maize, and made a list in her head of what had to be done; she was a very capable woman.

Then something struck her: if the man had forgotten, when applying for the job, to mention a wife, he was quite capable of forgetting children too. If they had children it wouldn't do; no, it wouldn't. She simply couldn't put up with a tribe of children – for Afrikaners never had less than twelve – running wild over the beautiful garden and teasing her goldfish. Anger spurted in her. De Wet – the name was hard on her tongue. Her husband should not have agreed to take on an Afrikaner. Really, really, Caroline, she chided herself humorously, stand-ing there in the deserted moonlit house, don't jump to con-clusions, don't be unfair.

She decided to arrange the house for a man and his wife, ignoring the possibility of children. She would arrange things, in kindness, for a woman who might be unused to living in loneliness; she would be good to this woman; so she scolded herself, to make atonement for her short fit of pettiness. But when she tried to form a picture of this woman who was coming to share her life, at least to the extent of taking tea with her in the mornings, and swapping recipes (so she supposed), imagin-ation failed her. She pictured a large Dutch frau, all homely comfort and sweating goodness, and was repulsed. For the first time the knowledge that she must soon, next week, take another woman into her life, came home to her; and she disliked it intensely.

Why must she? Her husband would not have to make a friend of the man. They would work together, that was all; but because they, the wives, were two women on an isolated farm, they would be expected to live in each other's pockets. All her instincts towards privacy, the distance which she had put between herself and other people, even her own husband, rebelled against it. And because she rebelled, rejecting this imaginary Dutch woman, to whom she felt so alien, she began to think of her friend Betty, as if it were she who would be coming to the farm.

Still thinking of her friend Betty she returned through the silent veld to her home, imagining them walking together over this road and talking as they had been used to do. The thought of Betty, who had turned into a shrewd, elderly woman doctor with kind eyes, sustained her through the frightening silences. At the gate she lifted her head to sniff the heavy perfume of the moonflowers, and became conscious that something else was invading her dream: it was a very bad smell, an odour of decay mingled with the odour from the flowers. Something had died on the veld, and the wind had changed and was bringing the smell towards the house. She made a mental note: I must send the boy in the morning to see what it is. Then the conflict between her thoughts of her friend and her own life presented itself sharply to her. You are a silly woman, Caroline, she said to herself. Three years before they had gone on holiday to England, and she had found she and Betty had nothing to say to each other. Their lives were so far apart, and had been for so long, that the weeks they spent together were an offering to a friendship that had died years before. She knew it very well, but tried not to think of it. It was necessary to her to have Betty remain, in imagination at least, as a counter-weight to her loneliness. Now she was being made to realize the truth. She resented that too, and somewhere the resentment was chalked up against Mrs De Wet, the Dutch woman who was going to invade her life with impertinent personal claims.

And next day, and the days following, she cleaned and swept and tidied the old house, not for Mrs De Wet, but for Betty. Otherwise she could not have gone through with it. And when it was all finished she walked through the rooms which she had furnished with things taken from her own home, and said to a visionary Betty (but Betty as she had been thirty years before): 'Well, what do you think of it?' The place was bare but clean now, and smelling of sunlight and air. The floors had coloured coconut matting over the brick; the beds, standing on opposite sides of the room, were covered with gaily striped counter-panes. There were vases of flowers everywhere. 'You would like living here,' Mrs Gale said to Betty, before locking the house up and returning to her own, feeling as if she had won a victory over herself.

The De Wets sent a wire saying they would arrive on Sunday after lunch. Mrs Gale noted with annoyance that this would spoil her rest, for she slept every day, through the afternoon heat. Major Gale, for whom every day was a working day (he hated idleness and found odd jobs to occupy him on Sundays), went off to a distant part of the farm to look at his cattle. Mrs Gale laid herself down on her bed with her eyes shut and listened for a car, all her nerves stretched. Flies buzzed drowsily over the window-panes; the breeze from the garden was warm and scented. Mrs Gale slept uncomfortably, warring all the afternoon with the knowledge that she should be awake. When she woke at four she was cross and tired, and there was still no sign of a car. She rose and dressed herself, taking a frock from the cupboard without looking to see what it was: her clothes were often fifteen years old. She brushed her hair absentmind-edly; and then, recalled by a sense that she had not taken enough trouble, slipped a large gold locket round her neck, as a conscientious mark of welcome. Then she left a message with the houseboy that she would be in the garden and walked away from the veranda with a strong excitement growing in her. This excitement rose as she moved through the crowding shrubs under the walls, through the rose garden with its wide green lawns where water sprayed all the year round, and arrived at her favourite spot among the fountains and the pools of water lilies. Her water-garden was an extravagance, for the pumping of the water from the river cost a great deal of money.

She sat herself on a shaded bench; and on one side were the glittering plumes of the fountains, the roses, the lawns, the house, and beyond them the austere wind-bitten high veld; on the other, at her feet, the ground dropped hundreds of feet sharply to the river. It was a rocky shelf thrust forward over the gulf, and here she would sit for hours, leaning dizzily outwards,

her short grey hair blown across her face, lost in adoration of
the hills across the river. Not of the river itself, no, she thought
of that with a sense of danger, for there, below her, in that
green-crowded gully, were suddenly the tropics: palm trees, a
slow brown river that eddied into reaches of marsh or curved
round belts of reeds twelve feet high. There were crocodiles,
and leopards came from the rocks to drink. Sitting there on her
exposed shelf, a smell of sun-warmed green, of hot decaying
water, of luxurious growth, an intoxicating heady smell rose in
waves to her face. She had learned to ignore it, and to ignore
the river, while she watched the hills. They were *her* hills: that
was how she felt. For years she had sat here, hours every day,
watching the cloud shadows move over them, watching them
turn blue with distance or come close after rain so that she
could see the exquisite brushwork of trees on the lower slopes.
They were never the same half an hour together. Modulating
light created them anew for her as she looked, thrusting one
peak forward and withdrawing another, moving them back so
that they were hazed on a smoky horizon, crouched in sullen
retreat; or raising them so that they towered into a brilliant
cleansed sky. Sitting here, buffeted by winds, scorched by the
sun or shivering with cold, she could challenge anything. They
were her mountains; they were what she was; they had made
her, had crystallized her loneliness into a strength, had sustained her and fed her.

And now she almost forgot the De Wets were coming, and
were hours late. Almost, not quite. At last, understanding that
the sun was setting (she could feel its warmth striking below
her shoulders), her small irritation turned to anxiety. Something might have happened to them? They had taken the wrong
road, perhaps? The car had broken down? And there was the
Major, miles away with their own car, and so there was no
means of looking for them. Perhaps she should send out
natives, along the roads? If they had taken the wrong turning,
to the river, they might be bogged in mud to the axles. Down
there, in the swampy heat, they could be bitten by mosquitoes
and then . . .

Caroline, she said to herself severely (thus finally withdrawing from the mountains), don't let things worry you so. She

stood up and shook herself, pushed the hair out of her face, and gripped her whipping skirts in a thick bunch. She stepped backwards away from the wind that raked the edges of the cliff, sighed a good-bye to her garden for that day, and returned to the house. There, outside the front door, was a car, an ancient jalopy bulging with luggage, its back doors tied with rope. And children! She could see a half-grown girl on the steps. No, really, it was too much. On the other side of the car stooped a tall, thin, fairheaded man, burnt as brown as toffee, looking for someone to come. He must be the father. She approached, adjusting her face to a smile, looking apprehensively about her for the children. The man slowly came forward, the girl after him. 'I expected you earlier,' began Mrs Gale briskly, looking reproachfully into the man's face. His eyes were cautious, blue, assessing. He looked her casually up and down, and seemed not to take her into account. 'Is Major Gale about?' he asked.

'I am Mrs Gale,' she replied. Then, again: 'I expected you earlier.' Really, four hours late, and not a word of apology!

'We started late,' he remarked. 'Where can I put our things?'

Mrs Gale swallowed her annoyance and said: 'I didn't know you had a family. I didn't make arrangements.'

'I wrote to the Major about my wife', said De Wet. 'Didn't he get my letter?' He sounded offended.

Weakly Mrs Gale said: 'Your wife?' and looked in wonderment at the girl, who was smiling awkwardly behind her husband. It could be seen, looking at her more closely, that she might perhaps be eighteen. She was a small creature, with delicate brown legs and arms, a brush of dancing black curls, and large excited black eyes. She put both hands round her husband's arm, and said, giggling: 'I am Mrs De Wet.'

De Wet put her away from him, gently, but so that she pouted and said: 'We got married last week.'

'Last week,' said Mrs Gale, conscious of dislike.

The girl said, with an extraordinary mixture of effrontery and shyness: 'He met me in the cinema and we got married next day.' It seemed as if she were in some way offering herself to the older woman, offering something precious of herself.

'Really,' said Mrs Gale politely, glancing almost apprehensively at this man, this slow-moving, laconic, shrewd South

African, who had behaved with such violence and folly. Distaste twisted her again.

Suddenly the man said, grasping the girl by the arm, and gently shaking her to and fro, in a sort of controlled exasperation: 'Thought I had better get myself a wife to cook for me, all this way out in the blue. No restaurants here, hey, Doodle?'

'Oh, Jack,' pouted the girl, giggling. 'All he thinks about is his stomach,' she said to Mrs Gale, as one girl to another, and then glanced with delicious fear up at her husband.

'Cooking is what I married you for,' he said, smiling down at her intimately.

There stood Mrs Gale opposite them, and she saw that they had forgotten her existence; and that it was only by the greatest effort of will that they did not kiss. 'Well,' she remarked dryly, 'this is a surprise.'

They fell apart, their faces changing. They became at once what they had been during the first moments: two hostile strangers. They looked at her across the barrier that seemed to shut the world away from them. They saw a middle-aged English lady, in a shapeless old-fashioned blue silk dress, with a gold locket sliding over a flat bosom, smiling at them coldly, her blue, misted eyes critically narrowed.

'I'll take you to your house,' she said energetically. 'I'll walk, and you go in the car – no, I walk it often.' Nothing would induce her to get into the bouncing rattle-trap that was bursting with luggage and half-suppressed intimacies.

As stiff as a twig she marched before them along the road, while the car jerked and ground along in bottom gear. She knew it was ridiculous; she could feel their eyes on her back, could feel their astonished amusement; but she could not help it.

When they reached the house, she unlocked it, showed them briefly what arrangements had been made, and left them. She walked back in a tumult of anger, caused mostly because of her picture of herself walking along that same road, meekly followed by the car, and refusing to do the only sensible thing, which was to get into it with them.

She sat on her veranda for half an hour, looking at the sunset sky without seeing it, and writhing with various emotions, none of which she classified. Eventually she called the houseboy, and gave him a note, asking the two to come to dinner. No sooner had the boy left, and was trotting off down the bushy path to the gate, than she called him back. 'I'll go myself,' she said. This was partly to prove that she made nothing of walking the half mile, and partly from contrition. After all, it was no crime to get married, and they seemed very fond of each other. That was how she put it.

When she came to the house, the front room was littered with luggage, paper, pots and pans. All the exquisite order she had created was destroyed. She could hear voices from the bedroom.

'But, Jack, I don't want you to. I want you to stay with me.' And then his voice, humorous, proud, slow, amorous: 'You'll do what I tell you, my girl. I've got to see the old man and find out what's cooking. I start work tomorrow, don't forget.'

'But, Jack . . .' Then came sounds of scuffling, laughter and a sharp slap.

'Well,' said Mrs Gale, drawing in her breath. She knocked on the wood of the door, and all sound ceased. 'Come in,' came the girl's voice. Mrs Gale hesitated, then went into the bedroom.

Mrs De Wet was sitting in a bunch on the bed, her flowered frock spread all around her, combing her hair. Mrs Gale noted that the two beds had already been pushed together. 'I've come to ask you to dinner,' she said briskly. 'You don't want to have to cook when you've just come.'

Their faces had already become blank and polite.

'Oh no, don't trouble, Mrs Gale,' said De Wet, awkwardly. 'We'll get ourselves something, don't worry.' He glanced at the girl, and his face softened. He said, unable to resist it: 'She'll get busy with the tin-opener in a minute, I expect. That's her idea of feeding a man.'

'Oh, Jack,' pouted his wife.

De Wet turned back to the washstand, and proceeded to swab lather on his face. Waving the brush at Mrs Gale, he said: 'Thanks all the same. But tell the Major I'll be over after dinner to talk things over.'

'Very well,' said Mrs Gale, 'just as you like.'

She walked away from the house. Now she felt rebuffed. After all, they might have had the politeness to come; yet she was pleased they hadn't; yet if they preferred making love to getting to know the people who were to be their close neighbours for what might be years, it was their own affair . . .

Mrs De Wet was saying, as she painted her toenails, with her knees drawn up to her chin, and the bottle of varnish gripped between her heels: 'Who the hell does she think she is, anyway? Surely she could give us a meal without making such a fuss when we've just come.'

'She came to ask us, didn't she?'

'Hoping we would say no.'

And Mrs Gale knew quite well that this was what they were thinking, and felt it was unjust. She would have liked them to come: the man wasn't a bad sort, in his way; a simple soul, but pleasant enough; as for the girl, she would have to learn, that was all. They should have come, it was their fault. Nevertheless she was filled with that discomfort that comes of having done a job badly. If she had behaved differently they would have come. She was cross throughout dinner; and that meal was not half finished when there was a knock on the door. De Wet stood there, apparently surprised they had not finished, from which it seemed that the couple had, after all, dined off sardines and bread and butter.

Major Gale left his meal and went out to the veranda to discuss business. Mrs Gale finished her dinner in state, and then joined the two men. Her husband rose politely at her coming, offered her a chair, sat down and forgot her presence. She listened to them talking for some two hours. Then she interjected a remark (a thing she never did, as a rule, for women get used to sitting silent when men discuss farming) and did not know herself what made her say what she did about the cattle; but when De Wet looked round absently as if to say she should mind her own business, and her husband remarked absently, 'Yes, dear,' when a Yes dear did not fit her remark at all, she got up angrily and went indoors. Well, let them talk, then, she did not mind.

As she undressed for bed, she decided she was tired, because of her broken sleep that afternoon. But she could not sleep then, either. She listened to the sound of the men's voices, drifting brokenly round the corner of the veranda. They seemed to be thoroughly enjoying themselves. It was after twelve when she heard De Wet say, in that slow factious way of his: 'I'd better be getting home. I'll catch it hot, as it is.' And, with rage, Mrs Gale heard her husband laugh. He actually laughed. She realized that she herself had been planning an acid remark for when he came to the bedroom; so when he did enter, smelling of tobacco smoke, and grinning, and then proceeded to walk jauntily about the room in his underclothes, she said nothing, but noted that he was getting fat, in spite of all the hard work he did.

'Well, what do you think of the man?'

'He'll do very well indeed,' said Major Gale, with satisfaction. 'Very well. He knows his stuff all right. He's been doing mixed farming in the Transvaal for years.' After a moment he asked politely, as he got with a bounce into his own bed on the other side of the room. 'And what is she like?'

'I haven't seen much of her, have I? But she seems pleasant enough.' Mrs Gale spoke with measured detachment.

'Someone for you to talk to,' said Major Gale, turning himself over to sleep. 'You had better ask her over to tea.'

At this Mrs Gale sat straight up in her own bed with a jerk of annoyance. Someone for her to talk to, indeed! But she composed herself, said good night with her usual briskness, and lay awake. Next day she must certainly ask the girl to morning tea. It would be rude not to. Besides, that would leave the afternoon free for her garden and her mountains.

Next morning she sent a boy across with a note, which read: 'I shall be so pleased if you will join me for morning tea.' She signed it: Caroline Gale.

She went herself to the kitchen to cook scones and cakes. At eleven o'clock she was seated on the veranda in the green-dappled shade from the creepers, saying to herself that she believed she was in for a headache. Living as she did, in a long, timeless abstraction of growing things and mountains and silence, she had become very conscious of her body's responses to weather and to the slow advance of age. A small ache in her ankle when rain was due was like a cherished friend. Or she would sit with her eyes shut, in the shade, after a morning's pruning in the violent sun, feeling waves of pain flood back from her eyes to the back of her skull, and say with satisfaction: 'You deserve it, Caroline!' It was right she should pay for such pleasure with such pain.

At last she heard lagging footsteps up the path, and she opened her eyes reluctantly. There was the girl, preparing her face for a social occasion, walking primly through the bougainvillaea arches, in a flowered frock as vivid as her surroundings. Mrs Gale jumped to her feet and cried gaily: 'I am so glad you had time to come.' Mrs De Wet giggled irresistibly and said: 'But I had nothing else to do, had I?' Afterwards she said scornfully to her husband: 'She's nuts. She writes me letters with stuck-down envelopes when I'm five minutes away, and says Have I the time? What the hell else did she think I had to do?' And then, violently: 'She can't have anything to do. There was enough food to feed ten.'

'Wouldn't be a bad idea if you spent more time cooking,' said De Wet fondly.

The next day Mrs Gale gardened, feeling guilty all the time, because she could not bring herself to send over another note of invitation. After a few days, she invited the De Wets to dinner, and through the meal made polite conversation with the girl while the men lost themselves in cattle diseases. What could one talk to a girl like that about? Nothing! Her mind, as far as Mrs Gale was concerned, was a dark continent, which she had no inclination to explore. Mrs De Wet was not interested in recipes, and when Mrs Gale gave helpful advice about ordering clothes from England, which was so much cheaper than buying them in the local towns, the reply came that she had made all her own clothes since she was seven. After that there seemed nothing to say, for it was hardly possible to remark that these strapped sun-dresses and bright slacks were quite unsuitable for the farm, besides being foolish, since bare shoulders in this sun were dangerous. As for her shoes! She wore corded beach sandals which had already turned dust colour from the roads.

There were two more tea parties; then they were allowed to lapse. From time to time Mrs Gale wondered uneasily what on

One morning she was pricking seedlings into a tin when the houseboy came and said the little missus was on the veranda and she was sick.

At once dismay flooded Mrs Gale. She thought of a dozen tropical diseases, of which she had had unpleasant experience, and almost ran to the veranda. There was the girl, sitting screwed up in a chair, her face contorted, her eyes red, her whole body shuddering violently. 'Malaria,' thought Mrs Gale at once, noting that trembling.

'What is the trouble, my dear?' Her voice was kind. She put her hand on the girl's shoulder. Mrs De Wet turned and flung her arms around her hips, weeping, weeping, her small curly head buried in Mrs Gale's stomach. Holding herself stiffly away from this dismaying contact, Mrs Gale stroked the head and made soothing noises.

'Mrs Gale, Mrs Gale . . .'

'What is it?'

'I can't stand it. I shall go mad. I simply can't stand it.'

Mrs Gale, seeing that this was not a physical illness, lifted her up, led her inside, laid her on her own bed, and fetched cologne and handkerchiefs. Mrs De Wet sobbed for a long while, clutching the older woman's hand, and then at last grew silent. Finally she sat up with a small rueful smile, and said pathetically: 'I am a fool.'

'But what *is* it, dear?'

'It isn't anything, really. I am so lonely. I wanted to get my mother up to stay with me, only Jack said there wasn't room, and he's quite right, only I got mad, because I thought he might at least have had my mother . . .'

Mrs Gale felt guilt like a sword: she could have filled the place of this child's mother.

'And it isn't anything, Mrs Gale, not really. It's not that I'm not happy with Jack. I am, but I never see him. I'm not used to this kind of thing. I come from a family of thirteen counting my parents, and I simply can't stand it.'

Mrs Gale sat and listened, and thought of her own loneliness when she first began this sort of life.

'And then he comes in late, not till seven sometimes, and I know he can't help it, with the farm work and all that, and then he has supper and goes straight off to bed. I am not sleepy then. And then I get up sometimes and I walk along the road with my dog . . .'

Mrs Gale remembered how, in the early days after her husband had finished with his brief and apologetic embraces, she used to rise with a sense of relief and steal to the front room, where she lighted the lamp again and sat writing letters, reading old ones, thinking of her friends and of herself as a girl. But that was before she had her first child. She thought: This girl should have a baby; and could not help glancing downwards at her stomach.

Mrs De Wet, who missed nothing, said resentfully: 'Jack says I should have a baby. That's all he says.' Then, since she had to include Mrs Gale in this resentment, she transformed herself all at once from a sobbing baby into a gauche but armoured young woman with whom Mrs Gale could have no contact. 'I am sorry,' she said formally. Then, with a grating humour: 'Thank you for letting me blow off steam.' She climbed off the bed, shook her skirts straight, and tossed her head. 'Thank you. I am a nuisance.' With painful brightness she added: 'So, that's how it goes. Who would be a woman, eh?'

Mrs Gale stiffened. 'You must come and see me whenever you are lonely,' she said, equally bright and false. It seemed to her incredible that this girl should come to her with all her defences down, and then suddenly shut her out with this facetious nonsense. But she felt more comfortable with the distance between them, she couldn't deny it.

'Oh, I will, Mrs Gale. Thank you so much for asking me.' She lingered for a moment, frowning at the brilliantly polished table in the front room, and then took her leave. Mrs Gale watched her go. She noted that at the gate the girl started whistling gaily, and smiled comically. Letting off steam! Well, she said to herself, well . . . And she went back to her garden.

That afternoon she made a point of walking across to the other house. She would offer to show Mrs De Wet the garden. The two women returned together, Mrs Gale wondering if the girl regretted her emotional lapse of the morning. If so, she showed no signs of it. She broke into bright chatter when a topic mercifully occurred to her; in between were polite silences full of attention to what she seemed to hope Mrs Gale might say.

Mrs Gale was relying on the effect of her garden. They passed the house through the shrubs. There were the fountains, sending up their vivid showers of spray, there the cool mats of water lilies, under which the coloured fishes slipped, there the irises, sunk in green turf.

'This must cost a packet to keep up,' said Mrs De Wet. She stood at the edge of the pool, looking at her reflection dissolving among the broad green leaves, glanced obliquely up at Mrs Gale, and dabbed her exposed red toenails in the water.

Mrs Gale saw that she was thinking of herself as her husband's employer's wife. 'It does, rather,' she said dryly, remembering that the only quarrels she ever had with her husband were over the cost of pumping water. 'You are fond of gardens?' she asked. She could not imagine anyone not being fond of gardens.

Mrs De Wet said sullenly: 'My mother was always too busy having kids to have time for gardens. She had her last baby early this year.' An ancient and incommunicable resentment dulled her face. Mrs Gale, seeing that all this beauty and peace meant nothing to her companion that she would have it mean, said, playing her last card: 'Come and see my mountains.' She regretted the pronoun as soon as it was out – *so* exaggerated.

But when she had the girl safely on the rocky verge of the escarpment, she heard her say: 'There's my river.' She was leaning forward over the great gulf, and her voice was lifted with excitement. 'Look,' she was saying, 'Look, there it is.' She turned to Mrs Gale, laughing, her hair spun over her eyes in a fine iridescent rain, tossing her head back, clutching her skirts down, exhilarated by the tussle with the wind.

'Mind, you'll lose your balance.' Mrs Gale pulled her back.

'You have been down to the river, then?'

'I go there every morning.'

Mrs Gale was silent. The thing seemed preposterous. 'But it is four miles there and four back.'

'Oh, I'm used to walking.'

'But . . .' Mrs Gale heard her own sour, expostulating voice and stopped herself. There was after all no logical reason why the girl should not go to the river. 'What do you do there?'

'I sit on the edge of a big rock and dangle my legs in the water, and I fish, sometimes. I caught a barble last week. It tasted foul, but it was fun catching it. And I pick water lilies.'

'There are crocodiles,' said Mrs Gale sharply. The girl was wrong-headed; anyone was who could like that steamy bath of vapours, heat, smells and – what? It was an unpleasant place. 'A native girl was taken there last year, at the ford.'

'There couldn't be a crocodile where I go. The water is clear, right down. You can see right under the rocks. It is a lovely pool. There's a kingfisher, and water-birds, all colours. They are so pretty. And when you sit there and look, the sky is a long narrow slit. From here it looks quite far across the river to the other side, but really it isn't. And the trees crowding close make it narrower. Just think how many millions of years it must have taken for the water to wear down the rock so deep.'

'There's bilharzia, too.'

'Oh, bilharzia!'

'There's nothing funny about bilharzia. My husband had it. He had injections for six months before he was cured.'

The girl's face dulled. 'I'll be careful,' she said irrationally, turning away, holding her river and her long hot dreamy mornings away from Mrs Gale, like a secret.

'Look at the mountains,' said Mrs Gale, pointing. The girl glanced over the chasm at the foothills, then bent forward again, her face reverent. Through the mass of green below were glimpses of satiny brown. She breathed deeply: 'Isn't it a lovely smell?' she said.

'Let's go and have some tea,' said Mrs Gale. She felt cross and put out; she had no notion why. She could not help being brusque with the girl. And so at last they were quite silent together; and in silence they remained on that veranda above the beautiful garden, drinking their tea and wishing it was time for them to part.

Soon they saw the two husbands coming up the garden. Mrs De Wet's face lit up; and she sprang to her feet and was off down the path, running lightly. She caught her husband's arm and clung there. He put her away from him, gently. 'Hullo,' he remarked good-humouredly. 'Eating again?' And then he turned back to Major Gale and went on talking. The girl lagged up the path behind her husband like a sulky small girl, pulling at Mrs Gale's beloved roses and scattering crimson petals everywhere.

On the veranda the men sank at once into chairs, took large cups of tea, and continued talking as they drank thirstily. Mrs Gale listened and smiled. Crops, cattle, disease; weather, crops and cattle. Mrs De Wet perched on the veranda wall and swung her legs. Her face was petulant, her lips trembled, her eyes were full of tears. Mrs Gale was saying silently under her breath, with ironical pity, in which there was also cruelty: You'll get used to it, my dear; you'll get used to it. But she respected the girl, who had courage: walking to the river and back, wandering round the dusty flowerbeds in the starlight, trying to find peace – at least, she was trying to find it.

She said sharply, cutting into the men's conversation: 'Mr De Wet, did you know your wife spends her mornings at the river?'

The man looked at her vaguely, while he tried to gather the sense of her words: his mind was on the farm. 'Sure,' he said at last. 'Why not?'

'Aren't you afraid of bilharzia?'

He said laconically: 'If we were going to get it, we would have got it long ago. A drop of water can infect you, touching the skin.'

'Wouldn't it be wiser not to let the water touch you in the first place?' she enquired with deceptive mildness.

'Well, I told her. She wouldn't listen. It is too late now. Let her enjoy it.'

'But . . .'

'About that red heifer,' said Major Gale, who had not been aware of any interruption.

'No,' said Mrs Gale sharply. 'You are not going to dismiss it like that.' She saw the three of them look at her in astonishment. 'Mr De Wet, have you ever thought what it means to a woman being alone all day, with not enough to do? It's enough to drive anyone crazy.'

Major Gale raised his eyebrows; he had not heard his wife speak like that for so long. As for De Wet, he said with a slack good-humour that sounded brutal: 'And what do you expect me to do about it?'

'You don't realize,' said Mrs Gale futilely, knowing perfectly well there was nothing he could do about it. 'You don't understand how it is.'

'She'll have a kid soon,' said De Wet. 'I hope so, at any rate. That will give her something to do.'

Anger raced through Mrs Gale like a flame along petrol. She was trembling. 'She might be that red heifer,' she said at last.

'What's the matter with having kids?' asked De Wet. 'Any objection?'

'You might ask me first,' said the girl bitterly.

Her husband blinked at her, comically bewildered. 'Hey, what is this?' he enquired. 'What have I done? You said you wanted to have kids. Wouldn't have married you otherwise.'

'I never said I didn't.'

'Talking about her as if she were . . .'

'When, then?' Mrs Gale and the man were glaring at each other.

'There's more to women than having children,' said Mrs Gale at last, and flushed because of the ridiculousness of her words.

De Wet looked her up and down, up and down. 'I want kids,' he said at last. 'I want a large family. Make no mistake about that. And when I married her' – he jerked his head at his wife – 'I told her I wanted them. She can't turn round now and say I didn't.'

'Who is turning round and saying anything?' asked the girl, fine and haughty, staring away over the trees.

'Well, if no one is blaming anyone for anything,' asked Major Gale, jauntily twirling his little moustache, 'what is all this about?'

'God knows, I don't,' said De Wet angrily. He glanced sullenly at Mrs Gale. 'I didn't start it.'

Mrs Gale sat silent, trembling, feeling foolish, but so angry she could not speak. After a while she said to the girl: 'Shall we go inside, my dear?' The girl, reluctantly, and with a lingering backward look at her husband, rose and followed Mrs Gale. 'He didn't mean anything,' she said awkwardly, apologizing for her husband to her husband's employer's wife. This room, with its fine old furniture, always made her apologetic.

At this moment, De Wet stooped into the doorway and said: 'Come on, I am going home.'

'Is that an order?' asked the girl quickly, backing so that she came side by side with Mrs Gale: she even reached for the other woman's hand. Mrs Gale did not take it: this was going too far.

'What's got into you?' he said, exasperated. 'Are you coming or are you not?'

'I can't do anything else, can I?' she replied, and followed him from the house like a queen who has been insulted.

Major Gale came in after a few moments. 'Lovers' quarrel,' he said, laughing awkwardly. This phrase irritated Mrs Gale.

'That man!' she exclaimed. 'That man!'

'Why, what is wrong with him?' She remained silent, pretending to arrange her flowers. This silly scene, with its hinterlands of emotion, made her furious. She was angry with herself, angry with her husband, and furious at that foolish couple who had succeeded in upsetting her and destroying her peace. At last she said: 'I am going to bed. I've such a headache, I can't think.'

'I'll bring you a tray, my dear,' said Major Gale, with a touch of exaggeration in his courtesy that annoyed her even more. 'I don't want anything, thank you,' she said, like a child, and marched off to the bedroom.

There she undressed and went to bed. She tried to read, found she was not following the sense of the words, put down the book, and blew out the light. Light streamed into the room from the moon; she could see the trees along the fence banked black against stars. From next door came the clatter of her husband's solitary meal.

Later she heard voices from the veranda. Soon her husband came into the room and said: 'De Wet is asking whether his wife has been here.'

'What!' exclaimed Mrs Gale, slowly assimilating the implications of this. 'Why, has she gone off somewhere?'

'She's not at home,' said the Major uncomfortably. For he always became uncomfortable and very polite when he had to deal with situations like this.

Mrs Gale sank back luxuriously on her pillow. 'Tell that fine young man that his wife often goes for long walks by herself when he's asleep. He probably hasn't noticed it.' Here she gave a deadly look at her husband. 'Just as I used to,' she could not prevent herself adding.

Major Gale fiddled with his moustache, and gave her a look which seemed to say: 'Oh lord, don't say we are going back to all that business again?' He went out, and she heard him saying: 'Your wife might have gone for a walk, perhaps?' Then the young man's voice: 'I know she does sometimes. I don't like her being out at night, but she just walks around the house. And she takes the dogs with her. Maybe she's gone farther this time – being upset, you know.'

'Yes, I know,' said Major Gale. Then they both laughed. The laughter was of a quite different quality from the sober responsibility of their tone a moment before: and Mrs Gale found herself sitting up in bed, muttering: 'How *dare* he?'

She got up and dressed herself. She was filled with premonitions of unpleasantness. In the main room her husband was sitting reading, and since he seldom read, it seemed he was also worried. Neither of them spoke. When she looked at the clock, she found it was just past nine o'clock.

After an hour of tension, they heard the footsteps they had been waiting for. There stood De Wet, angry, worried sick, his face white, his eyes burning.

'We must get the boys out,' he said, speaking directly to Major Gale, and ignoring Mrs Gale.

'I am coming too,' she said.

'No, my dear,' said the Major cajolingly. 'You stay here.'

'You can't go running over the veld at this time of night,' said De Wet to Mrs Gale, very blunt and rude.

'I shall do as I please,' she returned.

The three of them stood on the veranda, waiting for the natives. Everything was drenched in moonlight. Soon they heard a growing clamour of voices from over a ridge, and a little while later the darkness there was lighted by flaring torches held high by invisible hands: it seemed as if the night were scattered with torches advancing of their own accord. Then a crowd of dark figures took shape under the broken lights. The farm natives, excited by the prospect of a night's chasing over the veld, were yelling as if they were after a small buck or hare.

Mrs Gale sickened. 'Is it necessary to have all these natives in it?' she asked. 'After all, have we even considered the possibilities? Where can a girl run *to* on a place like this?'

'That is the point,' said Major Gale frigidly.

'I can't bear to think of her being – pursued, like this, by a crowd of natives. It's horrible.'

'More horrible still if she has hurt herself and is waiting for help,' said De Wet. He ran off down the path, shouting to the natives and waving his arms. The Gales saw them separate into three bands, and soon there were three groups of lights jerking away in different directions through the hazy dark, and the yells and shouting came back to them on the wind.

Mrs Gale thought: She could have taken the road back to the station, in which case she could be caught by car, even now. She commanded her husband: 'Take the car along the road and see.'

'That's an idea,' said the Major, and went off to the garage. She heard the car start off, and watched the rear light dwindle redly into the night.

But that was the least ugly of the possibilities. What if she had been so blind with anger, grief, or whatever emotion it was that had driven her away, that she had simply run off into the veld not knowing where she went? There were thousands of acres of trees, thick grass, gullies, kopjes. She might at this moment be lying with a broken arm or leg; she might be pushing her way through grass higher than her head, stumbling over roots and rocks. She might be screaming for help some- where for fear of wild animals, for if she crossed the valley into the hills there were leopards, lions, wild dogs. Mrs Gale suddenly caught her breath in an agony of fear: the valley! What if she had mistaken her direction and walked over the edge of the escarpment in the dark? What if she had forded the river and been taken by a crocodile? There were so many things: she might even be caught in a game trap. Once, taking her walk, Mrs Gale herself had come across a tall sapling by the path where the spine and ribs of a large buck dangled, and on the ground were the pelvis and legs, fine eroded bones of an animal trapped and forgotten by its trapper. Anything might have happened. And worse than any of the actual physical dangers was the danger of falling a victim to fear: being alone on the veld, at night, knowing oneself lost: this was enough to send anyone off balance.

The silly little fool, the silly little fool: anger and pity and terror confused in Mrs Gale until she was walking crazily up and down her garden through the bushes, tearing blossoms and foliage to pieces in trembling fingers. She had no idea how time was passing; until Major Gale returned and said that he had taken the ten miles to the station at seven miles an hour, turning his lights into the bush this way and that. At the station everyone was in bed; but the police were standing on the alert for news.

It was long after twelve. As for De Wet and the bands of searching natives, there was no sign of them. They would be miles away by this time.

'Go to bed,' said Major Gale at last.

'Don't be ridiculous,' she said. After a while she held out her hand to him, and said: 'One feels so helpless.'

There was nothing to say; they walked together under the stars, their minds filled with horrors. Later she made some tea and they drank it standing; to sit would have seemed heartless. They were so tired they could hardly move. Then they got their second wind and continued walking. That night Mrs Gale hated her garden, that highly-cultivated patch of luxuriant growth, stuck in the middle of a country that could do this sort of thing to you suddenly. It was all the fault of the country! In a civilized sort of place, the girl would have caught the train to her mother, and a wire would have put everything right. Here, she might have killed herself, simply because of a passing fit of despair. Mrs Gale began to get hysterical. She was weeping softly in the circle of her husband's arm by the time the sky lightened and the redness of dawn spread over the sky.

As the sun rose, De Wet returned over the veld. He said he

had sent the natives back to their huts to sleep. They had found nothing. He stated that he also intended to sleep for an hour, and that he would be back on the job by eight. Major Gale nodded: he recognized this as a necessary discipline against collapse. But after the young man walked off across the veld towards his house, the two older people looked at each other and began to move after him. 'He must not be alone,' said Mrs Gale sensibly. 'I shall make him some tea and see that he drinks it.'

'He wants sleep,' said Major Gale. His own eyes were red and heavy.

'I'll put something in his tea,' said Mrs Gale. 'He won't know it is there.' Now she had something to do, she was much more cheerful. Planning De Wet's comfort, she watched him turn in at his gate and vanish inside the house: they were some two hundred yards behind.

Suddenly there was a shout, and then a commotion of screams and yelling. The Gales ran fast along the remaining distance and burst into the front room, white-faced and expecting the worst, in whatever form it might choose to present itself.

There was De Wet, his face livid with rage, bending over his wife, who was huddled on the floor and shielding her head with her arms, while he beat her shoulders with his closed fists.

Mrs Gale exclaimed: 'Beating your wife!'

De Wet flung the girl away from him, and staggered to his feet. 'She was here all the time,' he said, half in temper, half in sheer wonder. 'She was hiding under the bed. She told me. When I came in she was sitting on the bed and laughing at me.' The girl beat her hands on the floor and said, laughing and crying together: 'Now you have to take some notice of me. Looking for me all night over the veld with your silly natives! You looked so stupid, running about like ants, looking for me.'

'My God,' said De Wet simply, giving up. He collapsed backwards into a chair and lay there, his eyes shut, his face twitching.

'So now you have to notice me,' she said defiantly, but beginning to look scared. 'I have to pretend to run away, but then you sit up and take notice.'

'Be quiet,' said De Wet, breathing heavily. 'Be quiet, if you don't want to get hurt bad.'

'Beating your wife,' said Mrs Gale. 'Savages behave better.'

'Caroline, my dear,' said Major Gale awkwardly. He moved towards the door.

'Take that woman out of here if you don't want me to beat her too,' said De Wet to Major Gale.

Mrs Gale was by now crying with fury. 'I'm not going,' she said. 'I'm not going. This poor child isn't safe with you.'

'But what was it all about?' said Major Gale, laying his hand kindly on the girl's shoulder. 'What was it, my dear? What did you have to do it for, and make us all so worried?'

She began to cry. 'Major Gale, I am sorry. I forgot myself. I got mad. I told him I was going to have a baby. I told him when I got back from your place. And all he said was: that's fine. That's the first of them, he said. He didn't love me, or say he was pleased, or nothing.'

'Dear Christ in hell,' said De Wet wearily, with the exasperation strong in his voice, 'what do you make me do these things for? Do you think I want to beat you? Did you think I wasn't pleased: I keep telling you I want kids, I love kids.'

'But you don't care about me,' she said, sobbing bitterly.

'Don't I?' he said helplessly.

'Beating your wife when she is pregnant,' said Mrs Gale. 'You ought to be ashamed of yourself.' She advanced on the young man with her own fists clenched, unconscious of what she was doing. 'You ought to be beaten yourself, that's what you need.'

Mrs De Wet heaved herself off the floor, rushed on Mrs Gale, pulled her back so that she nearly lost balance, and then flung herself on her husband. 'Jack,' she said, clinging to him desperately, 'I am so sorry, I am so sorry, Jack.'

He put his arms round her. 'There,' he said simply, his voice thick with tiredness, 'don't cry. We got mixed up, that's all.'

Major Gale, who had caught and steadied his wife as she staggered back, said to her in a low voice: 'Come, Caroline. Come. Leave them to sort it out.'

'And what if he loses his temper again and decides to kill her this time?' demanded Mrs Gale, her voice shrill.

De Wet got to his feet, lifting his wife with him. 'Go away now, Mrs Major,' he said. 'Get out of here. You've done enough damage.'

'I've done enough damage?' she gasped. 'And what have I done?'

'Oh nothing, nothing at all,' he said with ugly sarcasm. 'Nothing at all. But please go and leave my wife alone in future, Mrs Major.'

'Come, Caroline, *please*,' said Major Gale.

She allowed herself to be drawn out of the room. Her head was aching so that the vivid morning light invaded her eyes in a wave of pain. She swayed a little as she walked.

'Mrs Major,' she said, 'he was upset,' said her husband judiciously.

She snorted. Then, after a silence: 'So, it was all my fault.'

'He didn't say so.'

'I thought that was what he was saying. He behaves like a brute and then says it is my fault.'

'It was no one's fault,' said Major Gale, patting her vaguely on shoulders and back as they stumbled back home.

They reached the gate, and entered the garden, which was now musical with birds.

'A lovely morning,' remarked Major Gale.

'Next time you get an assistant,' she said finally, 'get people of our kind. These might be savages, the way they behave.'

And that was the last word she would ever say on the subject.

Little Tembi

Jane McCluster, who had been a nurse before she married, started a clinic on the farm within a month of arriving. Though she had been born and brought up in town, her experience of natives was wide, for she had been a sister in the native wards of the city hospital, by choice, for years; she liked nursing natives, and explained her feeling in the words: 'They are just like children, and appreciate what you do for them.' So, when she had taken a thorough, diagnosing kind of look at the farm natives, she exclaimed, 'Poor things!' and set about turning an old dairy into a dispensary. Her husband was pleased; it would save money in the long run by cutting down illness in the compound.

Willie McCluster, who had also been born and raised in South Africa, was nevertheless unmistakably and determinedly Scottish. His accent might be emphasized for loyalty's sake, but he had kept all the fine qualities of his people unimpaired by a slowing and relaxing climate. He was shrewd, vigorous, earthy, practical and kind. In appearance he was largely built, with a square bony face, a tight mouth, and eyes whose fierce blue glance was tempered by the laughter wrinkles about them. He became a farmer young, having planned the step for years: he was not one of those who drift on to the land because of discontent with an office, or because of failure, or vague yearnings towards 'freedom'. Jane, a cheerful and competent girl who knew what she wanted, trifled with her numerous suitors with one eye on Willie, who wrote her weekly letters from the farming college in the Transvaal. As soon as his four years' training were completed, they married.

They were then twenty-seven, and felt themselves well-equipped for a useful and enjoyable life. Their house was planned for a family. They would have been delighted if a baby had been born the old-fashioned nine months after marriage. As it was, a baby did not come; and when two years had passed Jane took a journey into the city to see a doctor. She was not so much unhappy as indignant to find she needed an operation before she could have children. She did not associate illness with herself, and felt as if the whole thing were out of character. But she submitted to the operation, and to waiting a further two years before starting a family, with her usual practical good sense. But it subdued her a little. The uncertainty preyed on her, in spite of herself; and it was because of her rather wistful, disappointed frame of mind at this time that her work in the clinic became so important to her. Whereas, in the beginning, she had dispensed medicines and good advice as a routine, every morning for a couple of hours after breakfast, she now threw herself into it, working hard, keeping herself at full stretch, trying to attack causes rather than symptoms.

The compound was the usual farm compound of insanitary mud and grass huts; the diseases she had to deal with were caused by poverty and bad feeding.

Having lived in the country all her life, she did not make the mistake of expecting too much; she had that shrewd, ironical patience that achieves more with backward people than any amount of angry idealism.

First she chose an acre of good soil for vegetables, and saw to the planting and cultivating herself. One cannot overthrow the customs of centuries in a season, and she was patient with the natives who would not at first touch food they were not used to. She persuaded and lectured. She gave the women of the compound lessons in cleanliness and baby care. She drew up diet sheets and ordered sacks of citrus from the big estates; in fact, it was not long before it was Jane who organized the feeding of Willie's two-hundred-strong labour force, and he was glad to have her help. Neighbours laughed at them; for it is even now customary to feed natives on maize meal only, with an occasional slaughtered ox for a feasting; but there was no doubt Willie's natives were healthier than most and he got far more work out of them. On cold winter mornings Jane would stand dispensing cans of hot cocoa from a petrol drum with a

slow fire burning under it to the natives before they went to the
fields; and if a neighbour passed and laughed at her, she set her
lips and said good-humouredly: 'It's good sound common
sense, that's what it is. Besides – poor things, poor things!'
Since the McClusters were respected in the district, they were
humoured in what seemed a ridiculous eccentricity.

But it was not easy, not easy at all. It was of no use to cure
hookworm-infested feet that would become reinfected in a
week, since none wore shoes; nothing could be done about
bilharzia, when all the rivers were full of it; and the natives
continued to live in the dark and smoky huts.

But the children could be helped; Jane most particularly
loved the little black piccanins. She knew that fewer children
died in her compound than in any for miles around, and this
was her pride. She would spend whole mornings explaining to
the women about dirt and proper feeding; if a child became ill,
she would sit up all night with it, and cried bitterly if it died.
The name for her among the natives was The Goodhearted
One. They trusted her. Though mostly they hated and feared
the white man's medicines,* they let Jane have her way,
because they felt she was prompted by kindness; and day by
day the crowds of natives waiting for medical attention became
larger. This filled Jane with pride; and every morning she made
her way to the big stone-floored, thatched building at the back
of the house that smelled always of disinfectants and soap,
accompanied by the houseboy who helped her, and spent there
many hours helping the mothers and the children and the
labourers who had hurt themselves at work.

Little Tembi was brought to her for help at the time when
she knew she could not hope to have a child of her own for at
least two years. He had what the natives call 'the hot weather
sickness'. His mother had not brought him soon enough, and
by the time Jane took him in her arms he was a tiny wizened
skeleton, loosely covered with harsh greyish skin, the stomach
painfully distended. 'He will die,' moaned the mother from
outside the clinic door, with that fatalistic note that always

* This story was written in 1950.

annoyed Jane. 'Nonsense!' she said briskly – even more briskly because she was so afraid he would.

She laid the child warmly in a lined basket, and the houseboy and she looked grimly into each other's faces. Jane said sharply to the mother, who was whimpering helplessly from the floor where she squatted with her hands to her face: 'Stop crying. That doesn't do any good. Didn't I cure your first child when he had the same trouble?' But that other little boy had not been nearly as sick as this one.

When Jane had carried the basket into the kitchen, and set it beside the fire for warmth, she saw the same grim look on the cookboy's face as she had seen on the houseboy's – and could feel on her own. 'This child is *not* going to die,' she said to herself. 'I won't let it! I won't let it.' It seemed to her that if she could pull little Tembi through, the life of the child she herself wanted so badly would be granted her.

She sat beside the basket all day, willing the baby to live, with medicines on the table beside her, and the cookboy and the houseboy helping her where they could. At night the mother came from the compound with her blanket; and the two women kept vigil together. Because of the fixed, imploring eyes of the black woman Jane was even more spurred to win through; and the next day, and the next, and through the long nights, she fought for Tembi's life even when she could see from the faces of the house natives that they thought she was beaten. Once, towards dawn of one night when the air was cold and still, the little body chilled to the touch, and there seemed no breath in it, Jane held it close to the warmth of her own breast, murmuring fiercely over and over again: 'You *will* live, you will live!' – and when the sun rose the infant was breathing deeply and its feet were pulsing in her hand.

When it became clear that he would not die, the whole house was pervaded with a feeling of happiness and victory. Willie came to see the child, and said affectionately to Jane: 'Nice work, old girl. I never thought you'd do it.' The cookboy and the houseboy were warm and friendly towards Jane, and brought her gratitude presents of eggs and ground meal. As for the mother, she took her child in her arms with trembling joy and wept as she thanked Jane.

· Jane herself, though exhausted and weak, was too happy to rest or sleep: she was thinking of the child she would have. She was not a superstitious person, and the thing could not be described in such terms: she felt that she had thumbed her nose at death, that she had sent death slinking from her door in defeat, and now she would be strong to make life, fine strong children of her own; she could imagine them springing up beside her, lovely children conceived from her own strength and power against sneaking death.

Little Tembi was brought by his mother up to the house every day for a month, partly to make sure he would not relapse, partly because Jane had grown to love him. When he was quite well, and no longer came to the clinic, Jane would ask the cookboy after him, and sometimes sent a message that he should be fetched to see her. The native woman would then come smiling to the back door with the little Tembi on her back and her older child at her skirts, and Jane would run down the steps, smiling with pleasure, waiting impatiently as the cloth was unwound from the mother's back, revealing Tembi curled there, thumb in mouth, with great black solemn eyes, his other hand clutching the stuff of his mother's dress for security. Jane would carry him indoors to show Willie. 'Look,' she would say tenderly, 'here's my little Tembi. Isn't he a sweet little piccanin?'

He grew into a fat shy little boy, staggering uncertainly from his mother's arms to Jane's. Later, when he was strong on his legs, he would run to Jane and laugh as she caught him up. There was always fruit or sweets for him when he visited the house, always a hug from Jane and a good-humoured, amused smile from Willie.

He was two years old when Jane said to his mother: 'When the rains come this year I shall also have a child.' And the two women, forgetting the difference in colour, were happy together because of the coming children: the black woman was expecting her third baby.

Tembi was with his mother when she came to visit the cradle of the little white boy. Jane held out her hand to him and said: 'Tembi, how are you?' Then she took her baby from the cradle and held it out, saying: 'Come and see my baby, Tembi.' But

Tembi backed away, as if afraid, and began to cry. 'Silly Tembi,' said Jane affectionately; and sent the houseboy to fetch some fruit as a present. She did not make the gift herself, as she was holding her child.

She was absorbed by this new interest, and very soon found herself pregnant again. She did not forget little Tembi, but thought of him rather as he had been, the little toddler whom she had loved wistfully when she was childless. Once she caught sight of Tembi's mother walking along one of the farm roads, leading a child by the hand, and said: 'But where's Tembi?' Then she saw the child was Tembi. She greeted him; but afterwards said to Willie: 'Oh dear, it's such a pity when they grow up, isn't it?' He could hardly be described as grown-up,' said Willie, smiling indulgently at her where she sat with her two infants on her lap. 'You won't be able to have them climbing all over you when we've a dozen,' he teased her – they had decided to wait another two years and then have some more; Willie came from a family of nine children. 'Who said a dozen?' exclaimed Jane tartly, playing up to him. 'Why not?' asked Willie. 'We can afford it.' 'How do you think I can do everything?' grumbled Jane pleasantly. For she was very busy. She had not let the work at the clinic lapse; it was still she who did the ordering and planning of the labourers' food; and she looked after her children without help – she did not even have the customary native nanny. She could not really be blamed for losing touch with little Tembi.

He was brought to her notice one evening when Willie was having the usual discussion with the bossboy over the farm work. He was short of labour again and the rains had been heavy and the lands were full of weeds. As fast as the gangs of natives worked through a field it seemed that the weeds were higher than ever. Willie suggested that it might be possible to take some of the older children from their mothers for a few weeks. He already employed a gang of piccanins, of between about nine and fifteen years old, who did lighter work; but he was not sure that all the available children were working. The bossboy said he would see what he could find.

As a result of this discussion Willie and Jane were called one day to the front door by a smiling cookboy to see Little Tembi, now about six years old, standing proudly beside his father, who was also smiling. 'Here is a man to work for you,' said Tembi's father to Willie, pushing forward Tembi, who jibbed like a little calf, standing with his head lowered and his fingers in his mouth. He looked so tiny, standing all by himself, that Jane exclaimed compassionately: 'But, Willie, he's just a baby still!' Tembi was quite naked, save for a string of blue beads cutting into the flesh of his fat stomach. Tembi's father explained that his older child, who was eight, had been herding the calves for a year now, and that there was no reason why Tembi should not help him.

'But I don't need two herdboys for the calves,' protested Willie. And then, to Tembi: 'And now, my big man, what money do you want?' At this Tembi dropped his head still lower, twisted his feet in the dust, and muttered: 'Five shillings.' 'Five shillings a month!' exclaimed Willie indignantly. 'What next! Why, the ten-year-old piccanins get that much.' And then, feeling Jane's hand on his arm, he said hurriedly: 'Oh, all right, four and sixpence. He can help his big brother with the calves.' Jane, Willie, the cookboy and Tembi's father stood laughing sympathetically as Tembi lifted his head, stuck out his stomach even farther, and swaggered off down the path, beaming with pride. 'Well,' sighed Jane, 'I never would have thought it. Little Tembi! Why, it seems only the other day . . .'

Tembi, promoted to a loincloth, joined his brother with the calves; and as the two children ran alongside the animals, everyone turned to look smiling after the tiny black child, strutting with delight, and importantly swishing the twig his father had cut him from the bush as if he were a full-grown driver with his team of beasts.

The calves were supposed to stay all day near the kraal; when the cows had been driven away to the grazing, Tembi and his brother squatted under a tree and watched the calves, rising to run, shouting, if one attempted to stray. For a year Tembi was apprentice to the job; and then his brother joined the gang of older piccanins who worked with the hoe. Tembi was then seven years old, and responsible for twenty calves, some standing higher than he. Normally a much older child had the

job; but Willie was chronically short of labour, as all the
farmers were, and he needed every pair of hands he could find,
for work in the fields.

'Did you know your Tembi is a proper herdsboy now?' Willie
said to Jane, laughing, one day. 'What!' exclaimed Jane. 'That
baby! Why, it's absurd.' She looked jealously at her own
children, because of Tembi; she was the kind of woman who
hates to think of her children growing up. But she now had
three, and was very busy indeed. She forgot the little black
boy.

Then one day a catastrophe happened. It was very hot, and
Tembi fell asleep under the trees. His father came up to the
house, uneasily apologetic, to say that some of the calves had
got into the mealie field and trampled down the plants. Willie
was angry. It was that futile, simmering anger that cannot be
assuaged, for it is caused by something that cannot be remedied
– children had to herd the calves because adults were needed
for more important work, and one could not be really angry
with a child of Tembi's age. Willie had Tembi fetched to the
house, and gave him a stern lecture about the terrible thing he
had done. Tembi was crying when he turned away; he stumbled
off to the compound with his father's hand resting on his
shoulder, because the tears were streaming so fast he could not
have directed his own steps. But in spite of the tears, and his
contrition, it all happened again not very long afterwards. He
fell asleep in the drowsily-warm shade, and when he woke,
towards evening, all the calves had strayed into the fields and
flattened acres of mealies. Unable to face punishment he ran
away, crying, into the bush. He was found that night by his
father who cuffed him lightly round the head for running away.
And now it was a very serious matter indeed. Willie was
angry. To have happened once – that was bad, but forgivable.
But twice, and within a month! He did not at first summon
Tembi, but had a consultation with his father. 'We must do
something he will not forget, as a lesson,' said Willie. Tembi's
father said the child had already been punished. 'You have
beaten him?' asked Willie. But he knew that Africans do not
beat their children, or so seldom it was not likely that Tembi
had really been punished. 'You say you have beaten him?' he

insisted; and saw, from the way the man turned away his eyes and said, 'Yes, baas,' that it was not true. 'Listen,' said Willie. 'Those calves straying must have cost me about thirty pounds. There's nothing I can do. I can't get it back from Tembi, can I? And now I'm going to stop it happening again.' Tembi's father did not reply. 'You will fetch Tembi up here, to the house, and cut a switch from the bush, and I will give him a beating.' 'Yes, baas,' said Tembi's father, after a pause.

When Jane heard of the punishment she said: 'Shame! Beating my little Tembi . . .'

When the hour came, she took away her children so that they would not have such an unpleasant thing in their memories. Tembi was brought up to the veranda, clutching his father's hand and shivering with fear. Willie said he did not like the business of beating; he considered it necessary, however, and intended to go through with it. He took the long light switch from the cookboy, who had cut it from the bush, since Tembi's father had come without it, and ran the sharply-whistling thing loosely through the air to frighten Tembi. Tembi shivered more than ever, and pressed his face against his father's thighs. 'Come here, Tembi.' Tembi did not move; so his father lifted him close to Willie. 'Bend down.' Tembi did not bend down, so his father bent him down, hiding the small face against his own legs. Then Willie glanced smilingly but uncomfortably at the cookboy, the houseboy and Tembi's father, who were all regarding him with stern, unresponsive faces, and swished the wand backwards and forwards over Tembi's back; he wanted them to see he was only trying to frighten Tembi for the good of his upbringing. But they did not smile at all. Finally Willie said in an awful, solemn voice: 'Now, Tembi!' And then, having made the occasion solemn and angry, he switched Tembi lightly, three times, across the buttocks, and threw the switch away into the bush. 'Now you will never do it again, Tembi, will you?' he said. Tembi stood quite still, shuddering, in front of him, and would not meet his eyes. His father gently took his hand and led him away back home.

'Is it over?' asked Jane, appearing from the house. 'I didn't hurt him,' said Willie crossly. He was annoyed, because he felt the black men were annoyed with him. 'They want to have it both ways,' he said. 'If the child is old enough to earn money, then he's old enough to be responsible. Thirty pounds!'

'I was thinking of our little Freddie,' said Jane emotionally. Freddie was their first child. Willie said impatiently: 'And what's the good of thinking of him?' 'Oh no good, Willie. No good at all,' agreed Jane tearfully. 'It does seem awful, though. Do you remember him, Willie? Do you remember what a sweet little thing he was?' Willie could not afford to remember the sweetness of the baby Tembi at that moment; and he was displeased with Jane for reminding him; there was a small constriction of feeling between them for a little while, which soon dissolved, for they were good friends, and were in the same mind about most things.

The calves did not stray again. At the end of the month, when Tembi stepped forward to take his four shillings and sixpence wages, Willie smiled at him and said: 'Well, Tembi, and how are things with you?' 'I want more money,' said Tembi boldly. 'Wha-a-at!' exclaimed Willie, astounded. He called to Tembi's father, who stepped out of the gang of waiting Africans, to hear what Willie wanted to say. 'This little rascal of yours, to hear the cattle stray twice, and then says he wants more money.' Willie said this loudly, so that everyone could hear; and there was laughter from the labourers. But Tembi kept his head high, and said defiantly: 'Yes, baas, I want more money.' 'You'll get your bottom tanned,' said Willie, only half-indignant; and Tembi went off sulkily, holding his silver in his hand, with amused glances following him.

He was now about seven, very thin and lithe, though he still carried his protuberant stomach before him. His legs were flat and spindly, and his arms broader below the elbow than above. He was not crying now, nor stumbling. His small thin shape was straight, and – so it seemed – angry. Willie forgot the incident.

But next month the child again stood his ground and argued stubbornly for an increase. Willie raised him to five and sixpence, saying resignedly that Jane had spoiled him. Tembi bit his lips in triumph, and as he walked off gave little joyous skipping steps, finally breaking into a run as he reached the trees. He was still the youngest of the working children, and was now earning as much as some three or four years older than he: this made them grumble, but it was recognized, because of Jane's attitude, that he was a favourite.

Now, in the normal run of things, it would have been a year, at least, before he got any more money. But the very month following, he claimed the right to another increase. This time the listening natives made sounds of amused protest; the lad was forgetting himself. As for Willie, he was really annoyed. There was something insistent, something demanding, in the child's manner that was almost impertinent. He said sharply: 'If you don't stop this nonsense, I'll tell your father to teach you a lesson where it hurts.' Tembi's eyes glowed angrily, and he attempted to argue, but Willie dismissed him curtly, turning to the next labourer.

A few minutes later Jane was fetched to the back door by the cook, and there stood Tembi, shifting in embarrassment from foot to foot, but grinning at her eagerly. 'Why, Tembi . . .' she said vaguely. She had been feeding the children, and her mind was filled with thoughts of bathing and getting them to bed – thoughts very far from Tembi. Indeed, she had to look twice before she recognized him, for she carried always in the back of her mind the picture of that sweet fat black baby who bore, for her, the name Tembi. Only his eyes were the same: large dark glowing eyes, now imploringly fixed on her. 'Tell the boss to give me more money,' he beseeched.

Jane laughed kindly. 'But, Tembi, how can I do that? I've nothing to do with the farm. You know that.'

'Tell him, missus. Tell him, my missus,' he beseeched.

Jane felt the beginnings of annoyance. But she chose to laugh again, and said, 'Wait a minute, Tembi.' She went inside and fetched from the children's supper table some slices of cake, which she folded into a piece of paper and thrust into Tembi's hand. She was touched to see the child's face spread into a beaming smile: he had forgotten about the wages, the cake did as well or better. 'Thank you, thank you,' he said; and, turning, scuttled off into the trees.

And now Jane was given no chance of forgetting Tembi. He would come up to the house on a Sunday with quaint little mud toys for the children, or with the feather from a brilliant bird he had found in the bush; even a handful of wild flowers tied with wisps of grass. Always Jane welcomed him, talked to him, and rewarded him with small gifts. Then she had another child, and was very busy again. Sometimes she was too occupied to go herself to the back door. She would send her servant with an apple or a few sweets.

Soon after, Tembi appeared at the clinic one morning with his toe bound up. When Jane removed the dirty bit of cloth, she saw a minute cut, the sort of thing no native, whether child or adult, would normally take any notice of at all. But she bound it properly for him, and even dressed it good-naturedly when he appeared again, several days later. Then, only a week afterwards, there was a small cut on his finger. Jane said impatiently: 'Look here, Tembi, I don't run this clinic for nonsense of this kind.' When the child stared up at her blankly, those big dark eyes fixed on her with an intensity that made her uncomfortable, she directed the houseboy to translate the remark into dialect, for she thought Tembi had not understood. He said, stammering: 'Missus, my missus, I come to see you only.' But Jane laughed and sent him away. He did not go far. Later, when all the other patients had gone, she saw him standing a little way off, looking hopefully at her. 'What is it?' she asked, a little crossly, for she could hear the new baby crying for attention inside the house.

'I want to work for you,' said Tembi. 'But, Tembi, I don't need another boy. Besides, you are too small for housework. When you are older, perhaps.' 'Let me look after the children.' Jane did not smile, for it was quite usual to employ small piccanins as nurses for children not much younger than themselves. She might even have considered it, but she said: 'Tembi, I have just arranged for a nanny to come and help me. Perhaps later on. I'll remember you, and if I need someone to help the nanny I'll send for you. First you must learn to work well. You must work well with the calves and not let them stray; and then we'll know you are a good boy, and you can come to the house and help me with the children.'

Tembi departed on this occasion with lingering steps, and some time later Jane, glancing from the window, saw him standing at the edge of the bush gazing towards the house. She despatched the houseboy to send him away, saying that she would not have him loitering round the house doing nothing.

Jane, too, was now feeling that she had 'spoiled' Tembi, that he had 'got above himself'.

And now nothing happened for quite a long time.

Then Jane missed her diamond engagement ring. She used often to take it off when doing household things; so that she was not at first concerned. After several days she searched thoroughly for it, but it could not be found. A little later a pearl brooch was missing. And there were several small losses, a spoon used for the baby's feeding, a pair of scissors, a silver christening mug. Jane said crossly to Willie that there must be a poltergeist. 'I had the thing in my hand and when I turned round it was gone. It's just silly. Things don't vanish like that.' 'A black poltergeist, perhaps,' said Willie. 'How about the cook?' 'Don't be ridiculous,' said Jane, a little too quickly. 'Both the houseboys have been with us since we came to the farm.' But suspicion flared in her, nevertheless. It was a well-worn maxim that no native, no matter how friendly, could be trusted; scratch any one of them, and you found a thief. Then she looked at Willie, understood that he was feeling the same, and was as ashamed of his feelings as she was. The houseboys were almost personal friends. 'Nonsense,' said Jane firmly. 'I don't believe a word of it.' But no solution offered itself, and things continued to vanish.

One day Tembi's father asked to speak to the boss. He untied a piece of cloth, laid it on the ground – and there were all the missing articles. 'But not Tembi, surely,' protested Jane. Tembi's father, awkward in his embarrassment, explained that he had happened to be passing the cattle kraals, and had happened to notice the little boy sitting on his antheap, in the shade, playing with his treasures. 'Of course he had no idea of their value,' appealed Jane. 'It was just because they were so shiny and glittering.' And indeed, as they stood there, looking down at the lamplight glinting on the silver and the diamonds, it was easy to see how a child could be fascinated. 'Well, and what are we going to do?' asked Willie practically. Jane did not reply directly to the question; she exclaimed helplessly: 'Do you realize that the little imp must have been watching me doing things round the house for weeks, nipping in when my back was turned for a moment – he must be quick as a snake.' 'Yes, but what are we going to do?' 'Just give him a good talking-to,' said Jane, who did not know why she felt so dismayed and lost. She was angry; but far more distressed – there was something ugly and persistent in this planned, deliberate thieving, that she could not bear to associate with little Tembi, whom she had saved from death.

'A talking-to won't do any good,' said Willie. Tembi was whipped again; this time properly, with no nonsense about making the switch whistle for effect. He was made to expose his bare bottom across his father's knees, and when he got up, Willie said with satisfaction: 'He's not going to be comfortable sitting down for a week.' 'But, Willie, there's blood,' said Jane. For as Tembi walked off stiffly, his legs straddled apart from the pain, his fists thrust into his streaming eyes, reddish patches appeared on the stuff of his trousers. Willie said angrily: 'Well, what do you expect me to do – make him a present of it and say: How clever of you?'

'But *blood*, Willie!'

'I didn't know I was hitting so hard,' admitted Willie. He examined the long flexible twig in his hands, before throwing it away, as if surprised at its effectiveness. 'That must have hurt,' he said doubtfully. 'Still, he deserved it. Now stop crying, Jane. He won't do that again.'

But Jane did not stop crying. She could not bear to think of the beating; and Willie, no matter what he said, was uncomfortable when he remembered it. They would have been pleased to let Tembi slip from their minds for a while, and have him reappear later, when there had been time for kindness to grow in them again.

But it was not a week before he demanded to be made nurse to the children: he was now big enough, he said; and Jane had promised. Jane was so astonished she could not speak to him. She went indoors, shutting the door on him; and when she knew he was still lingering there for speech with her, sent out the houseboy to say she was not having a thief as nurse for her children.

A few weeks later he asked again; and again she refused.

Then he took to waylaying her every day, sometimes several times a day: 'Missus, my missus, let me work near you, let me work near you.' Always she refused, and always she grew more angry.

At last, the sheer persistence of the thing defeated her. She said: 'I won't have you as a nurse, but you can help me with the vegetable garden.' Tembi was sullen, but he presented himself at the garden next day, which was not the one near the house, but the fenced patch near the compound, for the use of the natives. Jane employed a garden boy to run it, telling him when was the time to plant, explaining about compost and the proper treatment of soil. Tembi was to help him.

She did not often go to the garden; it ran of itself. Sometimes, passing, she saw the beds full of vegetables were running to waste; this meant that a new batch of Africans were in the compound, natives who had to be educated afresh to eat what was good for them. But now she had had her last baby, and employed two nannies in the nurseries, she felt free to spend more time at the clinic and at the garden. Here she made a point of being friendly to Tembi. She was not a person to bear grudges, though a feeling that he was not to be trusted barred him as a nurse. She would talk to him about her own children, and how they were growing, and would soon be going to school in the city. She would talk to him about keeping himself clean, and eating the right things; how he must earn good money so that he could buy shoes to keep his feet from the germ-laden dust; how he must be honest, always tell the truth and be obedient to the white people. While she was in the garden he would follow her around, his hoe trailing forgotten in his hand, his eyes fixed on her. 'Yes, missus; yes, my missus,' he repeated continually. And when she left, he would implore: '*When* are you coming again? Come again soon, my missus.' She took to bringing him her own children's books, when they were too worn for use in the nursery. 'You must learn to read, Tembi,' she would say. 'Then, when you want to get a job, you will earn more wages if you can say: "Yes, missus, I can read and write." You can take messages on the telephone then, and write down orders so that you don't forget them.' 'Yes, missus,' Tembi would say, reverently taking the books from her. When

she left the garden, she would glance back, always a little
uncomfortably, because of Tembi's intense devotion, and see
him kneeling on the rich red soil, framed by the bright green of
the vegetables, knitting his brows over the strange coloured
pictures and the unfamiliar print.

This went on for about two years. She said to Willie: 'Tembi
seems to have got over that funny business of his. He's really
useful in that garden. I don't have to tell him when to plant
things. He knows as well as I do. And he goes round the huts
in the compound with the vegetables, persuading the natives to
eat them.' 'I bet he makes a bit on the side,' said Willie,
chuckling. 'Oh no, Willie, I'm sure he wouldn't do that.'

And, in fact, he didn't. Tembi regarded himself as an apostle
of the white man's way of life. He would say earnestly,
displaying the baskets of carefully arranged vegetables to the
native women: 'The Goodhearted One says it is right we should
eat these things. She says eating them will save us from
sickness.' Tembi achieved more than Jane had done in years of
propaganda.

He was nearly eleven when he began giving trouble again.
Jane sent her two elder children to boarding-school, dismissed
her nannies, and decided to engage a piccanin to help with the
children's washing. She did not think of Tembi; but she engaged
Tembi's younger brother.

Tembi presented himself at the back door, as of old, his eyes
flashing, his body held fine and taut, to protest. 'Missus, missus,
you promised I should work for you.' 'But Tembi, you are
working for me, with the vegetables.' 'Missus, my missus, you
said when you took a piccanin for the house, that piccanin
would be me.' But Jane did not give way. She still felt as if
Tembi were on probation. And the demanding, insistent,
impatient thing in Tembi did not seem to her a good quality to
be near her children. Besides, she liked Tembi's little brother,
who was a softer, smiling, chubby Tembi, playing good-
naturedly with the children in the garden when he had finished
the washing and ironing. She saw no reason to change, and
said so.

Tembi sulked. He no longer took baskets of green stuff from
door to door in the compound. And he did as little work as he

need without actually neglecting it. The spirit had gone out of him.

'You know,' said Jane half indignantly, half amused, to Willie: 'Tembi behaves as if he had some sort of claim on us.'

Quite soon, Tembi came to Willie and asked to be allowed to buy a bicycle. He was then earning ten shillings a month, and the rule was that no native earning less than fifteen shillings could buy a bicycle. A fifteen-shilling native would keep five shillings of his wages, give ten to Willie, and undertake to remain on the farm till the debt was paid. That might take two years, or even longer. 'No,' said Willie. 'And what does a piccanin like you want with a bicycle? A bicycle is for big men.'

Next day, their eldest child's bicycle vanished from the house, and was found in the compound leaning against Tembi's hut. Tembi had not even troubled to conceal the theft; and when he was called for an interview kept silent. At last he said: 'I don't know why I stole it. I don't know.' And he ran off, crying, into the trees.

'He must go,' said Willie finally, baffled and angry.

'But his father and mother and the family live in our compound,' protested Jane.

'I'm not having a thief on the farm,' said Willie. But getting rid of Tembi was more than dismissing a thief: it was pushing aside a problem that the McClusters were not equipped to handle. Suddenly Jane knew that when she no longer saw Tembi's burning, pleading eyes, it would be a relief; though she said guiltily: 'Well, I suppose he can find work on one of the farms nearby.'

Tembi did not allow himself to be sacked so easily. When Willie told him he burst into passionate tears, like a very small child. Then he ran round the house and banged his fists on the kitchen door till Jane came out. 'Missus, my missus, don't let the baas send me away.' 'But Tembi, you must go, if the boss says so.' 'I work for you, missus, I'm your boy, let me stay. I'll work for you in the garden and I won't ask for any more money.' 'I'm sorry, Tembi,' said Jane. Tembi gazed at her while his face hollowed into incredulous misery: he had not believed she would not take his part. At this moment his little brother came round the corner of the house carrying Jane's youngest child, and Tembi flew across and flung himself on them, so that the little black child staggered back, clutching the white infant to himself with difficulty. Jane flew to rescue her baby, and then pulled Tembi off his brother, who was bitten and scratched all over his face and arms.

'That finishes it,' she said coldly. 'You will be off this farm in an hour, or the police will chase you off.'

They asked Tembi's father, later, if the lad had found work; the reply was that he was garden boy on a neighbouring farm. When the McClusters saw these neighbours they asked after Tembi, but the reply was vague: on this new farm Tembi was just another labourer without a history.

Later still, Tembi's father said there had been 'trouble', and that Tembi had moved to another farm, many miles away. Then, no one seemed to know where he was; it was said he had joined a gang of boys moving south to Johannesburg for work in the gold mines.

The McClusters forgot Tembi. They were pleased to be able to forget him. They thought of themselves as good masters; they had a good name with their labourers for kindness and fair dealing; while the affair of Tembi left something hard and unassimilable in them, like a grain of sand in a mouthful of food. The name 'Tembi' brought uncomfortable emotions with it; and there was no reason why it should, according to their ideas of right and wrong. So at last they did not even remember to ask Tembi's father what had become of him: he had become another of those natives who vanish from one's life after seeming to be such an intimate part of it.

It was about four years later that the robberies began again. The McClusters' house was the first to be rifled. Someone climbed in one night and took the following articles: Willie's big winter coat, his stick, two old dresses belonging to Jane, a quantity of children's clothing and an old and battered child's tricycle. Money left lying in a drawer was untouched. 'What extraordinary things to take,' marvelled the McClusters. For except for Willie's coat, there was nothing of value. The theft was reported to the police, and a routine visit was made to the compound. It was established that the thief must be someone who knew the house, for the dogs had not barked at him; and that it was not an experienced thief, who would certainly have taken money and jewellery.

Because of this, the first theft was not connected with the second, which took place at a neighbouring farmhouse. There, money and watches and a gun were stolen. And there were more thefts in the district of the same kind. The police decided it must be a gang of thieves, not the ordinary pilferer, for the robberies were so clever and it seemed as if several people had planned them. Watchdogs were poisoned; times were chosen when servants were out of the house; and on two occasions someone had entered through bars so closely set together that no one but a child could have forced his way through.

The district gossiped about the robberies; and because of them, the anger lying dormant between white and black, always ready to flare up, deepened in an ugly way. There was hatred in the white people's voices when they addressed their servants, that futile anger, for even if their personal servants were giving information to the thieves, what could be done about it? The most trusted servant could turn out to be a thief. During these months when the unknown gang terrorized the district, unpleasant things happened; people were fined more often for beating their natives; a greater number of labourers than usual ran away over the border to Portuguese territory; the dangerous, simmering anger was like heat growing in the air. Even Jane found herself saying one day: 'Why do we do it? Look how I spend my time nursing and helping these natives! What thanks do I get? They aren't grateful for anything we do for them.' This question of gratitude was in every white person's mind during that time.

As the thefts continued, Willie put bars in all the windows of the house, and bought two large fierce dogs. This annoyed Jane, for it made her feel confined and a prisoner in her own home.

To look at a beautiful view of mountains and shaded green bush through bars, robs the sight of joy; and to be greeted on her way from house to storerooms by the growling of hostile dogs who treated everyone, black and white, as an enemy, became daily more exasperating. They bit everyone who came near the house, and Jane was afraid for her children. However, it·was not more than three weeks after they were bought that they were found lying stretched in the sun, quite dead, foam at their mouths and their eyes glazing. They had been poisoned. 'It looks as if we can expect another visit,' said Willie crossly; for he was by now impatient of the whole business. 'However,' he said impatiently, 'if one chooses to live in a damned country like this, one has to take the consequences.' It was an exclamation that meant nothing, that could not be taken seriously by anyone. During that time, however, a lot of settled and contented people were talking with prickly anger about 'the damned country'. In short, their nerves were on edge.

Not long after the dogs were poisoned, it became necessary for Willie to make the trip into town, thirty miles off. Jane did not want to go; she disliked the long, hot, scurrying day in the streets. So Willie went by himself.

In the morning, Jane went to the vegetable garden with her younger children. They played around the water-butt, by themselves, while she staked out a new row of beds; her mind was lazily empty, her hands working quickly with twine and wooden pegs. Suddenly, however, an extraordinary need took her to turn around sharply, and she heard herself say: 'Tembi!' She looked wildly about her; afterwards it seemed to her she had heard him speak her name. It seemed to her that she would see a spindly earnest-faced black child kneeling behind her between the vegetable beds, poring over a tattered picture book. Time slipped and swam together; she felt confused; and it was only by looking determinedly at her two children that she regained a knowledge of how long it had been since Tembi followed her around the garden.

When she got back to the house, she sewed on the veranda. Leaving her chair for a moment to fetch a glass of water, she found her sewing basket had gone. At first she could not believe it. Distrusting her own senses, she searched the place for her basket, which she knew very well had been on the veranda not a few moments before. It meant that a native was lingering in the bush, perhaps a couple of hundred yards away, watching her movements. It wasn't a pleasant thought. An old uneasiness filled her; and again the name 'Tembi' rose into her mind. She took herself into the kitchen and said to the cookboy:

'Have you heard anything of Tembi recently?' But there had been no news, it seemed. He was 'at the gold mines'. His parents had not heard from him for years.

'But why a sewing basket?' muttered Jane to herself, incredulously. 'Why take such a risk for so little? It's insane.'

That afternoon, when the children were playing in the garden and Jane was asleep on her bed, someone walked quietly into the bedroom and took her big garden hat, her apron, and the dress she had been wearing   at morning. When Jane woke and discovered this, she began to tremble, half with anger, half with fear. She was alone in the house, and she had the prickling feeling of being watched. As she moved from room to room, she kept glancing over her shoulder behind the angles of wardrobe and cupboard, and fancied that Tembi's great imploring eyes would appear there, as unappeasable as a dead person's eyes, following her.

She found herself watching the road for Willie's return. If Willie had been there, she could have put the responsibility on to him and felt safe: Jane was a woman who depended very much on that invisible support a husband gives. She had not known, before that afternoon, just how much she depended on him; and this knowledge – which it seemed the thief shared – made her unhappy and restless. She felt that she should be able to manage this thing by herself, instead of waiting helplessly for her husband. I must do something, I must do something, she kept repeating.

It was a long, warm, sunny afternoon. Jane, with all her nerves standing to attention, waited on the veranda, shading her eyes as she gazed along the road for Willie's car. The waiting preyed on her. She could not prevent her eyes from returning again and again to the bush immediately in front of the house, which stretched for mile on mile, a low, dark scrubby green, darker because of the lengthening shadows of approaching evening. An impulse pulled her to her feet, and she marched towards the bush through the garden. At its edge she stopped, peering everywhere for those dark and urgent eyes, and called, 'Tembi, Tembi.' There was no sound. 'I won't punish you, Tembi,' she implored. 'Come here to me.' She waited, listening delicately, for the slightest movement of

branch or dislodged pebble. But the bush was silent under the
sun; even the birds were drugged by the heat; and the leaves
hung without trembling. 'Tembi!' she called again; at first
peremptorily, and then with a quaver in her voice. She knew
very well that he was there, flattening himself behind some tree
or bush, waiting for her to say the right word, to find the right
things to say, so that he could trust her. It maddened her to
think he was so close, and she could no more reach him than
she could lay her hands on a shadow. Lowering her voice
persuasively she said: 'Tembi, I know you are there. Come
here and talk to me. I won't tell the police. Can't you trust me,
Tembi?'

Not a sound, not a whisper of a reply. She tried to make her
mind soft and blank, so that the words she needed would
appear there, ready for using. The grass was beginning to shake
a little in the evening breeze, and the hanging leaves tremored
once or twice; there was a warm mellowing of the light that
meant the sun would soon sink; a red glow showed on the
foliage, and the sky was flaring high with light. Jane was
trembling so she could not control her limbs; it was a deep
internal trembling, welling up from inside, like a wound bleeding invisibly. She tried to steady herself. She said: This is silly,
I can't be afraid of little Tembi! How could I be? She made her
voice firm and loud and said: 'Tembi, you are being very
foolish. What's the use of stealing things like a stupid child?
You can be clever about stealing for a little while, but sooner
or later the police will catch you and you will go to prison. You
don't want that, do you? Listen to me, now. You come out
now and let me see you; and when the boss comes I'll explain
to him, and I'll say you are sorry, and you can come back and
work for me in the vegetable garden. I don't like to think of
you as a thief, Tembi. Thieves are bad people.' She stopped.
The silence settled around her; she felt the silence like a
coldness, as when a cloud passes overhead. She saw that the
shadows were thick about her and the light had gone from the
leaves, that had a cold grey look. She knew Tembi would not
come out to her now. She had not found the right things to say.
'You are a silly little boy,' she announced to the still listening
bush. 'You make me very angry, Tembi.' And she walked very

slowly back to the house, holding herself calm and dignified, knowing that Tembi was watching her, with some plan in his mind she could not conjecture.

When Willie returned from town, tired and irritable as he always was after a day of traffic, and interviewing people, and shopping, she told him carefully, choosing her words, what had happened. When she told how she had called to Tembi from the verges of the bush, Willie looked gently at her and said: 'My dear, what good do you think that's going to do?' 'But Willie, it's all so awful . . .' Her lips began to tremble luxuriously, and she allowed herself to weep comfortably on his shoulder. 'You don't know it is Tembi,' said Willie. 'Of course it's Tembi. Who else could it be? The silly little boy. My silly little Tembi . . .'

She could not eat. After supper she said suddenly: 'He'll come here tonight. I'm sure of it.'

'Do you think he will?' said Willie seriously, for he had a great respect for Jane's irrational knowledge. 'Well, don't worry, we'll be ready for him.' 'If he'd only let me talk to him,' said Jane. 'Talk to him!' said Willie. 'Like hell! I'll have him in prison. That's the only place for him.' 'But, *Willie* . . .' Jane protested, knowing perfectly well that Tembi must go to prison.

It was then not eight o'clock. 'I'll have my gun beside the bed,' planned Willie. 'He stole a gun, didn't he, from the farm over the river? He might be dangerous.' Willie's blue eyes were alight; he was walking up and down the room, his hands in his pockets, alert and excited: he seemed to be enjoying the idea of capturing Tembi, and because of this Jane felt herself go cold against him. It was at this moment that there was a sound from the bedroom next door. They sprang up, and reached the entrance together. There stood Tembi, facing them, his hands dangling empty at his sides. He had grown taller, but still seemed the same lithe, narrow child, with the thin face and great eloquent eyes. At the sight of those eyes Jane said weakly: 'Willie . . .'

Willie, however, marched across to Tembi and took that unresisting criminal by the arm. 'You young rascal,' he said angrily, but in a voice appropriate, not to a dangerous thief, who had robbed many houses, but rather to a naughty child caught pilfering fruit. Tembi did not reply to Willie: his eyes were fixed on Jane. He was trembling; he looked no more than a boy.

'Why didn't you come when I called you?' asked Jane. 'You are so foolish, Tembi.'

'I was afraid, missus,' said Tembi, in a voice just above a whisper. 'But I said I wouldn't tell the police,' said Jane.

'Be quiet, Jane,' ordered Willie. 'Of course we're calling the police. What are you thinking of?' As if feeling the need to remind himself of this important fact, he said: 'After all, the lad's a criminal.'

'I'm not a bad boy,' whispered Tembi imploringly to Jane. 'Missus, my missus, I'm not a bad boy.'

But the thing was out of Jane's hands; she had relinquished it to Willie.

Willie seemed uncertain what to do. Finally he strode purposefully to the wardrobe, and took his rifle from it, and handed it to Jane. 'You stay here,' he ordered. 'I'm calling the police on the telephone.' He went out, leaving the door open, while Jane stood there holding the big gun, and waiting for the sound of the telephone.

She looked helplessly down at the rifle, set it against the bed, and said in a whisper: 'Tembi, why do you steal?'

Tembi hung his head and said: 'I don't know, missus.' 'But you must know.' There was no reply. The tears poured down Tembi's cheeks.

'Tembi, did you like Johannesburg?' There was no reply. 'How long were you there?' 'Three years, missus.' 'Why did you come back?' 'They put me in prison, missus.' 'What for?' 'I didn't have a pass.' 'Did you get out of prison?' 'No, I was there one month and they let me go.' 'Was it you who stole all the things from the houses around here?' Tembi nodded, his eyes cast down to the floor.

Jane did not know what to do. She repeated firmly to herself: 'This is a dangerous boy, who is quite unscrupulous, and very clever,' and picked up the rifle again. But the weight of it, a cold hostile thing, made her feel sorry. She set it down sharply. 'Look at me, Tembi,' she whispered. Outside, in the passage,

Willie was saying in a firm confident voice: 'Yes, Sergeant, we've got him here. He used to work for us, years ago. Yes.'

'Look, Tembi,' whispered Jane quickly. 'I'm going out of the room. You must run away quickly. How did you get in?' This thought came to her for the first time. Tembi looked at the window. Jane could see how the bars had been forced apart, so that a very slight person could squeeze in, sideways. 'You must be strong,' she said. 'Now, there isn't any need to go out that way. Just walk out of that door,' she pointed at the door to the living-room, 'and go through into the veranda, and run into the bush. Go to another district and get yourself an honest job and stop being a thief. I'll talk to the baas. I'll tell him to tell the police we made a mistake. *Now then, Tembi . . .*' she concluded urgently, and went into the passage, where Willie was at the telephone, with his back to her.

He lifted his head, looked at her incredulously, and said: 'Jane, you're crazy.' Into the telephone he said: 'Yes, come quickly.' He set down the receiver, turned to Jane and said: 'You know he'll do it again, don't you?' He ran back to the bedroom.

But there had been no need to run. There stood Tembi, exactly where they had left him, his fists in his eyes, like a small child.

'I told you to run away,' said Jane angrily.

'He's nuts,' said Willie.

And now, just as Jane had done, Willie picked up the rifle, seemed to feel foolish holding it, and set it down again.

Willie sat on the bed and looked at Tembi with the look of one who has been outwitted. 'Well, I'm damned,' he said. 'It's got me beat, this has.'

Tembi continued to stand there in the centre of the floor, hanging his head and crying. Jane was crying too. Willie was getting angrier, more and more irritable. Finally he left the room, slamming the door, and saying: 'God damn it, everyone is mad.'

Soon the police came, and there was no doubt about what should be done. Tembi nodded at every question: he admitted everything. The handcuffs were put on him, and he was taken away in the police car.

At last Willie came back into the bedroom, where Jane lay crying on the bed. He patted her on the shoulder and said: 'Now stop it. The thing is over. We can't do anything.'

Jane sobbed out: 'He's only alive because of me. That's what's so awful. And now he's going to prison.'

'They don't think anything of prison. It isn't a disgrace as it is for us.'

'But he's going to be one of those natives who spend all their lives in and out of prison.'

'Well, what of it?' said Willie. With the gentle, controlled exasperation of a husband, he lifted Jane and offered her his handkerchief. 'Now stop it, old girl,' he reasoned. 'Do stop it. I'm tired. I want to go to bed. I've had hell up and down those damned pavements all day, and I've got a heavy day tomorrow with the tobacco.' He began pulling off his boots.

Jane stopped crying, and also undressed. 'There's something horrible about it all,' she said restlessly. 'I can't forget it.' And finally, 'What did he *want*, Willie? What is it he was *wanting*, all this time?'

Old John's Place

The people of the district, mostly solidly established farmers who intended to live and die on their land, had become used to a certain kind of person buying a farm, settling on it with a vagabond excitement, but with one eye always on the attractions of the nearest town, and then flying off again after a year or so, leaving behind them a sense of puzzled failure, a desolation even worse than usual, for the reason that they had taken no more than a vagabond's interest in homestead and stock and land.

It soon became recognized that the Sinclairs were just such persons in spite of, even because of, their protestations of love for the soil and their relief at the simple life. Their idea of the simple was not shared by their neighbours, who felt they were expected to measure up to standards which were all very well when they had the glamour of distance, but which made life uncomfortably complicated if brought too close.

The Sinclairs bought Old John's Farm, and that was an unlucky place, with no more chance of acquiring a permanent owner than a restless dog has. Although this part of the district had not been settled for more than forty years, the farm had changed hands so often no one could remember how it had got its name. Old John, if he had ever existed, had become merely a place, as famous people may do.

Mr Sinclair had been a magistrate before he retired, and was known to have private means. Even if this had not been known – he referred to himself humorously as 'another of these damned cheque-book farmers' – his dilettante's attitude towards farming would have proved the fact: he made no attempt at all to make money and did not so much as plough a field all the time he was there. Mrs Sinclair gardened and gave parties. Her very first party became a legend, remembered with admiration, certainly, but also with that grudging tolerance that is accorded to spendthrifts who can afford to think of extravagance as a necessity. It was a weekend affair, very highly organized, beginning with tennis on Saturday morning and ending on Sunday night with a lengthy formal dinner for forty people. It was not that the district did not enjoy parties, or give plenty of their own; rather it was, again, that they were expected to enjoy themselves in a way that was foreign to them. Mrs Sinclair was a realist. Her parties, after that, followed a more familiar routine. But it became clear, from her manner, that in settling here she had seen herself chiefly as a hostess, and now felt that she had not chosen her guests with discrimination. She took to spending two or three days of each week in town; and went for prolonged visits to farms in other parts of the country. Mr Sinclair, too, was seen in the offices of estate agents. He did not mention these visits; Mrs Sinclair was reticent when she returned from these other farms.

When people began to say that the Sinclairs were leaving, and for the most familiar reason, that Mrs Sinclair was not cut out for farm life, their neighbours nodded and smiled, very politely. And they made a point of agreeing earnestly with Mrs Sinclair when she said town life was after all essential to her.

The Sinclairs' farewell party was attended by perhaps fifty people who responded with beautiful tact to what the Sinclairs expected of them. The men's manner towards Mr Sinclair suggested a sympathy which the women, for once, regarded with indulgence. In the past many young men, angry and frustrated, had been dragged back to offices in town by their wives; and there had been farewell parties that left hostility between husbands and wives for days. The wives were unable to condemn a girl who was genuinely unable 'to take the life', as the men condemned her. They championed her, and something always happened then which was what those farmers perhaps dreaded most; for dig deep enough into any one of those wives, and one would find a willing martyr alarmingly apt to expose a bleeding heart in an effort to win sympathy from a husband supposed – for the purposes of this argument – not to have one at all.

But this substratum of feeling was not reached that evening. Here was no tragedy. Mrs Sinclair might choose to repeat, sadly, that she was not cut out for the life; Mr Sinclair could sigh with humorous resignation as much as he liked; but the whole thing was regarded as a nicely acted play. In corners people were saying tolerantly: 'Yes, they'll be much happier there.' Everyone knew the Sinclairs had bought another farm in a district full of cheque-book farmers, where they would be at home. The fact that they kept this secret – or thought they had – was yet another evidence of unnecessary niceness of feeling. Also, it implied that the Sinclairs thought them fools.

In short, because of the guards on everyone's tongue, the party could not take wings, in spite of all the drink and good food.

It began at sundown, on Old John's veranda, which might have been designed for parties. It ran two sides of the house, and was twenty feet deep.

Old John's house had been built on to and extended so often, by so many people with differing tastes and needs, that of all the houses in the district it was the most fascinating for children. It had rambling creeper-covered wings, a staircase climbing to the roof, a couple of rooms raised up a flight of steps here, another set of rooms sunk low, there; and through all these the children ran wild till they began to grow tired and fretful. They then gathered round their parents' chairs, where they were a nuisance, and the women roused themselves unwillingly from conversation, and began to look for places where they might sleep. By eight o'clock it was impossible to move anywhere without watching one's feet – children were bedded down on floors, in the bath, on sofas, any place, in fact, that had room for a child.

That done, the party was free to start properly, if it could. But there was always a stage when the women sat at one end of the veranda and the men at the other. The host would set bottles of whisky freely on window-ledges and on tables among them. As for the women, it was necessary, in order to satisfy convention, to rally them playfully so that they could expostulate, cover their glasses, and exclaim that really, they couldn't drink another mouthful. The bottles were then left unobtrusively near them, and they helped themselves, drinking no less than the men.

During this stage Mrs Sinclair played the game and sat with the women, but it was clear that she felt defeated because she had been unable to dissolve the ancient convention of the segregation of the sexes. She frequently rose, when it was quite unnecessary, to attend to the food and to the servants who were handing it round; and each time she did so, glances followed her which were as ambiguous as she was careful to keep her own.

Between the two separate groups wandered a miserable child, who was too old to be put to bed with the infants, and too young to join the party; unable to read because that was considered rude; unable to do anything but loiter on the edge of each group in turn, until an impatient look warned her that something was being suppressed for her benefit that would otherwise add to the gaiety of the occasion. As the evening advanced and the liquor fell in the bottles, these looks became more frequent. Seeing the waif's discomfort, Mrs Sinclair took her hand and said: 'Come and help me with the supper,' thus giving herself a philanthropic appearance in removing herself and the child altogether.

The big kitchen table was covered with cold roast chickens, salads and trifles. These were the traditional party foods of the district; and Mrs Sinclair provided them; though at that first party, two years before, the food had been exotic.

'If I give you a knife, Kate, you won't cut yourself?' she enquired; and then said hastily, seeing the child's face, which protested, as it had all evening, that such consideration was not necessary: 'Of course you won't. Then help me joint these chickens . . . not that the cook couldn't do it perfectly well, I suppose.'

While they carved, Mrs Sinclair chatted determinedly; and only once said anything that came anywhere near to what they were both thinking, when she remarked briskly: 'It is a shame. Really, arrangements should be made for you. Having you about is unfair to you and to the grown-ups.'

'What could they do with me?' enquired Kate reasonably.

'Heaven knows,' acknowledged Mrs Sinclair. She patted

Kate's shoulder encouragingly, and said in a gruff and friendly
voice: 'Well, I can't say anything helpful, except that you are
bound to grow up. It's an awful age, being neither one thing or
the other.' Kate was thirteen; and it was an age for which no
social provision was made. She was thankful to have the excuse
to be here, in the kitchen, with at least an appearance of
something to do. After a while Mrs Sinclair left her, saying
without any attempt at disguising her boredom, even though
Kate's parents were among those who bored her: 'I've got to
go back, I suppose.'

Kate sat on a hard kitchen chair, and waited for something
to happen, though she knew she could expect nothing in the
way of amusement save those odd dropped remarks which for
the past year or so had formed her chief education.

In the meantime she watched the cook pile the pieces of
chicken on platters, and hand trays and jugs and plates to the
waiters, who were now hurrying between this room and the
veranda. The sound of voices was rising steadily: Kate judged
that the party must be moving towards its second phase, in
which case she must certainly stay where she was, for fear of
the third.

During the second phase the men and women mingled,
pulling their chairs together in a wide circle; and it was likely
that some would dance, calling for music, when the host would
wind up an old portable gramophone. It was at this stage that
the change in the atmosphere took place which Kate acknowledged by the phrase: 'It is breaking up.' The sharply-defined
family units began to dissolve, and they dissolved always in the
same way, so that during the last part of each evening, from
about twelve o'clock, the same couples could be seen together
dancing, talking, or even moving discreetly off into dark rooms
or the night outside. This pattern was to Kate as if a veil had
been gently removed from the daytime life of the district,
revealing another truth, and one that was bare and brutal. Also
quite irrevocable, and this was acknowledged by the betrayed
themselves (who were also, in their own times and seasons,
betrayers) for nothing was more startling than the patient
discretion with which the whole thing was treated.

Mrs Wheatley, for instance, a middle-aged lady who played

the piano at church services and ran the Women's Institute, known as a wonderful mother and prize cook, seemed on these occasions not to notice how her husband always sought out Mrs Fowler (her own best friend) and how this partnership seemed to strike sparks out of the eyes of everyone present. When Andrew Wheatley emerged from the dark with Nan Fowler, their eyes heavy, their sides pressed close together, Mrs Wheatley would simply avert her eyes and remark patiently (her lips tightened a little, perhaps): 'We ought to be going quite soon.' And so it was with everyone else. There was something recognized as dangerous, that had to be given latitude, emerging at these parties, and existing only because if it were forbidden it would be even more dangerous.

Kate, after many such parties, had learned that after a certain time, no matter how bored she might be, she must take herself out of sight. This was consideration for the grown-ups, not for her; since she did not have to be present in order to understand. There was a fourth stage, reached very rarely, when there was an explosion of raised voices, quarrels and ugliness. It seemed to her that the host and hostess were always acting as sentinels in order to prevent this fourth stage being reached: no matter how much the others drank, or how husbands and wives played false for the moment, they had to remain on guard: at all costs Mrs Wheatley must be kept tolerant, for everything depended on her tolerance.

Kate had not been in the kitchen alone for long, before she heard the shrill thin scraping of the gramophone; and only a few minutes passed before both Mr and Mrs Sinclair came in. The degree of Kate's social education could have been judged by her startled look when she saw that neither were on guard and that anything might happen. Then she understood from what they said that tonight things were safe.

Mrs Sinclair said casually: 'Have something to eat, Kate?' and seemed to forget her. 'My God, they are a sticky lot,' she remarked to her husband.

'Oh, I don't know, they get around in their own way.'

'Yes, but what a way!' This was a burst of exasperated despair. 'They don't get going tonight, thank heavens. But one expects . . .' Here Mrs Sinclair's eyes fell on Kate, and she

lowered her voice. 'What I can't understand is the sameness of
it all. You press a button – that's sufficient alcohol – and then
the machinery begins to turn. The same things happen, the
same people, never a word said – it's awful.' She filled her glass
liberally from a bottle that stood among the denuded chicken
carcases. 'I needed that,' she remarked, setting the glass down.
'If I lived here much longer I'd begin to feel that I couldn't
enjoy myself unless I were drunk.'

'Well, my dear, we are off tomorrow.'

'How did I stick two years of it? It really is awful,' she
pursued petulantly. 'I don't know why I should get so cross
about it. After all,' she added reasonably, 'I'm no puritan.'

'No, dear, you are not,' said Mr Sinclair dryly; and the two
looked at each other with precisely that brand of discretion
which Kate had imagined Mrs Sinclair was protesting against.
The words opened a vista with such suddenness that the child
was staring in speculation at this plain, practical lady whose
bread and butter air seemed to leave even less room for the
romance which it was hard enough to associate with people like
the Wheatleys and the Fowlers.

'Perhaps it is that I like a little more – what? – grace? with
my sin?' enquired Mrs Sinclair, neatly expressing Kate's own
thought; and Mr Sinclair drove it home by saying, still very dry-
voiced: 'Perhaps at our age we ought not to be so demanding?'

Mrs Sinclair coloured and said quickly: 'Oh, you know what
I mean.' For a moment this couple's demeanour towards each
other was unfriendly; then they overcame it in a gulp of
laughter. 'Cat,' commented Mrs Sinclair, wryly appreciative;
and her husband slid a kiss on her cheek.

'You know perfectly well,' said Mrs Sinclair, slipping her
arm through her husband's, 'that what I meant was . . .'

'Well, we'll be gone tomorrow,' Mr Sinclair repeated.

'I think, on the whole,' said Mrs Sinclair after a moment,
'that I prefer worthies like the Copes to the others; they at any
rate have the discrimination to know what wouldn't become
them . . . except that one knows it is sheer, innate dullness . . .'

Mr Sinclair made a quick warning movement; Mrs Sinclair
coloured, looked confused, and gave Kate an irritated glance,
which meant: that child here again!

To hear her parents described as 'worthies' Kate took, defiantly, as a compliment; but the look caused the tears to suffuse her eyes, and she turned away.

'I am sorry, my dear,' said kindhearted Mrs Sinclair penitently. 'You dislike being your age as much as I do being mine, I daresay. We must make allowances for each other.'

With her hand still resting on Kate's shoulder, she remarked to her husband: 'I wonder what Rosalind Lacey will make of all this?' She laughed, with pleasurable maliciousness.

'I wouldn't be surprised if they didn't do very well.' His dryness now was astringent enough to sting.

'How could they?' asked Mrs Sinclair, really surprised. 'I shall be really astonished if they last six months. After all, she's not the type – I mean, she has at least some idea.'

'Which idea?' enquired Mr Sinclair blandly, grinning spitefully; and though Mrs Sinclair exclaimed: 'You are horrid, darling,' Kate saw that she grinned no less spitefully.

While Kate was wondering how much more 'different' (the word in her mind to distinguish the Sinclairs from the rest of the district) the coming Laceys would be from the Sinclairs, they all became aware that the music had stopped, and with it the sounds of scraping feet.

'Oh dear,' exclaimed Mrs Sinclair, 'you had better take out another case of whisky. What is the matter with them tonight? Say what you like, but it is exactly like standing beside a machine with an oil-can waiting for it to make grinding noises.'

'No, let them go. We've done what we should.'

'We must join them, nevertheless.' Mrs Sinclair hastily swallowed some more whisky, and sighing heavily, moved to the door. Kate could see through a vista of several open doors to the veranda, where people were sitting about with bored expressions which suggested surreptitious glances at the clock. Among them were her own parents, sitting side by side, their solidity a comment (which was not meant) on the way the others had split up. Mr Cope, who was described as The Puritan by his neighbours, a name he considered a great compliment, managed to enjoy his parties because it was quite possible to shut one's eyes to what went on at them. He was now smiling at Andrew Wheatley and Nan Fowler, as if the way they were interlaced was no more than roguish good fun. I like to see everyone enjoying themselves, his expression said, defiant of the gloom which was in fact settling over everyone.

Kate heard Mrs Sinclair say to her husband, this time impatiently: 'I suppose those Lacey people are going to spoil everything we have done here?' and this remark was sufficient food for thought to occupy her during the time she knew must elapse before she would be called to the car.

What had the Sinclairs, in fact, done here? Nothing – at least, to the mind of the district.

Kate supposed it might be something in the house; but, in fact, nothing had been built on, nothing improved; the place had not even been painted. She began to wander through the rooms, cautious of the sleeping children whose soft breathing could be heard from every darkened corner. The Sinclairs had brought in a great deal of heavy dark furniture, which everyone knew had to be polished by Mrs Sinclair herself, as the servants were not to be trusted with it. There was silver, solid and cumbersome stuff. There were brass trays and fenders and coal scuttles which were displayed for use even in the warm weather. And there were inordinate quantities of water-colours, engravings and oils whose common factor was a pervading heaviness, a sort of brownish sigh in paint. All these things were now in their packing-cases, and when the lorries came in the morning, nothing would be left of the Sinclairs. Yet the Sinclairs grieved for the destruction of something they imagined they had contributed. This paradox slowly cleared in Kate's mind as she associated it with that suggestion in the Sinclairs' manner that everything they did or said referred in some way to a standard that other people could not be expected to understand, a standard that had nothing to do with beauty, ugliness, evil or goodness. Looked at in this light, the couple's attitude became clear. Their clothes, their furniture, even their own persons, all shared that same attribute, which was a kind of expensive and solid ugliness that could not be classified in any terms that had yet been introduced to Kate.

So the child shelved that problem and considered the Laceys, who were to arrive next week. They, presumably, would be even more expensive and ugly, yet kind and satisfactory, than the Sinclairs themselves.

But she did not have time to think of the Laceys for long; for the house began to stir into life as the parents came to rouse their children, and the family units separated themselves off in the dark outside the house, where the cars were parked. For this time, that other pattern was finished with, for now ordinary life must go on.

In the back of the car, heavily covered by blankets, for the night was cold, Kate lay half asleep, and heard her father say: 'I wonder who we'll get this time?'

'More successful, I hope,' said Mrs Cope.

'Horses, I heard.' Mr Cope tested the word.

Mrs Cope confirmed the doubt in his voice by saying decisively: 'Just as bad as the rest, I suppose. This isn't the place for horses on that scale.'

Kate gained an idea of something unrespectable. Not only the horses were wrong; what her parents said was clearly a continuation of other conversations, held earlier in the evening. So it was that long before they arrived the Laceys were judged, and judged as vagrants.

Mr Cope would have preferred to have the kind of neighbours who become a kind of second branch of one's own family, with the children growing up together, and a continual borrowing back and forth of farm implements and books and so forth. But he was a gentle soul, and accepted each new set of people with a courtesy that only his wife and Kate understood was becoming an effort . . . it was astonishing the way all the people who came to Old John's Place were so much not the kind that the Copes would have liked.

Old John's House was three miles away, a comparatively short distance, and the boundary between the farms was a vlei which was described for the sake of grandness as a river, though most of the year there was nothing but a string of potholes caked with cracked mud. The two houses exchanged glances, as it were, from opposite ridges. The slope on the Copes' side was all ploughed land, of a dull yellow colour which deepened to glowing orange after rain. On the other side was a fenced expanse that had once been a cultivated field, and which was now greening over as the young trees spread and strengthened.

During the very first week of the Laceys' occupation this land became a paddock filled with horses. Mr Cope got out his binoculars, gazed across at the other slope, and dropped them after a while, remarking: 'Well, I suppose it is all right.' It was a grudging acceptance. 'Why shouldn't they have horses?' asked Kate curiously.

'Oh, I don't know, I don't know. Let's wait and see.' Mr Cope had met Mr Lacey at the station on mail day, and his report of the encounter had been brief, because he was a man who hated to be unfair, and he could not help disliking everything he heard about the Laceys. Kate gathered that the Laceys included a Mr Hackett. They were partners, and had been farming in the Argentine, in the Cape, and in England. It was a foursome, for there was also a baby. The first wagon load of furniture had consisted of a complete suite of furniture for the baby's nurseries, and many cases of saddles and stable equipment; and while they waited for the next load the family camped on the veranda without even so much as a teapot or a table for a meal. This tale was already making people smile. But because there was a baby the women warmed towards Mrs Lacey before they had seen her; and Mrs Cope greeted her with affectionate welcome when she arrived to make friends.

Kate understood at first glance that it was not Mrs Lacey's similarity to Mrs Sinclair that had caused the latter to accept her, in advance, as a companion in failure.

Mrs Lacey was not like the homely mothers of the district. Nor did she – like Mrs Sinclair – come into that category of leathery-faced and downright women who seemed more their husbands' partners than their wives. She was a tall, smooth-faced woman, fluidly moving, and bronze hair coiled in her neck with a demureness that seemed a challenge, taken with her grace, and with the way she used her eyes. These were large, grey, and very quick, and Kate thought of the swift glances, retreating immediately behind smooth lowered lids, as spies sent out for information. Kate was charmed, as her mother was; as her father was, too – though against his will; but she could not rid herself of distrust. All this wooing softness was an apology for something of which her parents had a premonition, while she herself was in the dark. She knew it was not the fact of the horses, in itself, that created disapproval; just as she knew that it was not merely Mrs Lacey's caressing manner that was upsetting her father.

When Mrs Lacey left, she drew Kate to her, kissed her on both cheeks, and asked her to come and spend the day. Warmth suddenly enveloped the child, so that she was head over ears in love, but distrusting the thing as a mature person does. Because the gesture was so clearly aimed, not at her, but at her parents, that first moment resentment was born with the love and the passionate admiration; and she understood her father when he said slowly, Mrs Lacey having left: 'Well, I suppose it is all right, but I can't say I like it.'

The feeling over the horses was explained quite soon: Mr Lacey and Mr Hackett kept these animals as other people might keep cats. They could not do without them. As with the Sinclairs, there was money somewhere. In this district people did not farm horses; they might keep a few for the races or to ride round the lands. But at Old John's Place now there were dozens of horses, and if they were bought and sold it was not for the sake of the money, but because these people enjoyed the handling of them, the business of attending sales and the slow, shrewd talk of men as knowledgeable as themselves. There was, in fact, something excessive and outrageous about the Laceys' attitude towards horses: it was a passionate business to be disapproved of, like gambling or women.

Kate went over to 'spend the day' a week after she was first asked; and that week was allowed to elapse only because she was too shy to go sooner. Walking up the road beside the paddock she saw the two men, in riding breeches, their whips looped over their arms, moving among the young animals with the seriousness of passion. They were both lean, tough, thin-flanked men, slow-moving and slow-spoken; and they appeared to be gripping invisible saddles with their knees even when they were walking. They turned their heads to stare at Kate, in the manner of those so deeply engrossed in what they are doing that outside things take a long time to grow in to their sight, but finally their whips cut a greeting in the air, and they shouted across to her. Their voices had a burr to them conveying again the exciting sense of things foreign; it was not the careful English voice of the Sinclairs, nor the lazy South African slur. It was an accent that had taken its timbre from many places and climates, and its effect on Kate was as if she had suddenly smelt the sea or heard a quickening strain of music.

She arrived at Old John's Place in a state of exaltation; and was greeted perfunctorily by Mrs Lacey, who then seemed to remind herself of something, for Kate once more found herself enveloped. Then, since the rooms were still scattered with packing-cases, she was asked to help arrange furniture and clear things up. By the end of that day her resentment was again temporarily pushed to the background by the necessity for keeping her standards sharp in her mind; for the Laceys, she knew, were to be resisted; and yet she was being carried away with admiration.

Mrs Sinclair might have brought something intangible here that to her was valuable, and she was right to have been afraid that Mrs Lacey would destroy it. The place was transformed. Mrs Lacey had colour-washed the walls sunny yellow, pale green, and rose, and added more light by the sort of curtains and hangings that Kate knew her own mother would consider frivolous. Such rooms were new in this district. As for Mrs Lacey's bedroom, it was outrageous. One wall had been ripped away, and it was now a sheet of glass; and across it had been arranged fifty yards of light transparent material that looked like crystallized sunlight. The floor was covered right over from wall to wall with a deep white carpet. The bed, standing out into the room in a way that drew immediate notice, was folded and looped into oyster-coloured satin. It was a room which had nothing to do with the district, nothing to do with the drifts of orange dust outside and the blinding sunlight, nothing to do with anything Kate had ever experienced. Standing just outside the door (for she was afraid she might leave orange-coloured footprints on that fabulous carpet) she stood and stared, and was unable to tear her eyes away even though she knew Mrs Lacey's narrowed grey gaze was fixed on her. 'Pretty?' she asked lightly, at last; and Kate knew she was being used as a test for what the neighbours might later say. 'It's lovely,' said

Kate doubtfully; and saw Mrs Lacey smile. 'You'll never keep it clean,' she added, as her mother would certainly do, when she saw this room. 'It will be difficult, but it's worth it,' said Mrs Lacey, dismissing the objection far too lightly, as Kate could see when she looked obliquely along the walls, for already there were films of dust in the grain of the plaster. But all through that day Kate felt as if she were continually being brought face to face with something new, used, and dismissed: she had never been so used; she had never been so ravaged by love, criticism, admiration and doubt.

Using herself (as Mrs Lacey was doing) as a test for other people's reactions, Kate could already hear the sour criticisms which would eventually defeat the Laceys. When she saw the nursery, however, she felt differently. This was something that the women of the district would appreciate. There were, in fact, three rooms for the baby, all conveying a sense of discipline and hygiene, with white enamel, thick cork floors and walls stencilled all over with washable coloured animals. The baby himself, at the crawling stage, was still unable to appreciate his surroundings. His nanny, a very clean, white-aproned native girl, sat several paces away and watched him. Mrs Lacey explained that this nanny had orders not to touch the baby; she was acting as a guard; it was against the principles which were bringing the child up that the germs (which certainly infested every native, washed or not) should come anywhere near him.

Kate's admiration grew; the babies she had known were carried about by piccanins or by the cook's wife. They did not have rooms to themselves, but cots set immediately by their mothers' beds. From time to time they were weighed on the kitchen scales, for feeding charts and baby scales had been encountered only in the pages of women's magazines that arrived on mail days from England.

When she went home that evening she told her mother first about the nurseries, and then about the bedroom: as she expected, the first fact slightly outweighed the second. 'She must be a good mother,' said Mrs Cope, adding immediately: 'I should like to know how she's going to keep the dust out of that carpet.' Mr Cope said: 'Well, I'm glad they've got money, because they are certainly going to need it.' These comments acted as temporary breakwaters to the flood that would later sweep through such very modified criticism.

For a while people discussed nothing but the Laceys. The horses were accepted with a shrug and the remark: 'Well, if they've money to burn . . .' Besides, that farm had never been properly used; this was merely a perpetuation of an existing fact. The word found for Mrs Lacey was that she was 'clever'. This was not often a compliment; in any case it was a tentative one. Mrs Lacey made her own clothes, but not in the way the other women made theirs. She cut out patterns from brown paper by some kind of an instinct; she made the desserts and salads from all kinds of unfamiliar substances; she grew vegetables profusely, and was generous with them. People were always finding a native at the back door, with a basket full of fresh things and Mrs Lacey's compliments. In fact, the women were going to Old John's House these days as they might have gone to raid a treasure cave; for they always returned with some fresh delight: mail order catalogues from America, new recipes, patterns for nightdresses. Mrs Lacey's nightdresses were discussed in corners at parties by the women, while the men called out across the room: 'What's that, eh? Let us in on the fun.' For a while it remained a female secret, for it was not so often that something new offered itself as spice to these people who knew each other far, far too well. At last, and it was at the Copes' house, one of the women stood up and demonstrated how Mrs Lacey's nightdresses were cut, while everyone applauded. For the first time Kate could feel a stirring, a quickening in the air; she could almost see it as a man slyly licking his lips. This was the first time, too, that Mr Cope openly disapproved of anything. He might be laughed at, but he was also a collective conscience; for when he said irritably: 'But it is so unnecessary, so unnecessary, this kind of thing . . .' everyone became quiet, and talked of something else. He always used that word when he did not want to condemn, but when he was violently uncomfortable. Kate remembered afterwards how the others looked over at him while they talked: their faces showed no surprise at his attitude, but also, for the moment, no agreement; it was as if a child looked at a parent to see how far it might go before forfeiting approval, for there was a lot of fun to be had out of the Laceys yet.

Mrs Lacey did not give her housewarming party until the place was finished, and that took several weeks. She did all the work herself. Kate, who was unable to keep away, helped her, and saw that Mrs Lacey was pleased to have her help. Mr Lacey was not interested in the beautiful house his wife was making; or, at any rate, he did not show it. Provided he was left enough room for books on horses, equipment for horses, and collections of sombreros, belts and saddles, he did not mind what she did. He once remarked: 'Well, it's your money, if you want to pour it down the sink.' Kate thought this sounded as if he wished to stop her; but Mrs Lacey merely returned, sharply: 'Quite. Don't let's go into that again, now.' And she looked meaningly at Kate. Several times she said: 'At last I can feel that I have a home. No one can understand what that is like.' At these moments Kate felt warm and friendly with her, for Mrs Lacey was confiding in her; although she was unable to see Old John's Place as anything but a kind of resthouse. Even the spirit of Mrs Sinclair was still strong in it, after all; for Kate summoned her, often, to find out what she would think of all this. She could positively see Mrs Sinclair standing there looking on, an ironical, pitying ghost. Kate was certain of the pity; because she herself could now hardly bear to look at Mrs Lacey's face when Mr Lacey and Mr Hackett came in to meals, and did not so much as glance at the work that had been done since they left. They would say: 'I heard there was a good thing down in Natal,' or 'that letter from old Perry, in California, made me think . . .' and they were so clearly making preparations for when the restless thing in them that had already driven them from continent to continent spoke again, that she wondered how Mrs Lacey could go on sewing curtains and ordering paints from town. Besides, Mrs Sinclair had known when she was defeated: she had chosen, herself, to leave. Turning the words over on her tongue that she had heard Mrs Sinclair use, she found the right ones for Mrs Lacey. But in the meantime, for the rest of the district, she was still 'clever'; and everyone looked forward to that party.

The Copes arrived late. As they climbed out of the car and moved to the door, they looked for the familiar groups on the veranda, but there was no one there, although laughter came from inside. Soon they saw that the veranda had been cleared of furniture, and the floor had been highly polished. There was no light, save for what fell through the windows; but this gave an appearance, not so much of darkness, but of hushed preparedness. There were tubs of plants set round the walls, forming wells of shadow, and chairs had been set in couples, discreetly, behind pillars and in corners.

Inside the room that opened from the veranda, there were men, but no women. Kate left her parents to assimilate themselves into the group (Mrs Cope protesting playfully that she was the only woman, and felt shy) and passed through the house to the nurseries. The women were putting the children to bed, under the direction of Mrs Lacey. The three rooms were arranged with camp-beds and stretchers, so that they looked like improvised dormitories, and the children were subdued and impressed, for they were not used to such organization. What Mrs Lacey represented, too, subdued them, as it was temporarily subduing their mothers.

Mrs Lacey was in white lace, and very pretty; but not only was she in evening dress and clearly put out because the other women were in their usual best dresses of an indeterminate floral crepiness that was positively a uniform for such occasions, there was that contrast, stronger now than ever, between what she seemed to want to appear, and what everyone felt of her. Those heavy down-looping, demure coils of hair, the discreet eyelids, the light white dress with childish puffed sleeves, were a challenge, but a challenge that was being held in reserve, for it was not directed at the women.

They were talking with the hurried forced laughter of nervousness. 'You have got yourself up, Rosalind,' said one of them; and this released a chorus of admiring remarks. What was behind the admiration showed itself when Mrs Lacey left the nurseries for a moment to call the native nanny. The same sycophantic lady said tentatively, as if throwing a bird into the air to be shot at: 'It is a sort of madonna look, isn't it? That oval face and smooth hair, I mean . . .' After a short silence someone said pointedly: 'Some madonna,' and then there was laughter, of a kind that sickened Kate, torn as she was between passionate partisanship and the knowledge that here was a lost cause.

Mrs Lacey returned with the native girl; and her brief glance at the women was brave; Kate could have sworn she had heard the laughter and the remark that prompted it. It was with an air of womanly dignity that fitted perfectly with her dress and appearance that she said: 'Now we have got the children into bed, we'll leave the girl to watch them and feel safe.' But this was not how she had said previously: 'Let's get them out of the way, and then we can enjoy ourselves.' The women, however, filed obediently out, ignoring the small protests of the children, who were not at all sleepy, since it was before their proper bedtime.

In the big room Mrs Lacey arranged her guests in what was clearly a planned compromise between the family pattern and the thing she intended should grow out of it. Husbands and wives were put together, yes; but in such a way that they had only to turn their heads to find other partners. Kate was astonished that Mrs Lacey could have learned so much about these people in such a short time. The slightest suggestion of an attraction, which had merited no more than a smile or a glance, was acknowledged frankly by Mrs Lacey in the way she placed her guests. For instance, while the Wheatleys were sitting together, Nan Fowler was beside Andrew Wheatley, and an elderly farmer, who had flirted mildly with Mrs Wheatley on a former occasion, was beside her. Mrs Lacey sat herself by Mr Fowler, and cried gaily: 'Now I shall console you, my dear – no, I shall be jealous if you take any notice of your wife tonight.' For a moment there was a laughing, but uneasy pause, and then Mr Lacey came forward with bottles, and Kate saw that everything was working as Mrs Lacey had intended. In half an hour she saw she must leave, if she wanted to avoid that uncomfortable conviction of being a nuisance. By now Mrs Lacey was beside Mr Lacey at the sideboard, helping him with the drinks; there was no help here – she had been forgotten by her hostess.

Kate slipped away to the kitchens. Here were tables laden

with chickens and trifles, certainly; but everything was a little dressed up; this was the district's party food elaborated to a stage where it could be admired and envied without causing suspicion.

Kate had had no time to do more than look for signs of the fatal aspics, sauces and creams when Mrs Lacey entered. Kate had to peer twice to make sure it was Mr Hackett and not Mr Lacey who came with her: the two men seemed to her so very alike. Mrs Lacey asked gaily: 'Having a good tuck-in?' and then the two passed through into the pantries. Here there was a good deal of laughter. Once Kate heard: 'Oh, do be careful . . .' and then Mrs Lacey looked cautiously into the kitchen. Seeing Kate she assumed a good-natured smile and said, 'You'll burst,' and then withdrew her head. Kate had eaten nothing; but she did what seemed to be expected of her, and left the kitchen, wondering just what this thing was that sprang up suddenly between men and women – no, not *what* it was, but what prompted it. The word love, which had already stretched itself to include so many feelings, atmospheres and occasions, had become elastic enough for Kate not to astonish her. It included, for instance, Mr Lacey and Mrs Lacey helping each other to pour drinks, with an unmistakable good feeling; and Mrs Lacey flirting with Mr Hackett in the pantry while they pretended to be looking for something. To look at Mrs Lacey this evening – that was no problem, for the bright expectancy of love was around her like sunlight. But why Mr Hackett, or Mr Lacey; or why either of them? And then Nan Fowler, that fat, foolish, capable dame who flushed scarlet at a word: what drew Andrew Wheatley to her, of all women, through years of parties, and kept him there?

Kate drifted across the intervening rooms to the door of the big living-room, feeling as if someone had said to her: 'Yes, this house is yours, go in,' but had forgotten to give her the key, or even to tell her where the door was. And when she reached the room she stopped again; through the hazing cigarette smoke, the hubbub, the leaning, laughing faces, the hands lying along chair-arms, grasping glasses, she could see her parents sitting side by side, and knew at once, from their faces, that they wanted only to go home, and that if she entered now, putting her to bed would be made an excuse for going. She went back to the nurseries; as she passed the kitchen door she saw Mr Hackett, Mr Lacey and Mrs Lacey, arms linked from waist to waist, dancing along between the heaped tables and singing: All I want is a *lit*tle bit of love, a *lit*tle bit of love, a *lit*tle bit of love. Both men were still in their riding things, and their boots thumped and clattered on the floor. Mrs Lacey looked like a species of fairy who had condescended to appear to cowhands – cowhands who, however, were cynical about fairies, for at the end of the dance Mr Lacey smacked her casually across her behind and said, 'Go and do your stuff, my girl,' and Mrs Lacey went laughing to her guests, leaving the men raiding the chickens in what appeared to be perfect good fellowship.

In the nurseries Kate was struck by the easy manner in which some twenty infants had been so easily disposed of: they were all asleep. The silence here was deepened by the soft, regular sounds of breathing, and the faint sound of music from beyond the heavy baize doors. Even now, with the extra beds, and the little piles of clothing at the foot of each, everything was so extraordinarily tidy. A great cupboard, with its subdued gleaming paint, presented to Kate an image of Mrs Lacey herself; and she went to open it. Inside it was orderly, and on the door was a list of its contents, neady typed; but if a profusion of rich materials, like satin and velvet, had tumbled out as the door opened, she would not have been in the least surprised. On the contrary, her feeling of richness restrained and bundled out of the way would have been confirmed, but there was nothing of the kind, not an article out of place anywhere, and on the floor sat the smiling native nanny, apologizing by her manner for her enforced uselessness, for the baby was whimpering and she was forbidden to touch it.

'Have you told Mrs Lacey?' asked Kate, looking doubtfully at the fat pink and white creature, which was exposed in a brief vest and napkin, for it was too hot an evening for anything more. The nanny indicated that she had told Mrs Lacey, who had said she would come when she could.

Kate sat beside the cot to wait, surrendering herself to self-pity: the grown-ups were rid of her, and she was shut into the nursery with the tiny children. Her tears gathered behind her eyes as the baby's cries increased. After some moments she sent the nanny again for Mrs Lacey, and when neither of them returned, she rather fearfully fetched a napkin from the cupboard and made the baby comfortable. Then she held it on her knee, for consolation. She did not much like small babies, but the confiding warmth of this one soothed her. When the nursery door swung open soundlessly, so that Mrs Lacey was standing over her before she knew it, she could not help wriggling guiltily up and exclaiming: 'I changed him. He was crying.' Mrs Lacey said firmly: 'You should never take a child out of bed once it is in. You should never alter a time-table.' She removed the baby and put it back into the cot. She was afloat with happiness, and could not be really angry, but went on: 'If you don't keep them strictly to a routine, they take advantage of you.' This was so like what Kate's own mother always said about her servants, that she could not help laughing; and Mrs Lacey said good-humouredly, turning round from the business of arranging the baby's limbs in an orderly fashion: 'It is all very well, but he is perfectly trained, isn't he? He never gives me any trouble. I am quite certain you have never seen such a well-trained baby around here before.' Kate admitted this was so, and felt appeased: Mrs Lacey had spoken as if there was at least a possibility of her one day reaching the status of being able to profit by the advice: she was speaking as if to an equal.

Kate watched her move to the window, adjust the angle of a pane so that the starlight no longer gleamed in it, and use it as a mirror: there was no looking-glass in the nurseries. The smooth folds of hair were unruffled, but the usually guarded, observant eyes were bright and reckless. There was a vivid glow about Mrs Lacey that made her an exotic in the nursery; even her presence there was a danger to the sleeping children. Perhaps she felt it herself, for she smoothed her forefinger along an eyebrow and said: 'Are you going to stay here?' Kate hesitated. Mrs Lacey said swiftly: 'I don't see why you shouldn't come in. It's your father, though. He's such an old . . .' She stopped herself, and smiled sourly. 'He doesn't approve of me. However, I can't help that.' She was studying Kate. 'Your mother has no idea, no idea at all,' she remarked impatiently, turning Kate about between her hands. Kate understood that had Mrs Lacey been her mother, her clothes would have been graded to suit her age. As it was, she wore a short pink cotton frock, reaching half-way down her thighs, that a child of six might have worn. That frock caused her anguished embarrassment, but loyalty made her say: 'I like pink,' very defiantly. Her eyes, though, raised in appeal to Mrs Lacey's, gained the dry reply: 'Yes, so I see.'

On her way out, Mrs Lacey remarked briskly: 'I've got a lot of old dresses that could be cut down for you. I'll help you with them.' Kate felt that this offer was made because Mrs Lacey truly loved clothes and materials; for a moment her manner to Kate had not been adjusted with an eye to the ridiculous, but powerful Mr Cope. She said gratefully: 'Oh, Mrs Lacey . . .'

'And that hair of yours . . .' she heard, as the door swung, and went on swinging, soundlessly. There was the crisp sound of a dress moving along the passage, and the sweet homely smell of the nursery had given way to a perfume as unsettling as the music that poured strongly through the house. The Laceys had a radiogram and the newest records. Feet were swishing and sliding, the voices were softer now, with a reckless note. The laughter, on the other hand, swept by in great gusts. Peering through the doors, Kate tried to determine what 'stage' the party had reached; she saw there had been no stages; Mrs Lacey had fused these people together from the beginning, by the force of wanting to do it, and because her manner seemed to take the responsibility for whatever might happen. Now her light gay voice sounded above the others; she was flirting with everyone, dancing with everyone. Now there was no criticism; they were all in love with her.

Kate could see that while normally at this hour the rooms would be half empty, tonight they were all there. Couples were moving slowly in the subdued light of the veranda, very close together, or sitting at the tables, looking on. Then she suddenly saw someone walking towards her, by herself, in a violent staggering way; and peering close, saw it was Mrs Wheatley. She was crying. 'I want to go home, I want to go home,' she was saying, her tongue loose in her mouth. She did not see

Kate, who ran quickly back to the baby, who was now asleep, lying quite still in its white cot, hands flexed at a level with its head, its fingers curled loosely over. Darling baby, whispered Kate, the tears stinging her cheeks. Darling, darling baby. The painful wandering emotion that had filled her for weeks, even since before the Laceys came, when she had felt held safe in Mrs Sinclair's gruff kindliness, spilled now into the child. With a fearful, clutching pounce, she lifted the sleeping child, and cuddled it. Darling, darling baby . . . Later, very much later, she woke to find Mr Lacey, looking puzzled, taking the baby from her; they had been lying asleep on the floor together. 'Your father wants you,' stated Mr Lacey carefully, the sickly smell of whisky coming strong from his mouth. Kate staggered up and gained the door on his arm; but it was not as strong a support as she needed, for he was holding on to tables and chairs as he passed them.

For a moment Kate's sleep-dazed eyes could find nothing to hold them, for the big room was quite empty; so, it seemed, was the veranda. Then she saw Mrs Lacey, dancing by herself down the dim shadowed space, weaving her arms and bending her body, and leaning her head to watch her white reflection move on the polished floor beside her. 'Who is going to dance with me?' she crooned. 'Who is going to dance?'

'You've worn us out,' said a man's voice from Kate's feet; and looking hazily round she saw that couples were sitting around the edges of the space, with their arms about each other. Another voice, a woman's this time, said: 'Oh what a beautiful dress, what a beautiful dress,' repeating it with drunken intensity; and someone answered in a low tone: 'Yes, and not much beneath it, either, I bet.'

Suddenly Kate's world was restored for her by her father's comment at her shoulder: 'So unnecessary!' And she felt herself pushed across the veranda in the path of the dancing Mrs Lacey, whose dim white skirts flung out and across her legs in a crisp caress. But she took no notice of Kate at all; nor did she answer Mr Cope when he said stiffly: 'Good-bye, Mrs Lacey. I am afraid we must take this child to bed.' She continued to dance, humming to herself, a drowsy happy look on her face.

In the car Kate lay wrapped in blankets and looked through

the windows at the sky moving past. There was a white blaze of moonlight and the stars were full and bright. It could not be so very late after all, for the night still had the solemn intensity of midnight; that feeling of glacial withdrawal that comes into the sky towards dawn was not yet there. But in the hollow of the veld, where the cold lay congealed, she shivered and sat up. Her parents' heads showed against the stars, and they were being quite silent for her benefit. She was waiting for them to say something; she wanted her confused, conflicting impressions sorted and labelled by them. In her mind she was floating with Mrs Lacey down the polished floor; she was also in the nursery with the fat and lovable baby; she could feel the grip of Mr Lacey's hand on her shoulder. But not a word was said, not a word; though she could almost feel her mother thinking: 'She has to learn for herself,' and her father answering it with a 'Yes, but how unpleasant!'

The next day Kate waited until her father had gone down to the lands in order to watch his labourers at their work, and her mother was in the vegetable garden. Then she said to the cook: 'Tell the missus I have gone to Old John's Place.' She walked away from her home and down to the river with the feeling that large accusing eyes were fixed on her back, but it was essential that she should see Mrs Lacey that day: she was feverish with terror that Mr Lacey had given her away – worse, that the baby had caught cold from lying on the floor beside her, and was ill. She walked slowly, as if dragged by invisible chains: if she left behind her unspoken disapproval, in front of her she sensed cruel laughter and anger.

Guilt, knowledge of having behaved ridiculously, and defiance churned through her; above the tumult another emotion rose like a full moon over a sky of storm. She was possessed by love; she was in love with the Laceys, with the house and its new luxuries, with Mrs Lacey and the baby – even with Mr Lacey and Mr Hackett, who took lustre from Mrs Lacey. By the time she neared the place, fear had subsided in her to a small wariness, lurking like a small trapped animal, with bared teeth; she could think of nothing but that in a moment she would again have entered the magical circle. The drowsy warmth of a September morning, the cooing of the pigeons in the trees all about, the dry smell of sun-scorched foliage – all these familiar scents and sounds bathed her, sifted through her new sensitiveness and were reissued, as it were, in a fresh currency: around Mrs Lacey's house the bush was necessarily more exciting than it could be anywhere else.

The picture in her mind of the veranda and the room behind it, as she had seen them the night before, dissolved like the dream it had appeared to be as she stepped through the screen door. Already at ten in the morning, there was not a sign of the party. The long space of floor had been polished anew to a dull gleaming red; the chairs were in their usual circle at one end, against a bank of ferns, and at the other Mrs Lacey sat sewing, the big circular table beside her heaped with materials and neatly-folded patterns. For a moment she did not notice Kate, who was free to stand and gaze in devoted wonder. Mrs Lacey was in fresh green linen, and her head was bent over the white stuff in her lap in a charming womanly pose. This, surely, could never have been that wild creature who danced down this same veranda last night? She lifted her head and looked towards Kate; her long eyes narrowed, and something hardened behind them until, for a brief second, Kate was petrified by a vision of a boredom so intense that it was as if Mrs Lacey had actually said: 'What! Not you again?' Then down dropped those lids, so that her face wore the insufferable blank piety of a primitive Madonna. Then she smiled. Even that forced smile won Kate; and she moved towards Mrs Lacey with what she knew was an uncertain and apprehensive grin. 'Sit down,' said Mrs Lacey cordially, and spoiled the effect by adding immediately: 'Do your parents know you are here?' She watched Kate obliquely as she put the question. 'No,' said Kate honestly, and saw the lids drop smoothly downwards.

She was stiff with dislike; she could not help but want to accept this parody of welcome as real; but not when the illusion was destroyed afresh every time Mrs Lacey spoke. She asked timidly: 'How is the baby?' This time Mrs Lacey's look could not possibly be misinterpreted: she had been told by her husband; she had chosen, for reasons of her own, to say nothing. 'The baby's very well,' she said neutrally, adding after a moment: 'Why did you come without telling your mother?'

Kate could not give any comfort. 'They would be angry if they knew I was here. I left a message.' Mrs Lacey frowned, laughed with brave, trembling gaiety, and then reached over and touched the bell behind her. Far away in the kitchens of that vast house there was a shrill peal; and soon a padding of bare feet announced the coming of the servant. 'Tea,' ordered Mrs Lacey. 'And bring some cakes for the little missus.' She rearranged her sewing, put her hand to her eyes, laughed ruefully and said: 'I've got such a hangover I won't be able to eat for a week. But it was worth it.' Kate could not reply. She sat fingering the materials heaped on the table; and wondered if any of these were what Mrs Lacey had intended to give her; she even felt a preliminary gratitude, as it were. But Mrs Lacey seemed to have forgotten her promise. The white stuff was for the baby. They discussed suitable patterns for children's vests: it went without saying that Mrs Lacey's pattern was one Kate had never seen before, combining all kinds of advantages, so that it appeared that not a binding, a tape or a fastener had escaped the most far-sighted planning.

The long hot morning had to pass at last; at twelve Mrs Lacey glanced at the folding clock which always stood beside her, and fetched the baby from where he lay in the shade under a big tree. She fed him orange juice, spoon by spoon, without taking him from the pram, while Kate watched him with all the nervousness of one who has betrayed emotion and is afraid it may be unkindly remembered. But the baby ignored her. He was a truly fine child, fat, firm, dimpled. When the orange juice was finished he allowed himself to be wheeled back to the tree without expostulating, and no one could have divined, from his placid look, the baffled affection that Kate was projecting into him.

That done, she accompanied Mrs Lacey to the nursery, where the cup and the spoon and the measuring-glass were boiled for germs and set to cool under a glass bell. The baby's rooms had a cool, ordered freshness; when the curtains blew out into the room, Kate looked instinctively at Mrs Lacey to see if she would check such undisciplined behaviour, but she was looking at the time-table which hung on the inside of the baize door. This time-table began with: 'Six A.M., orange juice';

continued through 'Six-thirty, rusk and teething ring, seven, wash and dress'; and ended at 'five P.M., mothering hour and bed'. Somewhere inside of Kate bubbled a disloyal and incredulous laughter, which astonished her; the face she turned towards Mrs Lacey was suddenly so guilty that it was met with a speculative lift of the smooth wide brows. 'What is wrong with you now, Kate?' said Mrs Lacey.

Soon after, the men appeared, in their breeches and trailing their whips behind them across the polished floors. They smiled at Kate, but for a moment their pupils narrowed as Mrs Lacey's had done. Then they all sat on the veranda, not at the sewing end, but at the social part, where the big grass chairs were. The servant wheeled out a table stacked with drinks; Kate could not think of any other house where gin and vermouth were served as a routine, before meals. The men were discussing a gymkhana that was due shortly; Mrs Lacey did not interrupt. When they moved indoors to the dining-room, Kate again felt the incongruity between the orderly charm created by Mrs Lacey and the casual way the men took it, even destroying it by refusing to fit in. Lunch was a-cool, lazy affair, with jugs of frosted drinks and quantities of chilled salads. Mr Lacey and Mr Hackett were scribbling figures on pieces of paper and talking together all through the meal; and it was not until it was over that Kate understood that the scene had been like a painted background to the gymkhana which to the men was far more real than anything Mrs Lacey said or did.

As soon as it was over, they offered their wide lazy good-humoured grin, and slouched off again to the paddock. Kate could have smiled; but she knew there would be no answering smile from Mrs Lacey.

In silence they took their places at the sewing-table; and at two o'clock to the minute Mrs Lacey looked at the clock and brought the baby in for his nap, leaving the nanny crouched on the floor to guard him.

Afterwards Kate's discomfort grew acute. In the district 'coming over for the day' meant either one of two things: something was arranged, like tennis or swimming, with plenty to eat and drink: or the women came by themselves to sew and cook and knit, and this sharing of activity implied a deeper sharing. Kate used to think that her mother came back from a day with one of her women friends wearing the same relaxed softened expression as she did after a church service.

But Kate was at a hopelessly loose end, and Mrs Lacey did not show it only because it suited her book not to. She offered to sew, and did not insist when Mrs Lacey rather uncomfortably protested. Mrs Lacey sewed exquisitely, and anything she could do would be bungling in comparison.

At last the baby woke. Kate knew the time-table said: 'Three to five: walk or playpen', and offered to push the pram. Again she had to face up to the shrewd, impatient look, while Mrs Lacey warned: 'Remember, babies don't like being messed about.' 'I know,' said Kate consciously, colouring. When the baby was strapped in and arranged, Kate was allowed to take the handles of the pram. Leading away from the house in the opposite direction from the river was a long avenue of reeds where the shade lay cool and deep. 'You mustn't go away from the trees,' directed Mrs Lacey; and Kate saw her return to the house, her step quickening with relief; whatever her life was, the delicious, devoted secret life that Kate imagined, she was free to resume it now that Kate was gone: it seemed impossible this lovely and secret thing should not exist: for it was the necessary complement to the gross practicality of her husband and Mr Hackett. But when Kate returned at five o'clock, after two hours of steady walking up and down the avenue, pushing the pram and suppressing her passionate desire to cuddle the indifferent baby, Mrs Lacey was baking tarts in the kitchen.

If she was to be back home before it grew dark, she must leave immediately. She lingered, however, till five past five: during those two hours she had, in fact, been waiting for the moment when Mrs Lacey would 'mother' the baby. But Mrs Lacey seated herself with a book and left the child to crawl on a rug at her feet. Kate set off on the road home; and this time the eyes she felt follow her were irritated and calculating.

At the gate stood her mother. 'You shouldn't have gone off without telling me!' she exclaimed reproachfully. Now, Kate was free to roam as she willed over the farm, so this was unjust, and both sides knew it to be so. 'I left a message,' said Kate, avoiding her mother's eyes.

· Next morning she was loitering about the gate looking out over the coloured slopes to the Laceys' house, when her mother came up behind her, apparently cutting zinnias, but in fact looking for an opportunity to express her grievance. 'You would live there, if you could, wouldn't you, dear?' she said, smiling painfully. 'All those fashions and new clothes and things, we can't compete, can we?' Kate's smile was as twistingly jealous as hers; but she did not go to the Laceys that day. After all, she couldn't very well: there were limits. She remained in that part of the farm which lay beside the Laceys', and looked across at the trees whose heavy greenness seemed to shed a perfume that was more than the scent of sunheated leaves, and where the grass beckoned endlessly as the wind moved along it. Love, still unrecognized, still unaccepted in her, flooded this way and that, leaving her limp with hatred or exalted with remembrance. And through it all she thought of the baby while resentment grew in her. Whether she stood with the binoculars stuck to her eyes, hour after hour, hoping for a glimpse of Mrs Lacey on the veranda, or watching the men lean against the fence as the horses moved about them, the baby was in the back of her mind; and the idea of it was not merely the angry pity that is identification with suffering, but also a reflection of what other people were thinking. Kate knew, from a certain tone in her mother's voice when she mentioned that child, that she was not wholly convinced by time-tables and hygiene.

The ferment of the last party had not settled before Mrs Lacey issued invitations for another; there had only been a fortnight's interval. Mr Cope said, looking helplessly across at his wife: 'I suppose we ought to go?' and Mrs Cope replied guardedly: 'We can't very well not, when they are our nearest neighbours, can we?' 'Oh Lord!' exclaimed Mr Cope, moving irritably in his chair. Then Kate felt her parents' eyes come to rest on her; she was not surprised when Mr Cope asked: 'When does Kate go back to school?' 'The holidays don't end for another three weeks.'

So the Copes all went to Mrs Lacey's second party, which began exactly as the first had done: everything was the same. The women whisked their children into the improvised dormitory without showing even a formal uneasiness. One of them said: 'It is nice to be free of them for once, isn't it?' and Kate saw Mrs Lacey looking humorous before she turned away her face. That evening Mrs Lacey wore a dress of dim green transparent stuff, as innocent and billowing, though as subtly indiscreet as the white one, and the women – save for Mrs Cope – were in attempts at evening dress.

Mrs Lacey saw Kate standing uncertainly in the passage, grasped her by the shoulder, and pushed her gently into the room where all the people were. 'I shall find you a boy friend,' she stated gaily; and Kate looked apprehensively towards her parents, who were regarding her, and everyone else, with helpless disapproval. Things had gone beyond their censure already: Mrs Lacey was so sure of herself that she could defy them about their own daughter before their eyes. But Kate found herself seated next to a young assistant recently come to the district, who at eighteen was less likely to be tolerant of little girls than an older man might have been. Mrs Lacey had shown none of her usual shrewdness in the choice. After a few painful remarks, Kate saw this young man turn away from her, and soon she tried to slip away. Mr Hackett, noticing her, put his arm round her and said, 'Don't run away, my dear,' but the thought of her watching parents stiffened her to an agony of protest. He dropped his arm, remarked humorously to the rest of the room – for everyone was looking over at them and laughing: 'These girlish giggles!' and turned his attention to the bottle he was holding. Kate ran to the kitchens. Soon she fled from there, as people came in. She crept furtively to the baby's cot, but he was asleep; and it was not long before Mrs Lacey glanced in and said: 'Do leave him alone, Kate,' before vanishing again. Kate took herself to that set of rooms that Mrs Lacey had not touched at all. They were still roughly white-washed, and the cement floors, though polished, were bare. Saddles of various patterns hung in rows in one room; another was filled with beautifully patterned belts with heavy silver buckles and engraved holsters. There were, too, rows and rows of guns of all kinds, carved, stamped, twisted into strange shapes. They came from every part of the world, and were worth a fortune, so people said.

· These rooms were where Mr Lacey and Mr Hackett liked to sit; and they had heavy leather armchairs, and a cupboard with a private supply of whisky and siphons. Kate sat stiffly on the edge of one of the chairs, and looked at the rows of weapons: she was afraid the men might be angry to find her there. And in fact it was not long before Mr Lacey appeared in the doorway, gave an exclamation, and withdrew. He had not been alone. Kate, wondering who the lady was, and whether Mrs Lacey would mind, left the house altogether and sat in the back of their car. Half asleep, she watched the couples dancing along the veranda, and saw how at one end a crowd of natives gathered outside in the dark, pressing their noses to the wire gauze, in curious admiration at the white people enjoying themselves. Sometimes a man and a woman would come down the steps, their arms about each other, and disappear under the trees; or into the cars. She shrank back invisibly, for in the very next car were a couple who were often visitors at their house, though as members of their own families; and she did not want them to have the embarrassment of knowing she was there. Soon she stuck her fingers in her ears; she felt sick, and she was also very hungry.

But it was not long before she heard shouts from the house, and the shouts were angry. Peering through the back window of the car she could see people standing around two men who were fighting. She saw legs in riding breeches, and then Mrs Lacey came and stood between them. 'What nonsense,' Kate heard her exclaim, her voice still high and gay, though strained. Almost immediately Kate heard her name called, and her mother appeared, outlined against the light. Kate slipped from the car so that the couple in the next car might not see her and ran to tug at her mother's arm.

'So there you are!' exclaimed Mrs Cope in a relieved voice. 'We are going home now. Your father is tired.'

In the car Kate asked: 'What were Mr Hackett and Mr Lacey fighting about?' There was a pause before Mrs Cope replied: 'I don't know, dear.' 'Who won?' insisted Kate. Then, when she got no answer, she said: 'It's funny, isn't it, when in the daytime they are such friends?' In the silence the sound of her own words tingled in her ears, and Kate watched something unexpected, yet familiar, emerge. Here it was again, the other pattern. It was of Mr Hackett that she thought as the car nosed its way through the trees to their own farm, and her wonder crystallized at last into exclamation: 'But they are so much alike!' She felt as she would have done if she had seen a little girl, offered a doll, burst into tears because she had not been given another that was identical in every way. 'Don't bother your head about it,' soothed Mrs Cope. 'They aren't very nice people. Forget about it.'

The next Sunday was Church Sunday. The ministers came in rotation: Presbyterian, Church of England, Roman Catholic. Sometimes there was a combined service. The Copes never missed the Church of England Sundays.

The services were held in the district hall, near the station. The hall is a vast barn of a place, and the small group of worshippers crowded at one end, near the platform, where Nan Fowler perched to play the hymns, like a thin flock of birds in a very large tree. The singing rose meagrely over the banging of the piano and dissolved in the air above their heads: even from the door the music seemed to come from a long way off.

The Laceys and Mr Hackett arrived late that day, tiptoeing uncomfortably to the back seats and arranging themselves so that Mrs Lacey sat between the men. This was the first time they had been to church. Kate twisted her neck and saw that for once the men were not in riding things; released, thus, from their uniforms, looking ordinary in brown suits, it was easier to see them as two different people. But even so, they were alike, with the same flat slouching bodies and lean humorous faces. They hummed tunelessly, making a bumblebee noise, and looked towards the roof. Mrs Lacey, who held the hymn book for all three of them, kept her eyes on the print in a manner which seemed to be directing the men's attention to it. She looked very neat and sober today, and her voice, a pretty contralto, was stronger than anyone's, so that in a little while she was leading the singing. Again, irresistibly, the subterranean laughter bubbled in Kate, and she turned away, glancing doubtfully at her mother, who hissed in her ear: 'It's rude to stare.'

When the service was over, Mrs Lacey came straight to Mrs

Cope and held out her hand. 'How are you?' she asked
winningly. Mrs Cope replied stiffly: 'It is nice to see you at
church.' Kate saw Mrs Lacey's face twitch, and sympathy told
her that Mrs Lacey, too, was suffering from the awful need to
laugh. However, her face straightened, and she glanced at Mr
Cope and flushed. She stood quietly by and watched while Mrs
Cope issued invitations to everyone who passed to come home
to Sunday lunch. She was expecting an invitation too, but none
was offered. Mrs Cope finally nodded, smiled, and climbed
into the car. There was suddenly a look of brave defiance about
Mrs Lacey that tugged at Kate's heart: if it had not been for
the stoic set of her shoulders as she climbed into the car with
her two men, Kate would have been able to bear the afternoon
better. When lunch was over, things arranged themselves as
usual with the men on one side of the room and the women on
the other. Kate stood for a while behind her father's chair;
then, with burning cheeks, she moved over to the women who
had their heads together around her mother's chair. They
glanced up at her, and then behaved as grown-up people do
when they wish to talk and children are in the way; they simply
pretended she was not there. In a few moments Kate sped from
the house and ran through the bush to her place of refuge,
which was a deep hollow over which bushes knotted and
tangled. Here she flung herself and wept.

Nobody mentioned the Laceys at supper. People seemed to
have been freed from something. There was a great deal of
laughter at the comfortable old jokes at which they had been
laughing for years. The air had been cleared: something final
had happened, or was going to happen. Later, when these
farmers and their wives, carrying their children rolled in
blankets, went to find their cars, Kate lifted the curtain and
looked over at the cluster of lights on the opposite ridge, and
wondered if Mrs Lacey was watching the headlights of the cars
swing down the various roads home, and if so, what it was she
was thinking and feeling.

Next morning a basket arrived at the back door, full of fresh
vegetables and roses. There was also a note addressed to Miss
Catherine Cope. It said: 'If you have nothing better to do,
come and spend the day. I have been looking over some of my

old dresses for you.' Kate read this note, feeling her mother's reproachful eyes fixed on her, and reluctantly handed it over. 'You are not going, surely!' exclaimed Mrs Cope. 'I might as well, for the last time,' said Kate. When she heard what it was she had said, the tears came into her eyes, so that she could not turn round to wave good-bye to her mother.

That last day she missed nothing of the four miles' walk: she felt every step.

The long descent on their side was through fields which were now ploughed ready for the wet season. A waste of yellow clods stretched away on either side, and over them hung a glinting haze of dust. The road itself was more of a great hogsback, for the ditches on either side had eroded into cracked gullies fifteen feet deep. Soon, after the rains, this road would have to be abandoned and another cut, for the water raced turbulently down here during every storm, swirling away the soil and sharpening the ridge. At the vlei, which was now quite dry, the gullies had cut down into a double pothole, so that the drift was unsafe even now. This time next year the old road to the Laceys would be a vivid weal down the slope where no one could walk.

On the other side the soil changed: here it was pale and shining, and the dews of each night hardened it so that each step was a small crusty subsidence. Because the lands had not been farmed for years and were covered with new vegetation, the scars that had been cut down this slope, too, were healing, for the grasses had filmed over them and were gripping the loose soil.

Before Kate began to ascend this slope she took her cretonne hat that her mother had made to 'go' with her frock, and which stuck up in angles round her face, and hid it in an antbear hole, where she could find it on the way home; she could not bear Mrs Lacey to see her in it.

Being October, it was very hot, and the top of her head began to feel as if a weight were pressing on it. Soon her shoulders ached too, and her eyes dazzled. She could hardly see the bright swift horses in the bushy paddock for glare, and her tight smile at Mr Hackett and Mr Lacey was more like a grimace of pain. When she arrived on the veranda, Mrs Lacey, who was sewing, gave her a concerned glance, and exclaimed: 'What have you done with your hat?' 'I forgot it,' said Kate.

On the sewing table were piles of Mrs Lacey's discarded frocks. She said kindly: 'Have a look at these and see which you would like.' Kate blinked at the glare outside and slid thankfully into a chair; but she did not touch the frocks. After a while her head cleared and she said: 'I can't take them. My mother wouldn't like it. Thank you all the same.' Mrs Lacey glanced at her sharply, and went on sewing for a while in silence. Then she said lightly: 'I don't see why you shouldn't, do you?' Kate did not reply. Now that she had recovered, and the pressure on her head had gone, she was gazing about her, consciously seeing everything for the last time, and wondering what the next lot of people would be like.

'Did you have a nice time yesterday?' asked Mrs Lacey, wanting to be told who had spent the day with the Copes, what they had done, and – most particularly – what they had said. 'Very nice, thank you,' said Kate primly; and saw Mrs Lacey's face turn ugly with annoyance before she laughed and asked: 'I am in disgrace, am I?'

But Kate could not now be made an ally. She said cautiously: 'What did you expect?'

Mrs Lacey said, with amused annoyance: 'A lot of hypocritical old fogeys.' The word 'hypocrite' isolated itself and stood fresh and new before Kate's eyes, and it seemed to her all at once that Mrs Lacey was wilfully misunderstanding.

She sat quietly, watching the sun creep in long warm streaks towards her over the shining floor, and waited for Mrs Lacey to ask what she so clearly needed to ask. There would be some question, some remark, that would release her, so that she could go home, feeling a traitor no longer: she did not know it, but she was waiting for some kind of an apology, something that would heal the injustice that burned in her: after all, for Mrs Lacey's sake she had let her own parents dislike her.

But there was no sound from Mrs Lacey, and when Kate looked up, she saw that her face had changed. It was peaked, and diminished, with frail blue shadows around the mouth and eyes. Kate was looking at an acute, but puzzled fear, and could not recognize it; though if she had been able to search inside herself, now, thinking of how she feared to return home, she would have found pity for Mrs Lacey.

After a while she said: 'Can I take the baby for a walk?' It was almost midday, with the sun beating directly downwards; the baby was never allowed out at this hour; but after a short hesitation Mrs Lacey gave her an almost appealing glance and said: 'If you keep in the shade.' The baby was brought from the nursery and strapped into the pram. Kate eased the pram down the steps, but instead of directing her steps towards the avenue, where there might possibly have been a little shade, even at this hour, went down the road to the river. On one side, where the bushes were low, sun-glare fell about the grassroots. On the other infrequent patches of shade stood under the trees. Kate dodged from one patch to the next, while the baby reclined in the warm airless cave under the hood.

She could not truly care: she knew Mrs Lacey was watching her and did not turn her head; she had paid for this by weeks of humiliation. When she was out of sight of the house she unstrapped the baby and carried it a few paces from the road into the bush. There she sat, under a tree, holding the child against her. She could feel sweat running down her face, and did not lift her hand to find whether tears mingled with it: her eyes were smarting with the effort of keeping her lids apart over the pressure of tears. As for the baby, beads of sweat stood all over his face. He looked vaguely about and reached his hands for the feathery heads of grasses and seemed subdued. Kate held him tight, but did not caress him; she was knotted tight inside with tears and anger. After a while she saw a tick crawl out of the grass on to her leg, and from there to the baby's leg. For a moment she let it crawl; from that dark region of her mind where the laughter spurted, astonishingly, came the thought: He might get tick fever. She could see Mrs Lacey very clearly, standing beside a tiny oblong trench, her head bent under the neat brown hat. She could hear women saying, their admiration and pity heightened by contrition: 'She was so brave, she didn't give way at all.'

Kate brushed off the tick and stood up. Carefully keeping the sun off the child – his cheek was already beginning to redden – she put him back in the pram, and began wheeling it back. Whatever it was she had been looking for, satisfaction, whether of pain, or love, she had not been given it. She could see Mrs Lacey standing on the veranda shading her eyes with her hand as she gazed towards them. Another thought floated up: she vividly saw herself pleading with Mrs Lacey: 'Let me keep the baby, you don't want him, not really.'

When she faced Mrs Lacey with the child, and looked up into the concerned eyes, guilt swept her. She saw that Mrs Lacey's hands fumbled rapidly with the straps; she saw how the child was lifted out, with trembling haste, away from the heat and the glare. Mrs Lacey asked: 'Did you enjoy the walk?' but although she appeared to want to make Kate feel she had been willingly granted this pleasure, Mrs Lacey could not help putting her hand to the baby's head and saying: 'He's very hot.'

She sat down beside her sewing table; and for the first time Kate saw her actually hold her child in her arms, even resting her cheek against his head. Then the baby wriggled round towards her and put his arms around her neck and burrowed close, gurgling with pleasure. Mrs Lacey appeared taken aback; she looked down at her own baby with amazement in which there was also dismay. She was accepting the child's cuddling in the way a woman accepts the importunate approaches of someone whose feelings she does not want to hurt. She was laughing and protesting and putting down the baby's clutching arms. Still laughing, she said to Kate: 'You see, this is all your doing.' The words seemed to Kate so extraordinary that she could not reply. Through her mind floated pictures of women she had known from the district, and they flowed together to make one picture – her idea, from experience, of a mother. She saw a plump smiling woman holding a baby to her face for the pleasure of its touch. She remembered Nan Fowler one mail day at the station, just after the birth of her third child. She sat in the front seat of the car, with the bundled infant on her lap, laughing as it nuzzled to get to her breasts, where appeared two damp patches. Andrew Wheatley stood beside the car talking to her, but her manner indicated a smiling withdrawal from him. 'Look,' she seemed to be saying – not at all concerned for her stretched loose body and those shameless patches of milk – 'as you observe, I can't be really with you for the moment, but I'd like to see you later.'

Kate watched Mrs Lacey pull her baby's arms away from her neck, and then gently place it in the pram. She was frowning. 'Babies shouldn't be messed about,' she remarked; and Kate saw that her dislike of whatever had just happened was stronger even than her fear of Kate's parents.

Kate got up, saying: 'I feel funny.' She walked blindly through the house in the direction of the bedroom. The light had got inside her head: that was how it felt; her brain was swaying on waves of light. She got past Mrs Lacey's bed and collapsed on the stool of the dressing-table, burying her face in her arms. When she lifted her eyes, she saw Mrs Lacey standing beside her. She saw that her own shoes had left brownish patches on the carpet, and that along the folds of the crystalline drapery at the windows were yellowish streaks.

Gazing into the mirror, her own face stared back. It was a narrow face, pale and freckled; a serious lanky face, and incongruously above it perched a large blue silk bow from which pale lanky hair straggled. Kate stood up and looked at her body in shame. She was long, thin, bony. The legs were a boy's legs still, flat lean legs set on to a plumping body. Two triangular lumps stood out from her tight child's bodice. Kate turned in agony from this reflection of herself, which seemed to be rather of several different young boys and girls haphazardly mingled, and fixed her attention to Mrs Lacey, who was frowning as she listened to the baby's crying from the veranda: this time he had not liked being put down. 'There!' she exclaimed angrily, 'that's what happens if you give in to them.' Something rose in a wave to Kate's head: 'Why did they say the baby is exactly like Mr Hackett?' she demanded, without knowing she had intended to speak at all. Looking wonderingly up at Mrs Lacey she saw the shadows round her chin deepen into long blue lines that ran from nose to chin; Mrs Lacey had become as pinched and diminished as her room now appeared. She drew in her breath violently: then held herself tight, and smiled. 'Why, what an extraordinary thing for them to say,' she commented, walking away from Kate to fetch a handkerchief from a drawer, where she stood for a while with her back turned, giving them both an opportunity to recover. Then, turning, she looked long and closely at Kate, trying to determine whether the child had known what it was she had said.

Kate faced her with wide and deliberately innocent eyes; inside she was gripped with amazement at the strength of her own desire to hurt the beloved Mrs Lacey, who had hurt her so badly: it was this that the innocence was designed to conceal.

They both moved away from the room to the veranda, with the careful steps of people conscious of every step, every action. There was, however, not a word spoken.

As they passed through the big room Mrs Lacey took a photograph album from a bookstand and carried it with her to the chairs. When Kate had seated herself, the album was deposited on her lap; and Mrs Lacey said: 'Look at these; here are pictures of Mr Lacey when he was a baby; you can see that the baby is the image of him.' Kate looked dutifully at several pages of photographs of yet another fat, smiling, contented baby, feeling more and more surprised at Mrs Lacey. The fact was that whether the baby did or did not look like Mr Hackett was not the point; it was hard to believe that Mrs Lacey did not understand this, had not understood the truth, which was that the remark had been made in the first place as a sort of stick snatched up to beat her with. She put down the album and said: 'Yes, they do look alike, don't they?' Mrs Lacey remarked casually: 'For the year before the baby was born I and Mr Lacey were living alone on a ranch. Mr Hackett was visiting his parents in America.' Kate made an impatient movement which Mrs Lacey misinterpreted. She said reproachfully: 'That was a terrible thing to say, Kate.' 'But I didn't say it.' 'No matter who said it, it was a terrible thing.' Kate saw that tears were pouring down Mrs Lacey's cheeks.

'But . . .'

'But what?'

'It isn't the point.'

'What isn't the point?'

Kate was silent: there seemed such a distance between what she felt and how Mrs Lacey was speaking. She got up, propelled by the pressure of these unsayable things, and began wandering about the veranda in front of Mrs Lacey. 'You see,' she said helplessly, 'we've all been living together so long. We all know each other very well.'

'You are telling me,' commented Mrs Lacey, with an unpleasant laugh. 'Well?'

Kate sighed. 'Well, we have all got to go on living together, haven't we? I mean, when people have *got* to live together . . .' She looked at Mrs Lacey to see if she had understood.

She had not.

Kate had, for a moment, a vivid sense of Mrs Sinclair standing there beside her; and from this reinforcement she gained new words: 'Don't you see? It's not what people do, it's how they do it. It can't be broken up.'

Mrs Lacey's knotted forehead smoothed, and she looked ruefully at Kate: 'I haven't a notion of what I've done, even now.' This note, the playful note, stung Kate again: it was as if Mrs Lacey had decided that the whole thing was too childish to matter.

She walked to the end of the veranda, thinking of Mrs Sinclair. 'I wonder who will live here next?' she said dreamily, and turned to see Mrs Lacey's furious eyes. 'You might wait till we've gone,' she said. 'What makes you think we are going?'

Kate looked at her in amazement: it was so clear to her that the Laceys would soon go.

Seeing Kate's face, Mrs Lacey grew sober. In a chastened voice she said: 'You frighten me.' Then she laughed, rather shrilly.

'Why did you come here?' asked Kate unwillingly.

'But why on earth shouldn't we?'

'I mean, why *this* district. Why so far out, away from everything?'

Mrs Lacey's eyes bored cruelly into Kate's. 'What have they been saying? What are they saying about us?'

'Nothing,' said Kate, puzzled, seeing that there was a new thing here, that people could have said.

'I suppose that old story about the money? It isn't true. It isn't true, Kate.' Once again tears poured down Mrs Lacey's face and her shoulders shook.

'No one has said anything about money. Except that you must have a lot,' said Kate. Mrs Lacey wiped her eyes dry and peered at Kate to see if she were telling the truth. Then her face hardened. 'Well, I suppose they'll start saying it now,' she said bitterly.

Kate understood that there was something ugly in this, and directed at her, but not what it could be. She turned away from Mrs Lacey, filled again with the knowledge of injustice.

'Aren't I ever to have a home? Can't I ever have a home?' wept Mrs Lacey.

'Haven't you ever had one?'

'No, never. This time I thought I would be settled for good.'

'I think you'll have to move again,' said Kate reasonably. She looked around her, again trying to picture what would happen to Old John's Place when the new people came. Seeing that look, Mrs Lacey said quickly: 'That's superstition. It isn't possible that places can affect people.'

'I didn't say they did.'

'What are you saying, then?'

'But you get angry when I do say. I was just thinking that . . .'

'Well?'

Kate stammered: 'You ought to go somewhere where . . . that has your kind of people.' She saw this so clearly.

Mrs Lacey glared at her and snapped: 'When I was your age I thought of nothing but hockey.' Then she picked up her sewing as she might have swallowed an aspirin tablet, and sat stitching with trembling, angry fingers.

Kate's lips quivered. Hockey and healthy games were what her own mother constantly prescribed as prophylactics against the little girl she did not want to be.

Mrs Lacey went on: 'Don't you go to school?'

'Yes.'

'Do you like it?'

Kate replied: Yes, knowing it was impossible to explain what school meant to her: it was a recurring episode in the city where time raced by, since there was nothing of importance to slow it. School had so little to do with this life, on the farm, and the things she lived by, that it was like being taken to the pictures as a treat. One went politely, feeling grateful, then sat back and let what happened on the screen come at you and flow over you. You left with relief, to resume a real life.

She said slowly to Mrs Lacey, trying to express that injustice that was corroding her: 'But if I had been – like you want – you wouldn't have been able to – find out what you wanted, would you?'

Mrs Lacey stared. 'If you were mine I'd . . .' She bit off her thread angrily.

'You'd dress me properly,' said Kate sarcastically, quivering with hate, and saw Mrs Lacey crimson from throat to hairline.

'I think I'd better be going home,' she remarked, sidling to the door.

'You must come over again sometime,' remarked Mrs Lacey brightly, the fear lying deep in her eyes.

'You know I can't come back,' said Kate awkwardly.

'Why not?' said Mrs Lacey, just as if the whole conversation had never happened.

'My parents won't let me. They say you are bad for me.'

'Do you think I am bad for you?' asked Mrs Lacey, with her high gay laugh.

Kate stared at her incredulously. 'I'm awfully glad to have met you,' she stammered finally, with embarrassment thick in her tongue. She smiled politely, through tears, and went away down the road to home.

'Leopard' George

George Chester did not earn his title for some years after he first started farming. He was well into middle age when people began to greet him with a friendly clout across the shoulders and the query: 'Well, what's the score now?' Their faces expressed the amused and admiring tolerance extorted by a man who has proved himself in other ways, a man entitled to eccentricities. But George's passion for hunting leopards was more than a hobby. There was a period of years when the District Notes in the local paper were headed, Friday after Friday, by a description of his week-end party: 'The Four Winds' Hunt Club bag this Sunday was four jackals and a leopard' – or a wild dog and two leopards, as the case might be. All kinds of game make good chasing; the horses and dogs went haring across the veld every week after whatever offered itself. As for George, it was a recognized thing that if there was a chance of a leopard, the pack must be called off its hare, its duiker, its jackal, and directed after the wily spotted beast, no matter what the cost in time or patience or torn dogs. George had been known to climb a kopje alone, with a wounded leopard waiting for him in the tumbled chaos of boulder and tree; they told stories of how he walked once into a winding black cave (his ammunition finished and his torch smashed) and finally clouted the clawing spitting beast to death with the butt of his rifle. The scars of that fight were all over his body. When he strode into the post office or store, in shorts, his sleeves rolled up, people looked at the flesh that was raked from shoulder to knuckle and from thigh to ankle with great white weals, and quickly turned their eyes away. Behind his back they might smile, their lips compressed forbearingly.

But that was when he was one of the wealthiest men in the

district: one of those tough, shrewd farmers who seem ageless, for sun and hard work and good eating have shaped their bodies into cases of muscle that time can hardly touch.

George was the child of one of the first settlers. He was bred on a farm, and towns made him restless. When the First World War began he set off at once for England where he joined up in a unit that promised plenty of what he called fun. After five years of fighting he had collected three decorations, half a dozen minor wounds and the name 'Lucky George'. He allowed himself to be demobilized with the air of one who does not insist on taking more than his fair share of opportunities.

When he returned to Southern Rhodesia, it was not to that part of it he had made his own as a child; that was probably because his father's name was so well known there, and George was not a man to be the mere son of his father.

He saw many farms before finally choosing Four Winds. The agent was a man who had known his father well: this kind of thing still counts for more than money in places where there is space and time for respect of the past, and George was offered farms at prices which broke the agent's businessman's heart. Besides, he was a war hero. But the agent was defeated by George. He had been selling farms long enough to recognize the look that comes into a man's face when he is standing on land that appeals to him, land which he will shape and knead and alter to the scale of his own understanding – the look of the creator. That look did not appear on George's face.

After months of visiting one district after another, the agent took George to buy a farm so beautiful that it seemed impossible he could refuse to buy it. It was low lying and thickly covered with trees, and the long fat strip of rich red land was held between two rivers. The house had gardens running away on two sides to vistas of water. Rivers and richness and unspoiled trees and lush grass for cattle – such farms are not to be had for whistling in Africa. But George stood there on a rise between the stretches of water where they ran close to each other, and moved his shoulders restlessly in a way which the agent had grown to understand. 'No good?' he said, sounding disgruntled. But by now there was that tolerance in him for George which he was always to make people feel: his standards were different. Incomprehensible they might be; but the agent at last saw that George was not looking for the fat ease promised by this farm. 'If you could only tell me what you are looking for,' he suggested, rather irritably.

'This is a fine farm,' said George, walking away from it, holding his shoulders rigid. The agent grabbed his elbow and made him stop. 'Listen to me,' he said. 'This must be one of the finest farms in the country.'

'I know,' said George.

'If you want me to get you a farm, you'll have to get your mind clear about what you need.'

George said: 'I'll know it when I see it.'

'Have I got to drive you to every free farm in a thousand miles of Africa? God damn it, man,' he expostulated, 'be reasonable. This is my job. I am supposed to be earning my living by it.'

George shrugged. The agent let go his arm, and the two men walked along beside each other, George looking away over the thick dark trees of the river to the slopes on the other side. There were the mountains, range on range of them, rising high and glistening into the fresh blue sky.

The agent followed that look, and began to think for himself. He peered hard at George. This man, in appearance, was what one might expect after such a childhood, all freedom and sunlight, and after five years of such fighting. He was very lean and brown, with loose broad shoulders and an easy swinging way of moving. His face was lean and angled, his eyes grey and shrewd, his mouth hard but also dissatisfied. He reminded the agent of his father at the same age; George's father had left everything familiar to him, in an old and comfortable country, to make a new way of living with new people. The agent said tentatively: 'Good to get away from people, eh? Too many people crowded together over there in the Old Country?' exactly as he might have done to the older man. George's face did not change: this idea seemed to mean nothing to him. He merely continued to stare, his eyes tightened, at the mountains. But now the agent knew what he had to do. Next day he drove him to Four Winds, which had just been surveyed for sale. It was five thousand acres of virgin bush, lying irregularly over the lower slopes of a range of kopjes that crossed high over a plain where there were still few farms. Four Winds was all rocky outcrops, scrubby trees and wastes of shimmering grass, backed by mountains. There was no house, no river, not so much as a fence; no one could call it a desirable farm. George's face cleared to content as he walked over it, and on it came that look for which the agent had been waiting.

He slouched comfortably all through that day over those bare and bony acres, rather in the way a dog will use to make a new place its own, ranging to pick up a smell here or a memory there, anything that can be formed into a shell of familiarity for comfort against strangeness. But white men coming to Africa take not only what is there, but also impose on it a pattern of their own, from other countries. This accounts for the fine range of variation one can find in a day's travelling from farm to farm across any district. Each house will be different, suggesting a different country, climate, or way of speech.

Towards late afternoon, with the blaze of yellow sunlight falling directly across his face and dazzling into his eyes, and glazing the wilderness of rock and grass and tree with the sad glitter of sunset, George stooped suddenly in a place where gullies ran down from all sides into a flat place among bushes. 'There should be water here, for a borehole,' he said. And, after a moment: 'There was a windmill I caught sight of in Norfolk from a train. I liked the look of it. The shape of it, I mean. It would do well here . . .'

It was in this way that George said he was buying the farm, and showed his satisfaction at the place. The restless, rather wolfish look had gone from the long bony face.

'Your nearest neighbour is fifteen miles away,' was the last warning the agent gave.

George answered indifferently: 'This part of the country is opening up, isn't it?' And the next day he signed the papers.

He was no recluse after all, or at least, not in the way the agent had suspected.

He went round to what farms there were, as is the custom, paying his respects, saying he had bought Four Winds, and would be a neighbour, though not a near one. And the house he built himself was not a shack, the sort of house a man throws together to hold off the weather for a season.

He intended to live there, though it was not finished. It looked as if it had been finely planned and then cut in half. There were, to begin with, three large rooms, raftered with that timber that sends out a pungent fragrance when the weather changes, and floored with dark red wood. These were furnished properly, there were no makeshifts here, either. And he was seen at the station on mail days, not often, but often enough, where he was greeted in the way proper not only to his father's son and to his war record, but because people approved what he was doing. For after both wars there has been a sudden appearance of restless young men whose phrases: 'I want to be my own boss', and 'I'm not going to spend my life wearing out the seat of my trousers on a stool', though clichés, still express the spirit that opened up the country in the first place. Between wars there is a different kind of immigrant, who use their money as spades to dig warm corners to sleep in. Because of these people who have turned an adventurous country into a sluggish one, and because of the memory of something different, restless young men find there is no need to apologize for striking out for themselves. It is as if they are regarded as a sort of flag, or even a conscience. When people heard that George had bought Four Winds, a bare, gusty rocky stretch of veld on the side of a mountain, they remarked, 'Good luck to him,' which is exactly how they speak when a returning traveller says: 'There is a man on the shores of Lake Nyasa who has lived alone in a hut by himself for twenty years,' or 'I heard of someone who has gone native in the Valley – he goes away into the bush if a white person comes near him.' There is no condemnation, but rather a recognition of something in themselves to which they pay tribute by proxy.

George's first worry was whether he would get sufficient native labour; but he had expected an anxious time, and, knowing the ropes, he sat tight, built his house, sank his borehole and studied his land. A few natives did come, but they were casual labourers, and were not what he was waiting for. He was more troubled, perhaps, than he let himself know. It is so easy to get a bad name as an employer. A justly dismissed man can spitefully slash a tree on the boundary of a farm where the migrating natives walk, in such a way that they read in the pattern of the gashes on the bark: This is a bad farm with a bad master. Or there may be a native in the compound who frightens or tyrannizes over the others, so that they slowly leave, with excuses, for other farms, while the farmer himself never finds out what is wrong. There can be a dozen reasons why a fair man, just to his natives according to the customs of the time, can get a bad name without ever knowing the reason for it.

George knew this particular trouble was behind him when one day he saw coming up the road to his front door an old native who had worked many years for his own father. He waited on the steps, smoking comfortably, smiling his greeting.

'Morning,' he said.

'Morning, baas.'

'Things go well with you, old Smoke?'

'Things go well, baas.'

George tapped out his pipe, and motioned to the old man to seat himself. The band of young men who had followed Smoke along the road were waiting under some trees at a short distance for the palaver to finish. George could see they had come a long way for they were dusty, weary with the weight of their big bundles. But they looked a strong lot and good for work, and George settled himself in the big chair he used for audiences with satisfaction growing in him.

'You have come a long way?' he asked.

'A long way, baas. I heard the Little Baas had come back from the war and was wanting me. I have come to the Little Baas.'

George smiled affectionately at old Smoke, who looked not a day older now than he had ten years, or even twenty years back, when he had lifted the small boy for rides on the mealie wagon, or carried him, when he was tired, on his back. He seemed always to have been a very old man, with grizzling hair and filming eyes but as light and strong and erect as a youth.

'How did you know I had come back?'

'One of my brothers told me.'

George smiled again, acknowledging that this was all he would ever be told of the mysterious way the message had travelled from mouth to mouth across hundreds of miles. 'You will send messages to all your brothers to work for me? I need a great many boys.'

'I have brought twenty. Later, others will come. I have other relations coming after the rains from Nyasaland.'

'You will be my bossboy, Smoke? I need a bossboy.'

'I am too old, much too old, baas.'

'Do you know how old you are?' asked George, knowing he would get no satisfactory answer, for natives of Smoke's generation had no way of measuring their age.

'How should I know, baas? Perhaps fifty. Perhaps a hundred. I remember the days of the fighting well, I was a young man.' He paused, and added carefully, having averted his eyes: 'Better we do not remember those days, perhaps.'

The two men laughed, after a moment during which their great liking for each other had time to take the unpleasantness from the reminder of war. 'But I need a bossboy,' repeated George. 'Until I find a younger man as capable as you are, will you help me?'

'But I am too old,' protested Smoke again, his eyes brightening.

Thus it was settled, and George knew his labour troubles were over. Smoke's brothers would soon fill his compound. It must be explained that relationships, among Africans, are not understood as they are among white people. A native can travel a thousand miles in strange country, and find his clan brothers in every village, and be made welcome by them.

George allowed these people a full week to build themselves a village and another week as earnest of good feeling. Then he pulled the reins tight and expected hard work. He got it. Smoke was too old to work hard himself; also he was something of an old rascal with his drinking and his women – he had got his name because he smoked dagga, which bleared his eyes and set his hands shaking – but he held the obedience of the younger men, and because of this was worth any amount of money to George.

Later, a second man was chosen to act as bossboy under Smoke. He was a nephew, and he supervised the gangs of natives, but it was understood that Smoke was the real chief. When George held his weekly palavers to discuss farm matters, the two men came up from the compound together, and the younger man (who had in fact done the actual hard work) deferred to the older. George brought a chair from the house to the foot of the great flight of stone steps that led up to the living-rooms, and sat there at ease smoking, while Smoke sat cross-legged on the ground before him. The nephew stood behind his uncle, and his standing was not so much an act of deference to George – though of course it was that too – as respect for his tribal superior. (This was in the early 'twenties, when a more gentle, almost feudal relationship was possible between good masters and their servants: there was space, then, for courtesy; bitterness had not yet crowded out affection.)

During these weekly talks it was not only farm matters that were discussed, but personal ones also. There was always a short pause when crops, weather, plans, had been finished; then Smoke turned to the young man behind him and spoke a few dismissing words. The young man said, 'Good night, baas,' to George, and went away.

George and Smoke were then free to talk about things like the head driver's quarrels with his new wife, or how Smoke himself was thinking of taking a young wife. George would laugh and say: 'You old rascal. What do you want with a wife at your age?' And Smoke would reply that an old man needed a young body for warmth during the cold weather.

Nor was old Smoke afraid of becoming stern, though reproachful, as if he momentarily regarded himself as George's father, when he said: 'Little Baas, it is time you got married. It is time there was a woman on this farm.' And George would laugh and reply that he certainly agreed he should get married, but that he could find no woman to suit him.

Once Smoke suggested: 'The baas will perhaps fetch himself a wife from England?' And George knew then that it was discussed in the compound how he had a photograph of a girl on his dressing-table: old Smoke's son was cookboy in George's house.

The girl had been his fiancée for a week or so during the war, but the engagement was broken off after one of those practical dissecting discussions that can dissolve a certain kind of love like mist. She was a London girl, who liked her life, with no desire for anything different. There was no bitterness left after the affair; at least not against each other. George remained with a small bewildered anger against himself. He was a man, after all, who liked things in their proper place. It was the engagement he could not forgive himself for: he had been temporarily mad; it was that he could not bear to think of. But he remembered the girl sometimes with an affectionate sensuality. She had married and was living the kind of life he could not imagine any sane person choosing. Why he kept her picture – which was a very artificial posed affair – he did not ask himself. For he had cared for other women more, in his violent intermittent fashion.

However, there was her picture in his room, and it was seen not only by the cookboy and the houseboys but by the rare visitors to the house. There was a rumour in the district that George had a broken heart over a woman in England; and this explanation did as well as any other for George's cheerful but determined self-isolation, for there are some people the word loneliness can never be made to fit. George was alone, and seemed not to know it. What surprised people was that the frame of his life was so much larger than he needed, and for what he was. The three large rooms had been expanded, after a few years, into a dozen. It was the finest house for many miles. Outhouses, storehouses, washhouses and poultry yards spread about the place, and he had laid out a garden, and paid two boys handsomely to keep it beautiful. He had scooped out the soil between a cluster of boulders, and built a fine natural swimming pool over which bamboos hung, reflecting patterns of green foliage and patches of blue sky. Here he swam every morning at sun-up, summer or winter, and at evening, too, when he came from the day's work. He built a row of stables, sufficient to house a dozen beasts, but actually kept only two, one of which was ridden by old Smoke (whose legs were now

too feeble to carry him far) and one which he used himself.
This was a mare of great responsiveness and intelligence but
with no beauty, chosen with care after weeks of attending sales
and following up advertisements: she was for use, not show.
George rode her round the farm, working her hard, during the
day, and when he stabled her at night patted her as if he were
sorry she could not come into the house with him. After he had
come from the pool, he sat in the glow from the rapidly fading
sunset, looking out over the wild and beautiful valley, and
ceremoniously drinking beside a stinkwood table laden with
decanters and siphons. Nothing here of the bachelor's bottle
and glass on a tin tray; and his dinner was served elaborately
by two uniformed men, with whom he chatted or kept silence,
as he felt inclined. After dinner coffee was brought to him, and
having read farming magazines for half an hour or so, he went
to bed. He was asleep every night by nine, and up before the
sun.

That was his life. It was his life for years, one of exhausting
physical toil, twelve hours a day of sweat and effort in the sun,
but surrounded by a space and comfort that seemed to ask for
something else. It asked, in short, for a wife. But it is not easy
to ask of such a man, living in such a way, what it is he misses,
if he misses anything at all.

To ask would mean entering into what he feels during the
long hours riding over the ridges of kopje in the sunshine, with
the grass waving about him like blond banners. It would mean
understanding what made him one of mankind's outriders in
the first place.

Even old Smoke himself, ambling beside him on the other
horse, would give him a long look on certain occasions, and
quietly go off, leaving him by himself.

Sloping away in front of the house was a three-mile-long
expanse of untouched grass, which sprang each year so tall that
even from their horses the two men could not see over it. There
was a track worn through it to a small knoll, a cluster of rocks
merely, with trees breaking from the granite for shade. Here it
was that George would dismount and, leaning his arm on the
neck of his mare, stand gazing down into the valley which was
in itself a system of other hills and valleys, so high did Four

Winds stand above the rest of the country. Twenty miles away other mountains stood like blocks of tinted crystal, blocking the view; between there were trees and grass, trees and rocks and grass, with the rivers marked by lines of darker vegetation. Slowly, as the years passed, this enormous reach of pure country became marked by patches of cultivation; and smudges of smoke showed where new houses were going up, with the small glittering of roofs. The valley was being developed. Still George stood and gazed, and it seemed as if these encroaching lives affected him not at all. He would stay there half the morning, with the crooning of the green-throated wood pigeons in his ears, and when he rode back home for his meal, his eyes were heavy and veiled.

But he took things as they came. Four Winds, lifted high into the sky among the great windswept sun-quivering mountains, tumbled all over with boulders, offering itself to storms and exposure and invasion by baboons and leopards – this wilderness, this pure, heady isolation, had not affected him after all.

For when the valley had been divided out among new settlers, and his neighbours were now five miles, and not fifteen, away, he began going to their houses and asking them to his. They were very glad to come, for though he was an eccentric, he was harmless enough. He chose to live alone: that piqued the women. He had become very rich; which pleased everyone. For the rest, he was considered mildly crazy because he would not allow an animal to be touched on his farm; and any native caught setting traps for game would be beaten by George himself and then taken to the police afterwards: George considered the fine that he incurred for beating the native well worth it. His farm was as good as a game reserve; and he had to keep his cattle in what were practically stockades for fear of leopards. But if he lost an occasional beast, he could afford it.

George used to give swimming parties on Sundays; he kept open house on that day, and everyone was welcome. He was a good host, the house was beautiful, and his servants were the envy of every housewife; perhaps this was what people found it difficult to forgive him, the perfection of his servants. For they never left him to go 'home' as other people's boys did; their home was here, on this farm, under old Smoke, and the compound was a proper native village, and not the usual collection of shambling huts about which no one cared, since no one lived in them long enough to care. For a bachelor to have such well-trained servants was a provocation to the women of the district; and when they teased him about the perfection of his arrangements, their voices had an edge on them. They used to say: 'You damned old bachelor, you.' And he would reply, with calm good-humour: 'Yes, I must think about getting me a wife.'

Perhaps he really did feel he ought to marry. He knew it was suspected that this new phase, of entertaining and being entertained, was with a view to finding himself a girl. And the girls, of course, were only too willing. He was nothing, if not a catch; and it was his own fault that he was regarded, coldly, in this light. He would sometimes look at the women sprawled half-naked around the swimming pool under the bamboos – sprawling with deliberate intent, and for his benefit – and his eyes would narrow in a way that was not pleasant. Nor was it even fair, for if a man will not allow himself to be approached by sympathy and kindness, there is only one other approach. But the result of all this was simply that he set that photograph very prominently on the table beside his bed; and when girls remarked on it he replied, letting his eyelids half-close in a way which was of course exasperatingly attractive: 'Ah, yes, Betty – now *there* was a woman for you.'

At one time it was thought he was 'caught' after all. One of his boundaries was shared with a middle-aged woman with two grown daughters; she was neither married, nor unmarried, for her husband seemed not to be able to make up his mind whether to divorce her or not, and the girls were in their early twenties, horse-riding, whisky-drinking, flat-bodied tomboys who were used to having their own way with the men they fancied. They would make good wives for men like George, people said: they would give back as good as they got. But they continued to be spoken of in the plural, for George flirted with them both and they were extraordinarily similar. As for the mother, she ran the farm, for her husband was too occupied with a woman in town to do this, and drank a little too much, and could be heard complaining fatalistically: 'Christ, why did

I have daughters? After all, sons are expected to behave badly.'
She used to complain to George, who merely smiled and
offered her another drink. 'God help you if you marry either of
them,' she would say, gloomily. 'May I be forgiven for saying
it, but they are fit for nothing but enjoying themselves.'

'At their age, Mrs Whately, that seems reasonable enough.'
Thus George retreated, into a paternally indulgent attitude that
nevertheless had a hint in it of cruel relish for the girls'
discomfiture.

He used to look for Mrs Whately when he entered a room,
and stay beside her for hours, apparently enjoying her company; and she seemed to enjoy his. She did all the talking,
while he stretched himself beside her, his eyes fixed thoughtfully on his glass, which he swung lightly between finger and
thumb, occasionally letting out an amused grunt. She spoke
chiefly of her husband whom she had turned from a liability
into an asset, for the whole room would become silent to hear
her humorous, grumbling tales of him. 'He came home last
week-end,' she would say, fixing wide astonished eyes on
George, 'and do you know what he said? My God, he said, I
don't know what I'd do without you, old girl. If I can't get out
of town for a spot of fresh air, sometimes, I'd go mad. And
there I was, waiting for him with my grievance ready to air.
What can one do with a man like that?' 'And are you prepared
to be a sort of week-end resort?' asked George. 'Why, Mr
Chester!' exclaimed Mrs Whately, widening her eyes to an
incredibly foolish astonishment, 'after all, he's my husband, I
suppose.' But this handsome, battered matron was no fool, she
could not have run the farm so capably if she had been; and on
these occasions George would simply laugh and say: 'Have
another drink.'

At his own swimming parties Mrs Whately was the only
woman who never showed herself in a swimming suit. 'At my
age,' she explained, 'it is better to leave it to one's daughters.'
And with an exaggerated sigh of envy she gazed across at the
girls. George would gaze, too, non-committally; though on the
whole it appeared he did not care for the spare and boyish
type. He had been known, however, during those long hot days
when thirty or forty people lounged for hours in their swimming

suits on the edge of the pool, eating, drinking, and teasing each other, to rise abruptly, looking inexplicably irritated, and walk off to the stables. There he saddled his mare – who, one would have thought, should have been allowed her Sunday's rest, since she was worked so hard the rest of the week – swung himself up, and was off across the hillsides, riding like a maniac. His guests did not take this hardly; it was the sort of thing one expected of him. They laughed – most particularly the women – and waited for him to come back, saying: 'Well, old George, you know . . .'

They used to suggest it would be nice to go riding together, but no one ever succeeded in riding with George. Now that the farms had spread up from the valley over the foothills, George often saw people on horses in the early morning, or at evening; and on these occasions he would signal a hasty greeting with his whip, rise in his stirrups and flash out of sight. This was another of the things people made allowances for: George, that lean, slouching, hard-faced man, riding away along a ridge with his whip raised in perfunctory farewell was positively as much a feature of the landscape as his own house, raised high on the mountain in a shining white pile, or the ten-foot-high notices all along the boundaries saying: Anyone found shooting game will be severely prosecuted.

Once, at evening, he came on Mrs Whately alone, and as instinctively he turned his horse to flee, heard her shout: 'I won't bite.' He grinned unamiably at her expectant face and shouted back: 'I'm no more of a fool than you are, my dear.'

At the next swimming party she acknowledged this incident by saying to him thoughtfully, her eyes for once direct and cool: 'There are many ways of being a fool, Mr Chester, and you are the sort of man who would starve himself to death because he once overate himself on green apples.'

George crimsoned with anger. 'If you are trying to hint that there are, there really *are*, some *sweet*, *charming* women, if I took the trouble to look, I promise you women have suggested that before.'

She did not get angry. She merely appeared genuinely surprised. 'Worse than I thought,' she commented amicably.

And then she began talking about something else in her familiar, rather clowning manner.

It was at one of these swimming parties that the cat came out of the bag. Its presence had of course been suspected, and accorded the usual tolerance. In fact, the incident was not of importance because of his friends' reactions to it, but because of George's own reactions.

It was one very warm December morning with the rains due to break at any moment. All the farmers had their seed-beds full of tobacco ready to be planted out and their attention was less on the excellence of the food and drink and the attractions of the women, than on the sky, which was filled with heavy masses of dull cloud. Thunder rolled behind the kopjes, and the air was charged and tense. Under the bamboos round the pool, whose fronds hung without a quiver, people tended to be irritable because of the feeling of waiting; for the last few weeks before the season are a bad time in any country where rain is uncertain.

George was sitting dressed on a small rock: he always dressed immediately he had finished bathing. The others were still half-naked. They had all lifted their heads and were looking with interested but non-committal expressions past him into the trees when he noticed the direction of their gaze, and turned himself to look. He gave a brief exclamation; then said, very deliberately: 'Excuse me,' and rose. Everyone watched him walk across the garden, and through the creeper-draped rocks beyond to where a young native woman stood, hand on hips provocatively, swinging herself a little as if wishing to dance. Her eyes were lowered in the insolently demure manner of the native woman; and she kept them down while George came to a standstill in front of her and began to speak. They could not make out from his gestures, or from his face, what he was saying; but after a little while the girl looked sulky, shrugged, and then moved off again towards the compound, which could be seen through trees and past the shoulder of a big kopje, perhaps a mile away. She walked dragging her feet, and swinging her hands to loosely clutch at the grassheads: it was a beautiful exhibition of unwilling departure; that was the impression given, that this was not only how she felt, but how she intended to show she felt. The long ambiguous look over her bare shoulder (she wore native-style dress, folded under the armpits) directed at the group of white people, could be interpreted in a variety of ways. No one chose to interpret it. No one spoke; and eyes were turned carefully to sky, trees, water or fingernails, when George returned. He looked at them briefly, without any hint of apology, then sat himself down again and reached for his glass. He took a swallow, and went on speaking where he had left off. They were quick to answer him; and in a moment conversation was general, though it was a conscious and controlled conversation: these people were behaving as if for the benefit of an invisible observer who was standing somewhere at a short distance and chuckling irresistibly as he called out: 'Bravo! Well done!'

What they felt towards George – an irritation which was a reproach for not preserving appearances – was not allowed to appear in their manner. The women, however, were noticeably acid; and George's acknowledgement of this was a faint smile, so diminishing of their self-respect that by that evening, when the party broke up (it would rain before midnight and they would all have to be up early for a day's hard planting), relations were as usual. In fact, George would be able to count on their saying, or implying: 'Oh, George! Well, it is all very well for him, I suppose.'

But that did not end the matter for him. He was very angry. He summoned old Smoke to the house when the visitors had gone, and this showed how angry he was, for it was a rule of his never to disturb the labourers on a Sunday.

The girl was Smoke's daughter (or grand-daughter, George did not know), and the arrangement – George's attitude towards the thing forbade any other term – had come about naturally enough. The only time it had ever been mentioned between the two men was when shortly after the girl had set herself in George's path one evening when he was passing from swimming pool to house, Smoke had remarked, without reproach, but sternly enough, that a half-caste child would not be welcome among his people. George had replied with equal affability, that he gave his assurance there would be no child. The old man replied, half-sighing, that he understood the white people had means at their disposal. There the thing had ended. The girl came to George's room when he sent for her, two or three times a week. She used to arrive when George's dinner was finished, and she left at sun-up, with a handful of small change. George kept a supply of sixpences and threepenny bits under his handkerchiefs, for he had noticed she preferred several small coins to one big one. This discrimination was the measure of his regard for her, of her needs and nature. He liked to please her in these little ways. For instance, recently, when he had gone into town and was down among the Kaffir-truck shops buying a supply of aprons for his houseboys, he had made a point of buying her a headcloth of a colour she particularly liked. And once, she had been ill, and he drove her himself to hospital. She was not afraid to come to him to ask for especial favours to her family. This had been going on for five years.

Now, when old Smoke came to the house, with the lowered eyes and troubled manner that showed he knew of the incident, George said simply that he wished the girl to be sent away, she was making trouble. Smoke sat cross-legged before George for some minutes before replying, looking at the ground. George had time to notice that he was getting a very old man indeed. He had a shrunken, simian appearance; even the flesh over his skull was crinkled under the dabs of white wool; his face was withered to the bone; and his small eyes peered with difficulty. At last he spoke, and his voice was resigned and trembling: 'Perhaps the Little Baas could speak to the girl? She will not do it again.'

But George was not taking the chance of it happening again.

'She is my child,' pleaded the old man.

George, suddenly irritable, said: 'I cannot have this sort of thing happening. She is a very foolish girl.'

'I understand, baas, I understand. She is certainly a foolish girl. But she is also young, and my child.' But even this last appeal, spoken in the old wheezy voice, did not move George.

It was finally arranged that George should pay the expenses of the girl at mission school, some fifty miles off. He would not see her before she left, though she hung about the back steps for days. She even attempted to get into his bedroom the night before she was to set off, accompanied by one of her brothers for escort, for the long walk to her new home. But George had locked his door. There was nothing to be said. In a way he blamed himself. He felt he might have encouraged the girl: one did not know, for example, how the matter of the headcloth might rearrange itself in a primitive woman's mind. He had been responsible, at any rate, for acting in a way that had 'put ideas into her head'. That appearance of hers at the swimming pool had been an act of defiance, a deliberate claiming of him, a provocation, whose implications appalled him. They appalled him precisely because the thing could never have happened if he had not treated her faultily.

During the week after she left, one evening, before going to bed, he suddenly caught the picture of the London girl off his dressing-table, and tossed it into a cupboard. He was thinking of old Smoke's daughter – grand-daughter, perhaps – with an uncomfortable aching of the flesh, for some weeks before another girl presented herself for his notice.

He had been waiting for this to happen; for he had no intention of incurring old Smoke's reproach by enticing a woman to him.

He was sitting on his veranda one night, smoking, his legs propped on the veranda wall, gazing at the great yellow moon that was rising over a long wooded spur to one side of the house, when a furtive, softly-gliding shape entered the corner of his vision. He sat perfectly still, puffing his pipe, while she came up the steps, and across the patch of light from the lamp inside. For a moment he could have sworn it was the same girl, but she was younger, much younger, not more than about sixteen. She was naked above the waist, for his inspection, and she wore a string of blue beads around her neck.

This time, in order to be sure of starting on the right basis, he pulled out a handful of small coins and laid them on the veranda wall before him. Without raising her eyes, the girl leaned over sideways, picked them up, and caused them to disappear in the folds of her skirt. An hour later she was turned out of the house, and the doors were locked for the night. She wept and pleaded to be allowed to stay till the first light came (as the other girl had always done) for she was afraid to go home by herself through the dark bush that was full of beasts and ghosts and the ancient terrors that were her birthright. George replied simply that if she came at all, she must resign herself to leaving when the business of the occasion was at an end. He remembered the nights with the other one, which had been spent wrapped close in each other's arms – *that* was where he had made his mistake, perhaps? In any case, it was not going to be allowed to happen again.

This girl wept pitifully the first night, and even more violently the second. George suggested that one of her brothers should come for her. She was shocked at the idea, so shocked that he understood things were with her as with him: the thing was permissible provided it was possible decently to ignore it. But she was sent home; and George did not allow himself to picture her gliding through the dark shadows of the moonlit path and whimpering with fear, as she had done in his arms before leaving him.

At their next weekly palaver, George waited for Smoke to speak, for he knew that he would. It was with a conscious determination not to show guilt (a reaction which surprised and annoyed him) that George watched the old man dismiss the nephew, wait for him to get well on his way on the path to the compound, and turn back to face him, in appeal. 'Little Baas,' he said, 'there are things that need not be said between us.' George did not answer. 'Little Baas, it is time that you took a wife from your own people.'

George replied: 'The girl came to me, of her own accord.'

Smoke said, as if it were an insult that he was forced to say such an obvious thing: 'If you had a wife, she would not have come.' The old man was deeply troubled; far more so than George had expected. For a while he did not answer. Then he said: 'I shall pay her well.' It seemed to him that he was speaking in that spirit of honesty that was in everything he said, or did, with this man who had been the friend of his father, and was his own good friend. He could not have said anything he did not feel. 'I'm paying her well; and will see that she is looked after. I am paying well for the other one.'

'Aie, aie,' sighed the old man, openly reproachful now, 'this is not good for our women, baas. Who will want to marry her?'

George moved uncomfortably in his chair. 'They both came to me, didn't they? I didn't go running after them.' But he stopped. Smoke so clearly considered this argument irrelevant that he could not pursue it, even though he himself considered it valid. If he had gone searching for a woman among those at the compound, he would have felt himself responsible. That old Smoke did not see things in this light made him angry.

'Young girls,' said Smoke reproachfully, 'you know how they are.' Again there was more than reproach. In the feeble ancient eyes there was a deeper trouble. He could not look straight at George. His gaze wavered this way and that, over George's face, away to the mountains, down to the valley, and his hands were plucking at his garments.

George smiled, with determined cheerfulness: 'And young men, don't you make allowances for them?'

Smoke suddenly flashed into anger: 'Young men, little boys, one expects nonsense from them. But you, baas, you – you should be married, baas. You should have grown children of your own, not spoiling mine . . .' the tears were running down his face. He scrambled to his feet with difficulty, and said, very dignified: 'I do not wish to quarrel with the son of my old friend, the Old Baas. I ask you to think, only, Little Baas. These girls, what happens to them? You have sent the other one to the mission school, but how long will she stay? She has been used to your money and to . . . she has been used to her own way. She will go into the town and become one of the loose women. No decent man will have her. She will get herself a town husband, and then another, and another. And now there is this one . . .' He was now grumbling, querulous, pathetic. His dignity could not withstand the weight of his grief. 'And now this one, this one! You, Little Baas, that you should take this woman . . .' A very old, tottering scarecrow man, he swayed off down the path.

For a moment George was impelled to call him back, for it was the first time one of their palavers had ended in unkindness, without courteous exchange in the old manner. But he watched the old man move uncertainly past the swimming pool through the garden, along the rockeries, and out of sight. He was feeling uncomfortable and irritated, but at the same time he was puzzled. There was a discrepancy between what had happened and what he had expected that he felt now as a sharp intrusion – turning over the scene in his mind, he knew there was something that did not fit. It was the old man's emotion. Over the first girl reproach could be gathered from his manner but a reproach that was fatalistic, and related not to George himself but rather to circumstances, some view of life George could not be expected to share. It had been an impersonal grief, a grief against life. This was different; Smoke had been accusing him, George, directly. It had been like an accusation of disloyalty. Reconstructing what had been said, George fastened upon the recurring words: 'wife' and 'husband'; and suddenly an idea entered George's head that was intolerable. It was so ugly that he rejected it and cast about for something else. But he could not refuse it for long; it crept back, and took possession of him, for it made sense of everything that had happened: a few months before old Smoke had taken to himself a new young wife.

After a space of agitated reflection George raised his voice and called loudly for his houseboy. This was a young man brought to the house by old Smoke himself, years before. His relations with George were formal, but warmed slightly by the fact that he knew of George's practical arrangements and treated them with an exquisite discretion. All this George now chose to throw aside. He asked directly: 'Did you see the girl who was here last night?'

'Yes, baas.'

'Is she old Smoke's new wife?'

His eyes directed to the ground, the youth replied: 'Yes, baas.'

George smothered an impulse to appeal: 'I didn't know she was,' an impulse which shocked him, and said: 'Very well, you can go.' He was getting more and more angry; the situation infuriated him; by no fault of his own he was in a cruel position.

That night he was in his room reading when the girl entered smiling faintly. She was a beautiful young creature, but for George this fact had ceased to exist.

'Why did you not tell me you were Smoke's new wife?' he asked.

She was not disconcerted. Standing just inside the door, still in that pose of shrinking modesty, she said: 'I thought the baas knew.' It was possible that she had thought so; but George insisted: 'Why did you come when you knew I didn't know?'

She changed her tone, and pleaded: 'He is an old man, baas,' seeming to shudder with repugnance.

George said: 'You must not come here again.'

She ran across the room to him, flung herself down, and embraced his legs. 'Baas, baas,' she murmured, 'don't send me away.'

George's violent anger, that had been diffused within him, now focused itself sharply, and he threw her away from him, and got to his feet. 'Get out,' he said. She slowly got to her feet, and stood as before, though now sullenness was mingled with her shrinking humility. She did not say a word. 'You are not to come back,' he ordered; and when she did not move, he took her arm with the extreme gentleness that is the result of controlled dislike, and pushed her out of the front door. He locked it, and went to bed.

He always slept alone in the house, for the cookboy and the houseboys went back to the compound every night after finishing the washing up, but one of the garden boys slept in a shed at the back with the dogs, as a guard against thieves. George's garden boys, unlike his personal servants, were not permanent, but came and went at short intervals of a few months. The present one had been with him for only a few weeks, and he had not troubled to make a friend of him.

Towards midnight there was a knock at the back door, and when George opened it he found this garden boy standing there, and there was a grin on his face that George had never seen on the face of a native before – at least, not directed at himself. He indicated a shadowy human shape that stood under a large tree which rose huge and glittering in the strong moonlight, and said intimately: 'She's there, baas, waiting for you.' George promptly cuffed him, in order to correct his expression, and then strode out into the moonlight. The girl neither moved nor looked at him. A statue of grief, she stood waiting with her hands hanging at her sides. Those hands – the helplessness of them – particularly infuriated George. 'I told you to get back to where you belong,' he said, in a low angry voice. 'But, baas, I am afraid.' She began to cry again.

'What are you afraid of?'

The girl, her eyeballs glinting in the gleams of moonlight that fell strong through the boughs overhead, looked along to the compound. It was a mile of bush, with kopjes rising on either side of the path, big rocks throwing deep shadows all the way. Somewhere a dog was howling at the moon; all the sounds of night rose from the bush, bird noises, insect noises, animal noises that could not be named: here was a vast protean life, and a cruel one. George, looking towards the compound, which in this unreal glinting light had shrunk back, absorbed, into the background of tree and rock, without even a glow of fire to indicate its presence, felt as he always did: it was the feeling which had brought him here so many years before. It was as if, while he looked, he was flowing softly outwards, diffused into the bush and the moonlight. He knew no terror; he could not understand fear; he contained that cruelty within himself, shut safe in some deep place. And this girl, who was bred of the bush and of the wildness, had no right to tremble with fright. That, obscurely, was what he felt.

With the moonlight pouring over him, showing how his lips were momentarily curled back from his teeth, he pulled the girl roughly towards him out of the shade, turned her round so that she faced the compound, and said: 'Go, now.'

She was trembling, in sharp spasms, from head to foot. He could feel her convulse against him as if in the convulsions of love, and he pushed her away so that she staggered. 'Go,' he ordered, again. She was now sobbing wildly, with her arm across her eyes. George called to the garden boy who was standing near the house watching the scene, his face expressing an emotion George did not choose to recognize. 'Take this woman back to the compound.'

For the first time in his life George was disobeyed by a native. The youth simply shook his head, and said with a directness that was not intended to be rude, but was rather a rebuke for asking something that could not be asked: 'No, baas.' George understood he could not press the point.

Impatiently he turned back to the girl and dismissed the matter by saying: 'I'm not going to argue with you.'

He went indoors, and to bed. There he listened futilely for sounds of conversation: he was hoping that the two people outside might come to some arrangement. After a few moments he heard the scraping of chains along earth, and the barking of dogs; then a door shut. The garden boy had gone back to his shed. George repressed a desire to go to the window and see if the girl was still there. He imagined that she might perhaps steal into one of the outhouses for shelter. Not all of them were locked.

It was hours before he slept. It was the first night in years that he had difficulty in sleeping. He was still angry, yes; he was uncomfortable because of his false relationship to old Smoke, because he had betrayed the old man; but beyond these emotions was another; again he felt that discrepancy, something discordant which expressed itself through him in a violent irritation; it was as if a fermenting chemical had been poured into a still liquid. He was intolerably restless, and his limbs twitched. It seemed as if something large and challenging were outside himself saying: And how are you going to include *me*? It was only by turning his back on that challenge that he eventually managed to sleep.

Before sunrise next day, before the smoke began to curl up from the huts in the compound, George called the garden boy, who emerged sleepy and red-eyed from the shed, the dogs at his heels, and told him to fetch old Smoke. George felt he had to apologize to him; he must put himself right with that human being to whom he felt closer than he had ever felt to anyone since his parents died.

He dressed while waiting. The house was quite empty, as the servants had not yet come from the compound. He was in a fever of unrest for the atonement it was necessary for him to make. But the old man delayed his coming. The sun was blazing over the kopjes, and the smells of coffee and hot fat were pervading the house from the kitchen when George, waiting impatiently on the veranda, saw a group of natives coming through the trees. Old Smoke was wrapped in a blanket, and supported on each side by a young man; and he

moved as if each step were an effort to him. By the time the
three natives had reached the steps, George was feeling like an
accused person. Nor did any of his accusers look at him directly.

He said at once: 'Smoke, I am very sorry. I did not know she
was your wife.' Still they did not look at him. Already irritation
was growing inside him, because they did not accept his
contrition. He repeated sternly: 'How was I to know? How
could I?'

Instead of answering directly, Smoke said in the feeble and
querulous tones of a very old man: 'Where is she?'

This George had not foreseen. Irritation surged through him
with surprising violence. 'I sent her home,' he said angrily. It
was the strength of his own anger that quieted him. He did not
know himself what was happening within him.

The group in front of him remained silent. The two young
men, each supporting Smoke with an arm under his shoulders,
kept their eyes down. Smoke was looking vaguely beyond the
trees and over the slopes of grass to the valley; he was looking
for something, but looking without hope. He was defeated.

With a conscious effort at controlling his voice, George said:
'Till last night I did not know she was your wife.' He paused,
swallowed, and continued, dealing with the point which he
understood now was where he stood accused: 'She came to me
last night, and I told her to go home. She came late. Has she
not returned to you?'

Smoke did not answer: his eyes were ranging over the kopjes
tumbled all about them. 'She did not come home,' said one of
the young men at last.

'She has not perhaps gone to the hut of a friend?' suggested
George futilely.

'She is not in the compound,' said the same young man,
speaking for Smoke.

After a delay, the old man looked straight at George for the
first time, but it was as if George were an object, a thing, which
had nothing to do with him. Then he moved himself against the
arms of the young man in an effort towards independence; and,
seeing what he wanted, his escort turned gently round with
him, and the three moved slowly off again to the compound.

George was quite lost; he did not know what to do. He stood

on the steps, smoking, looking vaguely about him at the scenery, the familiar wild scenery, and down to the valley. But it was necessary to do something. Finally he again raised his voice for the servant. When he came, orders were given that the garden boy should be questioned. The houseboy returned with a reflection of the garden boy's insolent grin on his face, and said: 'The garden boy says he does not know what happened, baas. He went to bed, leaving the girl outside – just as the baas did himself.' This final phrase showed itself as a direct repetition of the insolent accusation the garden boy had made. But George did not act as he would have done even the day before. He ignored the insolence.

'Where is she?' he asked the houseboy at last.

The houseboy seemed surprised; it was a question he thought foolish, and he did not answer it. But he raised his eyes, as Smoke had done, to the kopjes, in a questing hopeless way; and George was made to admit something to his mind he had been careful not to admit.

In that moment, while he stood following the direction of his servant's eyes with his own, a change took place in him; he was gazing at a towering tumbling heap of boulders that stood sharp and black against a high fresh blue, the young blue of an African morning, and it was as if that familiar and loved shape moved back from him, reared menacingly like an animal and admitted danger – a sharp danger, capable of striking from a dark place that was a place of fear. Fear moved in George; it was something he had not before known; it crept along his flesh with a chilling touch, and he shivered. It was so new to him that he could not speak. With the care that one uses for a fragile, easily destroyable thing he took himself inside for breakfast, and went through the meal conscious of being sustained by the ceremony he always insisted on. Inside him a purpose was growing, and he was shielding it tenderly; for he did not know what it was. All he knew was, when he had laid down his coffee cup, and rung the bell for the servants, and gone outside to the veranda, that there the familiar landscape was outside of him, and that something within him was pointing a finger at it. In the now strong sunlight he shivered again; and crossed his arms so that his hands cupped his shoulders: they

felt oddly frail. Till lately they had included the pushing
strength of mountains; till this morning his arms had been
branches and the birds sang in them; within him had been that
terror which now waited outside and which he must fight.

He spent that day doing nothing, sitting on his veranda with
his pipe. His servants avoided the front part of the house.

Towards sundown he fetched his rifle which he used only on
the rare occasions when there was a snake that must be killed,
for he had never shot a bird or a beast with it, and cleaned it,
very carefully. He ordered his dinner for an hour earlier than
usual, and several times during that meal went outside to look
at the sky. It was clear from horizon to horizon, and a luminous
glow was spreading over the rocks. When a heavy yellow moon
was separated from the highest boulder of the mountain by a
hairline, he said to the boys that he was going out with his gun.
This they accepted as a thing he must do; nor did they make
any move to leave the house for the compound: they were
waiting for him to return.

George passed the ruffling surface of the swimming pool,
picked his way through the rock garden, and came to where his
garden merged imperceptibly, in the reaching tendrils of the
creepers, with the bush. For a few yards the path passed
through short and trodden grass, and then it forked, one branch
leading off to the business part of the farm, the other leading
straight on through a grove of trees. Through the dense
shadows George moved steadily; for the grass was still short,
and the tree trunks glimmered low to the ground. Between the
edge of this belt of trees and the half mile of path that wound
in and around the big boulders of the kopje was a space filled
with low jagged rocks, that seemed higher and sharper than
they were because of the shadows of the moon. Here it was
clear moving. The moon poured down its yellow flood; and his
shadow moved beside him, lengthening and shortening with the
unevenness of the ground. Behind him were the trees in their
gulf of black, before him the kopje, the surfaces of granite
showing white and glittering, like plates of crusted salt.
Between, the broken shadows, of a dim purple colour, dappled
with moonlight. To the left of him the rocks swept up sharply
to another kopje; on the other side the ground fell away into a

gulley which in its turn widened into the long grass slope, which, moving gently in the breeze, presented a gently gleaming surface, flattening and lifting so that there was a perpetual sweeping movement of light across miles of descending country. Far below was the valley, where the lights of homesteads gleamed steadily.

The kopje in front of him was silent, dead silent. Not a bird stirred, and only the insects kept up their small shrilling. George moved into the shadows with a sharp tug of the heart, holding his fear in him cold and alive, like a weapon. But his rifle he handled carelessly.

With cautious, directed glances he moved along and up the path as it rose through the boulders on the side of the kopje. As he went he prayed. He was praying that the enemy might present itself and be slain. It was when he was on the height of the path so that half a mile behind showed the lit veranda of his house, and half a mile in front the illuminated shapes of the huts in the compound, that he stopped and waited. He remained quite still, and allowed his fear to grow inside him, a controlled fear, so that while his skin crept and his scalp tingled, yet his hands remained steady on the rifle. To one side of him was a large rock, leaning forward and over him in a black shelf. On the other was a rock-encumbered space, girt by a tangle of branches and foliage. There were, in fact, trees and rocks all about him; the thing might come from any side. But this was the place; he knew it by instinct. And he kept perfectly still for fear that his enemy might be scared away. He did not have to wait long. Before the melancholy howling of the moonstruck dogs in the compound had had time to set the rhythm of his nerves, before his neck had time to ache with the continual alert movements of his head from side to side, he saw one of the shadows a dozen paces from him lengthen gradually, and at last separate itself from the rock. The low, ground-creeping thing showed a green glitter of eyes, and a sheen of moonlight shifted with the moving muscles of the flank. When the shape stilled and flattened itself for a spring, George lifted his rifle and fired. There was a coughing noise, and the shape lay still. George lowered the rifle and looked at it, almost puzzled, and stood still. There lay the enemy, dead, not a couple of paces from him. Sprawled almost at his feet was the leopard, its body still tensing and convulsing in death. Anger sprang up again in George: it had all been so easy, so easy! Again he looked in wonder at his rifle; then he kicked the unresisting flesh of the leopard, first with a kind of curiosity, then brutally. Finally he smashed the butt of the rifle, again and again, in hard, thudding blows, against the head. There was no resistance, no sound, nothing.

Finally, as the smell of blood and flesh began to fill him, he desisted, weak and helpless. He was let down. He had not been given what he had come for. When he finally left the beast lying there and walked home again, his legs were weak under him and his breath was coming in sobs; he was crying the peevish, frustrated tears of a disappointed man.

The houseboys went out without complaint, into the temporarily safe night, to drag the body into the homestead. They began skinning the beast by lamplight. George slept heavily; and in the morning found the skin pegged in the sunshine, flesh side uppermost, and the fine papery inner skin was already blistering and puffing in the heat. George went to the kopje, and after a morning's search among thorn and blackjack and stinging-nettle, found the mouth of a cave. There were fresh human bones lying there, and the bones of cattle, and smaller bones, probably of buck and hare.

But the thing had been killed, and George was still left empty, a hungry man without possibility of food. He did not know what satisfaction it was he needed.

The farm boys came to him for instructions; and he told them, impatiently, not to bother him, but to go to old Smoke.

In a few days old Smoke himself came to see him, an evasive, sorrowful, dignified figure, to say he was going home: he was too old now to work for the Old Baas's son.

A few days later his compound was half empty. It was the urgent necessity of attracting new labour that pulled George together. He knew that an era was finished for him. While not all old Smoke's kinsmen had left, there was now no focus, no authority, in his compound. He himself, now, would have to provide that focus, with his own will, his own authority; and he knew very well the perpetual strain and worry he must face. He was in the position of his neighbours.

He patched things up, as he could; and while he was reordering his life, found that he was behaving towards himself as he might to a convalescent. For there was a hurt place in him, and a hungry anger that no work could assuage.

For a while he did nothing. Then he suddenly filled his stables with horses; and his home became a centre for the horse-loving people about him. He ran a pack of dogs, too, trained by himself; and took down those notices along his boundaries. For 'Leopard' George had been born. For him, now, the landscape was simply a home for leopards. Every week-end his big house was filled with people, young and old, male and female, who came for various reasons; some for the hospitality, some for love of George, some, indeed, for the fun of the Sunday's hunting, which was always followed by a gigantic feast of food and drink.

Quite soon George married Mrs Whately, a woman who had the intelligence to understand what she could and could not do if she wished to remain the mistress of Four Winds.

Winter in July

The three of them were sitting at their evening meal on the veranda. From behind, the living-room shed light on to the table, where their moving hands, the cutlery, the food, showed dimly, but clear enough for efficiency. Julia liked the half-tone. A lamp or candles would close them into a soft illuminated space, but obliterate the sky, which now bent towards them through the pillars of the veranda, a full deep sky, holding a yellowy bloom from an invisible moon that absorbed the stars into a faint far glitter.

Sometimes Tom said, grumbling humorously: 'Romantic, that's what she is'; and Kenneth would answer, but with an abrupt, rather grudging laugh: 'I like to see what I am eating.' Kenneth was altogether an abrupt person. That quick, quickly-checked laugh, the swift critical look he gave her (which she met with her own eyes, as critical as his) were part of the long dialogue between them. For Kenneth did not accept her. He resisted her. Tom accepted her, as he accepted everything. For Julia it was not a question of preference: the two men supported her in their different manners. And the things they said, the three of them, seemed hardly to matter. The real thing was the soft elastic tension that bound them close.

Her liking for the evening hour, before moving indoors to the brightly-lit room, was the expression of her feeling for them. The mingling lights, half from the night-sky, half from the lamp, softened their faces and subdued their voices, and she was free to feel what they were, rather than rouse herself by listening. This state was a continuation of her day, spent by herself (for the men were most of the time on the lands) in an almost trance-like condition where the soft flowing of the hours was marked by no necessities of action strong enough to wake her. As for them, she knew that returning to her was an entrance into that condition. Their day was hard and vigorous, full of practical details and planning. At sundown they entered her country, and the evening meal, where the outlines of fact were blurred by her passivity no less than by the illusion of indistinctness created by sitting under a roof which projected shadow-like into the African night, was the gateway to it.

They used to say to her sometimes: 'What do you do with yourself all day? Aren't you bored?' She could not explain how it was she could never become bored. All restlessness had died in her. She was content to do nothing for hours at a time; but it depended on her feeling of being held loosely in the tension between the two men. Tom liked to think of her content and peaceful in his life; Kenneth was irritated.

This particular evening, half-way through the meal, Kenneth rose suddenly and said: 'I must fetch my coat.' Dismay chilled Julia as she realized that she, too, was cold. She had been cold for several nights, but had put off the hour of recognizing the fact. Her thoughts were confirmed by Tom's remark: 'It's getting too cold to eat outside now, Julia.'

'What month is it?'

He laughed indulgently. 'We are reaping.'

Kenneth came back, shrugging himself quickly into the coat. He was a small, quick-moving, vital man; dark, dark-eyed, impatient; he did everything as if he resented the time he had to spend on it. Tom was large, fair, handsome, in every way Kenneth's opposite. He said with gentle persistence to Julia, knowing that she needed prodding: 'Better tell the boys to move the table inside tomorrow.'

'Oh, I suppose so,' she grumbled. Her summer was over: the long luminous warm nights, broken by swift showers, or obscured suddenly by heavy driving clouds – the tumultuous magical nights – were gone and finished for this year. Now, for the three months of winter, they would eat indoors, with the hot lamp over the table, the cold shivering about their legs, and outside a parched country, roofed by dusty freezing stars.

Kenneth said briskly: 'Winter, Julia, you'll have to face it.'

'Well,' she smiled, 'tomorrow you'll be able to see what you are eating.'

· There was a slight pause; then Kenneth said: 'I shan't be here tomorrow night. I'm taking the car into town in the morning.'

Julia did not reply. She had not heard. That is to say, she felt dismay deepening in her at the sound of his voice; then she wondered at her own forebodings, and then the words: 'Town. In the morning,' presented themselves to her.

They very seldom went into the city, which was fifty miles away. A trip was always planned in advance, for it would be a matter of buying things that were not available at the local store. The three of them had made the journey only last week. Julia's mind was now confronting and absorbing the fact that on that day Kenneth had abruptly excused himself and gone off on some business of his own. She remembered teasing him, a little, in her fashion. To herself she would have said (disliking the knowledge) that she controlled jealousy, like many jealous women, by becoming an accomplice, as it were, in Kenneth's adventures: the tormenting curiosity was eased when she knew what he had been doing. Last week he had disliked her teasing.

Now she looked over at Tom for reassurance, and saw that his eyes were expressing disquiet as great as her own. Doubly deserted, she gazed clearly and deliberately at both men; and because Kenneth's bald statement of his intentions seemed to her so gross a betrayal of their real relations, chose to say nothing, but in a manner of waiting for an explanation. None was offered, though Kenneth appeared uneasy. They finished their meal in silence and went indoors, passing through the stripped dining-room, which tomorrow would appear in its winter guise of arranged furniture and candles and bowls of fruit, into the living-room.

The house was built for heat. In the winter cold struck up from the floor and out of the walls. This room was very bare, very high, of dull red brick, flagged with stone. Tomorrow she would put down rugs. There was a large stone fireplace, in which stood an earthenware jar filled with Christ-thorn. Julia unconsciously crossed to it, knelt, and bent to the little glowing red flowers, holding out her hands as if to the comfort of fire. Realizing what she was doing, she lifted her head, smiled wryly at the two men, who were watching her with the same small smile, and said: 'I'll get a fire put in.' Shaking herself into a knowledge of what she did by action, she walked purposefully to the door, and called to the servants. Soon the houseboy entered with logs and kindling materials, and the three stood drinking their coffee, watching him as he knelt to make the fire. They were silent, not because of any scruples against letting their lives appear falsely to servants, but because they knew speech was necessary, and that what must be said would break their life together. Julia was trembling; it was as if a support had been cut away beneath her. Held as she was by these men, her life made for her by them, her instincts were free to come straight and present themselves to her without the necessity for disapproval or approval. Now she found herself glancing alternatively from Tom, that large gentle man, her husband, whose very presence comforted her into peace, to Kenneth, who was frowning down at his coffee cup, so as not to meet her eyes. If he had simply laughed and said what was needed! – he did not. He drank what remained in the cup with two large gulps, seemed to feel the need of something to do, and then went over to the fireplace. The native still knelt there, his bare legs projecting loosely behind him, his hands hanging loose, his body free and loose save for head and shoulders, into which all his energy was concentrated for the purpose of blowing up the fire, which he did with steady, bellow-like breathing. 'Here,' said Kenneth, 'I'll do that.' The servant glanced at him, accepted the white man's whim, and silently left the room, leaving the feeling behind him that he had said: 'White men can't make fires'; just as Julia could feel her cook saying, when she was giving orders in the kitchen: 'I can make better pastry than you.'

Kenneth knelt where the servant had knelt and began fiddling with the logs. But he was good with his hands, and in a moment the sparse beginnings of a fire flowered in the wall; while the crock of prickly red thorn blossoms, Julia's summer fire, was set to one side.

'Now,' said Kenneth, rather offhand, rather too loudly: 'You can warm your hands, Julia.' He gave his quick, grudging laugh. Julia found it offensive; and met his eyes. They were hostile. She flushed, walked slowly over to the fireplace, and sat down. The two men followed her example. For a while they did nothing; that unoffered explanation hung in the air between them. After a while Kenneth reached for a magazine and began to read. Julia looked over at her husband, whose kind blue eyes had always accepted everything she was, and raised her brows humorously. He did not respond, for he had turned again to Kenneth's now purposely bent head.

The fact that Kenneth had not spoken, that Tom was troubled, made Julia, thrown back on herself, ask: 'Why should you be so resentful? Surely he has a right to do as he pleases?' No, she answered herself. Not in this way. He shouldn't suddenly withdraw, shutting us out. Either one thing or the other. Doing it this way means that all our years together have been a lie; he simply repudiates them. But that was Kenneth, this continuous alternation between giving and withdrawal. Julia felt tears welling up inside her from a place that for a long time had remained dry. They were the tears of trembling insecurity. The thin, cold air in the great stone room, just beginning to be warmed by the small fire, was full of menace for Julia. But Kenneth did not speak: he was reading as if his future depended on the advertisements for tractors: and Tom soon began to read too, ignoring Julia.

She pulled herself together, and lay back in her chair, making herself think. She was thinking consciously of her life and what she was. There had been no need for her to consider herself for so long, and she hated having to do it.

She was the daughter to a small-town doctor in the North of England. To say that she had been ambitious would be false: the word ambition implies purpose; she was rather critical and curious, and her rebellion against the small-town atmosphere, and the prospect of marrying into it was no more conscious than the rebellion of most young people who think vaguely: Surely life can be better than this?

Yet she escaped. She was clever: at the end of her schooling she was better educated than most. She learned French and German because languages came easily to her, but mostly because at eighteen she fell in love with a French student, and at twenty became secretary to a man who had business connections in Germany, and she liked to please men. She was an excellent secretary, not merely because she was competent, but because of her peculiar fluid sympathy for the men she worked with. Her employers found that she quickly, intuitively, fitted in with what they wanted: it was a sort of directed passivity, a receptiveness towards people. So she earned well, and soon had the opportunity of leaving her home town and going to London.

Looking back now from the age she had reached (which was nearly forty) on the life she had lived (which had been varied and apparently adventurous) she could not put her finger on any point in her youth when she had said to herself: 'I want to travel; I want to be free.' Yet she had travelled widely, moving from one country to the next, from one job to the next; and all her relations with people, whether men or women, had been coloured by the brilliance of impermanence. When she left England she had not known it would be final. It was on a business trip with her employer, and her relations with him were almost those of a wife with a husband, excepting for sex: she could not work with a man unless she offered a friendly, delicate sympathy.

In France she fell in love, and stayed there for a year. When that came to an end, the mood took her to go to Italy – no, that is the wrong way of putting it. When she described it like that to herself, she scrupulously said: That's not the truth. The fact was that she had been very seriously in love; and yet could not bring herself to marry. Going to Italy (she had not wanted to go in the least) had been a desperate but final way of ending the affair. She simply could not face the idea of marriage. In Italy she worked in a travel agency; and there she met a man whom she grew to love. It was not the desperate passion of a year before, but serious enough to marry. Later, she moved to America. Why America? Why not? – she was offered a good job there at the time she was looking for some place to go.

She stayed there two years, and had, as they say, a wonderful time. She was now a little bit more cautious about falling in love; but nevertheless, there was a man who almost persuaded her to stay in New York. At the last moment a wild, trapped feeling came over her: what have I got to do with this country? she asked herself. This time, leaving the man was a destroying effort; she did not want to leave him. But she went south to the Argentine, and her state of mind was not a pleasant one.

Also, she found she was not as efficient as she had been. This was because she had become more wary, less adaptable. Afraid of falling in love, she was conscious of pulling away from the people she worked for; she gave only what she was paid to give, and this did not satisfy her. What, then, was going to satisfy her? After all, she could not spend all her life moving from continent to continent; yet there seemed no reason why she should settle in one place rather than another, even why it should be one man rather than another. She was tired. She was very tired. The springs of her feeling had run dry. This particular malaise is not so easily cured.

And now, for the first time, she had an affair with a man for whom she cared nothing: this was a half-conscious choice, for she understood that she could not have chosen a man whom she would grow to love. And so it went on, for perhaps two years. She was associating only with people who moved her not at all; and this was because she did not want to be moved.

There came a point when she said to herself that she must decide now, finally, what she wanted, and make sacrifices to get it. She was twenty-eight. She had spent the years since leaving school moving from hotel to furnished flat, from one job to the next, from one country to another. She seemed to have a tired affectionate remembrance of so many people, men and women, who had once filled her life. Now it was time to make something permanent. But what?

She said to herself that she was getting hard; yet she was not hard; she was numbed and tired. She must be very careful, she decided; she must not fall in love, lightly, again. Next time, it must matter.

All this time she was leading a full social life: she was attractive, well-dressed, amusing. She had the reputation of being brilliant and cold. She was also very lonely and she had never been lonely before, since there had always been some man to whom she gave warmth, affection, sympathy.

There was one morning when she had a vision of evil. It was at the window of a large hotel, one warm summer's day, when she was looking down through the streets of the attractive

modern city in South America, with the crowds of people and
the moving traffic . . . it might have been almost any city, on a
bright warm day, from a hotel window, with the people blowing
like leaves across her vision, as rootless as she, as impermanent;
their lives meaning as little. For the first time in her life, the
word, evil, meant something to her: she looked at it, coldly,
and rejected it. This was sentiment, she said; the result of being
tired, and nearly thirty. The feeling was not related to anything.
She could not feel – why should one feel? She disliked what she
was – well, it was at any rate honest to accept oneself as
unlikeable. Her brain remarked dispassionately that if one lived
without rules, one should be prepared to take the consequences
even if that meant moments of terror at hotel windows, with
death beckoning below and whispering: Why live? Anyway,
who was responsible for the way she was? Had she ever planned
it? \ .iy should one be one thing rather than another?

It was chance that took her to Cape Town. At a party she
met a man who offered her a job as his secretary on a business
trip, and it was easy to accept, for she had come to hate South
America.

During the trip over she found, with a groan, that she had
never been more efficient, more responsible, more gently
responsive. He was an unhappy man, who needed sympathy
. . . she gave it. At the end of the trip he asked her to marry
him; and she understood she would have felt much the same if
he had asked her to dinner. She fled.

She had enough money saved to live without working, so for
months she stayed by herself, in a small hotel high over Cape
Town, where she could watch the ships coming and going in
the harbour and think: they are as restless as I am. She lived
gently, testing every emotion she felt, making no contact save
the casual ones inevitable in a hotel, walking by herself for
hours of every day, soaking herself in the sea and the sun as if
the beautiful peninsula could heal her by the power of its
beauty. And she ran away from any possibility of liking some
other human being as if love itself were poisoned.

One warm afternoon when she was walking along the side of
a mountain, with the blue sea swinging and lifting below, and a
low sun sending a sad red pathway from the horizon, she was

overtaken by two walkers. There was no one else in sight, and it was inevitable they should continue together. She found they were farmers on holiday from Rhodesia, half-brothers, who had worked themselves into prosperity; this was the first holiday they had taken for years, and they were in a loosened, warm, adventurous mood. She sensed they were looking for wives to take back with them.

She liked Tom from the first, though for a day or so she flirted with Kenneth. This was an automatic response to his laughing, challenging antagonism. It was Kenneth who spoke first, in his brusque, offhand way, and she felt attracted to him: theirs was the relationship of people moving towards a love affair. But she did not really want to flirt; with Kenneth it seemed anything else was impossible. She was struck by the way Tom, the elder brother, listened while they sparred, smiling uncritically, almost indulgently: his was an almost protective attitude. It was more than protective. A long while afterwards she told Tom that on that first afternoon he had reminded her of the peasant who uses a bird to catch a fish for him. Yet there was a moment during the long hike back to the city through the deepening evening, when Julia glanced curiously at Tom and saw his warm blue glance resting kindly on her in a slow, speculative way, and she chose him, then, in her mind, even while she continued the exchange with Kenneth. Because of that kindness, she let herself sink towards the idea of marriage. It was what she wanted, really; and she did not care where she lived. Emotionally there was no country of which she could say: this is my home.

For several days the three of them went about together, and all the time she bantered with Kenneth and watched Tom. That defensive, grudging thing she could feel in Kenneth, which attracted her, against her will, was what she was afraid of: she was watching half-fearfully, half-cynically, for its appearance in Tom. Then, slowly, Kenneth's treatment of her grew more offhand and brutal: he knew he was being made use of. There came a point when in his sarcastic frank way he shut himself off from her; and for a while the three were together without contact. It had been Kenneth and she, with Tom as urbane onlooker; now it was she, by herself, drifting alone, floating loose, waiting, as it were, to be gathered in; and it was possible to mark the point when Tom and Kenneth looked at each other sardonically, in understanding, before Tom moved into Kenneth's place, in his warm and deliberate fashion, claiming her.

He was nicer than she had believed possible. There was suddenly no conflict. He listened to her tales about her life with detached interest, as if they could not possibly concern him. He remarked once, in his tender, protective way: 'You must have been hurt hard at some time. That's the trouble with you independent women. Actually, you are quite a nice woman, Julia.' She laughed at him scornfully, as an arrogant male who has to make some kind of a picture of a woman so as to be able to fit her into his life. He treated her laughter tolerantly. When she said things like this he found it merely a sort of piquancy, a sign of her wit. Half-laughingly, half-despairingly, she said to Kenneth: 'You do realize that Tom hasn't any idea of what I'm like? Do you think it's fair to marry him?'

'Well, why not, if he wants to be married?' returned Kenneth briskly. 'He's romantic. He sees you as a wanderer from city to city, and from bed to bed, because you are trying to heal a broken heart or something of the kind. That appeals to him.'

Tom listened to this silently, smiling with disquiet. But there were times when Julia liked to think she had a broken heart; it certainly felt bruised. It was restful to accept Tom's idea of her. She said in a piqued way to Kenneth: 'I suppose *you* understand perfectly easily why I've lived the way I have?'

Kenneth raised his brows. 'Why? Because you enjoyed it of course. What better reason?'

She could not help laughing, even while she said crossly, feeling misunderstood: 'The fact is, you are as bad as Tom. You make up stories about women, too, to suit yourself. You like thinking of women as hard and decided, cynically making use of men.'

'Certainly,' said Kenneth. 'Much better than letting yourself be made use of. I like women to know what they want and get it.'

This kind of conversation irritated and saddened Julia: it was rather like the froth whipping on the surface of the sea, with the currents underneath dark and unknown.

She did not like being reminded how much better Kenneth understood her than Tom did. She was pleased to get the business of the ceremony over. Tom married her in a purposeful, unhurrying way; but he remarked that it must be before a certain date because he wanted to start planting soon.

Kenneth attended as best man with a glint of malice in his eye, and the air of a well-wishing onlooker, interested to see how things would turn out. Julia and he exchanged a glance of pure understanding, very much against their wills, for their attitude towards each other was now one of brisk friendship. From the security of Tom's arms, she allowed herself to think that if Kenneth were not the kind of man to feel protective towards a woman simply because he enjoyed feeling protective, then it was so much the worse for him. This was slightly vindictive in her; but on the whole good-natured enough – good-nature was necessary; the three of them would be living together in one house, on the same farm, seeing other people seldom.

It was quite easy, after all. Kenneth did not have to efface himself. Tom effortlessly claimed Julia as his wife, from his magnificent, lazy self-assurance, and she was glad to be claimed. Kenneth and she maintained a humorous understanding. He was given three rooms to himself in one wing of the house; but it was not long before they became disused. It seemed silly for him to retire after dinner by himself. In the evenings, the fact that Julia was Tom's wife was marked by their two big chairs set side by side, with Kenneth's opposite. He used to sit there watching them with his observant, slightly sarcastic smile.

After a while Julia understood she was feeling uneasy; she put it down to the fact that she had expected subtle antagonism between the two men, which she would have to smooth over, while in fact there was no antagonism. It went deeper than that. Those first few nights, when Kenneth tactfully withdrew to his rooms, but looking amused, Tom was restless: he missed Kenneth badly. Julia watched them; and saw with a curious humorous sinking of the heart that they were so close to each other they could not bear to be apart for long. In the evenings it was they who talked, in the odd bantering manner they used even when serious: particularly when serious. Tom liked it when Kenneth sat there opposite, looking shrewd and sceptical about this marriage: they would tease each other in a way that, had they been man and woman, would have seemed positively flirtatious. Listening to them, Julia felt an extraordinary unease, as at a perversity. She chose not to think about it. Better to be affectionately amused at Tom's elder brother attitude towards Kenneth; there was often something petulant, rebellious, childish, in Kenneth's attitude towards Tom. Why, Tom was even elder-brotherish to her, who had been managing her own life, so efficiently, for years all over the world. Well, and was not that why she had married him?

She accepted it. They all accepted it. They grew into a silent comfortable understanding. Tom, so to speak, was the head of the family, commanding, strong, perhaps a little obtuse, as authority has to be; and Julia and Kenneth deferred to him, with the slightest hint of mockery, to gloss the fact that they were glad to defer: how pleasant to let the responsibility rest on someone else!

Julia even learned to accept the knowledge that when Tom was busy, and she walked with Kenneth, or swam with Kenneth, or took trips into town with Kenneth, it was not only with Tom's consent: more, he liked it, even needed it. Sometimes she felt as if he were urging her to be with his brother. Kenneth felt it and rebelled, shying away in his petulant younger-brother manner. He would exclaim: 'Good Lord, man, Julia's your wife, not mine.' And Tom would laugh uneasily and say: 'I don't like the idea of being possessive.' The thought of Tom being possessive was so absurd that Julia and Kenneth began giggling helplessly, like conspiring and wise children. And when Tom had departed, leaving them together, she would say to Kenneth, in her troubled serious fashion: 'But I don't understand this. I don't understand any of it. It flies in the face of nature.'

'So it does,' Kenneth would return easily. He looked at her with a quizzical glint. 'You must take things as they come, my dear sister-in-law.' But Julia felt she had been doing just that: she had relaxed, without thinking, drifting warmly and luxuriously inside Tom's warm and comfortable grasp: which was also Kenneth's, and because Tom wanted it that way.

In spite of Tom, she maintained with Kenneth a slight but strong barrier, because they were people who could be too strongly attracted to each other. Once or twice, when they had been left alone together by Tom, Kenneth would fly off irritably: 'Really, why I bother to be loyal in the circumstances I can't think.'

'But what are the circumstances?' Julia asked, puzzled.

'Oh Lord, Julia . . .' Kenneth expostulated irritably.

Once, when he was brutal with irritability, he made the curious remark: 'The fact is, it was just about time Tom and I had a wife.' He began laughing, not very pleasantly.

Julia did not understand. She thought it sounded ugly.

Kenneth regarded her ironically and said: 'Fortunately for Tom, he doesn't know anything at all about himself.'

But Julia did not like this said about her husband, even though she felt it to be true. Instinctively this particular frontier in their mutual relations was avoided in future; and she was careful with Kenneth, refusing to discuss Tom with him.

From time to time during those two years before Tom left for the war, Kenneth investigated (his own word) the girls on surrounding farms, with a view to marrying. They bored him. He had a prolonged affair with a married woman whose husband bored her. To Julia and Tom he made witty remarks about his position as a lover. Sometimes the three of them would become helpless with laughter at this description of himself being gallant: the lady was romantic, and liked being courted. Kenneth was not romantic, and his interest in the lady was confined to an end which he could not prevent himself describing in his pungent, sour, resigned fashion during those long evenings with the married couple. Again, Julia got the uneasy feeling that Tom was really too interested – no, that was not the word; it was not the easygoing interest of an amused outsider that Tom displayed; while he listened to Kenneth being witty about his affair, it was almost as if he were participating himself, as if he were silently urging Kenneth on to further revelations. On these occasions Julia felt a revulsion from Tom. She said to herself that she was jealous, and repressed the feeling.

When the war started Tom became restless; Julia knew that he would soon go. He volunteered before there was conscription; and she watched, with a humorous sadness, the scene (an uncomfortable one) between her two men, when it seemed that Tom felt impelled to apologize to Kenneth for taking the advantage of him in grasping a rare chance of happiness. Kenneth was unfit: the two brothers had come to Africa in the first place because of Kenneth's delicate lungs. Kenneth did not at all want to go to the war. 'Lord!' he exclaimed to Tom, 'there's no need to sound so apologetic. You're welcome. I'm not a romantic. I don't like getting killed unless in a good cause. I can't see any point in the thing.' In this way he appeared to dismiss the war and the world's turmoil. As for Tom, he didn't really care about the issues of the war, either. It was sufficient that there was a war. For both men it was axiomatic that it was impossible England could ever be beaten in a war; they might laugh at their own attitude (which they did, when Julia, from her liberal travelled internationalism, mocked at them), but that was what they felt, nevertheless.

As for Julia, she was more unhappy about the war than either of them. She had grown into security on the farm; now the world, which she had wanted to shut out, pressed in on her again; and she thought of her many friends, in so many countries, in the thick of things, feeling strange partisan emotions which seemed to her absurd. For she thought in terms of people, not of nations or issues; and the war, to her, was a question of mankind gone mad, killing each other pointlessly. Always the pointlessness of everything! And now she was not allowed to forget it.

To her credit, all her unhappiness and female resentment at being so lightly abandoned by Tom at the first sound of a bugle calling adventure down the wind was suppressed. She merely said scornfully to him: 'What a baby you are! As if there hadn't been the last war! And look at all the men in the district, pleased as punch because something exciting is going to happen. If you really cared two hoots about the war, I might respect you. But you don't. Nor do most of the people we know.'

Tom did not like this. The atmosphere of war had stirred him into a superficial patriotism. 'You sound like a newspaper leader,' Julia mocked him. 'You don't really believe a word you say. The truth is that most people like us, in all the countries I've been in, haven't a notion what we believe about anything. We don't believe in the slogans and the lies. It makes me sick, to see the way you all get excited the moment war comes.'

This made Tom angry, because it was true; and because he had suddenly remembered his sentimental attachment to England, in the Rupert Brooke fashion. They were on edge with each other, in the days before he left. He was glad to go, particularly as Kenneth was being no less caustic. This was the first time the two men had ever been separated; and Julia felt that Kenneth was as hurt as she because Tom left them so easily. In fact, they were all pleased when Tom was able to leave the farm, and put an end to the misery of their tormenting each other.

But after he had gone, Julia was very unhappy. She missed him badly. Marrying had been a greater peace than she had imagined possible for her. To let the restless critical part of one die; to drift; to relax; to enjoy Africa as a country, the way it looked and the way it felt; to enjoy the physical things slowly, without haste – learning all this had, she imagined, healed her. And now, without Tom, she was nothing. She was unsupported and unwarmed; and she knew that marrying had after all cured her of nothing. She was still floating rootlessly, without support; she belonged nowhere; and even Africa, which she had grown to love, meant nothing to her really: it was another country she had visited as lightly as a migrant bird.

And Kenneth was no help at all. With Tom on the farm she might have been able to drift with the current, to take the conventional attitude towards the war. But Kenneth used to switch on the wireless in the evenings and pungently translate the news of the war into the meaningless chaotic brutality which was how she herself saw it. He spoke with the callous cynicism that means people are suffering, and which she could hear in her own voice.

'It's all very well,' she would say to him. 'It's all very well for us. We sit here out of it all. Millions of people are suffering.'

'People like suffering,' he would retort, angrily. 'Look at Tom. There he sits in the desert, bored as hell. He'll be talking about the best years of his life in ten years' time.'

Julia could hear Tom's voice, nostalgically recalling adventure, only too clearly. At the same time Kenneth made her angry, because he expressed what she felt, and she did not like the way she felt. She joined the local women's groups and started knitting and helping with district functions; and flushed up when she saw Kenneth's cold eyes resting on her. 'By God, Julia, you are as bad as Tom . . .'

'Well, surely, one must be part of it, surely, Kenneth?' She tried hard to express what she was feeling.

'Just what are you fighting for?' he demanded. 'Can you tell me that?'

'I feel we ought to find out . . .'

He wouldn't listen. He flounced off down the farm saying: 'I'm going to make a new dam. Unless they bomb it, it's something useful done in all this waste and chaos. You can go and knit nice woollies for those poor devils who are getting themselves killed and listen to the dear women talking about the dreadful Nazis. My God, the hypocrisy. Just tell them to take a good look at South Africa, from me, will you?'

The fact was, he missed Tom. When he was approached to subscribe to war charities he gave generously, in Tom's name, sending the receipts carefully to Tom, with sarcastic intention. As the war deepened and the dragging weight of death and suffering settled in their minds, Julia would listen at night to angry pacing footsteps up and down, up and down the long stone passages of the house, and going out in her dressing-gown, would come on Kenneth, his eyes black with anger, his face tense and white: 'Get out of my way, Julia. I shall kill you or somebody. I'd like to blow the whole thing up. Why not blow it up and be finished with it? It would be good riddance.'

Julia would gently take him by the arm and lead him back to bed, shutting down her own cold terror at the world. It was necessary for one of them to remain sane. Kenneth at that time was not quite sane. He was working fourteen hours a day; up long before sunrise, hastening back up the road home after sundown, for an evening's studying: he read scientific stuff about farming. He was building dams, roads, bridges; he planted hundreds of acres of trees; he contour-ridged and drained. He would listen to the news of so many thousands killed and wounded, so many factories blown up, and turn to Julia, face contracted with hate, saying: 'At any rate I'm building not destroying.'

'I hope it comforts you,' Julia would remark, mildly sarcastic, though she felt bitter and futile.

He would look at her balefully and stride out again, away on some work for his hands.

They were quite alone in the house. For a short while after Tom left they discussed whether they would get an assistant, for conventional reasons. But they disliked the idea of a stranger, and the thing drifted. Soon, as the men left the farms to go off to the war, many women were left alone, doing the work themselves, or with assistants who were unfit for fighting, and there was nothing really outrageous in Kenneth and Julia living together by themselves. It was understood in the district, that for the duration of the war, this kind of situation should not be made a subject for gossip.

It was inevitable they should be lovers. From the moment Tom left they both knew it.

Tom was away three years. She was exhausted by Kenneth. His mood was so black and bitter and she knew that nothing she could do or say might help him, for she was as bad herself. She became the kind of woman he wanted: he did not want a warm, consoling woman. She was his mistress. Their relationship was a complicated fencing game, conducted with irony, tact, and good sense – except when he boiled over into hatred and vented it on her. There were times when suddenly all vitality failed her, and she seemed to sink swiftly, unsupported, to lie helpless in the depths of herself, looking up undesirously at the life of emotion and warmth washing gently over her head. Then Kenneth used to leave her alone, whereas Tom would have gently coaxed her into life again.

·'I wish Tom would come back, oh dear Christ, I wish he'd come back,' she would sigh.

'Do you imagine I don't?' Kenneth would enquire bitterly. Then, a little piqued, but not much: 'Don't I do?'

'Well enough, I suppose.'

'What do you want then?' he enquired briefly, giving what small amount of attention he could spare from the farm to the problem of Julia, the woman.

'Tom,' Julia replied simply.

He considered this critically. 'The fact is, you and I have far more in common than you and Tom.'

'I don't see what "in common" has to do with it.'

'You and I are the same kind of animal. Tom doesn't know the first thing about you. He never could.'

'Perhaps that's the reason.'

Dislike began welling between them, tempered, as always, by patient irony. 'You don't like women at all,' complained Julia suddenly. 'You simply don't like me. You don't trust me.'

'Oh if it comes to liking . . .' He laughed, resentfully. 'You don't trust me either, for that matter.'

It was the truth; they didn't trust each other; they mistrusted the destructive nihilism that they had in common. Conversations like these, which became far more frequent as time went on, left them hardened against each other for days, in a condition of watchful challenge. This was part of their long, exhausting exchange, which was a continual resolving of mutual antagonism in tired laughter.

Yet, when Tom wrote saying he was being demobilized, Kenneth, in a mood of tenderness, asked Julia to marry him. She was shocked and astonished. 'You know quite well you don't want to marry me,' she expostulated. 'Besides, how could you do that to Tom?' Catching his quizzical glance, she began laughing helplessly.

'I don't know whether I want to marry you or not,' admitted Kenneth honestly, laughing with her.

'Well, I know. You don't.'

'I've got used to you.'

'I haven't got used to you. I never could.'

'I don't understand what it is Tom gives you that I don't.'

'Peace,' said Julia simply. 'You and I fight all the time, we never do anything else.'

'We don't fight,' protested Kenneth. 'We have never, as they say, exchanged a cross word.' He grimaced. 'Except when I get wound up, and that's a different thing.'

Julia saw that he could not imagine a relationship with a woman that was not based on antagonism. She said, knowing it was useless: 'Everything is so easy with Tom.'

'Of course it's easy,' he said angrily. 'The whole damn thing is a lie from beginning to end. However, if that's what you like . . .' He shrugged, his anger evaporating. He said drily: 'I imagined I was qualifying as a husband.'

'Some men can't ever be husbands. They'll always be lovers.'

'I thought women liked that?'

'I wasn't talking about women, I was talking about me.'

'Well, I intend to get married, for all that.'

After that they did not discuss it. Speaking of what they felt left them confused, angry, puzzled.

Before Tom came back Kenneth said: 'I ought to leave the farm.'

She did not trouble to answer, it was so insincere.

'I'll get a farm over the other side of the district.'

She merely smiled. Kenneth had written long letters to Tom every week of those three years, telling him every detail of what was happening on the farm. Plans for the future were already worked out.

It was arranged that Julia should go and meet Tom in town, where they would spend some weeks before the three began life together again. As Kenneth said, sarcastically, to Julia: 'It will be just like a second honeymoon.'

It was. Tom returned from the desert toughened, sunburnt, swaggering a little because he was unsure of himself with Julia. But she was so happy to see him that in a few hours they were back where they had been. 'About Kenneth . . .' began Tom warily, after they had edged round this subject for some days.

'Much better not talk about it,' said Julia quickly.

Tom's blue eyes rested on her, not critically, but appealingly. 'Is it going to be all right?' he asked after a moment. She could see he was terrified she might say that Kenneth had decided to go away. She said drily: 'I didn't want you to go off to the wars like a hero, did I?'

'There's something in that,' he admitted; admitting at the same time that they were quits. Actually, he was rather subdued because of his years as a soldier. He was quick to drop the subject. It would not be just yet that he would begin talking about the happiest years of his life. He had still to forget how bored he had been and how he had missed his farm.

For a few days there was awkwardness between the three. Kenneth was jealous because of the way Julia had gladly turned back to Tom. But there was so much work to do, and Kenneth and Tom were so pleased to be back together, that it was not long before everything was as easy as before. Julia thought it was easier: now that her attraction for Kenneth, and his for her, had been slaked, the restlessness that had always been between them would vanish. Perhaps not quite . . . Julia and Kenneth's eyes would meet sometimes in that instinctive, laughing understanding that she could never have with Tom, and then she would feel guilty.

Sometimes Kenneth would 'take out' a girl from a near farm; and they would afterwards discuss his getting married. 'If only I could fall in love,' he would complain humorously. 'You are the only woman I can bear the thought of, Julia.' He would say this before Tom, and Tom would laugh: they had reached such a pitch of complicity.

Very soon there were plans for expanding the farm. They bought several thousands of acres of land next door. They would grow tobacco on a large scale: this was the time of the tobacco boom. They were getting very rich.

There were two assistants on the new farm, but Tom spent most of his days there. Sometimes his nights, too. Julia, after three days spent alone with Kenneth, with the old attraction strong between them, said to him: 'I wish you would let Kenneth run that farm.'

Tom, who was absorbed and fascinated by the new problems, said rather impatiently: 'Why?'

'Surely that's obvious.'

'That's up to you, isn't it?'

'Perhaps it isn't, always.'

It was the business of the war over again. He seemed a slow, deliberate man, without much fire. But he liked new problems to solve. He got bored. Kenneth, the quick, lively, impatient one, liked to be rooted in one place, liked to develop what he had.

Julia had the helpless feeling again that Tom simply didn't care about herself and Kenneth. She grew to accept the knowledge that really, it was Kenneth that mattered to him. Except for the war, they had never been separated. Tom's father had died, and his mother married Kenneth's father. Tom had always been with Kenneth, he could not remember a time when he had not been protectively guarding him. Once Julia asked him: 'I suppose you must have been very jealous of him, that was it, wasn't it?' and she was astonished at his quick flare of rage at the suggestion. She dropped the thing: what did it matter now?

The two boys had gone through various schools and to university together. They had started farming in their early twenties, when they hadn't a penny between them, and had to borrow money to support their mother, for whom they shared a deep love, which was also half-exasperated admiration; she had apparently been a helpless, charming lady with many admirers who left her children to the care of nurses.

When Tom was away one evening, and would not be back till next day, Kenneth said brusquely, with the roughness that is the result of conflict: 'Coming to my room tonight, Julia?'

'How can I?' she protested.

'Well, I don't like the idea of coming to the marriage bed,' he said practically, and they began to laugh. To Julia, Kenneth would always be the laughter of inevitability.

Tom said nothing, though he must have known. When Julia again appealed that he should stay on this farm and send Kenneth to the other, he turned away, frowning, and did not reply. His manner to her did not change. And she still felt: this is my husband, and compared to that feeling, Kenneth was nothing. At the same time a grim anxiety was taking possession of her: it seemed that in some perverse way the two men were brought even closer together, for a time, by sharing the same woman. That was how Julia put it, to herself: the plain and brutal fact.

It was Kenneth who pulled away in the end. Not from Julia: from the situation. There came a time when it was possible for Kenneth to say, as he stood smiling sardonically opposite Julia and Tom, who were sitting like an old married couple on their side of the fire: 'You know it is quite essential I should get married. Things can't go on like this.'

'But you can't marry without being in love,' protested Julia; and immediately checked herself with an annoyed laugh – she realized that what she was protesting against was Kenneth going away from her.

'You must see that I should.'

'I don't like the idea,' said Tom, as if it were his marriage that was under discussion.

'Look at you and Tom,' said Kenneth peaceably, but not without maliciousness. 'A very satisfactory marriage. You weren't in love.'

'Weren't we in love, Julia?' asked Tom, rather surprised.

'Actually, I was "in love" with Kenneth,' said Julia, with the sense that this was an unnecessary thing to say.

'You wanted a wife. Julia wanted a husband. All very sensible.'

'One can be "in love" once too often,' said Julia, aiming this at Kenneth.

'Are you in love with Kenneth now?'

Julia did not answer; it annoyed her that Tom should ask it, after virtually handing her over to Kenneth. After a moment she remarked: 'I suppose you are right. You really ought to get married.' Then, thoughtfully: 'I couldn't be married to you, Kenneth. You destroy me.' The word sounded heightened and absurd. She hurried on: 'I didn't know it was possible to be as happy as I have been with Tom.' She smiled at her husband and reached over and took his hand: he returned the pressure gratefully.

'Ergo, I have to get married,' said Kenneth caustically.

'But you say so yourself.'

'I don't seem to be feeling what I ought to feel,' said Tom at last, laughing in a bewildered way.

'That's what's wrong with the three of us,' said Julia; then, feeling as if she were on the edge of that dangerous thing that might destroy them, she stopped and said: 'Let's not talk about it. It doesn't do any good to talk about it.'

That conversation had taken place a month ago. Kenneth had not mentioned getting married since; and Julia had secretly hoped he had shelved it. Not long since, during that trip to town, he had spent a day away from Tom and herself – and with whom? Tomorrow he was making the trip again, and for the first time for years, since they had been together, it was not the three of them, close in understanding, but Tom and Julia, with Kenneth deliberately excluding himself and putting up barriers.

Kenneth did not open his mouth the whole evening; though both Tom and Julia waited for him to break the silence. Julia did not read; she moiled over the facts of her life unhappily; and from time to time looked over at Tom, who smiled back affectionately, knowing she wanted this of him.

In spite of the fire, that now roared and crackled in the wall, Julia was cold. The thin frosty air of the high veld was of an electric dryness in the big bare room. The roof was crackling with cold; every time the tin snapped overhead it evoked the arching, myriad-starred, chilly night outside, and the drying, browning leaves, the tan waving grass that was now a dull parched colour. Julia's skin crinkled and stung with dryness.

Suddenly she said: 'It won't do, Kenneth. You can't behave like this.' She got up, and stood with her back to the fire, gazing levelly at them. She felt herself to be parching and withering within; she felt no heavier than a twig; the sap did not run in her veins. Because of Kenneth's betrayal, she was wounded in some place she could not name. She had no substance. That was how she felt.

What they saw was a tall, rather broad woman, big-framed, the bones of her face strongly supporting the flesh. Her eyes were blue and candid, now clouded by trouble, but still humorously troubled. She was forcing them to look at her; to make comparisons; she was challenging them. She was forcing them even to break the habit of loyalty which, blithely tender, continually recreative, blinds the eyes of lovers to change.

They saw this strong, ageing woman, the companion of their lives, standing there in front of them, still formed in the shape of beauty, for she was pleasant to look at, but with the light of beauty gone. They remembered her, perhaps, on that afternoon by the sea when they had first encountered her, or when she was newly arrived at the farm: young, vivid, a slender and rather boyish girl, with sleek, close-cropped hair and quick amused blue eyes.

Now, around the firm and bony face the soft hair fell in dressed waves, she wore a soft flowery dress: they saw a disquieting incongruity between this expression of femininity and what they knew her to be. They were irritated. To stand there, reminding them (when they did not want to be reminded) that she was facing the sorrowful abdication of middle age, and facing it alone, seemed to them irrelevant, even unfair.

Kenneth said resentfully: 'Oh, Lord, you are very much a woman, after all, Julia. Must you make a scene?'

Her quick laugh was equally resentful. 'Why shouldn't I make a scene? I feel entitled to it.'

Kenneth said: 'We all know there's got to be a change. Can't we go through with it without this sort of thing?'

'Surely,' she said helplessly, 'everything can't be changed without some sort of explanation . . .' She could not go on.

'Well, what sort of explanation do you want?'

She shrugged hopelessly. After a moment she said, as if continuing an old conversation: 'Perhaps I should have had children, after all?'

'I always said so,' remarked Tom mildly.

'You are nearly forty,' said Kenneth practically.

'I wouldn't make a good mother,' she said. 'I couldn't compete with yours. I wouldn't have the courage to take it on, knowing I should fail by comparison with your so perfect mother.' She was being sarcastic, but there were tears in her voice.

'Let's leave our mother out of it,' said Tom coldly.

'Of course, we always leave everything important out of it.'

Neither of them said anything; they were closed away from her in hostility. She went on: 'I wonder, why did you want me at all, Tom? You didn't really want children particularly.'

'Yes, I did,' said Tom, rather bewildered.

'Not enough to make me feel you cared one way or the other. Surely a woman is entitled to that, to feel that her children matter. I don't know what it is you took me into your life *for*?'

After a moment Kenneth said lightly, trying to restore the comfortable surface of flippancy: 'I have always felt that we ought to have children.'

Neither Tom nor Julia responded to this appeal. Julia took a candle from the mantelpiece, bent to light it at the fire, and said: 'Well, I'm off to bed. The whole situation is beyond me.'

'Very well then,' said Kenneth. 'If you must have it: I'm getting married soon.'

'Obviously,' said Julia drily.

'What did you want me to say?'

'Who is it?' Tom sounded so resentful that it changed the weight of the conversation: now it was Tom and Kenneth as antagonists.

'Well, she's a girl from England. She came out here a few months ago on this scheme for importing marriageable women to the Colonies . . . well, that's what the scheme amounts to.'

'Yes, but the girl?' asked Julia, amused in spite of herself at Kenneth's invincible distaste at the idea of marrying.

'Well . . .' Kenneth hesitated, his dark bright eyes on Julia's face, his mouth already beginning to twist into dry amusement. 'She's fair. She's pretty. She seems capable. She wants to be married . . . what more do I want?' That last phrase was savage. They had come to a dead end.

'I'm going to bed!' exclaimed Julia suddenly, the tears pouring down her face. 'I can't bear this.'

Neither of them said anything to prevent her leaving. When she had gone, Kenneth made an instinctive defensive movement towards Tom. After a moment Tom said irritably, but commandingly: 'It's absurd for you to get married when there's no need.'

'Obviously there's a need,' said Kenneth angrily. He rose, taking another candle from the mantelpiece. As he left the room – and it was clear that he left in order to forestall the scene Tom was about to make – he said: 'I want to have

children before I get an old man. It seems to be the only thing
left.'

When Tom went into the bedroom, Julia was lying dry-eyed
on the pillow, waiting for him. She was waiting for him to
comfort her into security of feeling. He had never failed her.
When he was in bed, she found herself comforting him: it gave
her such a perverse, topsy-turvy feeling she could not sleep.

Soon after breakfast Kenneth left for town. He was dressed
smartly: normally he did not care how he looked, and his
clothes seemed to have been put on in the spirit of one picking
up tools for a job. All three acknowledged his appearance with
small, constricted smiles; and Kenneth reddened as he got into
the car. 'I might not be back tonight,' he called back, driving
away without looking back.

Tom and Julia watched the big car nose its way through the
trees, and turned back to face each other. 'Like to come down
the lands with me?' he asked. 'Yes, I would,' she accepted
gratefully. Then she saw, and was thrown back on to herself by
the knowledge of it, that he was asking her, not for her comfort,
but for his own.

It was a windy, sunlit morning, and very cold; winter had
taken possession of the veld overnight.

The house was built on a slight ridge, with the country falling
away on either side. The landscape was dulling for the dry
season into olive green and thin yellows; there was that
extraordinary contrast of limpid sparkling skies, with sunshine
pouring down like a volatile spirit, and dry cold parching the
face and hands that made Julia uneasy in winter. It was as if
the dryness tightened the cold into rigid fetters on her, so that
a perpetual inner shivering had to be suppressed. She walked
beside Tom over the fields with hunched shoulders and arms
crossed tight over her chest. Yet she was not cold, not in the
physical sense. Around the house the mealie fields, now a
gentle silvery-gold colour, swept into runnels of light as the
wind passed over them, and there was a dry tinkling of parched
leaves moving together, like rat's feet over grass. Tom did not
speak; but his face was heavy and furrowed. When she took his
hand he responded, but listlessly. She wanted him to turn to
her, to say: Now he's going to make something of his own, you

must come to me, and we'll build up again.' She wanted him to claim her, heal her, make her whole. But he was uneasy and restless; and she said at last diffidently: 'Why should you mind so much? It ought to be me who's unhappy.'

'Don't you?' he asked, sounding like a person angry at dishonesty.

'Yes, of course,' she said; and tried to find the words to say that if only he could take her gently into his own security, as he had years ago, things would be right for them.

But that security no longer existed in him.

All that day they hardly spoke, not because of animosity between them, but because of a deep, sad helplessness. They could not help each other.

That night Kenneth did not come back from town. Next day Tom went off by himself to the second farm, leaving her with a gentle apologetic look, as if to say: 'Leave me alone, I can't help it.'

Kenneth telephoned in the middle of the morning from town. His voice was offhand; it was also subtly defensive. That small voice coming from such a distance down the wires, conjured up such a clear vision of Kenneth himself, that she smiled tenderly.

'Well?' she asked warily.

'I'll be back sometime. I don't know when.'

'That means it's definite?'

'I think so.' A pause. Then the voice dropped into dry humour. 'She's such a nice girl that things take a long time, don't you know.' Julia laughed. Quickly he added: 'But she really is, you know, Julia. She's awfully nice.'

'Well, you must do as you think,' she said cautiously.

'How's Tom?' he asked.

'I suddenly don't know anything about Tom,' she answered.

There was such a long silence that she clicked the telephone.

'I'm still here,' said Kenneth. 'I was trying to think of the right things to say.'

'Has it come to the point where we have to think of the right things?'

'Looks like it, doesn't it?'

'Good-bye,' she said quickly, putting down the receiver. 'Let me know when you're coming and I'll get your things ready.'

As usual in the mornings, she passed on a tour of inspection from room to room of the big bare house, where the windows stood open all day, showing blocks of blue crystal round the walls, or views of veld, as if the building, the very bricks and iron, were compounded with sky and landscape to form a new kind of home. When she had made her formal inspection, and found everything cleaned and polished and arranged, she went to the kitchen. Here she ordered the meals, and discussed the state of the pantry with her cook. Then she went back to the veranda; at this hour she would normally read, or sew, till lunch-time.

The thought came into her mind, with a destroying force, that if she were not in the house, Tom would hardly notice it, from a physical point of view: the servants would create comfort without her. She suppressed an impulse to go into the kitchen and cook, or tidy a cupboard to find some work for the hands: that was not what she sought, a temporary salve for feeling useless. She took her large light straw hat from the nail in the bare, stone-floored passage, and went out into the garden. As she did not care for gardening, the ground about the house was arranged with groups of shrubs, so that there would be patches of blossom at any time of the year. The garden boy kept the lawns fresh and green. Over the vivid emerald grass spread the flowers of dryness, the poinsettias, loose scattering shapes of bright scarlet, creamy pink, light yellow. On the fine, shiny-brown stems fluttered light green leaves. In a swift gusty wind the quickly moving blossoms and leaves danced and shook; they seemed to her the very essence of the time of year, the essence of dry cold, of light thin sunshine, of high cold-blue skies.

She passed quietly down the path through the lawns and flowers to the farm road, and turned to look back at the house. From the outside it appeared such a large, assertive, barn of a place, with its areas of shiny tin roof, the hard pink of the walls, the glinting angled shapes of the windows. Although shrubs grew sparsely around it, and it was shaded by a thick clump of trees, it looked naked, raw, crude. 'That is my home,' said Julia to herself, testing the word. She rejected it. In that house she had lived ten years – more. She turned away from it,

walking lightly through the sifting pink dust of the roads like a
stranger. There had always been times when Africa rejected
her, when she felt like a critical ghost. This was one of those
times. Through the known and loved scenes of the veld she saw
Buenos Aires, Rome, Cape Town – a dozen cities, large and
small, merging and mingling as the country rose and fell about
her. Perhaps it is not good for human beings to live in so many
places? But it was not that. She was suffering from an unfamiliar dryness of the senses, an unlocated, unfocused ache that,
if she were young, would have formed itself about a person or
place, but now remained locked within her. 'What am I?' she
kept saying to herself as she walked through the veld, in the
moving patch of shade that fell from the large drooping hat.
On either side the long grass moved and whispered sibilantly;
the doves throbbed gently from the trees; the sky was a flower-
blue arch over her – it was, as they say, a lovely morning.

She passed like a revenant along the edges of the mealie
fields, watching the working gangs of natives; at the well she
paused to see the women with their groups of naked children;
at the cattle sheds she leaned to touch the wet noses of the
thrusting soft-headed calves which butted and pushed at her
legs. There she stayed for some time, finding comfort in these
young creatures. She understood at last that it was nearly
lunch-time. She must go home, and preside at the lunch-table
for Tom, in case he should decide to return. She left the calves
thinking: Perhaps I ought to have children? She knew perfectly
well that she would not.

The road back to the house wound along the high hogsback
between two vleis that fell away on either side. She walked
slowly, trying to recover that soft wonder she had felt when she
first arrived on the farm and learned how living in cities had
cheated her of the knowledge of the shapes of sky and land.
Above her, in the great bright bell of blue sky, the wind
currents were marked by swirls of cloud, the backwaters of the
air by heavy sculptured piles of sluggish white. Around her the
skeleton of rock showed under the thin covering of living soil.
The trees thickened with the fall or rise of the ground, with the
running of underground rivers; the grass – the long blond hair
of the grass – struggled always to heal and hold whatever

wounds were made by hoof of beast or thoughtlessness of man.
The sky, the land, the swirling air, closed around her in an
exchange of water and heat, and the deep multitudinous
murmuring of living substance sounded like a humming in her
blood. She listened, half-passively, half-rebelliously, and asked:
'What do I contribute to all this?'

That afternoon she walked again, for hours; and throughout
the following day; returning to the house punctually for meals,
and greeting Tom across the distance that puts itself between
people who try to support themselves with the mental knowledge of a country, and those who work in it. Once Tom said,
with tired concern, looking at her equally tired face: 'Julia, I
didn't know you would mind so much. I suppose it was conceit.
I always thought I came first.'

'You do,' she said quickly, 'believe me, you do.'

She went to him, so that he could put his arms about her. He
did, and there was no warmth in it for either of them. 'We'll
come right again,' he promised her. But it was as though he
listened to the sound of his own voice for a message of
assurance.

Kenneth came back unexpectedly on the fourth evening. He
was alone; and he appeared purposeful and decided. During
dinner no one spoke much. After dinner, in the bare, gaunt,
firelit room, the three waited for someone to speak.

At last Julia said: 'Well, Kenneth?'

'We are getting married next month.'

'Where?'

'In church,' he said. He smiled constrictedly. 'She wants a
proper wedding. I don't mind, if she likes it.' Kenneth's attitude
was altogether brisk, down-to-earth and hard. At the same
time he looked at Julia and Tom uneasily: he hated his position.

'How old is she?' asked Julia.

'A baby. Twenty-three.'

This shocked Julia. 'Kenneth, you can't do that.'

'Why not?'

Julia could not really see why not.

'Has she money of her own?' asked Tom practically, causing
the other two to look at him in surprise. 'After all,' he said
quickly, 'we must know about her, before she comes?'

'Of course she hasn't,' said Kenneth coldly. 'She wouldn'' e coming out to the Colonies on a subsidized scheme for importing marriageable women, would she?'

Tom grimaced. 'You two are brutal,' he remarked.

Kenneth and Julia glanced at each other; it was like a shrug. 'I didn't mention money in the first place,' he pointed out. 'You did. Anyway, what's wrong with it? If I were a surplus woman in England I should certainly emigrate to find a husband. It's the only sensible thing to do.'

'What is she living on now?' asked Julia.

'She has a job in an office. Some such nonsense.' Kenneth dismissed this. 'Anyway, why talk about money? Surely we have enough?'

'How much have we got?' asked Julia, who was always rather vague about money.

'A hell of a lot,' said Tom, laughing. 'The last three years we've made thousands.'

'Difficult to say, there's so much going back into the farms. Fifty thousand perhaps. We'll make a lot more this year.'

Julia smiled. The words 'fifty thousand' could not be made to come real in her mind. She thought of how she had earned her living for years, in offices, budgeting for everything she spent. 'I suppose we could be described as rich?' she asked wonderingly at last, trying to relate this fact to the life she lived, to the country around them, to their future.

'I suppose we could,' agreed Tom, snorting with amused laughter. He liked it when Julia made it possible for him to think of her as helpless. 'Most of the credit goes to Kenneth,' he added. 'All the work he did during the war is reaping dividends now.'

Julia looked at him; then sardonically at Kenneth, who was shifting uncomfortably in his chair. Tom persisted with good-natured sarcasm, getting his own back for Kenneth's gibes over the war: 'This is getting quite a show-place; I got a letter from the Government asking me if they could bring a collection of distinguished visitors from Home to see it, next week. You'll have to act as hostess. They're coming to see Kenneth's war effort.' He laughed. 'It's also been very profitable.'

Kenneth shut his mouth hard; and kept his temper. 'We are discussing my future wife,' he said coldly.

'So we are,' said Julia.

'Well, let's finish with the thing. I shall give the girl a thumping, expensive honeymoon in the most glossy and awful hotels in the sub-continent,' continued Kenneth grimly. 'She'll love it.'

'Why shouldn't she?' asked Julia. 'I should have loved it too, at her age.'

'I didn't say she shouldn't.'

'And then?' asked Julia again. She was wanting to hear what sort of plans Kenneth had for another farm. He looked at her blankly. 'And then what?'

'Where will you go?'

'Go?'

It came to her that he did not intend to leave the farm. This was such a shock she could not speak. She collected herself at last, and said slowly: 'Kenneth, surely you don't intend to live here?'

'Why not?' he asked quickly, very much on the defensive.

The atmosphere had tightened so that Julia saw, in looking from one man to the other, that this was the real crisis of the business, something she had not expected, but which they had both been waiting, consciously or unconsciously, for her to approach.

'Good God,' she said slowly, in rising anger. 'Good God.' She looked at Tom, who at once averted his eyes. She saw that Tom was longing uneasily for her to make it possible for Kenneth to stay.

She understood at last that, if it had occurred to either of them that another woman could not live here, it was a knowledge neither of them was prepared to face. She looked at these two men and hated them, for the way they took their women into their lives, without changing a thought or a habit to meet them.

She got up, and walked away from them slowly, standing with her back to them, gazing out of the window at the heavily-starred winter's night. She said: 'Kenneth, you are marrying .

this girl because you intend to have a family. You don't care
tuppence for her, really.'

'I've got to be very fond of her,' protested Kenneth.

'At bottom, you don't care tuppence.'

He did not reply. 'You are going to bring her here to me.
She'll feel with her instinct if not with her head that she's being
made use of. And you bring her here to me.' It seemed to her
that she had made her sense of outrage clear enough. She
turned to face them.

'The prospect of bringing her "to you" doesn't seem to me as
shocking as apparently it does to you,' said Kenneth dryly.

'Can't you see?' she said desperately. 'She couldn't
compete . . .'

'You flatter yourself,' said Kenneth briskly.

'Oh, I don't mean that. I mean we've been together for so
long. There's nothing we don't know about each other. Have I
got to say it . . .'

'No,' said Kenneth quietly. 'Much better not.'

Through all this Tom, that large, fair, comfortable man,
leaned back in his chair, looking from his wife to his half-
brother with the air of one suddenly transported to a foreign
country.

He said stubbornly: 'I don't see why you shouldn't adjust
yourself, Julia. After all, both Kenneth and I have had to
adjust ourselves to . . .'

'Quite,' said Kenneth quickly, 'quite.'

She turned on Kenneth furiously. 'Why do you always cut
the conversation short? Why shouldn't we talk about it? It's
what's real, isn't it, for all of us?'

'No point talking about it,' said Kenneth, with a sullen look.

'No,' she said coldly. 'No point.' She turned away from them,
fighting back tears. 'At bottom neither of you really cared
tuppence. That's what it is.' At the moment this seemed to her
true.

'What do you mean by "really caring"?' asked Kenneth.   ·

Julia turned slowly from the window, jerking the light
summer curtains across the stars. 'I mean, we don't care. We
just don't care.'

'I don't know what you are talking about,' said Tom, sounding bewildered and angry. 'Haven't you been happy with me? Is that what you are saying, Julia?'

At this both Kenneth and Julia began laughing with an irresistible and painful laughter.

'Of course I've been happy with you,' she said flatly, at last.

'Well then?' asked Tom.

'I don't know why I was happy then and why I'm unhappy now.'

'Let's say you're jealous,' said Kenneth briskly.

'But I don't think I am.'

'Of course you are.'

'Very well then, I am. That's not the point. What are we going to do to the girl?' she asked suddenly, her feeling finding expression.

'I shall make her a good husband,' said Kenneth. The three of them looked at each other, with raised brows, with humorous, tightened lips.

'Very well then,' amended Kenneth. 'But she'll have plenty of nice children. She'll have you for company, Julia, a nice intelligent woman. And she'll have plenty of money and pretty clothes and all that sort of nonsense, if she wants them.'

There was a silence so long it seemed that nothing could break it.

Julia said slowly and painfully: 'I think it is terrible we shouldn't be able to explain what we feel or what we are.'

'I wish you'd stop trying to,' said Kenneth. 'I find it unpleasant. And quite useless.'

Tom said: 'As for me, I would be most grateful if you'd try to explain what you are feeling, Julia. I haven't an idea.'

Julia stood up with her back to the fire and began gropingly: 'Look at the way we are. I mean, what do we add up to? What are we doing here, in the first place?'

'Doing where?' asked Tom kindly.

'Here, in Africa, in this district, on this land.'

'Ohhh,' groaned Tom humorously.

'Oh *Lord*, Julia,' protested Kenneth impatiently.

'I feel as if we shouldn't be here.'

'Where should we be then?'

·'We've as much right as anybody else.'

'I suppose so.' Julia dismissed it. It was not her point, after all, it seemed. She said slowly: 'I suppose there are comparatively very few people in the world as secure and as rich as we are.'

'It takes a couple of bad seasons or a change in the international set-up,' said Kenneth. 'We could get poor as easily as we've got rich. If you want to call it easy. We've worked hard enough, Tom and I.'

'So do many other people. In the meantime we've all the money we want. Why do we never talk about money, never think about it? It's what we are.'

'Speak for yourself, Julia,' said Tom. 'Kenneth and I spend all our days thinking and talking about nothing else. How else do you suppose we've got rich?'

'How to make it. Not what it all adds up to.'

The two men did not reply; they looked at each other with resignation. Kenneth lit a cigarette, Tom a pipe.

'I've been getting a feeling of money the last few days. Perhaps not so much money as . . .' She stopped. 'I can't say what I feel. It's no use. What do our lives add up to? That's what I want to know.'

'Why do you expect us to tell you?' asked Kenneth curiously at last.

This was a new note. Julia looked at him, puzzled. 'I don't know,' she said at last. Then, very dryly: 'I suppose I should be prepared to take the consequences for marrying the pair of you.' The men laughed uneasily though with relief that the worst seemed to be over. 'If I left this place tomorrow,' she said sadly, 'you simply wouldn't miss me.'

'Ah, you love Kenneth,' groaned Tom suddenly. The groan was so sudden, coming just as the flippant note had been struck, and successfully, that Julia could not bear it. She continued quietly, lightly, to wipe away the naked pain of Tom's voice: 'No, I don't. I wish you wouldn't talk about love.'

'That's what all this is about,' said Kenneth. 'Love.'

Julia looked at him scornfully. She said: 'What sort of people are we? Let's use bare words for bare facts, just for once.'

'Must you?' breathed Kenneth.

'Yes, I must. The fact is that I have been a sort of high-class concubine for the two of you . . .' She stopped at once. Even the beginning of the tirade sounded absurd in her own ears.

'I hope that statement has cleared your mind for you,' said Kenneth ironically.

'No, it hasn't, I didn't expect it would.' But now Julia was fighting hard against that no-man's-land of feeling in which she had been living for so long, that under-sea territory where one thing confuses with another, where it is so easy to drift at ease, according to the pull of the tides.

'I should have had children,' she said at last, quietly. 'That's where we went wrong, Tom. It was children we needed.'

'Ah,' said Kenneth from his chair, suddenly deeply sincere, 'now you are talking sense.'

'Well,' said Tom, 'there's nothing to stop us.'

'I'm too old.'

'Other women of forty have children.'

'I'm too – tired. It seems to me, to have children, one needs . . .' She stopped.

'What does one need?' asked Tom.

Julia's eyes met Kenneth's; they exchanged deep, ironic, patient understanding.

'Thank God you didn't marry me,' he said suddenly. 'You are quite right. Tom's the man for you. In a marriage it's necessary for one side to be strong enough to create the illusion.'

'What illusion?' asked Tom petulantly.

'Necessity,' said Kenneth simply.

'Is that the office this girl is going to perform for you?' asked Tom.

'Precisely. She loves me, God help her. She really does, you know . . .' Kenneth looked at them in a manner of inviting them to share his surprise at this fact. 'And she wants children. She knows why she wants them. She'll make me know it too, bless her. Most of the time,' he could not prevent himself adding.

Now it seemed impossible to go on. They remained silent, each face expressing tired and bewildered unhappiness. Julia stood against the mantelpiece, feeling the warmth of the fire running over her body, but not reaching the chill within.

Kenneth recovered first. He got up and said: 'Bed, bed for all of us. This doesn't help. We mustn't talk. We must get on, dealing with the next thing.' He said good night, and went to the door. There he turned, looked clear and full at Julia with his black, alert, shrewd eyes, and remarked: 'You must be nice to that girl, Julia.'

'You know very well I can be "nice" to her, but I won't be "nice" for her. You are deliberately submitting her to it. You won't even move two miles away on to the next farm. You won't even take that much trouble to make her happy. Remember that.'

Kenneth flushed, said hastily: 'Well, I didn't say I wouldn't go to the other farm,' and went out. Julia knew that it would take a lot of unhappiness for the four of them before he would consent to move himself. He thought of this house as his home; and he could not bear to leave Tom, even now.

'Come here,' said Tom gently, when Kenneth had left the room. She went to him, and slipped down beside him into his chair. 'Do you find me stupid?' he asked.

'Not stupid.'

'What then?'

She held him close. 'Put your arms round me.'

He held her; but she did not feel supported: the arms were as light as wind about her, and as unsure.

In the middle of the night she rose from her bed, slipped on her gown and went along the winding passages to Kenneth's bedroom, which was at the other end of the house.

It was filled with the brightness of moonlight. Kenneth was sitting up against his pillows; he was awake; she could see the light glinting on his eyes.

She sat herself down on the foot of his bed.

'Well, Julia? It's no good coming to me, you know.'

She did not reply. The confusing dimness of the moon, which hung immediately outside the window, troubled her. She held a match to the candle, and watched a warm yellow glow fill the room, so that the moon retreated and became a small hard bright coin high among the stars.

She saw on the dressing-table a new framed photograph.

'If one acquires a wife,' she said sarcastically, 'one of course acquires a photo to put on one's dressing-table.' She went over and picked it up and returned to the bed with it. Kenneth watched her, alertly.

Slowly Julia's face spread into a compassionate smile.

'What's the matter?' asked Kenneth quickly.

She was not twenty-three, Julia could see that. She was well over thirty. It was a pretty enough face, very English, with flat broad planes and small features. Fair neatly-waved hair fell away regularly from the forehead.

There was anxiety in those too-serious eyes; the mouth smiled carefully in a prepared sweetness for the photographer; the cheeks were thin. Turning the photograph to the light Julia could see how the neck was creased and furrowed. No, she was by no means a girl. She glanced at Kenneth, and was filled slowly by a sweet irrational tenderness for him, a delicious irresponsible gaiety.

'Why,' she said, 'you're in love, after all, Kenneth.'

'Whoever said I wasn't?' he grinned at her, lying watchfully back in his bed and puffing at his cigarette.

She grinned back affectionately, still lifted on a wave of delight; then she turned, and felt it ebb as she looked down at the photograph, mentally greeting this other tired woman, coming to the great rich farm, like the poor girl in the fairy story.

'What are you amused at?' asked Kenneth cautiously.

'I was thinking of you as a refuge,' she explained dryly.

'I'm quite prepared to be.'

'You'd never be a refuge for anyone.'

'Not for you. But you forget she's younger.' He laughed: 'She'll be less critical.'

She smiled without replying, looking at the pictured face. It was such a humourless, earnest, sincere face, the eyes so serious, so searching.

Julia sighed. 'I'm terribly tired,' she said to Kenneth, turning back to him.

'I know you are. So am I. That's why I'm marrying.'

Julia had a clear mental picture of this Englishwoman, who was soon coming to the farm. For a moment she allowed herself to picture her in various situations, arriving with nervous tact, hiding her longing for a home of her own, hoping not to find Julia an enemy. She would find not strife, or hostility, or scenes – none of the situations which she might be prepared to face. She would find three people who knew each other so well that for the most part they found it hardly necessary to speak. She would find indifference to everything she really was, a prepared, deliberate kindness. She would be like a latecomer to a party, entering a room where everyone is already cemented by hours of warmth and intimacy. She would be helpless against Kenneth's need for her to be something she could not be: a young woman, with the spiritual vitality to heal him.

Looking at the pretty girl in the frame which she held between her palms, the girl under whose surface prettiness Julia could see the anxious, haunted woman, the knowledge came to her of what word it was she sought: it was as though those carefully smiling lips formed themselves into that word. 'Do you know what we are?' she asked Kenneth.

'Not a notion,' he replied jauntily.

Julia accepted the word evil from that humourless, homeless girl. Twice in her life it had confronted her; this time she took it gratefully. After all, none other had been offered.

'I know what evil is,' she said to Kenneth.

'How nice for you,' he returned impatiently. Then he added: 'I suppose, like most women who have lived their own lives, whatever that might mean, you are now beginning to develop an exaggerated conscience. If so, we shall both find you very tedious.'

'Is that what I'm doing?' she asked, considering it. 'I don't think so.'

He looked at her soberly. 'Go to bed, my dear. Do stop fussing. Are you prepared to do anything about it? You aren't, are you? Then stop making us all miserable over impossibilities. We have a pleasant enough life, taking it for what it is. It's not much fun being the fag-end of something but even that has its compensations.'

Julia listened, smiling, to her own voice speaking. 'You put it admirably,' she said, as she went out of the room.

A Home for the Highland Cattle

These days when people emigrate, it is not so much in search of sunshine or food, or even servants. It is fairly safe to say that the family bound for Australia, or wherever it may be, has in its mind a vision of a nice house, or a flat, with maybe a bit of garden. I don't know how things were a hundred or fifty years ago. It seems, from books, that the colonizers and adventurers went sailing off to a new life, a new country, opportunities, and so forth. Now all they want is a roof over their heads.

An interesting thing, this: how is it that otherwise reasonable people come to believe that this same roof, that practically vanishing commodity, is freely obtainable just by packing up and going to another country? After all, headlines like World Housing Shortage are common to the point of tedium; and there is not a brochure or pamphlet issued by immigration departments that does not say (though probably in small print, throwing it away, as it were) that it is undesirable to leave home, without first making sure of a place to live.

Marina Giles left England with her husband in just this frame of mind. They had been living where they could, sharing flats and baths, and kitchens, for some years. If someone remarked enviously: 'They say that in Africa the sky is always blue,' she was likely to reply absentmindedly: 'Yes, and won't it be nice to have a proper house after all these years.'

They arrived in Southern Rhodesia, and there was a choice of an immigrants' camp, consisting of mud huts with a communal water supply, or a hotel, and they chose the hotel, being what are known as people of means. That is to say, they had a few hundred pounds, with which they had intended to buy a house as soon as they arrived. It was quite possible to buy a house, just as it is in England, provided one gives up all idea of buying a home one likes, and at a reasonable price. For years Marina had been inspecting houses. They fell into two groups, those she liked, and those she could afford. Now Marina was a romantic, she had not yet fallen into that passive state of mind which accepts (as nine-tenths of the population do) that one should find a corner to live, anywhere, and then arrange one's whole life around it, schooling for one's children, one's place of work, and so on. And since she refused to accept it, she had been living in extreme discomfort, exclaiming: 'Why should we spend all the capital we are ever likely to have tying ourselves down to a place we detest!' Nothing could be more reasonable, on the face of it.

But she had not expected to cross an ocean, enter a new and indubitably romantic-sounding country, and find herself in exactly the same position.

The city, seen from the air, is half-buried in trees. Sixty years ago, this was all bare veld; and even now it appears not as if the veld encloses an area of buildings and streets, but rather as if the houses have forced themselves up, under and among the trees. Flying low over it, one sees greenness, growth, then the white flash of a high building, the fragment of a street that has no beginning or end, for it emerges from trees, and is at once reabsorbed by them. And yet it is a large town, spreading wide and scattered, for here there is no problem of space: pressure scatters people outwards, it does not force them perpendicularly. Driving through it from suburb to suburb, is perhaps fifteen miles – some of the important cities of the world are not much less; but if one asks a person who lives there what the population is, he will say ten thousand, which is very little. Why do so small a number of people need so large a space? The inhabitant will probably shrug, for he has never wondered. The truth is that there are not ten thousand, but more likely 150,000, but the others are black, which means that they are not considered. The blacks do not so much *live* here, as squeeze themselves in as they can – all this is very confusing for the newcomer, and it takes quite a time to adjust oneself.

Perhaps every city has one particular thing by which it is known, something which sums it up, both for the people who live in it, and those who have never known it, save in books or

legend. Three hundred miles south, for instance, old Loben-
gula's kraal had the Big Tree. Under its branches sat the
betrayed, sorrowful, magnificent King in his rolls of black fat
and beads and gauds, watching his doom approach in the white
people's advance from the south, and dispensing life and death
according to known and honoured customs. That was only sixty
years ago . . .

This town has The Kopje. When the Pioneers were sent
north, they were told to trek on till they reached a large and
noble mountain they could not possibly mistake; and there they
must stop and build their city. Twenty miles too soon, due to
some confusion of mind, or perhaps to understandable exhaustion, they stopped near a small and less shapely hill. This has
rankled ever since. Each year, when the ceremonies are held
to honour those pioneers, and the vision of Rhodes who sent
them forth, the thought creeps in that this is not really what the
Founder intended . . . Standing there, at the foot of that kopje,
the speech-makers say: Sixty years, look what we have accom-
plished in sixty years. And in the minds of the listeners springs
a vision of that city we all dream of, that planned and shapely
city without stain or slum – the city that could in fact have been
created in those sixty years.

The town spread from the foot of this hill. Around it are the
slums, the narrow and crooked streets where the coloured
people eke out their short swarming lives among decaying brick
and tin. Five minutes' walk to one side, and the street peters
out in long, soiled grass, above which a power chimney pours
black smoke, and where an old petrol tin lies in a gulley, so
that a diving hawk swerves away and up, squawking, scared out
of his nature by a flash of sunlight. Ten minutes the other way
is the business centre, the dazzling white blocks of concrete,
modern buildings like modern buildings the world over. Here
are the imported clothes, the glass windows full of cars from
America, the neon lights, the counters full of pamphlets
advertising flights Home – wherever one's home might be. A
few blocks farther on, and the business part of the town is left
behind. This was once the smart area. People who have grown
with the city will drive through here on a Sunday afternoon,
and, looking at the bungalows raised on their foundations and

ornamented with iron scrollwork, will say: In 1910 there was nothing beyond this house but bare veld.

Now, however, there are more houses, small and ugly houses, until all at once we are in the 'thirties, with tall houses eight to a block, like very big soldiers standing to attention in a small space. The verandas have gone. Tiny balconies project like eyelids, the roofs are like bowler hats, rimless. Exposed to the blistering sun, these houses crowd together without invitation to shade or coolness, for they were not planned for this climate, and until the trees grow, and the creepers spread, they are extremely uncomfortable. (Though, of course, very smart.) Beyond these? The veld again, wastes of grass clotted with the dung of humans and animals, a vlei that is crossed and criss-crossed by innumerable footpaths where the Africans walk in the afternoon from suburb to suburb, stopping to snatch a mouthful of water in cupped palms from potholes filmed with iridescent oil, for safety against mosquitoes.

Over the vlei (which is rapidly being invaded by building, so that soon there will be no open spaces left) is a new suburb. Now, this is something quite different. Where the houses, only twenty minutes' walk away, stood eight to a block, now there are twenty tiny, flimsy little houses, and the men who planned them had in mind the cheap houses along the ribbon roads of England. Small patches of roofed cement, with room, perhaps, for a couple of chairs, call themselves verandas. There is a hall a couple of yards square – for otherwise where should one hang one's hat? Each little house is divided into rooms so small that there is no space to move from one wall to the other without circling a table or stumbling over a chair. And white walls, glaring white walls, so that one's eyes turn in relief to the trees.

The trees – these houses are intolerable unless foliage softens and hides them. Any new owner, moving in, says wistfully: It won't be so bad when the shrubs grow up. And they grow very quickly. It is an extraordinary thing that this town, which must be one of the most graceless and inconvenient in existence, considered simply as an association of streets and buildings, is so beautiful that no one fails to fall in love with it at first sight. Every street is lined and double-lined with trees, every house screened with brilliant growth. It is a city of gardens.

Marina was at first enchanted. Then her mood changed. For the only houses they could afford were in those mass-produced suburbs, that were spreading like measles as fast as materials could be imported to build them. She said to Philip: 'In England, we did not buy a house because we did not want to live in a suburb. We uproot ourselves, come to a reputedly exotic and wild country, and the only place we can afford to live is another suburb. I'd rather be dead.'

Philip listened. He was not as upset as she was. They were rather different. Marina was that liberally-minded person produced so plentifully in England during the 'thirties, while Philip was a scientist, and put his faith in techniques, rather than in the inherent decency of human beings. He was, it is true, in his own way an idealist, for he had come to this continent in a mood of fine optimism. England, it seemed to him, did not offer opportunities to young men equipped, as he was, with enthusiasm and so much training. Things would be different overseas. All that was necessary was a go-ahead Government prepared to vote sufficient money to Science – this was just common sense. (Clearly, a new country was likely to have more common sense than an old one.) He was prepared to make gardens flourish where deserts had been. Africa appeared to him eminently suitable for this treatment; and the more he saw of it, those first few weeks, the more enthusiastic he became.

But he soon came to understand that in the evenings when he propounded these ideas to Marina, her mind was elsewhere. It seemed to him bad luck that they should be in this hotel, which was uncomfortable, with bad food, and packed by fellow-immigrants all desperately searching for that legendary roof. But a house would turn up sooner or later – he had been convinced of this for years. He would not have objected to buying one of those suburban houses. He did not like them, certainly, but he knew quite well that it was not the house, as such, that Marina revolted against. Ah, this feeling we all have about the suburbs! How we dislike the thought of being just like the fellow next door! Bad luck, when the whole world rapidly fills with suburbs, for what is a British Colony but a sort of highly-flavoured suburb to England itself? Somewhere in the back of Marina's mind had been a vision of herself and Philip living in a group of amiable people, pleasantly interested in the arts, who read the *New Statesman* week by week, and held that discreditable phenomena like the colour bar and the black–white struggle could be solved by sufficient goodwill . . . a delightful picture.

Temporarily Philip turned his mind from thoughts of blossoming deserts, and so on, and tried another approach. Perhaps they could buy a house through one of the Schemes for Immigrants? He would return from this Housing Board or that, and say in a worried voice: 'There isn't a hope unless one has three children.' At this, Marina was likely to become depressed; for she still held the old-fashioned view that before one has children one should have a house to put them in.

'It's all very well for you,' said Marina. 'As far as I can see you'll be spending half your time gallivanting in your lorry from one end of the country to the other, visiting native reserves, and having a lovely time. I don't *mind*, but I have to make some sort of life for myself while you do it.' Philip looked rather guilty; for in fact he was away three or four days a week, on trips with fellow experts, and Marina would be very often left alone.

'Perhaps we could find somewhere temporary, while we wait for a house to turn up?' he suggested.

This offered itself quite soon. Philip heard from a man he met casually that there was a flat available for three months, but he wouldn't swear to it, because it was only an overheard remark at a sundowner party – Philip followed the trail, clinched the deal, and returned to Marina. 'It's only for three months,' he comforted her.

138 Cecil John Rhodes Vista was in that part of the town built before the sudden expansion in the 'thirties. These were all old houses, unfashionable, built to no important recipe, but according to the whims of the first owners. On one side of 138 was a house whose roof curved down, Chinese fashion, built on a platform for protection against ants, with wooden steps. Its walls were of wood, and it was possible to hear feet tramping over the wooden floors even in the street outside. The other neighbour was a house whose walls were invisible under a mass of golden shower – thick yellow clusters, like smoky honey,

dripped from roof to ground. The houses opposite were hidden by massed shrubs.

From the street, all but the roof of 138 was screened by a tall and straggling hedge. The sidewalks were dusty grass, scattered with faggots of dogs' dirt, so that one had to walk carefully. Outside the gate was a great clump of bamboo reaching high into the sky, and all the year round weaverbirds' nests, like woven-grass cricket balls, dangled there bouncing and swaying in the wind. Near it reached the angled brown sticks of the frangipani, breaking into white and a creamy pink, as if a young coloured girl held armfuls of blossom. The street itself was double-lined with trees, first jacaranda, fine green lace against the blue sky, and behind heavy dark masses of the cedrilatoona. All the way down the street were bursts of colour, a drape of purple bougainvillaea, the sparse scarlet flowers of the hibiscus. It was very beautiful, very peaceful.

Once inside the unkempt hedge, 138 was exposed as a shallow brick building, tin-roofed, like an elongated barn, that occupied the centre of two building stands, leaving plenty of space for front and back yards. It had a history. Some twenty years back, some enterprising businessman had built the place, ignoring every known rule of hygiene, in the interests of economy. By the time the local authorities had come to notice its unfitness to exist, the roof was on. There followed a series of court cases. An exhausted judge had finally remarked that there was a housing shortage; and on this basis the place was allowed to remain.

It was really eight semi-detached houses, stuck together in such a way that standing before the front door of any one, it was possible to see clear through the two rooms which composed each, to the back yard, where washing flapped over the woodpile. A veranda enclosed the front of the building: eight short flights of steps, eight front doors, eight windows – but these windows illuminated the front rooms only. The back room opened into a porch that was screened in by dull green mosquito gauze; and in this way the architect had achieved the really remarkable feat of producing, in a country continually drenched by sunlight, rooms in which it was necessary to have the lights burning all day.

The back yard, a space of bare dust enclosed by parallel hibiscus hedges, was a triumph of individualism over communal living. Eight separate woodpiles, eight clothes-lines, eight short paths edged with brick leading to the eight lavatories that were built side by side like segments of chocolate, behind an enclosing tin screen: the locks (and therefore the keys) were identical, for the sake of cheapness, a system which guaranteed strife among the inhabitants. On either side of the lavatories were two rooms, built as a unit. In these four rooms lived eight native servants. At least officially there were eight, in practice far more.

When Marina, a woman who took her responsibilities seriously, as has been indicated, looked inside the room which her servant shared with the servant from next door, she exclaimed helplessly: 'Dear me, how awful!' The room was very small. The brick walls were unplastered, the tin of the roof bare, focusing the sun's intensity inwards all day, so that even while she stood on the threshold, she began to feel a little faint because of the enclosed heat. The floor was cement, and the blankets that served as beds lay directly on it. No cupboards or shelves: these were substituted by a string stretching from corner to corner. Two small, high windows, whose glass was cracked and pasted with paper. On the walls were pictures of the English royal family, torn out of illustrated magazines, and of various female film stars, mostly unclothed.

'Dear me,' said Marina again, vaguely. She was feeling very guilty, because of this squalor. She came out of the room with relief, wiping the sweat from her face, and looked around the yard. Seen from the back, 138 Cecil John Rhodes Vista was undeniably picturesque. The yard, enclosed by low, scarlet-flowering hibiscus hedges, was of dull red earth; the piles of grey wood were each surrounded by a patch of scattered chips, yellow, orange, white. The colourful washing lines swung and danced. The servants, in their crisp white, leaned on their axes, or gossiped. There was a little black nurse-girl seated on one of the logs, under a big tree, with a white child in her arms. A delightful scene, it would have done as it was for the opening number of a musical comedy. Marina turned her back on it; and with her stern reformer's eye looked again at the end of the yard. In the space between the lavatories and the servants' rooms stood eight rubbish cans, each covered by its cloud of flies, and exuding a stale sour smell. She walked through them into the sanitary lane. Now if one drives down the streets of such a city, one sees the trees, the gardens, the flowering hedges; the streets form neat squares. Squares (one might suppose) filled with blossoms and greenness, in which the houses are charmingly arranged. But each block is divided down the middle by a sanitary lane, a dust lane, which is lined by rubbish cans, and in this the servants have their social life. Here they go for a quick smoke, in the middle of the day's work; here they meet their friends, or flirt with the women who sell vegetables. It is as if, between each of the streets of the white man's city, there is a hidden street, ignored, forgotten. Marina, emerging into it, found it swarming with gossiping and laughing Africans. They froze, gave her a long suspicious stare, and all at once seemed to vanish, escaping into their respective back yards. In a moment she was alone.

She walked slowly back across the yard to her back door, picking her way among the soft litter from the woodpiles, ducking her head under the flapping clothes. She was watched, cautiously, by the servants, who were suspicious of this sudden curiosity about their way of life – experience had taught them to be suspicious. She was watched, also, by several of the women, through their kitchen windows. They saw a small Englishwoman, with a neat and composed body, pretty fair hair, and a pink and white face under a large straw hat, which she balanced in position with a hand clothed in a white glove. She moved delicately and with obvious distaste through the dust, as if at any moment she might take wings and fly away altogether.

When she reached her back steps, she stopped and called: 'Charlie! Come here a moment, please.' It was a high voice, a little querulous. When they heard the accents of that voice, saw the white glove, and noted that *please* the watching women found all their worst fears confirmed.

A young African emerged from the sanitary lane where he had been gossiping (until interrupted by Marina's appearance) with some passing friends. He ran to his new mistress. He wore white shorts, a scarlet American-style shirt, tartan socks which were secured by mauve suspenders, and white tennis shoes. He stopped before her with a polite smile, which almost at once spread into a grin of pure friendliness. He was an amiable and cheerful young man by temperament. This was Marina's first morning in her new home, and she was already conscious of the disproportion between her strong pity for her servant, and that inveterately cheerful face.

She did not, of course, speak any native language, but Charlie spoke English.

'Charlie, how long have you been working here?'

'Two years, madam.'

'Where do you come from?'

'Madam?'

'Where is your home?'

'Nyasaland.'

'Oh.' For this was hundreds of miles north.

'Do you go home to visit your family?'

'Perhaps this year, madam.'

'I see. Do you like it here?'

'Madam?' A pause; and he involuntarily glanced back over the rubbish cans at the sanitary lane. He hoped that his friends, who worked on the other side of the town, and whom he did not often see, would not get tired of waiting for him. He hoped, too, that this new mistress (whose politeness to him he did not trust) was not going to choose this moment to order him to clean the silver or do the washing. He continued to grin, but his face was a little anxious, and his eyes rolled continually backwards at the sanitary lane.

'I hope you will be happy working for me,' said Marina.

'Oh, yes, madam,' he said at once, disappointedly; for clearly she was going to tell him to work.

'If there is anything you want, you must ask me. I am new to this country, and I may make mistakes.'

He hesitated, handling the words in his mind. But they were difficult, and he let them slip. He did not think in terms of countries, of continents. He knew the white man's town – this town. He knew the veld. He knew the village from which he came. He knew, from his educated friends, that there was 'a

big water' across which the white man came in ships: he had
seen pictures of ships in old magazines, but this 'big water' was
confused in his mind with the great lake in his own country. He
understood that these white people came from places called
England, Germany, Europe, but these were names to him.
Once, a friend of his who had been three years to a mission
school had said that Africa was one of several continents, and
had shown him a tattered sheet of paper – one half of the map
of the world – saying: Here is Africa, here is England, here is
India. He pointed out Nyasaland, a tiny strip of country, and
Charlie felt confused and diminished, for Nyasaland was what
he knew, and it seemed to him so vast. Now, when Marina
used the phrase 'this country' Charlie saw, for a moment, this
flat piece of paper, tinted pink and green and blue – the world.
But from the sanitary lane came shouts of laughter – again he
glanced anxiously over his shoulder; and Marina was conscious
of a feeling remarkably like irritation. 'Well, you may go,' she
said formally; and saw his smile flash white right across his face.
He turned, and ran back across the yard like an athlete, clearing
the woodpile, then the rubbish cans, in a series of great bounds,
and vanished behind the lavatories. Marina went inside her
'flat' with what was, had she known it, an angry frown.
'Disgraceful,' she muttered, including in this condemnation the
bare room in which this man was expected to fit his life, the
dirty sanitary lane bordered with stinking rubbish cans, and
also his unreasonable cheerfulness.

Inside, she forgot him in her own discomfort. It was a truly
shocking place. The two small rooms were so made that the
inter-leading door was in the centre of the wall. They were
more like passages than rooms. She switched on the light in
what would be the bedroom, and put her hand to her cheek,
for it stung where the sun had caught her unaccustomed skin
through the chinks of the straw of her hat. The furniture was
really beyond description! Two iron bedsteads, on either side
of the door, a vast chocolate-brown wardrobe, whose door
would not properly shut, one dingy straw mat that slid this way
and that over the slippery boards as one walked on it. And the
front room! If possible, it was even worse. An enormous
cretonne-covered sofa, like a solidified flower bed, a hard and

shiny table stuck in the middle of the floor, so that one must walk carefully around it, and four straight, hard chairs, ranged like soldiers against the wall. And the pictures – she did not know such pictures still existed. There was a desert scene, done in coloured cloth, behind glass; a motto in woven straw, also framed in glass, saying: *Welcome all who come in here, Good luck to you and all good cheer.*

There was also a very large picture of highland cattle. Half a dozen of these shaggy and ferocious creatures glared down at her from where they stood knee-deep in sunset-tinted pools. One might imagine that pictures of highland cattle no longer existed outside of Victorian novels, or remote suburban boarding-houses – but no, here they were. Really, why bother to emigrate?

She almost marched over and wrenched that picture from the wall. A curious inhibition prevented her. It was, though she did not know it, the spirit of the building. Some time later she heard Mrs Black, who had been living for years in the next flat with her husband and three children, remark grimly: 'My front door handle has been stuck for weeks, but I'm not going to mend it. If I start doing the place up, it means I'm here for ever.' Marina recognized her own feeling when she heard these words. It accounted for the fact that while the families here were all respectable, in the sense that they owned cars, and could expect a regular monthly income, if one looked through the neglected hedge it was impossible not to conclude that every person in the building was born sloven or slut. No one really lived here. They might have been here for years, without prospect of anything better, but they did not live here.

There was one exception, Mrs Pond, who painted her walls and mended what broke. It was felt she let everyone else down. In front of *her* steps a narrow path edged with brick led to her segment of yard, which was perhaps two feet across, in which lilies and roses were held upright by trellis work, like a tall, green sandwich standing at random in the dusty yard.

Marina thought: Well, what's the point? I'm not going to *live* here. The picture could stay. Similarly, she decided there was no sense in unpacking her nice curtains or her books. And the furniture might remain as it was, for it was too awful to waste effort on it. Her thoughts returned to the servants' rooms at the back: it was a disgrace. The whole system was disgraceful.

At this point, Mrs Pond knocked perfunctorily and entered. She was a short, solid woman, tied in at the waist, like a tight sausage, by the string of her apron. She had hard red cheeks, a full hard bosom, and energetic red hands. Her eyes were small and inquisitive. Her face was ill-tempered, perhaps because she could not help knowing she was disliked. She was used to the disapproving eyes of her fellow tenants, watching her attend to her strip of 'garden'; or while she swept the narrow strip across the back yard that was her path from the back door to her lavatory. There she stood, every morning, among the washing and the woodpiles, wearing a pink satin dressing-gown trimmed with swansdown, among the clouds of dust stirred up by her yard broom, returning defiant glances for the disapproving ones; and later she would say: 'Two rooms is quite enough for a woman by herself. I'm quite satisfied.'

She had no right to be satisfied, or at any rate, to say so . . .

But for a woman contented with her lot, there was a look in those sharp eyes which could too easily be diagnosed as envy; and when she said, much too sweetly: 'You are an old friend of Mrs Skinner, maybe?' Marina recognized, with the exhaustion that comes to everyone who has lived too long in overfull buildings, the existence of conspiracy. 'I have never met Mrs Skinner,' she said briefly. 'She said she was coming here this morning to make arrangements.'

Now, arrangements had been made already, with Philip; and Marina knew Mrs Skinner was coming to inspect herself; and this thought irritated her.

'She is a nice lady,' said Mrs Pond. 'She's my friend. We two have been living here longer than anyone else.' Her voice was sour. Marina followed the direction of her eyes, and saw a large white door set into the wall. A built-in cupboard, in fact. She had already noted that cupboard as the only sensible amenity the 'flat' possessed.

'That's a nice cupboard,' said Mrs Pond.

'Have all the flats got built-in cupboards?'

'Oh, no. Mrs Skinner had this put in special last year. She

paid for it. Not the landlord. You don't catch the landlord paying for anything.'

'I see,' said Marina.

'Mrs Skinner promised me this flat,' said Mrs Pond.

Marina made no reply. She looked at her wrist-watch. It was a beautiful gesture; she even felt a little guilty because of the pointedness of it; but Mrs Pond promptly said: 'It's eleven o'clock. The clock just struck.'

'I must finish the unpacking,' said Marina.

Mrs Pond seated herself on the flowery sofa, and remarked: 'There's always plenty to do when you move in. That cupboard will save you plenty of space. Mrs Skinner kept her linen in it. I was going to put all my clothes in. You're Civil Service, so I hear?'

'Yes,' said Marina. She could not account for the grudging tone of that last apparently irrelevant question. She did not know that in this country the privileged class was the Civil Service, or considered to be. No aristocracy, no class distinctions – but alas, one must have something to hate, and the Civil Service does as well as anything. She added: 'My husband chose this country rather than the Gold Coast, because it seems the climate is better even though the pay is bad.'

This remark was received with the same sceptical smile that she would have earned in England had she been tactless enough to say to her charwoman: Death duties spell the doom of the middle classes.

'You have to be in the Service to get what's going,' said Mrs Pond, with what she imagined to be a friendly smile. 'The Service gets all the plums.' And she glanced at the cupboard.

'I think,' said Marina icily, 'that you are under some misapprehension. My husband happened to hear of this flat by chance.'

'There were plenty of people waiting for this flat,' said Mrs Pond reprovingly. 'The lady next door, Mrs Black, would have been glad of it. And she's got three children, too. You have no children, perhaps?'

'Mrs Pond, I have no idea at all why Mrs Skinner gave us this flat when she had promised it to Mrs Black . . .'

'Oh no, she had promised it to me. It was a faithful promise.'

At this moment another lady entered the room without knocking. She was an ample, middle-aged person, in tight corsets, with rigidly-waved hair, and a sharp, efficient face that was now scarlet from heat. She said peremptorily: 'Excuse me for coming in without knocking, but I can't get used to a stranger being here when I've lived here so long.' Suddenly she saw Mrs Pond, and at once stiffened into aggression. 'I see you have already made friends with Mrs Pond,' she said, giving that lady a glare.

Mrs Pond was standing, hands on hips, in the traditional attitude of combat; but she squeezed a smile on to her face and said: 'I'm making acquaintance.'

'Well,' said Mrs Skinner, dismissing her, 'I'm going to discuss business with my tenant.'

Mrs Pond hesitated. Mrs Skinner gave her a long, quelling stare. Mrs Pond slowly deflated, and went to the door. From the veranda floated back the words: 'When people make promises, they should keep them, that's what I say, instead of giving it to people new to the country, and civil servants . . .'

Mrs Skinner waited until the loud and angry voice faded, and then said briskly: 'If you take my advice, you'll have nothing to do with Mrs Pond, she's more trouble than she's worth.'

Marina now understood that she owed this flat to the fact that this highly-coloured lady decided to let it to a stranger simply in order to spite all her friends in the building who hoped to inherit that beautiful cupboard, if only for three months. Mrs Skinner was looking suspiciously around her; she said at last: 'I wouldn't like to think my things weren't looked after.'

'Naturally not,' said Marina politely.

'When I spoke to your husband we were rather in a hurry. I hope you will make yourself comfortable, but I don't want to have anything altered.'

Marina maintained a polite silence.

Mrs Skinner marched to the inbuilt cupboard, opened it, and found it empty. 'I paid a lot of money to have this fitted,' she said in an aggrieved voice.

'We only came in yesterday,' said Marina. 'I haven't unpacked yet.'

'You'll find it very useful,' said Mrs Skinner. 'I paid for it myself. Some people would have made allowances in the rent.'

'I think the rent is quite high enough,' said Marina, joining battle at last.

Clearly, this note of defiance was what Mrs Skinner had been waiting for. She made use of the familiar weapon: 'There are plenty of people who would have been glad of it, I can tell you.'

'So I gather.'

'I could let it tomorrow.'

'But,' said Marina, in the high formal voice, 'you have in fact let it to us, and the lease has been signed, so there is no more to be said, is there?'

Mrs Skinner hesitated, and finally contented herself by repeating: 'I hope my furniture will be looked after. I said in the lease nothing must be altered.'

Suddenly Marina found herself saying: 'Well, I shall of course move the furniture to suit myself, and hang my own pictures.'

'This flat is let furnished, and I'm very fond of my pictures.'

'But you will be away, won't you?' This, a sufficiently crude way of saying: 'But it is we who will be looking at the pictures, and not you,' misfired completely, for Mrs Skinner merely said: 'Yes, I like my pictures, and I don't like to think of them being packed.'

Marina looked at the highland cattle and, though not half an hour before she had decided to leave it, said now: 'I should like to take that one down.'

Mrs Skinner clasped her hands together before her, in a pose of simple devotion, compressed her lips, and stood staring mournfully up at the picture. 'That picture means a lot to me. It used to hang in the parlour when I was a child, back Home. It was my granny's picture first. When I married Mr Skinner, my mother packed it and sent it especially over the sea, knowing how I was fond of it. It's moved with me everywhere I've been. I wouldn't like to think of it being treated bad, I wouldn't really.'

'Oh, very well,' said Marina, suddenly exhausted. What, after all, did it matter?

Mrs Skinner gave her a doubtful look: was it possible she

had won her point so easily? 'You must keep an eye on Charlie,' she went on. 'The number of times I've told him he'd poke his broom-handle through that picture . . .'

Hope flared in Marina. There was an extraordinary amount of glass. It seemed that the entire wall was surfaced by angry shaggy cattle. Accidents did happen . . .

'You must keep an eye on Charlie, anyway. He never does a stroke more than he has to. He's bred bone lazy. You'd better keep an eye on the food too. He steals. I had to have the police to him only last month, when I lost my garnet brooch. Of course he swore he hadn't taken it, but I've never laid my hands on it since. My husband gave him a good hiding, but Master Charlie came up smiling as usual.'

Marina, revolted by this tale, raised her eyebrows disapprovingly. 'Indeed?' she said, in her coolest voice.

Mrs Skinner looked at her, as if to say: What are you making that funny face for? She remarked: 'They're all born thieves and liars. You shouldn't trust them farther than you can kick them. I'm warning you. Of course, you're new here. Only last week a friend was saying, I'm surprised at you letting to people just from England, they always spoil the servants, with their ideas, and I said: "Oh, Mr Giles is a sensible man, I trust him."' This last was said pointedly.

'I don't think,' remarked Marina coldly, 'that you would be well-advised to trust my husband to give people "hidings".' She delicately isolated this word. 'I rather feel, in similar circumstances, that even if he did, he would first make sure whether the man had, in fact, stolen the brooch.'

Mrs Skinner disentangled this sentence and in due course gave Marina a distrustful stare. 'Well,' she said, 'it's too late now, and everyone has his way, but of course this is my furniture, and if it is stolen or damaged, you are responsible.'

'That, I should have thought, went without saying,' said Marina.

They shook hands, with formality, and Mrs Skinner went out. She returned from the veranda twice, first to say that Marina must not forget to fumigate the native quarters once a month if she didn't want livestock brought into her own flat . . . ('Not that I care if they want to live with lice, dirty creatures, but you have to protect yourself . . .'); and the second time to say that after you've lived in a place for years, it was hard to leave it, even for a holiday, and she was really regretting the day she let it at all. She gave Marina a final accusing and sorrowful look, as if the flat had been stolen from her, and this time finally departed. Marina was left in a mood of defiant anger, looking at the highland cattle picture, which had assumed, during this exchange, the look of a battleground. 'Really,' she said aloud to herself. 'Really! One might have thought that one would be entitled to pack away a picture, if one rents a place . . .'

Two days later she got a note from Mrs Skinner, saying that she hoped Marina would be happy in the flat, she must remember to keep an eye on Mrs Pond, who was a real troublemaker, and she must remember to look after the picture – Mrs Skinner positively could not sleep for worrying about it.

Since Marina had decided she was not living here, there was comparatively little unpacking to be done. Things were stored. She had more than ever the appearance of a migrating bird who dislikes the twig it has chosen to alight on, but is rather too exhausted to move to another.

But she did read the advertisement columns every day, which were exactly like those in the papers back home. The *accommodation wanted* occupied a full column, while the *accommodation offered* usually did not figure at all. When houses were advertised they usually cost between five and twelve thousand – Marina saw some of them. They were very beautiful; if one had five thousand pounds what a happy life one might lead – but the same might be said of any country. She also paid another visit to one of the new suburbs, and returned shuddering. 'What!' she exclaimed to Philip. 'Have we emigrated in order that I may spend the rest of life gossiping and taking tea with women like Mrs Black and Mrs Skinner?'

'Perhaps they aren't all like that,' he suggested absent-mindedly. For he was quite absorbed in his work. This country was fascinating! He was spending his days in his Government lorry, rushing over hundreds of miles of veld, visiting native reserves and settlements. Never had soil been so misused! Thousands of acres of it, denuded, robbed, fit for nothing, cattle and human beings crowded together – the solution, of course, was perfectly obvious. All one had to do was – and if the Government had any sense –

Marina understood that Philip was acclimatized. One does not speak of the 'Government' with that particular mixture of affection and exasperation unless one feels at home. But she was not at all at home. She found herself playing with the idea of buying one of those revolting little houses. After all, one has to live somewhere . . .

Almost every morning, in 138, one might see a group of women standing outside one or other of the flats, debating how to rearrange the rooms. The plan of the building being so eccentric, no solution could possibly be satisfactory, and as soon as everything had been moved around, it was bound to be just as uncomfortable as before. 'If I move the bookcase behind the door, then perhaps . . .' Or: 'It might be better if I put it into the bathroom . . .'

The problem was: Where should one eat? If the dining-table was in the front room, then the servant had to come through the bedroom with the food. On the other hand, if one had the front room as bedroom, then visitors had to walk through it to the living-room. Marina kept Mrs Skinner's arrangement. On the back porch, which was the width of a passage, stood a collapsible card-table. When it was set up, Philip sat crouched under the window that opened inwards over his head, while Marina shrank sideways into the bathroom door as Charlie came past with the vegetables. To serve food, Charlie put on a starched white coat, red fez, and white cotton gloves. In between courses he stood just behind them, in the kitchen door, while Marina and Philip ate in state, if discomfort.

Marina found herself becoming increasingly sensitive to what she imagined was his attitude of tolerance. It seemed ridiculous that the ritual of soup, fish, and sweet, silver and glass and fish-knives, should continue under such circumstances. She began to wonder how it all appeared to this young man, who, as soon as their meal was finished, took an enormous pot of mealie porridge off the stove and retired with it to his room, where he shared it (eating with his fingers and squatting on the floor) with the servant from next door, and any of his friends or relatives who happened to be out of work at the time.

That no such thoughts entered the heads of the other inhabitants was clear; and Marina could understand how necessary it was to banish them as quickly as possible. On the other hand . . .

There was something absurd in a system which allowed a healthy young man to spend his life in her kitchen, so that she might do nothing. Besides, it was more trouble than it was worth. Before she and Philip rose, Charlie walked around the outside of the building, and into the front room, and cleaned it. But as the wall was thin and he energetic, they were awakened every morning by the violent banging of his broom and the scraping of furniture. On the other hand, if it were left till they woke up, where should Marina sit while he cleaned it? On the bed, presumably, in the dark bedroom, till he had finished? It seemed to her that she spent half her time arranging her actions so that she might not get in Charlie's way while he cleaned or cooked. But she had learned better than to suggest doing her own work. On one of Mrs Pond's visits, she had spoken with disgust of certain immigrants from England, who had so far forgotten what was due to their position as white people as to dispense with servants. Marina felt it was hardly worth while upsetting Mrs Pond for such a small matter. Particularly, of course, as it was only for three months . . .

But upset Mrs Pond she did, and almost immediately.

When it came to the end of the month, when Charlie's wages were due, and she laid out the twenty shillings he earned, she was filled with guilt. She really could not pay him such an idiotic sum for a whole month's work. But were twenty-five shillings, or thirty, any less ridiculous? She paid him twenty-five and saw him beam with amazed surprise. He had been planning to ask for a rise, since this woman was easygoing, and he naturally optimistic; but to get a rise without asking for it, and then a full five shillings! Why, it had taken him three months of hard bargaining with Mrs Skinner to get raised from seventeen and sixpence to nineteen shillings. 'Thank you, madam,' he said hastily; grabbing the money as if at any moment she might change her mind and take it back. Later that same day, she saw that he was wearing a new pair of crimson satin garters, and felt rather annoyed. Surely those five shillings might have been more sensibly spent? What these unfortunate people needed was an education in civilized values – but before she could pursue the thought, Mrs Pond entered looking aggrieved.

It appeared that Mrs Pond's servant had also demanded a rise, from his nineteen shillings. If Charlie could earn twenty-five shillings, why not he? Marina understood that Mrs Pond was speaking for all the women in the building.

'You shouldn't spoil them,' she said. 'I know you are from England, and all that, but . . .'

'It seems to me they are absurdly underpaid,' said Marina.

'Before the war they were lucky to get ten bob. They're never satisfied.'

'Well, according to the cost-of-living index, the value of money has halved,' said Marina. But as even the Government had not come to terms with this official and indisputable fact, Mrs Pond could not be expected to, and she said crossly: 'All you people are the same, you come here with your fancy ideas.'

Marina was conscious that every time she left her rooms, she was followed by resentful eyes. Besides, she was feeling a little ridiculous. Crimson satin garters, really!

She discussed the thing with Philip, and decided that payment in kind was more practical. She arranged that Charlie should be supplied, in addition to a pound of meat twice a week, with vegetables. Once again Mrs Pond came on a deputation of protest. All the natives in the building were demanding vegetables. 'They aren't used to it,' she complained. 'Their stomachs aren't like ours. They don't need vegetables. You're just putting ideas into their heads.'

'According to the regulations,' Marina pointed out in that high clear voice, 'Africans should be supplied with vegetables.'

'Where did you get that from?' said Mrs Pond suspiciously.

Marina produced the regulations, which Mrs Pond read in grim silence. 'The Government doesn't have to pay for it,' she pointed out, very aggrieved. And then, 'They're getting out of hand, that's what it is. There'll be trouble, you mark my words . . .'

Marina completed her disgrace on the day when she bought a second-hand iron bedstead and installed it in Charlie's room. That her servant should have to sleep on the bare cement floor, wrapped in a blanket, this she could no longer tolerate. As for Charlie, he accepted his good fortune fatalistically. He could not understand Marina. She appeared to feel guilty about telling him to do the simplest thing, such as clearing away cobwebs he had forgotten. Mrs Skinner would have docked his wages, and Mr Skinner cuffed him. This woman presented him with a new bed on the day that he broke her best cut-glass bowl.

He bought himself some new ties, and began swaggering around the back yard among the other servants, whose attitude towards him was as one might expect; one did not expect justice from the white man, whose ways were incomprehensible, but there should be a certain proportion: why should Charlie be the one to chance on an employer who presented him with a fine bed, extra meat, vegetables, and gave him two afternoons off a week instead of one? They looked unkindly at Charlie, as he swanked across the yard in his fine new clothes; they might even shout sarcastic remarks after him. But Charlie was too good-natured and friendly a person to relish such a situation. He made a joke of it, in self-defence, as Marina soon learned.

She had discovered that there was no need to share the complicated social life of the building in order to find out what went on. If, for instance, Mrs Pond had quarrelled with a neighbour over some sugar that had not been returned, so that all the women were taking sides, there was no need to listen to Mrs Pond herself to find the truth. Instead, one went to the kitchen window overlooking her back yard, hid oneself behind the curtain, and peered out at the servants.

There they stood, leaning on their axes, or in the intervals of pegging the washing, a group of laughing and gesticulating men, who were creating the new chapter in that perpetually unrolling saga, the extraordinary life of the white people, their masters, in 138 Cecil John Rhodes Vista . . .

February, Mrs Pond's servant, stepped forward, while the others fell back in a circle around him, already grinning appreciatively. He thrust out his chest, stuck out his chin, and over a bad-tempered face he stretched his mouth in a smile so poisonously ingratiating that his audience roared and slapped their knees with delight. He was Mrs Pond, one could not mistake it. He minced over to an invisible person, put on an attitude of supplication, held out his hand, received something in it. He returned to the centre of the circle, and looked at what he held with a triumphant smile. In one hand he held an invisible cup, with the other he spooned in invisible sugar. He was Mrs Pond, drinking her tea, with immense satisfaction, in small dainty sips. Then he belched, rubbed his belly, smacked his lips. Entering into the game another servant came forward, and acted a falsely amiable woman: hands on hips, the jutting elbows, the whole angry body showing indignation, but the face was smiling. February drew himself up, nodded and smiled, turned himself about, lifted something from the air behind him, and began pouring it out: sugar, one could positively hear it trickling. He took the container, and handed it proudly to the waiting visitor. But just as it was taken from him, he changed his mind. A look of agonized greed came over his face, and he withdrew the sugar. Hastily turning himself back, throwing furtive glances over his shoulder, he poured back some of the sugar, then, slowly, as if it hurt to do it, he forced himself round, held out the sugar, and again – just as it left his hand, he grabbed it and poured back just a little more. The other servants were rolling with laughter, as the two men faced each other in the centre of the yard, one indignant, but still polite, screwing up his eyes at the returned sugar, as if there were too small a quantity to be seen, while February held it out at arm's length, his face contorted with the agony it caused him to return it at all. Suddenly the two sprang together, faced each other like a pair of angry hens, and began screeching and flailing their arms.

'February!' came a shout from Mrs Pond's flat, in her loud, shrill voice, 'February, I told you to do the ironing!'

'Madam!' said February, in his politest voice. He walked backwards to the steps, his face screwed up in a grimace of martyred suffering; as he reached the steps, his body fell into the pose of a willing servant, and he walked hastily into the kitchen, where Mrs Pond was waiting for him.

But the other servants remained, unwilling to drop the game. There was a moment of indecision. They glanced guiltily at the back of the building: perhaps some of the other women were watching? No, complete silence. It was mid-morning, the sun poured down, the shadows lay deep under the big tree, the sap crystallized into little rivulets like burnt toffee on the wood chips, and sent a warm fragrance mingling into the odours of dust and warmed foliage. For the moment, they could not think of anything to do, they might as well go on with the wood-chopping. One yawned, another lifted his axe and let it fall into a log of wood, where it was held, vibrating. He plucked the handle, and it thrummed like a deep guitar note. At once, delightedly, the men gathered around the embedded axe. One twanged it, and the others began to sing. At first Marina was unable to make out the words. Then she heard:

> There's a man who comes to our house,
> When poppa goes away,
> Poppa comes back and . . .

The men were laughing, and looking at No. 4 of the flats, where a certain lady was housed whose husband worked on the railways. They sang it again:

> There's a man who comes to this house,
> Every single day,
> The baas comes back, and
> The man goes away . . .

Marina found that she was angry. Really! The thing had turned into another drama. Charlie, her own servant, was driving an imaginary engine across the yard, chuff chuff, like a child, while two of the others, seated on a log of wood, were really, it was positively obscene!

Marina came away from the window, and reasoned with herself. She was using, in her mind, one of the formulae of the country: *What can one expect?*

At this moment, while she was standing beside the kitchen table, arguing with her anger, she heard the shrill cry: 'Peas! Nice potatoes! Cabbage! Ver' chip!'

Yes, she needed vegetables. She went to the back door. There stood a native woman with a baby on her back, carefully unslinging the sacks of vegetables which she had supported over her shoulder. She opened the mouth of one, displaying the soft mass of green pea-pods.

'How much?'

'Only one sheeling,' said the woman hopefully.

'What!' began Marina, in protest; for this was twice what the shops charged. Then she stopped. Poor woman. No woman should have to carry a heavy child on her back, and great sacks of vegetables from house to house, street to street, all day 'Give me a pound,' she said. Using a tin cup, the woman ladled out a small quantity of peas. Marina nearly insisted on weighing them; then she remembered how Mrs Pond brought her scales out to the back door, on these occasions, shouting abuse at the vendor, if there was short weight. She took in the peas, and brought out a shilling. The woman, who had not expected this, gave Marina a considering look and fell into the pose of a suppliant. She held out her hands, palms upwards, her head bowed, and murmured: 'Present, missus, present for my baby.'

Again Marina hesitated. She looked at the woman, with her whining face and shifty eyes, and disliked her intensely. The phrase: What can one expect? came to the surface of her mind; and she went indoors and returned with sweets. The woman received them in open, humble palms, and promptly popped half into her mouth. Then she said: 'Dress, missus?'

'No,' said Marina, with energy. Why should she?

Without a sign of disappointment, the woman twisted the necks of the sacks around her hand, and dragged them after her over the dust of the yard, and joined the group of servants who were watching this scene with interest. They exchanged greetings. The woman sat down on a log, easing her strained back, and moved the baby around under her armpit, still in its sling, so it could reach her breast. Charlie, the dandy, bent over her, and they began a flirtation. The others fell back. Who, indeed, could compete with that rainbow tie, the satin garters? Charlie was persuasive and assured, the woman bridling and laughing. It went on for some minutes until the baby let the nipple fall from its mouth. Then the woman got up, still laughing, shrugged the baby back into position in the small of her back, pulled the great sacks over one shoulder, and walked off, calling shrilly back to Charlie, so that all the men laughed. Suddenly they all became silent. The nurse-girl emerged from Mrs Black's flat, and sauntered slowly past them. She was a little creature, a child, in a tight pink cotton dress, her hair braided into a dozen tiny plaits that stuck out all over her head, with a childish face that was usually vivacious and mischievous. But now she looked mournful. She dragged her feet as she walked past Charlie, and gave him a long reproachful look. Jealousy, thought Marina, there was no doubt of that! And Charlie was looking uncomfortable – one could not mistake that either. But surely not! Why, she wasn't old enough for this sort of thing. The phrase, *this sort of thing*, struck Marina herself as a shameful evasion, and she examined it. Then she shrugged and said to herself: All the same, where did the girl sleep? Presumably in one of these rooms, with the men of the place?

Theresa (she had been named after Saint Theresa at the mission school where she had been educated) tossed her head in the direction of the departing seller of vegetables, gave Charlie a final supplicating glance, and disappeared into the sanitary lane.

The men began laughing again, and this time the laughter was directed at Charlie, who received it grinning self-consciously.

Now February, who had finished the ironing, came from Mrs Pond's flat and began hanging clothes over the line to air. The white things dazzled in the sun and made sharp, black shadows across the red dust. He called out to the others – what interesting events had happened since he went indoors? They laughed, shouted back. He finished pegging the clothes and went over to the others. The group stood under the big tree, talking; Marina, still watching, suddenly felt her cheeks grow hot. Charlie had separated himself off and, with a condensing, bowed movement of his body, had become the African woman, the seller of vegetables. Bent sideways with the weight of sacks, his belly thrust out to balance the heavy baby, he approached a log of wood – her own back step. Then he straightened, sprang back, stretched upward, and pulled from the tree a frond of leaves. These he balanced on his head, and suddenly Marina saw herself. Very straight, precise, finicky, with a prim little face peering this way and that under the broad hat, hands clasped in front of her, she advanced to the log of wood and stood looking downwards.

'Peas, cabbage, potatoes,' said Charlie, in a shrill female voice.

'How much?' he answered himself, in Marina's precise, nervous voice.

'Ten sheelings a pound, missus, only ten sheelings a pound!' said Charlie, suddenly writhing on the log in an ecstasy of humility.

'How ridiculous!' said Marina, in that high, alas, absurdly high voice. Marina watched herself hesitate, her face showing mixed indignation and guilt and, finally, indecision. Charlie nodded twice, said nervously: 'Of course, but certainly.' Then, in a hurried, embarrassed way, he retreated, and came back, his arms full. He opened them and stood aside to avoid a falling shower of money. For a moment he mimed the African woman and, squatting on the ground, hastily raked in the money and stuffed it into his shirt. Then he stood up Marina again. He bent uncertainly, with a cross, uncomfortable face, looking down. Then he bent stiffly and picked up a leaf – a single pea-pod, Marina realized – and marched off, looking at the leaf, saying: 'Cheap, very cheap!' one hand balancing the leaves on his hand, his two feet set prim and precise in front of him.

As the laughter broke out from all the servants, Marina, who was not far from tears, stood by the window and said to herself: Serve you right for eavesdropping.

A clock struck. Various female voices shouted from their respective kitchens:

'February!' 'Noah!' 'Thursday!' 'Sixpence!' 'Blackbird!'

The morning lull was over. Time to prepare the midday meal for the white people. The yard was deserted, save for Theresa the nurse-girl returning disconsolately from the sanitary lane, dragging her feet through the dust. Among the stiff quills of hair on her head she had perched a half-faded yellow flower that she had found in one of the rubbish-cans. She looked hopefully at Marina's flat for a glimpse of Charlie; then slowly entered Mrs Black's.

It happened that Philip was away on one of his trips. Marina ate her lunch by herself, while Charlie, attired in his waiter's outfit, served her food. Not a trace of the cheerful clown remained in his manner. He appeared friendly, though nervous; at any moment, he seemed to be thinking, this strange white woman might revert to type and start scolding and shouting.

As Marina rose from the card-table, being careful not to bump her head on the window, she happened to glance out at the yard and saw Theresa, who was standing under the tree with the youngest of her charges in her arms. The baby was reaching up to play with the leaves. Theresa's eyes were fixed on Charlie's kitchen.

'Charlie,' said Marina, 'where does Theresa sleep?'

Charlie was startled. He avoided her eyes and muttered: 'I don't know, madam.'

'But you must know, surely,' said Marina, and heard her own voice climb to that high, insistent tone which Charlie had so successfully imitated.

He did not answer.

'How old is Theresa?'

'I don't know.' This was true, for he did not even know his own age. As for Theresa, he saw the spindly, little-girl body, with the sharp young breasts pushing out the pink stuff of the dress she wore; he saw the new languor of her walk as she passed him. 'She is nurse for Mrs Black,' he said sullenly, meaning: 'Ask Mrs Black. What's it got to do with me?'

Marina said: 'Very well,' and went out. As she did so she saw Charlie wave to Theresa through the gauze of the porch. Theresa pretended not to see. She was punishing him, because of the vegetable woman.

In the front room the light was falling full on the highland cattle, so that the glass was a square, blinding glitter. Marina shifted her seat, so that her eyes were no longer troubled by it, and contemplated those odious cattle. Why was it that Charlie, who broke a quite fantastic number of cups, saucers, and vases, never – as Mrs Skinner said he might – put that vigorously jerking broom-handle through the glass? But it seemed he liked the picture. Marina had seen him standing in front of it, admiring it. Cattle, Marina knew from Philip, played a part in native tribal life that could only be described as religious – might it be that . . .

Some letters slapped on to the cement of the veranda, slid over its polished surface, and came to rest in the doorway. Two letters. Marina watched the uniformed postboy cycle slowly down the front of the building, flinging in the letters, eight times, slap, slap, slap, grinning with pleasure at his own skill. There was a shout of rage. One of the women yelled after him: 'You lazy black bastard, can't you even get off your bicycle to deliver the letters?' The postman, without taking any notice, cycled slowly off to the next house.

This was the hour of heat, when all activity faded into somnolence. The servants were away at the back, eating their midday meal. In the eight flats, separated by the flimsy walls which allowed every sound to be heard, the women reclined, sleeping, or lazily gossiping. Marina could hear Mrs Pond, three rooms away, saying: 'The fuss she made over half a pound of sugar, you would think . . .'

Marina yawned. What a lazy life this was! She decided, at that moment, that she would put an end to this nonsense of hoping, year after year, for some miracle that would provide her, Marina Giles, with a nice house, a garden, and the other vanishing amenities of life. They would buy one of those suburban houses and she would have a baby. She would have several babies. Why not? Nursemaids cost practically nothing. She would become a domestic creature and learn to discuss servants and children with women like Mrs Black and Mrs Skinner. Why not? What had she expected? Ah, what had she not expected! For a moment she allowed herself to dream of that large house, that fine exotic garden, the free and amiable life released from the tensions and pressures of modern exist-ence. She dreamed quite absurdly – but then, if no one dreamed these dreams, no one would emigrate, continents would remain undeveloped, and then what would happen to Charlie, whose salvation was (so the statesmen and newspapers continually proclaimed) contact with Mrs Pond and Mrs Skinner – white civilization, in short.

But the phrase 'white civilization' was already coming to affect Marina as violently as it affects everyone in that violent continent. It is a phrase like 'white man's burden', 'way of life' or 'colour bar' – all of which are certain to touch off emotions better not classified. Marina was alarmed to find that these phrases were beginning to produce in her a feeling of fatigued distaste. For the liberal, so vociferously disapproving in the first six months, is quite certain to turn his back on the whole affair before the end of a year. Marina would soon be finding herself profoundly bored by politics.

But at this moment, having taken the momentous decision, she was quite light-hearted. After all, the house next door to this building was an eyesore, with its corrugated iron and brick and wood flung hastily together; and yet it was beautiful, covered with the yellow and purple and crimson creepers. Yes, they would buy a house in the suburbs, shroud it with greenery, and have four children; and Philip would be perfectly happy rushing violently around the country in a permanent state of moral indignation, and thus they would both be usefully occupied.

Marina reached for the two letters, which still lay just inside the door, where they had been so expertly flung, and opened the first. It was from Mrs Skinner, written from Cape Town, where she was, rather uneasily, it seemed, on holiday.

> I can't help worrying if everything is all right, and the furniture. Perhaps I ought to have packed away the things, because no stranger understands. I hope Charlie is not getting cheeky, he needs a firm hand, and I forgot to tell you you must deduct one shilling from his wages because he came back late one afternoon, instead of five o'clock as I said, and I had to teach him a lesson.
> Yours truly,
> Emily Skinner.
> P.S. I hope the picture is continuing all right.

The second was from Philip.

> I'm afraid I shan't be back tomorrow as Smith suggests while we are here we might as well run over to the Nwenze reserve. It's only just across the river, about seventy miles as the crow flies, but the roads are anybody's guess, after the wet season. Spent

this morning as planned, trying to persuade these blacks it is better to have one fat ox than ten all skin and bone, never seen such erosion in my life, gullies twenty feet deep, and the whole tribe will starve next dry season, but you can talk till you are blue, they won't kill a beast till they're forced, and that's what it will come to, and then imagine the outcry from the people back home . . .

At this point Martha remarked to herself: Well, well; and continued:

You can imagine Screech-Jones or one of them shouting in the House: Compulsion of the poor natives. My eye. It's for their own good. Until all this mystical nonsense about cattle is driven out of their fat heads, we might as well save our breath. You should have seen where I was this morning! To get the reserve back in use, alone, would take the entire Vote this year for the whole country, otherwise the whole place will be a desert, it's all perfectly obvious, but you'll never get this damned Government to see that in a hundred years, and it'll be too late in five.
In haste,
Phil.
P.S. I do hope everything is all right, dear, I'll try not to be late.

That night Marina took her evening meal early so that Charlie might finish the washing-up and get off. She was reading in the front room when she understood that her ear was straining through the noise from the wirelesses all around her for a quite different sort of music. Yes, it was a banjo, and loud singing, coming from the servants' rooms, and there was a quality in it that was not to be heard from any wireless set. Marina went through the rooms to the kitchen window. The deserted yard, roofed high with moon and stars, was slatted and barred with light from the eight back doors. The windows of the four servants' rooms gleamed dully; and from the room Charlie shared with February came laughter and singing and the thumping of the banjo.

There's a man who comes to our house,
When poppa goes away . . .

Marina smiled. It was a maternal smile. (As Mrs Pond might remark, in a good mood: they are nothing but children.) She liked to think that these men were having a party. And women too: she could hear shrill female voices. How on earth did they all fit into that tiny room? As she returned through the back porch, she heard a man's voice shouting: 'Shut up there! Shut up, I say!' Mr Black from his back porch: 'Don't make so much noise.'

Complete silence. Marina could see Mr Black's long, black shadow poised motionless: he was listening. Marina heard him grumble: 'Can't hear yourself think with these bastards . . .' He went back into his front room, and the sound of his heavy feet on the wood was absorbed by their wireless playing: I love you, Yes I do, I love you . . . Slam! Mr Black was in a rage.

Marina continued to read. It was not long before once more her distracted ear warned her that riotous music had begun again. They were singing: Congo Conga Conga, we do it in the Congo . . .

Steps on the veranda, a loud knock, and Mr Black entered.

'Mrs Giles, your boy's gone haywire. Listen to the din.'

Marina said politely: 'Do sit down, Mr Black.'

Mr Black who in England (from whence he had come as a child) would have been a lanky, pallid, genteel clerk, was in this country an assistant in a haberdasher's; but because of his sunfilled and energetic week-ends, he gave the impression, at first glance, of being that burly young Colonial one sees on advertisements for Empire tobacco. He was thin, bony, muscular, sunburnt; he had the free and easy Colonial manner, the back-slapping air that is always just a little too conscious. 'Look,' it seems to say, 'in this country we are all equal (among the whites, that is – that goes without saying) and I'll fight the first person who suggests anything to the contrary.' Democracy, as it were, with one eye on the audience. But alas, he was still a clerk, and felt it; and if there was one class of person he detested it was the civil servant; and if there was another, it was the person new from 'Home'.

Here they were, united in one person, Marina Giles, wife of Philip Giles, soil expert for the Department of Lands and Afforestation, Marina, whose mere appearance acutely irritated him, every time he saw her moving delicately through the red dust, in her straw hat, white gloves, and touch-me-not manner.

'I say!' he said aggressively, his face flushed, his eyes hot. 'I say, what are you going to do about it, because if you don't, I shall.'

'I don't doubt it,' said Marina precisely; 'but I really fail to see why these people should not have a party, if they choose, particularly as it is not yet nine o'clock, and as far as I know there is no law to forbid them.'

'Law!' said Mr Black violently. 'Party! They're on our premises, aren't they? It's for us to say. Anyway, if I know anything they're visiting without passes.'

'I feel you are being unreasonable,' said Marina, with the intention of sounding mildly persuasive; but in fact her voice had lifted to that fatally querulous high note, and her face was as angry and flushed as his.

'Unreasonable! My kids can't sleep with that din.'

'It might help if you turned down your own wireless,' said Marina sarcastically.

He lifted his fists, clenching them unconsciously. 'You people . . .' he began inarticulately. 'If you were a man, Mrs Giles, I tell you straight . . .' He dropped his fists and looked around wildly as Mrs Pond entered, her face animated with delight in the scene.

'I see Mr Black is talking to you about your boy,' she began, sugarily.

'And your boy too,' said Mr Black.

'Oh, if I had a husband,' said Mrs Pond, putting on an appearance of helpless womanhood, 'February would have got what's coming to him long ago.'

'For that matter,' said Marina, speaking with difficulty because of her loathing for the whole thing, 'I don't think you really find a husband necessary for this purpose, since it was only yesterday I saw you hitting February yourself . . .'

'He was cheeky,' began Mrs Pond indignantly.

Marina found words had failed her; but none were necessary for Mr Black had gone striding out through her own bedroom, followed by Mrs Pond, and she saw the pair of them cross the shadowy yard to Charlie's room, which was still in darkness, though the music was at a crescendo. As Mr Black shouted: 'Come out of there, you black bastards!' the noise stopped, the door swung in, and half a dozen dark forms ducked under Mr Black's extended arm and vanished into the sanitary lane. There was a scuffle, and Mr Black found himself grasping, at arm's length, two people – Charlie and his own nursemaid, Theresa. He let the girl go and she ran after the others. He pushed Charlie against the wall. 'What do you mean by making all that noise when I told you not to?' he shouted.

'That's right, that's right,' gasped Mrs Pond from behind him, running this way and that around the pair so as to get a good view.

Charlie, keeping his elbow lifted to shield his head, said: 'I'm sorry, baas, I'm sorry, I'm sorry . . .'

'Sorry!' Mr Black, keeping a firm grasp of Charlie's shoulder, lifted his other hand to hit him; Charlie jerked his arm up over his face. Mr Black's fist, expecting to encounter a cheek, met instead the rising arm and he was thrown off balance and staggered back. 'How dare you hit me?' he shouted furiously, rushing at Charlie; but Charlie had escaped in a bound over the rubbish-cans and away into the lane.

Mr Black sent angry shouts after him; then turned and said indignantly to Mrs Pond: 'Did you see that? He hit me!'

'He's out of hand,' said Mrs Pond in a melancholy voice. 'What can you expect? He's been spoilt.'

They both turned to look accusingly at Marina.

'As a matter of accuracy,' said Marina breathlessly, 'he did not hit you.'

'What, are you taking that nigger's side?' demanded Mr Black. He was completely taken aback. He looked, amazed, at Mrs Pond, and said: 'She's taking his side!'

'It's not a question of sides,' said Marina in that high, precise voice. 'I was standing here and saw what happened. You know quite well he did not hit you. He wouldn't dare.'

'Yes,' said Mr Black, 'that's what a state things have come to, with the Government spoiling them, they can hit us and get away with it, and if we touch them we get fined.'

'I don't know how many times I've seen the servants hit since

I've been here,' said Marina angrily. 'If it is the law, it is a remarkably ineffective one.'

'Well, I'm going to get the police,' shouted Mr Black, running back to his own flat. 'No black bastard is going to hit me and get away with it. Besides, they can all be fined for visiting without passes after nine at night . . .'

'Don't be childish,' said Marina, and went inside her rooms. She was crying with rage. Happening to catch a glimpse of herself in the mirror as she passed it, she hastily went to splash cold water on her face, for she looked – there was no getting away from it – rather like a particularly genteel school-marm in a temper. When she reached the front room, she found Charlie there throwing terrified glances out into the veranda for fear of Mr Black or Mrs Pond.

'Madam,' he said. 'Madam, I didn't hit him.'

'No, of course not,' said Marina; and she was astonished to find that she was feeling irritated with him, Charlie. 'Really,' she said, 'must you make such a noise and cause all this fuss?'

'But, madam . . .'

'Oh, all right,' she said crossly. 'All right. But you aren't supposed to . . . who were all those people?'

'My friends.'

'Where from?' He was silent. 'Did they have passes to be out visiting?' He shifted his eyes uncomfortably. 'Well, really,' she said irritably, 'if the law is that you must have passes, for heaven's sake . . .' Charlie's whole appearance had changed; a moment before he had been a helpless small boy; he had become a sullen young man: this white woman was like all the rest.

Marina controlled her irritation and said gently: 'Listen, Charlie, I don't agree with the law and all this nonsense about passes, but I can't change it, and it does seem to me . . .' Once again her irritation rose, once again she suppressed it, and found herself without words. Which was just as well, for Charlie was gazing at her with puzzled suspicion since he saw all white people as a sort of homogeneous mass, a white layer, as it were, spread over the mass of blacks, all concerned in making life as difficult as possible for him and his kind; the idea that a white person might not agree with passes, curfew, and so on was so outrageously new that he could not admit it to his mind at once. Marina said: 'Oh, well, Charlie, I know you didn't mean it, and I think you'd better go quietly to bed and keep out of Mr Black's way, if you can.'

'Yes, madam,' he said submissively. As he went, she asked: 'Does Theresa sleep in the same room as Mr Black's boy?'

He was silent. 'Does she sleep in your room perhaps?' And, as the silence persisted: 'Do you mean to tell me she sleeps with you and February?' No reply. 'But Charlie . . .' She was about to protest again: But Theresa's nothing but a child; but this did not appear to be an argument which appealed to him.

There were loud voices outside, and Charlie shrank back: 'The police!' he said, terrified.

'Ridiculous nonsense,' said Marina. But looking out she saw a white policeman; and Charlie fled out through her bedroom and she heard the back door slam. It appeared he had no real confidence in her sympathy.

The policeman entered, alone. 'I understand there's been a spot of trouble,' he said.

'Over nothing,' said Marina.

'A tenant in this building claims he was hit by your servant.'

'It's not true. I saw the whole thing.'

The policeman looked at her doubtfully and said: 'Well, that makes things difficult, doesn't it?' After a moment he said: 'Excuse me a moment,' and went out. Marina saw him talking to Mr Black outside her front steps. Soon the policeman came back. 'In view of your attitude the charge has been dropped,' he said.

'So I should think. I've never heard of anything so silly.'

'Well, Mrs Giles, there was a row going on, and they all ran away, so they must have had guilty consciences about something, probably no passes. And you know they can't have women in their rooms.'

'The woman was Mr Black's own nursemaid.'

'He says the girl is supposed to sleep in the location with her father.'

'It's a pity Mr Black takes so little interest in his servants not to know. She sleeps here. How can a child that age be expected to walk five miles here every morning, to be here at seven, and walk five miles back at seven in the evening?'

The policeman gave her a look: 'Plenty do it,' he said. 'It's not the same for them as it is for us. Besides, it's the law.'

'The law!' said Marina bitterly.

Again the policeman looked uncertain. He was a pleasant young man, he dealt continually with cases of this kind, he always tried to smooth things over, if he could. He decided on his usual course, despite Marina's hostile manner. 'I think the best thing to do,' he said, 'is if we leave the whole thing. We'll never catch them now, anyway – miles away by this time. And Mr Black has dropped the charge. You have a talk to your boy and tell him to be careful. Otherwise he'll be getting himself into trouble.'

'And what are you going to do about the nurse? It amounts to this: It's convenient for the Blacks to have her here, so they can go out at night, and so on, so they ask no questions. It's a damned disgrace, a girl of that age expected to share a room with the men.'

'It's not right, not right at all,' said the policeman. 'I'll have a word with Mr Black.' And he took his leave, politely.

That night Marina relieved her feelings by writing a long letter about the incident to a friend of hers in England, full of phrases such as 'police state', 'despotism', and 'fascism'; which caused that friend to reply, rather tolerantly, to the effect that she understood these hot climates were rather upsetting and she did so hope Marina was looking after herself, one must have a sense of proportion, after all.

And, in fact, by the morning Marina was wondering why she had allowed herself to be so angry about such an absurd incident. What a country this was! Unless she was very careful she would find herself flying off into hysterical states as easily, for instance, as Mr Black. If one was going to make a life here, one should adjust oneself . . .

Charlie was grateful and apologetic. He repeated: 'Thank you, madam. Thank you.' He brought her a present of some vegetables and said: 'You are my father and my mother.' Marina was deeply touched. He rolled up his eyes and made a half-rueful joke: 'The police are no good, madam.' She discovered that he had spent the night in a friend's room some streets away for fear the police might come and take him to prison. For, in Charlie's mind, the police meant only one thing. Marina tried to explain that one wasn't put in prison without a trial of some sort; but he merely looked at her doubtfully, as if she were making fun of him. So she left it.

And Theresa? She was still working for the Blacks. A few evenings later, when Marina went to turn off the lights before going to bed, she saw Theresa gliding into Charlie's room. She said nothing about it: what could one expect?

Charlie had accepted her as an ally. One day, as he served vegetables, reaching behind her ducked head so that they might be presented, correctly, from the left, he remarked: 'That Theresa, she very nice, madam.'

'Very nice,' said Marina, uncomfortably helping herself to peas from an acute angle, sideways.

'Theresa says, perhaps madam give her a dress?'

'I'll see what I can find,' said Marina, after a pause.

'Thank you very much, thank you, madam,' he said. He was grateful; but certainly he had expected just that reply: his thanks were not perfunctory, but he thanked her as one might thank one's parents, for instance, from whom one expects such goodness, even takes it a little for granted.

Next morning, when Marina and Philip lay as usual, trying to sleep through the cheerful din of cleaning from the next room, which included a shrill and sprightly whistling, there was a loud crash.

'Oh, damn the man,' said Philip, turning over and pulling the clothes over his ears.

'With a bit of luck he's broken that picture,' said Marina. She put a dressing-gown on, and went next door. On the floor lay fragments of white porcelain – her favourite vase, which she had brought all the way from England. Charlie was standing over it. 'Sorry, madam,' he said, cheerfully contrite.

Now that vase had stood on a shelf high above Charlie's head – to break it at all was something of an acrobatic feat . . . Marina pulled herself together. After all, it was only a vase. But her favourite vase, she had had it ten years: she stood there, tightening her lips over all the angry things she would

have liked to say, looking at Charlie, who was carelessly
sweeping the pieces together. He glanced up, saw her face, and
said hastily, really apologetic: 'Sorry madam, very, very sorry,
madam.' Then he added reassuringly: 'But the picture is all
right.' He gazed admiringly up at the highland cattle which he
clearly considered the main treasure of the room.

'So it is,' said Marina, suppressing the impulse to say:
Charlie, if you break that picture I'll give you a present. 'Oh,
well,' she said, 'I suppose it doesn't matter. Just sweep the
pieces up.'

'Yes, missus, thank you,' said Charlie cheerfully; and she
left, wondering how she had put herself in a position where it
became impossible to be legitimately cross with her own
servant. Coming back into the room some time later to ask
Charlie why the breakfast was so late, she found him still
standing under the picture. 'Very nice picture,' he said, reluctantly leaving the room. 'Six oxes. Six fine big oxes, in one
picture!'

The work in the flat was finished by mid-morning. Marina
told Charlie she wanted to bake; he filled the old-fashioned
stove with wood for her, heated the oven and went off into the
yard, whistling. She stood at the window, mixing her cake,
looking out into the yard.

Charlie came out of his room, sat down on a big log under
the tree, stretched his legs before him, and propped a small
mirror between his knees. He took a large metal comb and
began to work on his thick hair, which he endeavoured to make
lie flat, white man's fashion. He was sitting with his back to the
yard.

Soon Theresa came out with a big enamel basin filled with
washing. She wore the dress Marina had given her. It was an
old black cocktail dress which hung loosely around her calves,
and she had tied it at the waist with a big sash of printed cotton.
The sophisticated dress, treated thus, hanging full and shapeless, looked grandmotherly and old-fashioned; she looked like
an impish child in a matron's garb. She stood beside the
washing-line gazing at Charlie's back; then slowly she began
pegging the clothes, with long intervals to watch him.

It seemed Charlie did not know she was there. Then his pose

of concentrated self-worship froze into a long, close inspection in the mirror, which he began to rock gently between his knees so that the sunlight flashed up from it, first into the branches over his head, then over the dust of the yard to the girl's feet, up her body: the ray of light hovered like a butterfly around her, then settled on her face. She remained still, her eyes shut, with the teasing light flickering on her lids. Then she opened them and exclaimed, indignantly: 'Hau!'

Charlie did not move. He held the mirror sideways on his knees, where he could see Theresa, and pretended to be hard at work on his parting. For a few seconds they remained thus, Charlie staring into the mirror, Theresa watching him reproachfully. Then he put the mirror back into his pocket, stretched his arms back in a magnificent slow yawn, and remained there, rocking back and forth on his log.

Theresa looked at him thoughtfully: and – since now he could not see her – darted over to the hedge, plucked a scarlet hibiscus flower, and returned to the washing-line, where she continued to hang the washing, the flower held lightly between her lips.

Charlie got up, his arms still locked behind his head, and began a sort of shuffle dance in the sunny dust, among the fallen leaves and chips of wood. It was a crisp, bright morning, the sky was as blue and fresh as the sea: this idyllic scene moved Marina deeply, it must be confessed.

Still dancing, Charlie let his arms fall, turned himself round, and his hands began to move in time with his feet. Jerking, lolling, posing, he slowly approached the centre of the yard, apparently oblivious of Theresa's existence.

There was a shout from the back of the building: 'Theresa!' Charlie glanced around, then dived hastily into his room. The girl, left alone, gazed at the dark door into which Charlie had vanished, sighed, and blinked gently at the sunlight. A second shout: 'Theresa, are you going to be all day with that washing?'

She tucked the flower among the stiff quills of hair on her head and bent to the basin that stood in the dust. The washing flapped and billowed all around her, so that the small, wiry form appeared to be wrestling with the big, ungainly sheets. Charlie ducked out of his door and ran quickly up the hedge, out of sight of Mrs Black. He stopped, watching Theresa, who was still fighting with the washing. He whistled, she ignored him. He whistled again, changing key; the long note dissolved into a dance tune, and he sauntered deliberately up the hedge, weight shifting from hip to hip with each step. It was almost a dance: the buttocks sharply protruding and then withdrawn inwards after the prancing, lifting knees. The girl stood motionless, gazing at him, tantalized. She glanced quickly over her shoulder at the building, then ran across the yard to Charlie. The two of them, safe for the moment beside the hedge, looked guiltily for possible spies. They saw Marina behind her curtain – an earnest English face, apparently wrestling with some severe moral problem. But she was a friend. Had she not saved Charlie from the police? Besides, she immediately vanished.

Hidden behind the curtain, Marina saw the couple face each other, smiling. Then the girl tossed her head and turned away. She picked a second flower from the hedge, held it to her lips, and began swinging lightly from the waist, sending Charlie provocative glances over her shoulder that were half disdain and half invitation. To Marina it was as if a mischievous black urchin was playing the part of a coquette; but Charlie was watching with a broad and appreciative smile. He followed her, strolling in an assured and masterful way, and she went before him into his room. The door closed.

Marina discovered herself to be furious. Really the whole thing was preposterous!

'Philip,' she said energetically that night, 'we should do something.'

'What?' asked Philip, practically. Marina could not think of a sensible answer. Philip gave a short lecture on the problems of the indigenous African peoples who were half-way between the tribal society and modern industrialization. The thing, of course, should be tackled at its root. Since he was a soil expert, the root, to him, was a sensible organization of the land. (If he had been a churchman, the root would have been a correct attitude to whichever God he happened to represent; if an authority on money, a mere adjustment of currency would have provided the solution – there is very little comfort from experts these days.) To Philip, it was all as clear as daylight. These people had no idea at all how to farm. They must give up this old attitude of theirs, based on the days when the tribe worked out one piece of ground and moved on to the next; they must learn to conserve their soil and, above all, to regard cattle, not as a sort of spiritual currency, but as an organic part of farm-work. (The word *organic* occurred very frequently in these lectures by Philip.) Once these things were done, everything else would follow . . .

'But in the meantime, Philip, it is quite possible that some-thing may *happen* to Theresa, and she can't be more than fifteen, if that . . .'

Philip looked a little dazed as he adjusted himself from the level on which he had been thinking to the level of Theresa: women always think so personally! He said, rather stiffly: 'Well, old girl, in periods of transition, what can one expect?'

What one might expect did in fact occur, and quite soon. One of those long ripples of gossip and delighted indignation passed from one end to the other of 138 Cecil John Rhodes Vista. Mrs Black's Theresa had got herself into trouble; these girls had no morals; no better than savages; besides, she was a thief. She was wearing clothes that had not been given her by Mrs Black. Marina paid a formal visit to Mrs Black in order to say that she had given Theresa various dresses. The air was not at all cleared. No one cared to what degree Theresa had been corrupted, or by whom. The feeling was: if not Theresa, then someone else. Acts of theft, adultery, and so on were necessary to preserve the proper balance between black and white; the balance was upset, not by Theresa, who played her allotted part, but by Marina, who insisted on introducing these Fabian scruples into a clear-cut situation.

Mrs Black was polite, grudging, distrustful. She said: 'Well, if you've given her the dresses, then it's all right.' She added: 'But it doesn't alter what she's done, does it now?' Marina could make no reply. The white women of the building con-tinued to gossip and pass judgement for some days: one must, after all, talk about something. It was odd, however, that Mrs Black made no move at all to sack Theresa, that immoral person, who continued to look after the children with her usual good-natured efficiency, in order that Mrs Black might have time to gossip and drink tea.

So Marina, who had already made plans to rescue Theresa when she was flung out of her job, found that no rescue was necessary. From time to time Mrs Black overflowed into reproaches, and lectures about sin. Theresa wept like the child she was, her fists stuck into her eyes. Five minutes afterwards she was helping Mrs Black bath the baby, or flirting with Charlie in the yard.

For the principals of this scandal seemed the least concerned about it. The days passed, and at last Marina said to Charlie: 'Well, and what are you going to do now?'

'Madam?' said Charlie. He really did not know what she meant.

'About Theresa,' said Marina sternly.

'Theresa she going to have a baby,' said Charlie, trying to look penitent, but succeeding only in looking proud.

'It's all very well,' said Marina. Charlie continued to sweep the veranda, smiling to himself. 'But Charlie . . .' began Marina again.

'Madam?' said Charlie, resting on his broom and waiting for her to go on.

'You can't just let things go on, and what will happen to the child when it is born?'

His face puckered, he sighed, and finally he went on sweeping, rather slower than before.

Suddenly Marina stamped her foot and said: 'Charlie, this really won't do!' She was really furious.

'Madam!' said Charlie reproachfully.

'Everybody has a good time,' said Marina. 'You and Theresa enjoy yourselves, all these females have a lovely time, gossiping, and the only thing no one ever thinks about is the baby.' After a pause, when he did not reply, she went on: 'I suppose you and Theresa think it's quite all right for the baby to be born here, and then you two, and the baby, and February, and all the rest of your friends who have nowhere to go, will all live together in that room. It really is shocking, Charlie.'

Charlie shrugged as if to say: 'Well, what do you suggest?'

'Can't Theresa go and live with her father?'

Charlie's face tightened into a scowl. 'Theresa's father, he no good. Theresa must work, earn money for father.'

'I see.' Charlie waited; he seemed to be waiting for Marina to solve this problem for him; his attitude said: I have unbounded trust and confidence in you.

'Are any of the other men working here married?'

'Yes, madam.'

'Where are their wives?'

'At home.' This meant, in their kraals, in the native reserves. But Marina had not meant the properly married wives who usually stayed with the clan, and were visited by their men perhaps one month in a year, or in two years. She meant women like Theresa, who lived in town.

'Now listen, Charlie. Do be sensible. What happens to girls like Theresa when they have babies. Where do they live?'

He shrugged again, meaning: they live as they can, and is it my fault the white people don't let us have our families with us when they work? Suddenly he said grudgingly: 'The nannie next door, she has her baby, she works.'

'Where is her baby?'

Charlie jerked his head over at the servants' quarters of the next house.

'Does the baas know she has her baby there?'

He looked away, uncomfortably. 'Well, and what happens when the police find out?'

He gave her a look which she understood. 'Who is the father of that baby?'

He looked away; there was an uncomfortable silence; and then he quickly began sweeping the veranda again.

'Charlie!' said Marina, outraged. His body had become defensive, sullen; his face was angry. She said energetically: 'You should marry Theresa. You can't go on doing this sort of thing.'

'I have a wife in my kraal,' he said.

'Well, there's nothing to stop you having two wives, is there?'

Charlie pointed out that he had not yet finished paying for his first wife.

Marina thought for a moment. 'Theresa's a Christian, isn't she? She was educated at the mission.' Charlie shrugged. 'If you marry Theresa Christian-fashion, you needn't pay lobola, need you?'

Charlie said: 'The Christians only like one wife. And Theresa's father, he wants lobola.'

Marina found herself delighted. At any rate he had tried to marry Theresa, and this was evidence of proper feeling. The fact that whether the position was legalized or not the baby's future was still uncertain, did not at once strike her. She was carried away by moral approval. 'Well, Charlie, that's much better,' she said warmly.

He gave her a rather puzzled look and shrugged again.

'How much lobola does Theresa's father want for her?'

'Plenty. He wants ten cattle.'

'What nonsense!' exclaimed Marina energetically. 'Where does he suppose you are going to find cattle, working in town, and where's he going to keep them?'

This seemed to annoy Charlie. 'In my kraal, I have fine cattle,' he pointed out. 'I have six fine oxen.' He swept, for a while, in silence. 'Theresa's father, he mad, he mad old man. I tell him I must give three oxen this year for my own wife. Where do I find ten oxen for Theresa?'

It appeared that Charlie, no more than Theresa's father, found nothing absurd about this desire for cattle on the part of an old man living in the town location. Involuntarily she looked over her shoulder as if Philip might be listening: this conversation would have plunged him into irritated despair. Luckily he was away on one of his trips, and was at this moment almost certain to be exhorting the Africans, in some distant reserve, to abandon this irrational attitude to 'fine oxen' which in fact were bound to be nothing but skin and bone, and churning whole tracts of country to dust.

'Why don't you offer Theresa's father some money?' she suggested, glancing down at Charlie's garters which were, this morning, of cherry-coloured silk.

'He wants cattle, not money. He wants Theresa not to marry, he wants her to work for him.' Charlie rapidly finished sweeping the veranda and moved off, with relief, tucking the broom under his arm, with an apologetic smile which said: I know you mean well, but I'm glad to end this conversation.

But Marina was not at all inclined to drop the thing. She interviewed Theresa who, amid floods of tears, said Yes, she wanted to marry Charlie, but her father wanted too much lobola. The problem was quite simple to her, merely a question of lobola; Charlie's other wife did not concern her; nor did she, apparently, share Charlie's view that a proper wife in the kraal was one thing, while the women of the town were another.

Marina said: 'Shall I come down to the location and talk to your father?'

Theresa hung her head shyly, allowed the last big tears to roll glistening down her cheeks and go splashing to the dust. 'Yes, madam,' she said gratefully.

Marina returned to Charlie and said she would interview the old man. He appeared restive at this suggestion. 'I'll advance you some of your wages and you can pay for Theresa in instalments,' she said. He glanced down at his fine shirt, his gay socks, and sighed. If he were going to spend years of life paying five shillings a month, which was all he could afford, for Theresa, then his life as a dandy was over.

Marina said crossly: 'Yes, it's all very well, but you can't have it both ways.'

He said hastily: 'I'll go down and see the father of Theresa, madam. I go soon.'

'I think you'd better,' she said sternly.

When she told Philip this story he became vigorously indignant. It presented in little, he said, the whole problem of this society. The Government couldn't see an inch in front of its nose. In the first place, by allowing the lobola system to continue, this emotional attitude towards cattle was perpetuated. In the second, by making no proper arrangements for these men to have their families in the towns it made the existence of prostitutes like Theresa inevitable.

'Theresa isn't a prostitute,' said Marina indignantly. 'It isn't her fault.'

'Of course it isn't her fault, that's what I'm saying. But she will be a prostitute, it's inevitable. When Charlie's fed up with her she'll find herself another man and have a child or two by him, and so on . . .'

'You talk about Theresa as if she were a vital statistic,' said

Marina, and Philip shrugged. That shrug expressed an attitude of mind which Marina would very soon find herself sharing, but she did not yet know that. She was still very worried about Theresa, and after some days she asked Charlie: 'Well, and did you see Theresa's father? What did he say?'

'He wants cattle.'

'Well, he can't have cattle.'

'No,' said Charlie brightening. 'My own wife, she cost six cattles. I paid three last year. I pay three more this year, when I go home.'

'When are you going home?'

'When Mrs Skinner comes back. She no good. Not like you, madam, you are my father and mother,' he said, giving her his touching, grateful smile.

'And what will happen to Theresa?'

'She stay here.' After a long, troubled silence, he said: 'She my town wife. I come back to Theresa.' This idea seemed to cheer him up.

And it seemed he was genuinely fond of the girl. Looking out of the kitchen window, Marina could see the pair of them, during lulls in the work, seated side by side on the big log under the tree – charming! A charming picture! 'It's all very well . . .' said Marina to herself, uneasily.

Some mornings later she found Charlie in the front room, under the picture, and looking at it this time, not with reverent admiration, but rather nervously. As she came in he quickly returned to his work, but Marina could see he wanted to say something to her.

'Madam . . .'

'Well, what is it?'

'This picture costs plenty money?'

'I suppose it did, once.'

'Cattles cost plenty money, madam.'

'Yes, so they do, Charlie.'

'If you sell this picture, how much?'

'But it is Mrs Skinner's picture.'

His body drooped with disappointment. 'Yes, madam,' he said politely, turning away.

'But wait, Charlie – what do you want the picture for?'

'It's all right, madam.' He was going out of the room.

'Stop a moment – why do you want it? You do want it, don't you?'

'Oh, yes,' he said, his face lit with pleasure. He clasped his hands tight, looking at it. 'Oh, yes, yes, madam!'

'What would you do with it? Keep it in your room?'

'I give it to Theresa's father.'

'Wha-a-a-t?' said Marina. Slowly she absorbed this idea. 'I see,' she said. And then, after a pause: 'I see . . .' She looked at his hopeful face, thought of Mrs Skinner, and said suddenly, filled with an undeniably spiteful delight: 'I'll give it to you, Charlie.'

'Madam!' exclaimed Charlie. He even gave a couple of involuntary little steps, like a dance. 'Madam, thank you, thank you.'

She was as pleased as he. For a moment they stood smiling delightedly at each other. 'I'll tell Mrs Skinner that I broke it,' she said. He went to the picture and lifted his hands gently to the great carved frame. 'You must be careful not to break it before you get it to her father.' He was staggering as he lifted it down. 'Wait!' said Marina suddenly. Checking himself, he stood politely: she saw he expected her to change her mind and take back the gift. 'You can't carry that great thing all the way to the location. I'll take it for you in the car!'

'Madam,' he said. 'Madam . . .' Then, looking helplessly around him for something, someone he could share his joy with, he said: 'I'll tell Theresa now . . .' And he ran from the room like a schoolboy.

Marina went to Mrs Black and asked that Theresa might have the afternoon off. 'She had her afternoon off yesterday,' said that lady sharply.

'She's going to marry Charlie,' said Marina.

'She can marry him next Thursday, can't she?'

'No, because I'm taking them both down in the car to the location, to her father, and . . .'

Mrs Black said resentfully: 'She should have asked me herself.'

'It seems to me,' said Marina in that high, acid voice, replying not to the words Mrs Black had used, but to what she had meant: 'It seems to me that if anyone employs a child of fifteen, and under such conditions, the very least one can do is to assume the responsibility for her; and it seems to me quite extraordinary that you never have the slightest idea what she does, where she lives, or even that she is going to get married.'

'You swallowed the dictionary?' said Mrs Black, with an ingratiating smile. 'I'm not saying she shouldn't get married; she should have got married before, that's what I'm saying.'

Marina returned to her flat, feeling Mrs Black's resentful eyes on her back: *Who the hell does she think she is, anyway?*

When Marina and Philip reached the lorry that afternoon that was waiting outside the gate, Theresa and Charlie were already sitting in the back, carefully balancing the picture on their knees. The two white people got in the front and Marina glanced anxiously through the window and said to Philip: 'Do drive carefully, dear, Theresa shouldn't be bumped around.'

'I'd be doing her a favour if I did bump her,' said Philip grimly. He was accompanying Marina unwillingly. 'Well, I don't know what you think you're going to achieve by it . . .' he had said. However, here he was, looking rather cross.

They drove down the tree-lined, shady streets, through the business area that was all concrete and modernity, past the slums where the half-caste people lived, past the factory sites, where smoke poured and hung, past the cemetery where angels and crosses gleamed white through the trees – they drove five miles, which was the distance Theresa had been expected to walk every morning and evening to her work. They turned off the main road into the location, and at once everything was quite different. No tarmac road, no avenues of beautiful trees here. Dust roads, dust paths, led from all directions inwards to the centre, where the housing area was. Dust lay thick and brown on the veld trees, the great blue sky was seen through a rust-coloured haze, dust gritted on the lips and tongue, and at once the lorry began to jolt and bounce. Marina looked back and saw Charlie and Theresa jerking and sliding with the lorry, under the great picture, clinging to each other for support, and laughing because of the joy-ride. It was the first time Theresa had ridden in a white man's car; and she was waving and calling shrill greetings to the groups of black children who ran after them.

They drove fast, bumping, so as to escape from the rivers of dust that spurted up from the wheels, making a whirling red cloud behind them, from which crowds of loitering Africans ran, cursing and angry. Soon they were in an area that was like a cheap copy of the white man's town; small houses stood in blocks, intersected by dust streets. They were two-roomed shacks with tin roofs, the sun blistering off them; and Marina said angrily: 'Isn't it awful, isn't it terrible?'

Had she known that these same houses represented years of campaigning by the liberals of the city, against white public opinion, which obstinately held that houses for natives were merely another manifestation of that *Fabian* spirit from England which was spoiling the fine and uncorrupted savage, she might have been more respectful. Soon they left this new area and were among the sheds and barns that housed dozens of workers each, a state of affairs which caused Marina the acutest indignation. Another glance over her shoulder showed Theresa and Charlie giggling together like a couple of children as they tried to hold the picture still on their knees, for it slid this way and that as if it had a spiteful life of its own. 'Ask Charlie where we must go,' said Philip; and Marina tapped on the glass till Charlie turned his head and watched her gestures till he understood and pointed onwards with his thumb. More of these brick shacks, with throngs of Africans at their doors, who watched the car indifferently until they saw it was a Government car, and then their eyes grew wary, suspicious. And now, blocking their way, was a wire fence, and Marina looked back at Charlie for instructions, and he indicated they should stop. Philip pulled the lorry up against the fence and Charlie and Theresa jumped down from the back, came forward, and Charlie said apologetically: 'Now we must walk, madam.' The four went through a gap in the fence and saw a slope of soiled and matted grass that ended in a huddle of buildings on the banks of a small river.

Charlie pointed at it, and went ahead with Theresa. He held the picture on his shoulders, walking bent under it. They passed through the grass, which smelled unpleasant and was covered by a haze of flies, and came to another expanse of dust, in which were scattered buildings – no, not buildings, shacks, extraordinary huts thrown together out of every conceivable substance, with walls perhaps of sacking, or of petrol boxes, roofs of beaten tin, or bits of scrap iron.

'And what happens when it rains?' said Marina, as they wound in and out of these dwellings, among scratching chickens and snarling native mongrels. She found herself profoundly dispirited, as if something inside her said: What's the use? For this area, officially, did not exist. The law was that all the workers, the servants should live inside the location, or in one of the smaller townships. But there was never enough room. People overflowed into such makeshift villages everywhere, but as they were not supposed to be there the police might at any moment swoop down and arrest them. Admittedly the police did not often swoop, as the white man must have servants, the servants must live somewhere – and so it all went on, year after year. The Government, from time to time, planned a new housing estate. On paper, all round the white man's city, were fine new townships for the blacks. One had even been built, and to this critical visitors (usually those Fabians from overseas) were taken, and came away impressed. They never saw these slums. And so all the time, every day, the black people came from their reserves, their kraals, drawn to the white man's city, to the glitter of money, cinemas, fine clothes; they came in their thousands, no one knew how many, making their own life, as they could, in such hovels. It was all hopeless, as long as Mrs Black, Mr Black, Mrs Pond were the voters with the power; as long as the experts and administrators such as Philip had to work behind Mrs Pond's back – for nothing is more remarkable than that democratic phenomenon, so clearly shown in this continent, where members of Parliament, civil servants (experts, in short) spend half their time and energy earnestly exhorting Mrs Pond: For heaven's sake have some sense before it is too late; if you don't let us use enough money to house and feed these people, they'll rise and cut your throats. To which reasonable plea for self-preservation, Mrs Pond merely turns a sullen and angry stare, muttering: They're getting out of hand, that's what it is, they're getting spoilt.

In a mood of grim despair, Marina found herself standing with Philip in front of a small shack that consisted of sheets of corrugated iron laid loosely together, resting in the dust, like a child's card castle. It was bound at the corners with string, and big stones held the sheet of iron that served as roof from flying away in the first gust of wind.

'Here, madam,' said Charlie. He thrust Theresa forward. She went shyly to the dark oblong that was the door, leaned inwards, and spoke some words in her own language. After a moment an old man stooped his way out. He was perhaps not so old – impossible to say. He was lean and tall, with a lined and angry face, and eyes that lifted under heavy lids to peer at Marina and Philip. Towards Charlie he directed a long, deadly stare, then turned away. He wore a pair of old khaki trousers, an old, filthy singlet that left his long, sinewed arms bare: all the bones and muscles of his neck and shoulders showed taut and knotted under the skin.

Theresa, smiling bashfully, indicated Philip and Marina; the old man offered some words of greeting; but he was angry, he did not want to see them, so the two white people fell back a little.

Charlie now came forward with the picture and leaned it gently against the iron of the shack in a way which said: 'Here you are, and that's all you are going to get from me.' In these surroundings those fierce Scottish cattle seemed to shrink a little. The picture that had dominated a room with its expanse of shining glass, its heavy carved frame, seemed not so enormous now. The cattle seemed even rather absurd, shaggy creatures standing in their wet sunset, glaring with a false challenge at the group of people. The old man looked at the picture, and then said something angry to Theresa. She seemed afraid, and came forward, unknotting a piece of cloth that had lain in the folds at her waist. She handed over some small change – about three shillings in all. The old man took the money, shaking it contemptuously in his hand before he slid it into his pocket. Then he spat, showing contempt. Again he spoke to Theresa, in short angry sentences, and at the end he flung out his arm, as if throwing something away; and she began to cry and shrank back to Charlie. Charlie laid his hand on her shoulder and pressed it; then left her standing alone and went forward to his father-in-law. He smiled, spoke persuasively, indicated Philip and Marina. The old man listened without speaking, his eyes lowered. Those eyes slid sideways to the big picture, a gleam came into them; Charlie fell silent and they all looked at the picture.

The old man began to speak, in a different voice, sad, and hopeless. He was telling how he had wooed his second wife, Theresa's mother. He spoke of the long courting, according to the old customs, how, with many gifts and courtesies between the clans, the marriage had been agreed on, how the cattle had been chosen, ten great cattle, heavy with good grazing; he told how he had driven them to Theresa's mother's family, carefully across the country, so that they might not be tired and thinned by the journey. As he spoke to the two young people he was reminding them, and himself, of that time when every action had its ritual, its meaning; he was asking them to contrast their graceless behaviour with the dignity of his own marriages, symbolized by the cattle, which were not to be thought of in terms of money, of simply buying a woman – not at all. They meant so much: a sign of good feeling, a token of union between the clans, an earnest that the woman would be looked after, an acknowledgement that she was someone very precious, whose departure would impoverish her family – the cattle were all these things, and many more. The old man looked at Charlie and Theresa and seemed to say: 'And what about you? What are you in comparison to what we were then?' Finally he spat again, lifted the picture and went into the dark of his hut. They could see him looking at the picture. He liked it: yes, he was pleased, in his way. But soon he left it leaning against the iron and returned to his former pose – he drew a blanket over his head and shoulders and squatted down inside the door, looking out, but not as if he still saw them or intended to make any further sign towards them.

The four were left standing there, in the dust, looking at each other.

Marina was feeling very foolish. Was that all? And Philip answered by saying brusquely, but uncomfortably: 'Well, there's your wedding for you.'

Theresa and Charlie had linked fingers and were together looking rather awkwardly at the white people. It was an awkward moment indeed – this was the end of it, the two were married, and it was Marina who had arranged the thing. What now?

But there was a more immediate problem. It was still early in the afternoon, the sun slanted overhead, with hours of light in it still, and presumably the newly-married couple would want to be together? Marina said: 'Do you want to come back with us in the lorry, or would you rather come later?'

Charlie and Theresa spoke together in their own language, then Charlie said apologetically: 'Thank you, madam, we stay.'

'With Theresa's father?'

Charlie said: 'He won't have Theresa now. He says Theresa can go away. He not want Theresa.'

Philip said: 'Don't worry, Marina, he'll take her back, he'll take her money all right.' He laughed, and Marina was angry with him for laughing.

'He very cross, madam,' said Charlie. He even laughed himself, but in a rather anxious way.

The old man still sat quite motionless, looking past them. There were flies at the corners of his eyes; he did not lift his hand to brush them off.

'Well . . .' said Marina. 'We can give you a lift back if you like.' But it was clear that Theresa was afraid of going back now; Mrs Black might assume her afternoon off was over and make her work.

Charlie and Theresa smiled again and said: 'Good-bye. Thank you, madam. Thank you, baas.' They went slowly off across the dusty earth, between the hovels, towards the river, where a group of tall brick huts stood like outsize sentry-boxes. There, though neither Marina nor Philip knew it, was sold illicit liquor; there they would find a tinny gramophone playing dance music from America; there would be singing, dancing, a good time. This was the place the police came first if they were in search of criminals. Marina thought the couple were going down to the river, and she said sentimentally: 'Well, they have this afternoon together, that's something.'

'Yes,' said Philip dryly. The two were angry with each other.

they did not know why. They walked in silence back to the lorry and drove home, making polite, clear sentences about indifferent topics.

Next day everything was as usual. Theresa back at work with Mrs Black, Charlie whistling cheerfully in their own flat.

Almost immediately Marina bought a house that seemed passable, about seven miles from the centre of town, in a new suburb. Mrs Skinner would not be returning for two weeks yet, but it was more convenient for them to move into the new home at once. The problem was Charlie. What would he do during that time? He said he was going home to visit his family. He had heard that his first wife had a new baby and he wanted to see it.

'Then I'll pay you your wages now,' said Marina. She paid him, with ten shillings over. It was an uncomfortable moment. This man had been working for them for over two months, intimately, in their home, they had influenced each other's lives – and now he was off, he disappeared, the thing was finished. 'Perhaps you'll come back and work for me when you come back from your family?' said Marina.

Charlie was very pleased. 'Oh, yes, madam,' he said. 'Mrs Skinner very bad, she no good, not like you.' He gave a comical grimace, and laughed.

'I'll give you our address.' Marina wrote it out and saw Charlie fold the piece of paper and place it carefully in an envelope which also held his official pass, a letter from her saying he was travelling to his family, and a further letter, for which he had asked, listing various bits of clothing that Philip had given him, for otherwise, as he explained, the police would catch him and say he had stolen them.

'Well, good-bye, Charlie,' said Marina. 'I do so hope your wife and your new baby are all right.' She thought of Theresa, but did not mention her; she found herself suffering from a curious disinclination to offer further advice or help. What would happen to Theresa? Would she simply move in with the first man who offered her shelter? Almost Marina shrugged.

'Good-bye, madam,' said Charlie. He went off to buy himself a new shirt with the ten shillings, and some sweets for Theresa. He was sad to be leaving Theresa. On the other hand, he was looking forward to seeing his new child and his wife; he expected to be home after about a week's walking, perhaps sooner if he could get a lift.

But things did not turn out like this.

Mrs Skinner returned before she was expected. She found the flat locked and the key with Mrs Black. Everything was very clean and tidy, but – where was her favourite picture? At first she saw only the lightish square patch on the dimming paint – then she thought of Charlie. Where was he? No sign of him. She came back into the flat and found the letter Marina had left, enclosing eight pounds for the picture 'which she had unfortunately broken'. The thought came to Mrs Skinner that she would not have got ten shillings for the picture if she had tried to sell it; then the phrase 'sentimental value' came to her rescue, and she was furious. Where was Charlie? For, looking about her, she saw various other articles were missing. Where was her yellow earthen vase? Where was the wooden door-knocker that said *Welcome Friend*? Where was . . . she went off to talk to Mrs Black, and quite soon all the women dropped in, and she was told many things about Marina. At last she said: 'It serves me right for letting to an immigrant. I should have let it to you, dear.' The dear in question was Mrs Pond. The ladies were again emotionally united: the long hostilities that had led to the flat being let to Marina were forgotten; that they were certain to break out again within a week was not to be admitted in this moment of pure friendship.

Mrs Pond told Mrs Skinner that she had seen the famous picture being loaded on to the lorry. Probably Mrs Giles had sold it – but this thought was checked, for both ladies knew what the picture was worth. No, Marina must have disposed of it in some way connected with her *Fabian* outlook – what could one expect from these white kaffirs?

Fuming, Mrs Skinner went to find Theresa. She saw Charlie, dressed to kill in his new clothes, who had come to say good-bye to Theresa before setting off on his long walk. She flew out, grabbed him by the arm, and dragged him into the flat. 'Where's my picture?' she demanded.

At first Charlie denied all knowledge of the picture. Then he said Marina had given it to him. Mrs Skinner dropped his arm and stared: 'But it was my picture . . .' She reflected rapidly: that eight pounds was going to be very useful; she had returned from her holiday, as people do, rather short of money. She exclaimed instead: 'What have you done with my yellow vase? Where's my knocker?'

Charlie said he had not seen them. Finally Mrs Skinner fetched the police. The police found the missing articles in Charlie's bundle. Normally Mrs Skinner would have cuffed him and fined him five shillings. But there was this business of the picture – she told the police to take him off.

Now, in this city in the heart of what used to be known as the Dark Continent, at any hour of the day, women shopping, typists glancing up from their work out of the window, or the business men passing in their cars, may see (if they choose to look) a file of handcuffed Africans, with two policemen in front and two behind, followed by a straggling group of African women who are accompanying their men to the courts. These are the Africans who have been arrested for visiting without passes, or owning bicycles without lights, or being in possession of clothes or articles without being able to say how they came to own them. These Africans are being marched off to explain themselves to the magistrates. They are given a small fine with the option of prison. They usually choose prison. After all, to pay ten shillings fine when one earns perhaps twenty or thirty a month, is no joke, and it is something to be fed and housed, free, for a fortnight. This is an arrangement satisfactory to everyone concerned, for these prisoners mend roads, cut down grass, plant trees: it is as good as having a pool of free labour.

Marina happened to be turning into a shop one morning, where she hoped to buy a table for her new house, and saw, without really seeing them, a file of such handcuffed Africans passing her. They were talking and laughing among themselves, and with the black policemen who herded them, and called back loud and jocular remarks at their women. In Marina's mind the vision of that ideal table (for which she had been searching for some days, without success) was rather stronger than what she actually saw; and it was not until the prisoners had passed that she suddenly said to herself: 'Good heavens, that man looks rather like Charlie – and that girl behind there, the plump girl with the spindly legs, there was something about the back view of that girl that was very like Theresa . . .' The file had in the meantime turned a corner and was out of sight. For a moment Marina thought: Perhaps I should follow and see? Then she thought: Nonsense, I'm seeing things, of course it can't be Charlie, he must have reached home by now . . . And she went into the shop to buy her table.

Eldorado

Hundreds of miles south were the gold-bearing reefs of Johannesburg; hundreds of miles north, the rich copper mines. These the two lodestars of the great central plateau, these the magnets which drew men, white and black; drew money from the world's counting-house; concentrated streets, shops, gardens; attracted riches and misery – particularly misery.

But this, here, was farming country, true farming land, a pocket of good, dark, rich soil in the wastes of the light sandveld. A 'pocket' some hundreds of miles in depth, and only to be considered in such midget terms by comparison with those eternal sandy wastes which fed cattle, though poorly, and satisfied that shallow weed tobacco. For that is how a certain kind of farmer sees it; a man of the old-fashioned sort will think of farming as the making of food, and of tobacco as a nervous, unsatisfactory crop, geared to centres in London and New York; he will watch the fields fill and crowd with new, bright leaf, and imagine it crushed through factory and warehouse to end in a wisp of pale smoke, he will not like to imagine the substance of his soil dissipating in smoke. And if sensible people argue: Yes, but people must smoke, you smoke yourself, you're not being reasonable; he is likely to reply (rather irritably perhaps): 'Yes, of course, you're right but I want to grow food, the others can grow tobacco.'

When Alec Barnes came searching for a farm, he chose the rich maize soil, though cleverer, experienced men told him the big money was to be found only in tobacco. Tobacco and gold, gold and tobacco – these were the moneymakers. For this country had gold too, a great deal of it; but perhaps there is only room in one's mind for one symbol, one type; and when people say 'gold' they think of the Transvaal, and so it was with

Alec. There were many ways of seeing this new country, and Alec Barnes chose to see it with the eye of the food producer. He had not left England, he said, to worry about money and chase success. He wanted a slow, satisfying life, taking things easy.

He bought a small farm, about two thousand acres, from a man who had gone bankrupt. There was a house already built. It was a pleasant house, in the style of the country, of light red brick with a corrugated iron roof, big, bare rooms and a wide veranda. Shrubs and creepers, now rather neglected, showed scarlet against the dull green scrub, or hung in showers of gold and purple from the trees. The rainy season had sprung new grass high and thick over paths, over flower-beds. When the Barnes family came in they had to send an African ahead with a scythe to cut an opening through thickets of growth, and in the front room the bricks of the floor were being tumbled aside by the shoots from old tree roots. There was a great deal to do before the place could be comfortable, and Maggie Barnes set herself to work. She was the daughter of a small Glasgow shopkeeper, and it might be thought that everything would be strange to her; but her grandparents had farmed and she remembered visiting the old people as a child, playing with a shaggy old cart-horse, feeding the chickens. That way of farming could hardly be compared to this, but in a sense it was like returning to her roots. At least, that was how she thought of it. She would pause in her work, duster in hand, at a window or on the veranda, and look over the scrub to the mealie-fields, and it did not seem so odd that she should be here in this big house, with black servants to wait on her, not so outlandish that she might walk an hour across country and call the soil underfoot her soil. There was no domesticated cart-horse to take sugar from her hand, only teams of sharp-horned and wild-eyed oxen; but there were chickens and turkeys and geese – she had no intention of paying good money for what she could grow herself, not she who knew the value of money! Besides, a busy woman has no time for fainthearted comparisons, and there was so much to do; and she intended that all this activity should earn its proper reward. She had gone beyond her grandparents, with their tight, frugal farm, which earned a living but no more, had gone beyond her parents, counting their modest profits in the back rooms of the grocery shop. In a sense she included both generations, could see the merits and failings of both, but – she and her husband would 'get on', they would be prosperous as the farmers around them were prosperous. It was true that when the neighbours made doubtful faces at their growing small-scale maize, and said there could be no 'taking it easy' on that farm, she felt a little troubled. But she approved her husband's choice, the growing of food satisfied her ideas of what was right, and connected her with her religious and respectable grandparents. Besides, many of the things Alec said she simply did not take seriously. When he said, fiercely, how glad he was to be out of England, out of the fight for success and the struggle to be better than one's neighbours, she merely smiled: what was the matter with getting on and bettering oneself? They were just words to her. She would say, in her bluff, affectionate way, of Alec: 'He's a queer man, being English, I canna get used to the way of him.' For she put down his high-flown notions to his being English. Also, he was strange to her because of his gentleness: the men of her people were outspoken and determined and did not defer to their women. Alec deferred to her. Sometimes she could not understand him; but she was happy with him, and with her son, who was still a small child.

She sent Paul out with a native servant to play in the veld, while she worked, whitewashing the house, even climbing the roof herself to see to the guttering. Paul learned a new way of playing. He spread himself, ranging over the farm, so that the native youth who had the care of him found himself kept running. His toys, the substitutes for the real thing, mechanical lorries and bricks and dolls, were left in cupboards; and he made dams in the mud of the fields, plunged fearfully on the plough behind the oxen, rode high on the sacks of the wagons. He lost the pretty, sheltered look of the child from 'home', who must be nervous of streets and traffic, always conscious of the pressure of the neighbours. He grew fast and tall, big-boned and muscular, and lean and burnt. Sometimes Maggie would say, with that good-natured laugh: 'Well, and I don't know myself with this change-child!' Perhaps the laugh was a little uneasy, too. For she was not as thick-fibred as she looked. She was that Scots type, rather short, but finely made, even fragile, with the great blue eyes and easily-freckling fair skin and a mass of light black curls. Even after the hard work and the sunlight, which thickened her into a sturdy, energetic body of a woman, she kept, under the appearance of strength, that fine-boned delicacy and a certain shy charm. And here was her son shooting up into a lanky, bony youngster, the whites of his eyes always a little reddened by glare, his dark hair tumbling rough over his head with rusty bleached locks where the sun had struck. She looked at him in the bath, showing smooth dark-brown all over, save for the tender, milky skin like a loincloth where the strong khaki shorts kept the sun off. She felt a little perturbed, as if in some way he was most flagrantly betraying her by growing so, away from the fair, clear, open looks of her good Scots ancestors. There was something stubborn and secretive about him – perhaps even something a little coarse. But then – she reminded herself – he was half-English, too, and Alec was tall, long-headed, with a closed English face, and slow English speech which concealed more than it said. For a time she tried to change the child, to make him more depend-ent, until Alec noticed it and was angry. She had never seen him so angry before. He was a mild, easy man, who noticed very little, content to work at the farm and leave the rest to her. But now they fought. 'What are you coddling him for?' Alec shouted. 'What's the good of bringing him here to a country where he can grow up a man if you're going to fuss and worry all the time?' She gave him back as good; for to her women friends she would expound her philosophy of men: 'You've got to stand against them once in a way, it doesnae do to be too sweet to them.' But these remarks, she soon under-stood, sounded rather foolish; for when did she need to 'stand against' Alec? She had her own way over everything. Except in this, for the very country was against her. Soon she left the boy to do as he liked on the veld. He was at an age when children at 'home' would be around their mothers, but at seven and eight he was quite independent, had thrown off the attendant servant, and would spend all day on the fields, coming in for meals as if – so Maggie complained in that soft, pretty, Scots voice: 'As if I'm no better than a restaurant!' But she accepted it, she was not the complaining sort; it was only a comfortable grumble to her woman friends. Besides, living here had hardened her a little. Perhaps hardened was not the right word? It was a kind of fatalism, the easy atmosphere of the country which might bring in Paul and her husband an hour late for a meal, looking at her oddly if she complained of the time. What's an hour? they seemed to be asking; even: 'What's time at all?' She could understand it, she was beginning to feel a little that way herself. But in her heart she was determined that Paul would not grow up lax and happy-go-lucky, like a Colonial. Soon he would be going to school and he would 'have it knocked out of him'. She had that good sturdy Scottish attitude towards education. She expected children to work and win scholarships. And indeed, it would be necessary, for the farm could hardly support a son through the sort of schooling she visualized for him. She was beginning to understand that it never would. At the end of the first five years she understood that their neighbours had been right: this farm would never do more than make a scanty living.

When she spoke to Alec he seemed to turn against her, not noisily, in a healthy and understandable quarrel, but in a stubborn, silent way. Surely he wanted Paul to make something of himself? she demanded. Put like that, of course, Alec had to agree, but he agreed vaguely. It was this vagueness that upset Maggie, for there was no way of answering it. It seemed to be saying: All these things are quite irrelevant; I don't understand you.

Alec had been a clerk in a bank until the First World War. After the upheaval he could not go back into an office. He married Maggie and came to this new country. There were farmers in his family, too, a long way back, though he had only come to remember this when he felt a need to explain, even excuse, that dissident streak which had made a conventional English life impossible. He would talk of a certain great-uncle, who had ridden a wild black horse around the shires, fathering illegitimate children and drinking and behaving so that he ended in prison for smuggling. Yes, this was all very well, thought Maggie, but what has that old rascal got to do with

Alec, and what with my son? For Alec would talk of this unsatisfactory ancestor with pride and his eyes would rest speculatively on Paul – it gave Maggie goose-flesh to see him.

Alec grew even vaguer as time went by. He used to stand at the edge of a field, gazing dimly across it at a ridge of bush which rose sharp to the great blue sky; or at the end of the big vlei, which cut across the farm in a shallow, golden swathe of rustling grasses, with a sluggish watercourse showing green down its centre. He would stand on a moonlit night staring across the fields which now appeared like a diffusing green sea, the white crests of the maize shifting like foam; or at midday, looking over the stretching acres of brown and heaving clods, warm and rich with sunlight; or at sunset, when the miles of bush flared gold and red. Distance – that was what he needed. It was what he had left England to find.

He cleared new ground every year. When he first came it was mostly bush, with a few cleared patches. The house was bedded in trees. Now one walked from the house through Maggie's pretty garden, and the mealies stood like a green wall on three sides of the homestead. From a little hillock behind the house, the swaying green showed solid and unbroken, hundreds of acres of it, beautiful to look at until one remembered that the experts were warning against this kind of planting. Better small fields with trees to guard them from wind; better girdles of grass, so that the precious soil might be held by the roots and not wash away with the flooding storm-waters. But Alec's instinct was for space, and soon half the surface of the farm was exposed, and the plough drove a straight line from boundary to boundary, and the labourers worked in a straight line, like an advancing army, their hoes rising and falling and flashing like spears in the sun. The vivid green of the leaves rippled and glittered, or shone soft with moonlight; or at reaping time the land lay bare and hard, and over it the tarnished litter of the fallen husks; or at planting, a wide sweep of dark-brown clods which turned to harsh red under the rain. Beautiful it was and Maggie could understand Alec's satisfaction in it; but it was disturbing when the rains drove the soil along the gulleys; when the experts came from town and told Alec he was ruining his farm; when at the season's end the yield rose hardly at all in spite of the constantly increased acreage. But Alec set that obstinate face of his against the experts and the evidence of the books, and cut more trees, exposing the new soil which fed fine, strong plants, showing the richness of their growth in the heavy cobs. One could mark the newly-cleared area in the great field every year; the maize stood a couple of feet shorter on the old soil. Alec sent gangs of workers into the trees, and through the dry season the dull thud-thud of axes sounded across the wide, clean air, and the trees crashed one after another into the wreckage of their branches. Always a new field, or rather, the old one extended; always fine new soil ready for the planting, but there came a time when it was not possible to cut more trees, for where would the cattle graze? There must be sufficient veld left to feed them, for without them the ploughs and wagons could not move, and there wasn't sufficient capital for a tractor. So Alec rested on his laurels for a couple of years, working the great field, and Maggie sent her son off to school in town a hundred miles away. He would return only for the holidays – would return, she hoped, brisker, with purpose, the languor of the farm driven out of him. She missed him badly, but it was a relief that he was with other children, and this relief made up for the loss. As for Alec, Paul's going made him uneasy. Now he was actually at school, he must face his responsibility for the child's future. He wandered over his farm rather less vaguely and wondered how Paul thought of the town. For that was how he saw it; not that he was at school, but in town; and it was the reason why he had been so reluctant for him to go. He did not want him to grow into an office-worker, a pen-user, a city-cypher, the sort of person he had been himself and now disowned. But what if Paul did not feel as he did? Alec would stand looking at a tree, or a stretch of water, thinking: What does this mean to Paul, what does he think when he swims here? – in the secretive, nostalgic way of parents trying to guess at their children's souls. What sort of a creature *was* Paul? When he came to it, he had no idea at all, although the child was so like him, a long, lean, dark, silent boy, with contemplative dark eyes and a slow way of speaking. And here was Maggie, with such plans for him, determined that he must be an engineer, a scientist, a doctor, and nothing less than famous. The fame could be discounted, tolerantly, with her maternal pride and possessiveness, but scientists of any kind are not produced on the sort of profit he was making.

He thought worriedly about the farm. Perhaps he could lease adjoining land and graze his beasts there, and leave his own good land free for cutting? But all the land was taken up. He knew quite well, too, that the problem was deeper. He should change his way of farming. There were all sorts of things he could do – *should* do, at once; but at the idea of them a lassitude crept over him and he thought, obstinately: Why should I, why fuss and worry, when I'm free of all that, free of the competition in the Old Country? I didn't come here to fight myself into a shadow over getting rich . . . But the truth was, though he did not admit it to himself, not for a second, he was very bored. He had come to the limits of his old way, and now, to succeed, it would be going over the same ground, but in a different way – nothing new; that was the point. Rather guiltily he found himself daydreaming about pulling up his roots here and going off somewhere else – South America, China – why not? Then he pulled himself together. To postpone the problem he cut another small area of trees, and the cutting of them exposed all the ground to where the ridge lifted itself; they could see clear from the house across the vlei and up the other side; all mealies, all a shimmering mass of green; and on the ridge was the boundary of the next farm, a low barbed-wire fence, and against the fence was a small mine. It was nothing very grand; just a two-stamp affair, run by a single man who got what gold he could from a poor but steady seam. The mine had been there for years.The mine-stamp thudded day and night, coming loud or soft, according to the direction of the wind. But to Alec there was something new and even terrible about seeing the black dump of the mine buildings, seeing the black smoke drifting up into the blue, fresh sky. His deep and thoughtful eyes would often turn that way. How strange that from that cluster of black ugliness, under the hanging smoke, gold should come from the earth. It was unpleasant, too. This was farming land. It was outrageous that the good soil should be covered, even for a mere five acres or so, by buildings and iron gear and the sordid mine compound.

Alec felt as he did when people urged him to grow tobacco. It would be a betrayal, though what he would be betraying he could not say. And this mine was a betrayal of everything decent. They fetched up the ore, they washed the gold out, melted it to conveniently-handled shapes, thousands of workers spent their lives on it when they might be doing something useful on the land; and ultimately the gold was shipped off to America. He often made the old joke, these days, about digging up gold from one hole in the ground and sending it to America to be buried in another. Maggie listened and wondered at him. What a queer man he was! He noticed nothing until he was faced with it. For years she had been talking about Paul's future; and only when she packed him off to school did Alec begin to talk, just as if he had only that moment come to consider it, of how he should be educated. For years he had been living a couple of miles from a mine, with the sound of it always in his ears, but it was not until he could see it clear on the next ridge that he seemed to notice it. And yet for years the old miner had been dropping in of an evening. Alec would make a polite enquiry or two and then start farm-talk, which could not possibly interest him. 'Poor body,' Maggie had been used to say, half-scornfully, 'what's the use of talking seasons and prices to *him*?' For she shared Alec's feeling that mining was not a serious way of living – not this sort of mining, scratching in the dirt for a little gold. That was how she thought of it. But at least she had thought of it; and here was Alec like a man with a discovery.

When Paul came home for his holiday and saw the mine lifted black before him on the long, green ridge, he was excited, and made his longest journey afield. He spent a day at the mine and came home chattering about pennyweights and ounces of gold; about reefs and seams and veins; about ore and slimes and cyanide – a whole new language. Maggie poured brisk scorn on the glamour of gold; but she was secretly pleased at this practical new interest. He was at least talking about things, he wasn't mooning about the farm like a waif returned from exile. She dreamed of him becoming a mining engineer or a geologist. She sent to town for books about famous men of science and left them lying about. Paul hardly glanced at them. His practical experience of handling things, watching growth, seeing iron for implements shaped in a fire, made it so that his knowledge must come first-hand, and afterward be confirmed by reading. And he was roused to quite different thoughts. He would kick at an exposed rock, so that the sparks fell dull red under his boot-soles, and say: 'Daddy, perhaps this is gold rock?' Or he would come running with bits of decomposed stone that showed dull gleams of metal and say: 'Look, this is gold, isn't it?'

'Maybe,' said Alec, reluctantly. 'This is all gold country. The prospectors used to come through here. There is a big reef running across that ridge which is exactly the same formation as one of the big reefs on the Rand; once they thought they'd find a mine as big as that one here. But it didn't come to anything.'

'Perhaps we'll find it,' said Paul, obstinately.

'Perhaps,' said Alec, indulgently. But he was stirred, whether he liked it or not. He thought of the old prospectors wandering over the country with their meagre equipment, panning gold from the sand of river-beds, crushing bits of rock, washing the grit for those tiny grains that might proclaim a new Rand. Sometimes, when he came on a projecting ledge of rock, instead of cursing it for being on farmland at all, he would surreptitiously examine it, thinking: That bit there looks as if it had been broken off – perhaps one of the old hands used his hammer here twenty years ago. Or he might find an old digging, half-filled in by the rains, where someone had tried his luck, and he stood looking down at the way the rock lay in folds under the earth, sometimes flat, packed tidily one above the other, sometimes slanting in a crazy plunge where the subterranean forces had pushed and squeezed. And then he would shake himself and turn back to the business of farming, to the visible surfaces, the tame and orderly top-soil that was a shallow and understandable layer responsive to light and air and wetness, where the worms and air-bringing roots worked their miracles of decomposition and growth. He put his thoughts back to this malleable surface of the globe, the soil – or imagined that he did; and suppressed his furtive speculation about the fascinating underground structure – but not altogether. There was slowly growing in him another vision, another need, and he listened to the regular thud-thud of the mine-stamps from the opposite ridge as if they were drums beating from a country whose frontier he was forbidden to cross.

One evening an old weather-stained man appeared at the door and unslung from his back a great bundle of equipment and came in for the night, assuming the traveller's privilege of hospitality. He was, in fact, one of the vanishing race of wandering prospectors; and for most of the night he talked about his life on the veld. It was like a story from a child's adventure book in its simplicities of luck and bad fortune and persistent courage rewarded only by the knowledge of right-doing. For this old man spoke of the search for gold as a scientist might of discovery, or an artist of his art. Twice he had found gold and sold his riches trustingly, so that he was tricked by unscrupulous men who were now rich, while he was as poor as he had been forty years before. He spoke of this angrily, it is true, but it was that kind of anger we maintain from choice, like a relation whose unpleasantness has become, through the years, almost a necessity. There had been one brief period of months when he was very rich indeed, and squandered he did not know how much money in the luxury hotels of the golden city. He spoke of this indifferently, as of a thing which had chosen to visit him, and then as arbitrarily chosen to withdraw. Maggie, listening, was thankful that Paul was not there. And yet this was a tale any child might remember all his life, grateful for a glimpse of one of the old kind of adventurer, bred when there were still parts of the world unknown to map-makers and instrument-makers. This was a character bound to fire any boy; but Maggie thought, stubbornly: There is enough nonsense as it is. And by this she meant, making no bones about it: Alec is enough of a bad influence. For she had come to understand that if Paul was to have that purpose she wanted in him, she must plant it and nurture it herself. She did not like the way Alec listened to this old man, who might be a grand body in his way, but not in *her* way. He was listening to a siren song, she

could see that in his face. And later he began talking again
about that nuisance of a great-uncle of his who, in some queer
way, he appeared to link with the prospector. What more did
the man want? Most sensible people would think that gallivanting off to farm in Africa was adventure enough, twice as
adventurous as being a mere waster and ruffian, deceiving
honest girls and taking honest people's goods, and ending as a
common criminal!

Maggie, that eminently sensible woman, wept a little that
night when Alec was asleep, and perhaps her courage went a
little numb. Or rather, it changed its character, becoming more
like a shield than a spear, a defensive, not an attacking thing.
For when she thought of Alec she felt helpless; and the old
man asleep in the room made her angry. Why did he have to
come to this farm, why not take his dangerous gleam elsewhere? Long afterwards, she remembered that night and said,
tartly, to Alec: 'Yes, that was when the trouble started, when
that old nuisance came lolloping along here with his long
tongue wagging . . .' But 'the trouble' started long before; who
could say when? With the war, that so unsettled men and sent
them flying off to new countries, new women? With whatever
forces they were that bred men's silly wars? Something in Alec
himself: his long-dead ancestor stirring in him and whispering
along his veins of wildness and adventure? Well, she would
leave all that to Alec and see that her son became a respectable
lawyer, or a bridge-builder. That was enough adventure for
her.

When the old man left next day, trudging off through the
mealie fields with his pack over his shoulder, Alec watched him
from the veranda. And that evening he climbed the hillock
behind the house, and saw the small red glow of a fire down in
the vlei. There he was, after his day of rock-searching, rock-
chipping. He would be cooking his supper, or perhaps already
lying wrapped in his blanket beside the embers, a fold of it
across his face so that the moon would not trouble his eyelids
with its shifting, cold gleams. The old man was alone; he did
not even take an African with him to interpret the veld; he no
longer needed this intermediary, he understood the country as
well as the black men who lived on it. Alec went slowly to bed,

thinking of the old prospector who was free, bound to no one, owning nothing but a blanket and a frying-pan and his clothes.

Not long afterwards a package arrived from the station and Maggie watched Alec open it. It was a gold pan. Alec held it clumsily between his palms, as he had seen the prospector do. He had not yet got the feel of the thing. It was like a deep frying-pan, without a handle, of heavy black metal, with a fine groove round the inside of the rim. This groove was to catch the runnels of silt that should hold grains of gold, if there was any gold. Alec brought back fragments of rock from the lands and crushed them in a mortar and stood beside the water tanks swirling the muddy mixture around and around endlessly, swearing with frustration, because he was still so clumsy and could not get the movements right. Each sample took a long time, and he could not be sure, when he had finished, if it had been properly done. First the handfuls of crushed rock, as fine as face powder, must be placed in the pan and then the water run in. Afterwards it must be shaken so that the heavy metals should sink, and then with a strong sideways movement the lighter grit and dust must be flung out, with the water. Then more water added and the shaking repeated. Finally, there should be nothing but a wash of clean water, and the loose grit and bits of metal sliding along the groove: the dull, soft black of iron, a harder shine for chrome, the false glitter of pyrites, that might be taken for gold by a greenhorn, and finally, and in almost every sample, dragging slow and heavy behind the rest, would be the few dully-shining grains of true gold. But the movements had to be learned. The secret was a subtle little sideways jerk at the end, which separated the metals from the remnants of lighter rock. So stood Alec, methodically practising, with the heavy pan between his palms, the packets of crushed rock on the ground beside him, and on the other side the dripping water-taps. He was squandering the precious water that had to be brought from the well three times a week in the water-cart. The household was always expected to be niggardly with water, and now here was Alec swilling away gallons of it every day. An aggrieved Maggie watched him through the kitchen window.

But it was still a hobby. Alec worked as usual on the farm,

picking up interesting bits of rock if he came across them, and panned them at evening, or early in the morning before breakfast. The house was littered with lumps of rock, and Maggie handled them wonderingly, when she was alone, for she did not intend to encourage Alec in 'this nonsense'. She was fascinated by the rocks, and she did not want to be fascinated. There were round stones, worn smooth by the wash of water; red stones, marbled with black; green stones, dull like rough jade; blue stones, with a fire of metal when they were shifted against a light. They were beautiful enough to be cut and worn as jewels. Then there were lumps of rough substance, half-way between soil and rock, the colour of ox-blood, and some so rich with metal that they weighed the hand low. Most promising were the decomposing rocks, where the soft parts had been rotted out by wind and water, leaving a crumbling, veiny substance, like a skeleton of the soil, and in some of these the gold could be seen lying thick and close, like dirt along the seams of a garment.

Alec did not yet know the names of the rocks and minerals, and he was troubled by his ignorance. He sent for books; and in the meantime he moved like an explorer over the farm he imagined he knew as well as it could be known, learning to see it in a new way. That rugged jut of reef, for instance, which intersected the big vlei like the wall of a natural dam – what was the nature of that hard and determined rock, and what happened to it beneath the ground? Why was the soil dark and red at one end of the big field and a sullen orange at the other? He looked at this field when it was bared ready for the planters, and saw how the soil shaded and modulated from acre to acre, according to the varieties of rock from which it had been formed, and he no longer saw the fields, he saw the reefs and shales and silts and rivers of the underworld. He lifted his eyes from this vision and saw the kopjes six miles away; hard granite, they were; and the foothills, tumbled outposts of granite boulders almost to his own boundary – rock from another era, mountains erupted from an older time. On another horizon could be seen the long mountain where chrome was mined and exported to the countries which used it for war. Along the flanks of the mountains showed the scars and levels of the workings – it was another knowledge, another language of labour. He felt as if he had been blind half his life and only just discovered it. And on the slopes of his own farm were the sharp quartz reefs that the prospector told him were promise of gold. Quartz, that most lovely of rocks, coloured and weathered to a thousand shapes and tints, sometimes standing cold and glittering, like miniature snow mountains; sometimes milky, like slabs of opal, or delicate pink and amber with a smoky flush in its depths, as if a fire burnt there invisibly; marbled black, or mottled blue – there was no end to the strangeness and variety of those quartz reefs which for years he had been cursing because they made whole acres of his land unfit for the plough. Now he wandered there with a prospector's hammer, watching the fragments of rock fly off like chips of ice, or like shattering jewels. When he panned these pieces they showed traces of gold. But not enough: he had already learned how to measure the richness of a sample.

He sent for a geological map and tacked it to the wall of his farm office. Maggie found it and stood in front of it, studying it when he couldn't see her. Here was Africa, but in a new aspect. Instead of the shaded greens and browns and blues of the map she was accustomed to see, the colours of earth and growth, the colours of leaf and soil and grass and moving water, now they were harsh colours like the metallic hues of rock. An arsenic green showed the copper deposits of Northern Rhodesia, a cold yellow the gold of the Transvaal – but not only the Transvaal. She had had no idea how much gold there was, worked everywhere; the patches of yellow mottled the subcontinent. But Maggie had no feeling for gold; her sound instincts were against the useless stuff. She looked with interest at the black of the coalfields – one of the richest in the world, Alec said, and hardly touched; at the dull grey of the chrome deposits, whole mountains of it, lying unused; at the glittering light green of the asbestos, at the iron and the manganese and – but most of these names she had never heard, could not even pronounce.

When Alec's books came, she would turn over the pages curiously, gaining not so much a knowledge as an intimation of the wonderful future of this continent. Perhaps Alec should have been a scientist, she thought, and not a farmer at all? Perhaps, with this capacity of his for completely losing himself (as he had become lost) he might have been a great man? For this was how the vision narrowed down in her: all the rich potentialities of Africa she saw through her son, who might one day work with coal, or with copper; or through Alec, the man, who 'might have done well for himself' if he had had a different education. Education, that was the point. And she turned her thoughts steadily towards her son. All her interests had narrowed to him. She set her will hard like a prayer, towards him, as if her dammed forces could work on him a hundred miles away at school in the city.

When he came home from school he found his father using a new vocabulary. Alec was still attending to the farm with half his attention, but his passion was directed into this business of gold-finding. He had taken half a dozen labourers from the fields and they were digging trenches along the quartz reef on the ridge. Maggie made no direct comment, but Paul could feel her disapproval. The child was torn between loyalty to his mother and fascination for this new interest, and the trenches won. For some days Maggie hardly saw him, he was with his father, or over at the mine on the ridge.

'Perhaps we'll have a mine on our farm, too,' said Paul to Maggie; and then, scornfully: 'But we won't have a silly mine like that one, we'll have a big one, like Johannesburg.' And Maggie's heart sank, listening to him. Now was the time, she thought, to mould him, and she showed him the coloured map on the office wall and tried to make it come alive for him, as it had for her. She spoke of the need for engineers and experts, but he looked and listened without kindling. 'But my bairn,' said Maggie reproachfully, using the old endearment which was falling out of use now, with her other Scots ways of speech, 'my bairn, it's time you were making up your mind to what you want. You must know what you want to be.' He looked sulky and said if they found 'a big mine, like Johannesburg', he would be a gold-miner. 'Oh, no,' said Maggie, indignantly. 'That's just luck. Anyone can have a stroke of luck.' It takes a clever man to be educated and know about things.' So Paul evaded this and said all right then, he'd be a tobacco farmer.

'Oh, no,' said Maggie again; and wondered herself at the passion she put into it. Why should he not be a tobacco farmer? But it wasn't what she dreamed of for him. He would become a rich tobacco farmer? He would make his thousands and study the international money-juggling and buy more farms and more farms and have assistants until he sat in an office and directed others, just as if he were a business man? For with tobacco there seemed to be no half-way place, the tobacco farmers drove themselves through night-work and long hours on the fields, as if an invisible whip threatened them, and then they failed, or they succeeded suddenly, and paid others to do the slaving . . . it was no sort of a life, or at least, not for *her* son. 'What's the matter with having money?' asked Paul at last, in hostility. 'Don't you see,' said Maggie desperately, trying to convey something of her solid and honest values; 'anyone can be lucky, anyone can do it. Young men come out from England, with a bit of money behind them, and they needn't be anything, just fools maybe, and then the weather's with them, and the prices are good, and they're rich men – but there's nothing in that, you want to try something more worthwhile than that, don't you?' Paul swung the dark and stubborn eyes on her and asked, dourly: 'What do you think of my father, then?' She caught her breath, looked at him in amazement – surely he couldn't be criticizing his father! But he was; already his eyes were half-ashamed, however, and he said quickly, 'I'll think about it,' and made his escape. He went straight off to the diggings, and seemed to avoid his mother for a time. As for Alec, Maggie thought he'd lost his senses. He came rushing in and out of the house with bits of rock and announcements of imminent riches so that Paul became as bad, and spent half his day crushing stones and watching his father panning. Soon he learned to use the pan himself. Maggie watched the intent child at work beside the water-tanks, while the expensive water went sloshing over to the dry ground, so that there were always puddles, in spite of the strong heat. The tanks ran dry and Alec had to give orders for the water-carts to make an extra journey. Yes, thought Maggie, bitterly, all these years I've been saving water and now, over this foolishness, the water-carts can make two or three extra trips a week. Because of this. Alec began talking of sinking a new well; and Maggie grew more bitter still, for she had often asked for a well to be sunk close at the back of the house, and there had never been time or money to see to it. But now, it seemed, Alec found it justified.

People who live on the veld for a long time acquire an instinct for the places where one must sink for water. An old-timer will go snuffing and feeling over the land like a dog, marking the fall of the earth, the lie of a reef, the position of an anthill, and say at last: Here is the place. Likely enough he will be right, and often enough, of course, quite wrong.

Alec went through just such a morning of scenting and testing, through the bush at the back of the house, where the hillock erupted its boulders. If the underground forces had broken here, then there might be fissures where water could push its way; water was often to be found near a place of reefs and rocks. And there were antheaps; and ant galleries mostly ended, perhaps a hundred feet down, in an underground river. And there was a certain promising type of tree – yes, said Alec, this would be a good place for a well. And he had already marked the place and taken two labourers from the farm to do the digging when there appeared yet another of those danger-ous visitors; another vagrant old man, just as stained and weatherworn as the last; with just such a craziness about him, only this time even worse, for he claimed he was a water-diviner and would find Alec Barnes a well for the sum of one pound sterling.

That night Paul was exposed until dawn to the snares of magical possibilities. He could not be made to go to bed. The old man had many tales of travel and danger; for he had spent his youth as a big-game hunter, and later, when he was too old for that, became a prospector; and later still, by chance, found that the forked twig of a tree had strength in his hands. Chance! – it was always chance, thought Maggie, listening dubiously. These men lived from one stroke of luck to the next. It was bad luck that the elephant charged and left the old man lame for life, with the tusk-scars showing white from ankle to groin. It was good luck that he 'fell in' with old Thompson, who had happened to 'make a break' with diamonds in the Free State.

It was bad luck that malaria and then blackwater got him, so that he could no longer sleep in the bush at nights. It was good luck that made him try his chance with the twig, so that now he might move from farm to farm, with an assured welcome for a night behind mosquito netting . . . What an influence for Paul!

Paul sat quietly beside her and missed not a word. He blinked slow attention through those dark and watchful eyes; and he was critical, too. He rejected the old man's boasting, his insistence on the scientific certainties of the magic wand, all the talk of wells and watercourses, of which he spoke as if they were a species of underground animal that could be stalked and trapped; Paul was fixed by something else, by what kept his father still and alert all night, his eyes fixed on his guest. That *something else* – how well Maggie knew it! and how she distrusted it, and how she grieved for Paul, whose heart was beating (she could positively hear it) to the pulse of that dangerous *something else*. It was not the elephants and the lions and the narrow escapes; not the gold; not underground rivers; none of these things in themselves, and perhaps not even the pursuit of them. It was that oblique, unnameable quality in life which Maggie, trying to pin it down safely in homely words, finally dismissed in the sour and nagging phrase: Getting something for nothing. That's all they wanted, she said to herself, sadly; and when she kissed Paul and put him to bed she said, in her sensible voice: 'There isn't anything to be proud of in getting something for nothing.' She saw that he did not know what she meant; and so she left him.

Next morning, when they all went off to the projected well, Maggie remained a little way off, her apron lifted over her head against the sun, arms folded on her breast, in that ancient attitude of a patient and ironic woman; and she shook her head when the diviner offered her the twig and suggested she should try. But Paul tried, standing on his two planted feet, elbows tight into his sides, as he was shown, with the angles of the fork between palm and thumb. The twig turned over for him and he cried, delightedly: 'I'm a diviner, I'm a diviner,' and the old man agreed that he had the gift.

Alec indicated the place and the old man walked across and around it with the twig, and at last he gave his sanction to dig –

the twig turned down, infallibly, at just that spot. Alex paid
him twenty shillings, and the old man wandered off to the next
farm. Maggie said: 'In a country the like of this, where
everyone is parched for water, a man who could tell for sure
where the water is would be nothing but a millionaire. And
look at this one, his coat all patches and his boots going.' She
knew she might as well save her breath, for she found two pairs
of dark and critical eyes fixed on her, and it was as good as if
they said: Well, woman, and what has the condition of his
boots got to do with it?

Late that evening she saw her husband go secretly along the
path to the hillock with a twig, and later still he came back with
an excited face, and she knew that he, too, 'had the gift'.

It was that term that Maggie got a letter from Paul's
headmaster saying that Paul was not fitted for a practical
education, nor yet did he have any especial facility for examin-
ations. If he applied himself he might win a scholarship,
however, and become academically educated . . . and so on. It
was a tactful letter, and its real sense Maggie preferred not to
examine, for it was too wounding to her maternal pride. Its
surface sense was clear; it meant that Paul was going to cost
them a good deal of money. She wrote to say that he must be
given special coaching, and went off to confront Alec. He was
rather irritable with her, for his mind was on the slow descent
of the well. He spent most of his time watching the work. And
what for? Wells were a routine. One set a couple of men to
dig, and if there was no water by a certain depth, one pulled
them out and tried again elsewhere. No need to stand over the
thing like a harassed mother hen. So thought Maggie as she
watched her husband walking in his contemplative way around
the well with his twig in his hands. At thirty feet they came on
water. It was not a very good stream, and might even fail in the
dry season, but Alec was delighted. 'And if that silly old man
hadnae come at all the well would have been sunk just that
place, and no fiddle-faddle with the divining rod,' Maggie
pointed out. Alec gave her a short answer and went off to the
mine on the ridge, taking his twig with him. The miner said,
tolerantly, that he could divine a well if he liked. Alec chose a
place, and came home to tell Maggie he would earn a guinea if

there turned out to be water. 'But man,' said Maggie in amazement, 'you aren't going to keep the family in shoe-leather on guineas earned that way!' She asked again about the money for Paul's coaching, and Alec said: 'What's the matter with the boy, he's doing all right.' She persisted, and he gave in; but he seemed to resent it, this fierce determination of hers that her son must be something special in the world. But when it came to the point, Alec could not find the money, it was just not in the bank. Maggie roused herself and sold eggs and poultry to the store at the station, to earn the extra few pounds that were needed. And she went on scraping shillings together and hoarding them in a drawer, though money from chickens and vegetables would not send Paul through university.

She said to Alec: 'The wages of the trench-boys would save up for Paul's education.' She did not say, since she could not think of herself as a nagging woman: And if you put your mind to it there'd be more money at the end of a season. But although she did not say it, Alec heard it, and replied with an aggrieved look and dogged silence. Later he said: 'If I find another Rand here the boy can go to Oxford, if you want that.' There was not a grain of humour in it, he was quite in earnest.

He spent all his time at the mine while the well was being sunk. They found water and he earned his guinea, which he put carefully with the silver for paying the labourers. What Maggie did not know was that during that time he had been walking around the mine-shaft with his divining rod. It was known how the reefs lay underground, and how much gold they carried.

He remarked, thoughtfully: 'Lucky the mine is just over the way for testing. The trouble with this business is it's difficult to check theories.'

Maggie did not at first understand; for she was thinking of water. She began: 'But the well on the mine is just the same as the one . . .' She stopped, and her face changed as the outrageous suspicion filled her. 'But Alec,' she began, indignantly; and saw him turning away, shutting out her carping and doubt. 'But Alec,' she insisted, furiously, 'surely you aren't thinking of . . .'

'People have been divining for water for centuries,' he said simply, 'so why not gold?' She saw that it was all quite clear to him, like a religious faith, and that nothing she could say would reach him at all. She remained silent; and it was at that moment the last shreds of her faith in him dissolved; and she was filled with the bitterness of a woman who has no life of her own outside husband and children, and must see everything that she could be destroyed. For herself she did not mind; it was Paul – he would have to pay for this lunacy. And she must accept that too; she had married Alec, and that was the end of it; for the thought of leaving him did not enter her mind: Maggie was too old-fashioned for divorce. There was nothing she could do; one could not argue with a possessed person, and Alec was possessed. And in this acceptance, which was like a slow shrug of the shoulders, was something deeper, as if she felt that the visionary moon-chasing quality in Alec – even though it was ridiculous – was something necessary, and that there must always be a moment when the practical-minded must pay tribute to it. From that day, Alec found Maggie willing to listen, though ironically; she might even enquire spontaneously after his 'experiments'. Well, why not? she would catch herself thinking; perhaps he may discover something new after all. Then she pulled herself up, rather angrily; she was becoming infected by the lunacy. In her mind she was lowering the standards she had for Paul.

When Paul next returned from school he found the atmosphere again altered. The exhilaration had gone out of Alec; the honeymoon phase of discovery was past; he was absorbed and grim. His divining rod had become an additional organ; for he was never seen without it. Now it was made of iron wire, because of some theory to do with the attraction of gold for iron; and this theory and all the others were difficult to follow. Maggie made no comment at all; and this Paul would have liked to accept at its surface value, for it would have left him free to move cheerfully from one parent to the other without feeling guilt. But he was deeply disturbed. He saw his mother, with the new eyes of adolescence, for the first time, as distinct from feeling her, as the maternal image. He saw her, critically, as a fading, tired woman, with grey hair. He watched her at evening sitting by the lamp, with the mending on her lap, in the shabby living-room; he saw how she knitted her brows and peered to thread a needle; and how the sock or shirt might lie forgotten while she went off into some dream of her own which kept her motionless, her face sad and pinched, for half an hour at a time, while her hands rubbed unconsciously in a hard and nervous movement over the arms of the chair. It is always a bad time when a son grows up and sees his mother as an elderly lady; but this did not last longer than a few days with Paul; because at once the pathos and tiredness of her gripped him, and with it, a sullen anger against his own father. Paul had become a young man when he was hardly into his teens; he took a clear look at his father and hated him for murdering the gay and humorous Maggie. He looked at the shabby house, at the neat but faded clothes of the family, and at the neglected farm. That holiday he spent down on the lands with the labourers, trying to find out what he should do. To Maggie, the new protective gentleness of her son was sweet, and also very frightening, because she did not know how to help him. He would come to her and say: 'Mother, there's a gulley down the middle of that land, what should I tell the bossboy to do?' or 'We should plant some trees, there's hardly any timber on the place, he's gone and cut it all down.' He referred to his father, with hostility, as *he*; all those weeks, and Maggie said over and over again that he should not worry, he was too young. She was mortally afraid he would become absorbed by the farm and never be able to escape. When he went back to school he wrote desperate letters full of appeals like this one: 'Do, please, *make* him see to that fence before the rains, please, mother, don't be soft and good-natured with him.' But Alec was likely to be irritable about details such as fences; and Maggie would send back the counter-appeal: 'Be patient, Paul. Finish your studies first, there'll be plenty of time for farming.'

He scraped through his scholarship examination with three marks to spare, and Maggie spoke to him very seriously. He appeared to be listening and perhaps he tried to; but in the end he broke in impatiently: 'Oh, mother, what's the use of me wasting time on French and Latin and English Literature? It just doesn't make sense in this country, you must see that.' Maggie could not break through this defence of impatient common sense, and planned to write him a long, authoritative letter when he got back to school. She still kept a touching belief in what schools could put in and knock out of children. At school, she thought, he might be induced into a serious consideration of his future, for the scholarship was a very small one, and would only last two years.

In the meantime he went to his father, since Maggie could not or would not help him, for advice about the farm. But Alec hardly listened to warnings about drains that needed digging and trees that should be planted; and in a fit of bitter disappointment, Paul wandered off to the mine: the boy needed a father, and had to find one somewhere. The miner liked the boy, and spoiled him with sweets and gave him the run of the workings, and let him take rides in the iron lift down the mine-shaft that descended through the soiled and sour-smelling earth. He went for a tour through the underground passages where the mine-boys worked in sodden grey loincloths, the water from the roof dripping and mingling with their running sweat. The muffled thudding of their picks sounded like marching men, a thudding that answered the beat of the mine-stamps overhead; and the lamps on their foreheads, as they moved cautiously through the half-dark tunnels, made them seem like a race of groping Cyclops. At evening he would watch the cage coming up to the sunlight full of labourers, soaked with dirt and sweat, their forehead lamps blank now, their eyes blinking painfully at the glare. Then everyone stood around expectantly for the blasting. At the very last moment the cage came racing up, groaning with the strain, and discharged the two men who had lit the fuse; and almost at once there was a soft, vibrating roar from far under their feet, and the faces and bodies of the watchers relaxed. They yawned and stretched, and drifted off in groups for their meal. Paul would lean over the shaft to catch the acrid whiff from the blasting; and then went off to eat with James, the miner. He lived in a little house with a native woman to cook for him. It was unusual to have a woman working in the house, and this plump creature, who smiled and smiled and gave him biscuits and called him darling, fascinated Paul. It was terrible cheek for a kaffir, and a kaffir woman at that, to call him darling; and Paul would never have dreamed of telling his mother, who had become so critical and impatient, and might forbid him to come again.

Several times his father appeared from the trenches down the ridge, walking straight and fast through the bush with his divining rod in his hand. 'So there you are, old son,' he would say to Paul, and forgot him at once. He nodded to James, asked: 'Do you mind?' and at once began walking back and forth around the mine-shaft with his rod. Sometimes he was pleased, and muttered: 'Looks as if I'm on the right track.' Or he might stand motionless in the sun, his old hat stuck on the back of his head, eyes glazed in thought. 'Contradictory,' he would mutter. 'Can't make it out at all.' Then he would say, briefly, 'Thanks!' nod again at James and Paul as if at strangers, and walk back just as fast and determined to the 'experimental' trenches. James watched him expressionlessly, while Paul avoided his eyes. He knew James found his father ridiculous, and he did not intend to show that he knew it. He would stare off into the bush, chewing at a grass-stem, or down at the ground, making patterns in the dust with his toes, and his face was flushed and unhappy. James, seeing it, would say, kindly: 'Your father'll make it yet, Paul.'

'Do you think there could be gold?' Paul asked, eagerly, for confirmation, not of the gold, but of his father's good sense.

'Why not? There's a mine right here, isn't there? There's half a dozen small-workers round and about.'

'How did you find this reef?'

'Just luck. I was after a wild pig, as it happened. It disappeared somewhere here and I put my rifle down against a rock to have a smoke, and when I picked it up the rock caught my eye, and it seemed a likely bit, so I panned it and it showed up well; I dug a trench or two and the reef went down well, and – so here I am.'

But Paul was still thinking of his father. He was looking away through the trees, over the wire fence to where the trenches were. 'My father says if he proves right he'll divine mines for everyone, all over the world, and not only gold but diamonds and coal – and everything!' maintained Paul proudly, with a defiant look at the miner.

'That's right, son,' said James nicely, meeting the look

seriously. 'Your Dad's all right,' he added, to comfort the boy. And Paul was grateful. He used to go over to James every day just after breakfast and return late in the evening when the sun had gone. Maggie did not know what to say to him. He could not be blamed for taking his troubles to someone who was prepared to spend time with him. It was not his fault for having Alec as a father – thus Maggie, secretly feeling disloyal.

One evening she paid a visit to Alec's trenches. The reef lay diagonally down the slope of the ridge for about a mile, jutting up slantingly, like a rough ledge. At intervals, trenches had been dug across it and in places it had been blown away by a charge of gelignite.

Maggie was astonished at the extent of the work. There were about twelve labourers, and the sound of picks on flinty earth sounded all around her. From shallow trenches protruded the shoulders and heads of some of the men, but others were out of sight, twelve or more feet down. She stood looking on, feeling sad and tired, computing what the labour must cost each month, let alone the money for gelignite and fuses and picks. Alec was moving through the scrub with his wire. He had a new way of handling it. As a novice he had gripped it carefully, elbows tight at his sides, and walked cautiously as if he were afraid of upsetting the magnetism. Now he strode fast over the ground, his loose bush-shirt flying around him, the wire held lightly between his fingers. He was zigzagging back and forth in a series of twenty-foot stretches, and Maggie saw he was tracking the course of a reef, for at the centre of each of these stretches the wire turned smartly downwards. Maggie could not help thinking there was something rather perfunctory in it. 'Let me try,' she asked, and for the first time she held the magic wand. 'Walk along here,' her husband ordered, frowning with the concentration he put into it; and she walked as bidden. It was true that the wire seemed to tug and strain her hands; but she tried again and it appeared to her that if she pulled the two ends apart, pressure tugged the point over and down, whereas if she held it without tension it remained unresponsive. Surely it could not be as simple as that? Surely Alec was not willing the wire to move as he wanted? He saw the doubt in her face and said quickly: 'Perhaps you haven't the electricity in you.' 'I daresay not,' she agreed, dryly; and then asked quickly, trying to sound interested, because at once he reacted like a child to the dry note in her voice: 'Is this water or a reef?'

'A reef.' His face had brightened pathetically at this sign of interest, and he explained: 'I've worked out that either an iron rod or a twig works equally well for water, but if you neutralize the current with an iron nut on the end there must be mineral beneath, but I don't know whether gold or just any mineral.'

Maggie digested this, with difficulty, and then said: 'You say an iron rod, but this is just called galvanized iron, it's just a name, it might be made of anything really, steel or tin – or anything,' she concluded lamely, her list of metals running out.

His face was perturbed. She saw that this, after all, very simple idea had never occurred to him. 'It doesn't matter,' he said, quickly, 'the point is that it works. I've proved it on the reefs at the mine.' She saw that he was looking thoughtful, nevertheless, and could not prevent herself thinking sarcastically that she had given birth to a new theory, probably based on the word *galvanized*. 'How do you know it isn't reacting to water? That mine is always having trouble with water, they say there's an underground river running parallel to the main reef.' But this was obvious enough to be insulting, and Alec said, indignantly: 'Give me credit for some sense. I checked that a long time ago.' He took the wire, slipped an iron nut on each bent end and gripped the ends tight. 'Like that,' he said. 'The iron neutralizes, do you see?' She nodded, and he took off the iron nuts and then she saw him reach into his pocket and take out his signet ring and put that on the wire.

'What are you doing?' asked Maggie, with the most curious feeling of dismay. That signet ring she had given him when they were married. She had bought it with money saved from working as a girl in her parents' shop, and it represented a great deal of sacrifice to her then. Even now, for that matter. And here he was using it as an implement, not even stopping to think how she might feel about it. When he had finished he slipped the gold ring, together with the two iron nuts, back into the pocket of his bush-shirt. 'You'll lose it,' she said, anxiously, but he did not hear her. 'If the iron neutralizes the water, which I've proved,' he said, worriedly, 'then the gold ring should neutralize the gold.' She did not follow the logic of this, though she could not doubt it all had been worked out most logically. He took her slowly along the great reef, talking in that slow, thoughtful way of his. She felt a thwarted misery – for what was the use of being miserable? She did not believe in emotions that were not useful in some way.

Later he began flying back and forth again over a certain vital patch of earth, and he dropped the signet ring and it rolled off among the long grasses, and she helped him to find it again. 'As a matter of fact,' he mused aloud, 'I'll give up the trenches here, I think, and sink a proper shaft. Not here. It's had a fair chance. I'll try somewhere new.'

Before they left at sundown she walked over to one of the deep trenches and stood looking down. It was like a grave, she thought. The mouth was narrow, a slit among the long, straggling grass, with the mounds of rubble banked at the ends, and the rosy evening sun glinted red on the grass-stems and flashed on the pebbles. The trees glowed, and the sky was a wash of colour. The side of the trench showed the strata of soil and stone. First a couple of feet of close, hard, reddish soil, hairy with root-structure; then a slab of pinkish stuff mixed with round white pebbles; then a narrow layer of smooth wl e that resembled the filling in a cake; and then a deep plunge of greyish shale that broke into flakes at the touch of the pick. There was no sign of any reef at the bottom of the trench; and as Alec looked down he was frowning; and she could see that there should have been a reef, and this trench proved something unsettling to the theory.

Some days later he remarked that he was taking the workers off the reef to a new site. She did not care to ask where; but soon she saw a bustle of activity in the middle of the great mealie-field. Yes, he had decided to sink a shaft just there, he, who had once lost his temper if he found even a small stone in a furrow which might nick the ploughshares.

It was becoming a very expensive business. The cases of explosive came out from the station twice a month on the wagon; and she had to order boxes of mining candles, instead of packets, from the store. And when Alec panned the samples there were twenty or more, instead of the half dozen, and he

would be working at the water-tanks half the morning. He was
very pleased with the shaft: he thought he was on the verge of
success. There were always a few grains of gold in the pan, and
one day a long trail of it, which he estimated at almost as much
as would be worth working. He sent a sample to the Mines
Department for a proper test, and it came back confirmed. But
this was literally a flash in the pan, for nothing fresh happened,
and soon that shaft was abandoned. Workers dragged an untidy
straggle of barbed wire around the shaft so that cattle should
not stray into it; and the ploughs detoured there; and in the
centre of the once unbroken field stood a tall thicket of grass
and scrub, which made Paul furious when he came home for
the holidays. He remonstrated with his father, who replied that
it had been justified, because from that shaft he had learned a
great deal, and one must be prepared to pay for knowledge.
He used just those words, very seriously, like a scientist.
Maggie remarked that the shaft had cost at least a hundred
pounds to sink, and she hoped the knowledge was worth that
much. It was the sort of remark she never made these days;
and she understood she had made it now because Paul was
there, who supported her. As soon as Paul came home she
always had the most uncomfortable feeling that his very presence tugged her away from her proper loyalty to Alec. She
found herself becoming critical and nagging; while the moment
Paul had gone she drifted back into a quiet acceptance, like
fatalism. It was not long after that bitter remark that Alec
finally lost his signet ring; and because it was necessary to work
with a gold ring, asked her for her wedding ring. She had never
taken it off her finger since they married, but she slipped it off
now and handed it to him without a word. As far as she was
concerned it was a moment of spiritual divorce; but a divorce
takes two and if the partner doesn't even notice it, what then?

He lost that ring too, of course, but it did not matter by then,
for he had amended his theory, and gold rings had become a
thing of the past. He was now using a rod of fine copper wire
with shreds of asbestos wound about it. Neither Maggie nor
Paul asked for explanations, for there were pages of detailed
notes on his farm desk, and books about magnetic fields and
currents and the sympathy of metals, and they could not have

understood the terms he used, for his philosophy had become
the most extraordinary mixture of alchemy and magic and the
latest scientific theories. His office, which for years had held
nothing but a safe for money and a bookshelf of farming
magazines, was now crammed with lumps of stone, crucibles,
mortars, and the walls were covered with maps and diagrams,
while divining rods in every kind of metal hung from nails.
Next to the newest geological map from the Government office
was an old map imagined by a seventeenth-century explorer,
with mammoth-like beasts scrolling the border; and the names
of the territories were fabulous, like El Dorado, and Golconda,
and Queen of Sheba's Country. There were shelves of retorts
and test-tubes and chemicals, and in a corner stood the skull of
an ox, for there was a period of months when Alec roamed the
farm with that skull dangling from his divining rod, to test a
belief that the substances of bone had affinities with probable
underground deposits of lime. The books ranged from the latest
Government publications to queer pamphlets with titles such
as *Metallurgy and the Zodiac*, or *Gold Deposits on Venus*.

It was in this room that Maggie confronted him with a letter
from Paul's headmaster. The scholarship money was finished.
Was it intended that the boy should try for a fresh one to take
him through university? In this case, he must change his
attitude, for, while he could not be described as stupid, he
'showed no real inclination for serious application'. If not, there
was 'no immediate necessity for reviewing the state of affairs',
but a list of employers was enclosed with whom Mrs Barnes
might care to communicate. In short, the headmaster thought
Paul was thick-witted. Maggie was furious. *Her* son become a
mere clerk! She informed Alec, peremptorily, that they must
find the money to send Paul through university. Alec was
engaged in making a fine diagram of his new shaft in cross-
section, and he lifted a blank face to say: 'Why spoon-feed the
boy? If he was any good he'd work.' The words struck Maggie
painfully, for they summed up her own belief; but she found
herself thinking that it was all Alec's fault for being English
and infecting her son with laziness. She controlled this thought
and said they must find the money, even if Alec curtailed his
experimenting. He looked at her in amazement and anger. She

saw that the anger was against her false scale of values. He was thinking: What is one child's future (even if he happens to be my own, which is a mere biological accident, after all) against a discovery which might change the future of the world? He maintained the silence necessary when dealing with little-minded people. But she would not give in. She argued and even wept, and gave him no peace, until his silence crumbled into violence and he shouted: 'Oh, all right then, have it your own way.'

At first Maggie thought that she should have done this before 'for his own good'. It was not long before she was sorry she had done it. For Alec went striding anxiously about the farm, his eyes worriedly resting on the things he had not really seen for so long – eroded soil, dragging fences, blocked drains – he had been driven out of that inward refuge where everything was clear and meaningful, and there was a cloud of fear on his face like a child with night-terrors. It hurt Maggie to look at him; but for a while she held out, and wrote a proud letter to the headmaster saying there was no need to trouble about a scholarship, they could pay the money. She wrote to Paul himself, a nagging letter, saying that his laziness was making his father ill, and the very least he could do 'after all his father had done for him' was to pass his matriculation well.

This letter shocked Paul, but not in the way she had intended. He knew quite well that his father would never notice whether he passed an examination or not. His mother's dishonesty made him hate her; and he came home from school in a set and defiant mood, saying he did not want to go to university. This betrayal made Maggie frantic. Physically she was passing through a difficult time, and the boy hardly recognized this hectoring and irritable mother. For the sake of peace he agreed to go to university, but in a way which told Maggie that he had no intention at all of doing any work. But his going depended, after all, on Alec, and when Maggie confronted him with the fact that money for fees was needed, he replied, vaguely, that he would have it in good time. It was not quite the old vagueness, for there was a fever and urgency in him that seemed hopeful to Maggie, and she looked every day at the fields for signs of reorganization. There were no changes yet.

Weeks passed, and again she went to him, asking what his new plans were. Alec replied, irritably, that he was doing what he could, and what did she expect, a miracle to order? There was something familiar in this tone and she looked closely at him and demanded: 'Alec, what exactly are you doing?'

He answered in the old, vague way: 'I'm on to it now, Maggie, I'm certain I'll have the answer inside a month.'

She understood that she had spurred him, not into working on the farm, but into putting fresh energies behind the gold-seeking. It was such a shock to her that she felt really ill, and for some days she kept to her bed. It was not real illness, but a temporary withdrawal from living. She pulled the curtains and lay in the hot half-dark. The servants took in her meals, for she could not bear the sight of either her son or her husband. When Paul entered tentatively, after knocking and getting no reply, he found her lying in her old dressing-gown, her eyes averted, her face flushed and exhausted, and she replied to his questions with nervous dislike. But it was Paul who coaxed her back into the family, with that gentle, protective sympathy which was so strange in a boy of his age. She came back because she had to; she took her place again and behaved sensibly, but in a tight and controlled way which upset Paul, and which Alec ignored, for he was quite obsessed. He would come in for meals, his eyes hot and glittering, and eat unconsciously, throwing out remarks like: Next week I'll know. I'll soon know for sure.

In spite of themselves, Paul and Maggie were affected by his certainty. Each was thinking secretly: Suppose he's right? After all, the great inventors are always laughed at to begin with.

There was a day when he came triumphantly in, loaded with pieces of rock. 'Look at this,' he said, confidently. Maggie handled them, to please him. They were of rough, heavy, crumbling substance, like rusty honeycomb. She could see the minerals glistening. She asked: 'Is this what you wanted?'

'You'll see,' said Alec, proudly, and ordered Paul to come with him to the shaft, to help bring more samples. Paul went, in his rather sullen way. He did not want to show that he half-believed his father. They returned loaded. Each piece of rock was numbered according to the part of the reef it had been taken from. Half of each piece was crushed in the mortar, and father and son stood panning all the afternoon.

Paul came to her and said, reluctantly: 'It seems quite promising, mother.' He was appealing to her to come and look. Silently she rose, and went with him to the water-tanks. Alec gave her a defiant stare, and thrust the pan over to her. There was the usual trail of mineral, and behind was a smear of dull gold, and behind that big grits of the stuff. She looked with listless irony over at Paul, but he nodded seriously. She accepted it from him, for he knew quite a lot by now. Alec saw that she trusted his son when she disbelieved him, and gave her a baffled and angry look. She hastened to smooth things over. 'Is it a lot?' she asked.

'Quite enough to make it workable.'

'I see,' she said, seriously. Hope flickered in her and again she looked over at Paul. He gave an odd, humorous grimace, which meant: Don't get excited about it yet; but she could see that he was really excited. They did not want to admit to each other that they were aroused to a half-belief, so they felt awkward. If this madness turned out to be no madness at all, how foolish they would feel!

'What are you going to do now?' she asked Alec.

'I'm sending in all these samples to the Department for proper assaying.'

'*All* of them . . .' she checked the protest, but she was thinking: That will cost an awful lot of money. 'And when will you hear?'

'In about a week.'

Again Paul and she exchanged glances, and they went indoors, leaving Alec to finish the panning. Paul said, with that grudging enthusiasm: 'You know, mother, if it's true . . .'

'If . . .' she scoffed.

'But he says if this works it means he can divine anything. He says Governments will be sending for him to divine their coalfields, water, gold – everything!'

'But Paul,' she said, wearily, 'they can find coalfields and minerals with scientific instruments, they don't need black magic.' She even felt a little mean to damp the boy in this way. 'Can they?' he asked, doubtfully. He didn't want to believe it, because it sounded so dull to him. 'But mother, even if he can't divine, and it's all nonsense, we'll have a rich mine on this farm.'

'That won't satisfy your father,' she said. 'He'll rest at nothing less than a universal theory.'

The rocks were sent off that same day to the station; and now they were restless and eager, even Maggie, who tried not to show it. They all went to examine this vital shaft one afternoon. It was in a thick patch of bush and they had to walk along a native path to reach the rough clearing, where a simple windlass and swinging iron bucket marked the shaft. Maggie leaned over. There being no gleam of water, as in a well, to mark the bottom, she could see nothing at first. For a short distance the circular hole plunged rockily, with an occasional flash of light from a faceted pebble; then a complete darkness. But as she looked there was a glow of light far below and she could see the tiny form of a man against the lit rock face. 'How deep?' she asked, shuddering a little.

'Over a hundred now,' said Alec, casually. 'I'll go down and have a look.' The Africans swung the bucket out into the centre of the shaft and Alec pulled the rope to him, so that the bucket inclined at the edge, slid in one leg and thrust himself out, so that he hung in space, clinging to the rope with one hand and using an arm and a leg to fend off the walls as the rope unwound him down into the blackness. Maggie found it frightening to watch so she pulled her head back from the shaft so as not to look; but Paul lay on his stomach and peered over.

At last Alec came up again. He scrambled lightly from the rocking bucket to safety, and Maggie suppressed a sigh of relief. 'You should see that reef,' he said, proudly. 'It's three feet wide. I've cross-cut in three places and it doesn't break at all.'

Maggie was thinking: Only three days of waiting gone! They were all waiting now, in a condition of hallucinatory calm, for the result to come back from the Assay Department. When only five days had passed Alec said: 'Let's send the boy in for the post.' She had been expecting this, and although she said 'Silly to send so soon,' she was eager to do so; after all, they might have replied, one never knew – and so the houseboy made the trip in to the station. Usually they only sent twice a week for letters. Next day he went again – nothing. And now a week had passed and the three of them were hanging helplessly about the house, watching the road for the post-boy. Eight days: Alec could not work, could not eat, and Paul lounged about the veranda, saying: 'Won't it be funny to have a big mine just down there, on our own farm. There'll be a town around it, and think what this land will be worth then!'

'Don't count your chickens,' said Maggie. But all kinds of half-suppressed longings were flooding up in her. It would be nice to have good clothes again; to buy nice linen, instead of the thin, washed-out stuff they had been using for years. Perhaps she could go to the doctor for her headaches, and he would prescribe a holiday, and they could go to Scotland for a holiday and see the old people . . .

Nine days. The tension was no longer pleasant. Paul and Alec quarrelled. Alec said he would refuse to allow a town to be built around the mine; it would be a pity to waste good farming land. Paul said he was mad – look at Johannesburg, the building lots there were worth thousands the square inch. Maggie again told them not to be foolish; and they laughed at her and said she had no imagination.

The tenth day was a regular mail-day. If there was no letter then Alec said he would telephone the Department; but this was a mere threat, because the Department dealt with hundreds of samples from hopeful gold-searchers all over the country and could not be expected to make special arrangements for one person. But Alec said: 'I'm surprised they haven't telephoned before. Just like a Government department not to see the importance of something like this.' The post was late. They sat on the darkening veranda, gazing down the road through the mealie-fields, and when the man came at last there was still no letter. They had all three expected it.

And now there was a feeling of anti-climax, and Maggie found a private belief confirmed: that nothing could happen to this family in neat, tidy events; everything must always drag itself out, everything declined and decayed and muddled itself along. Even if there is gold, she thought, secretly, there'll be all kinds of trouble with selling it, and it'll drag out for months and months! That eleventh day was a long torture. Alec sat in his office, anxiously checking his calculations, drinking cup after cup of strong, sweet tea. Paul pretended to read, and yawned, and watched the clock until Maggie lost her temper with him. The houseboy, now rather resentful because of these repeated trips of seven miles each way on foot, set off late after lunch to the station. They tried to sleep the afternoon away, but could not keep their eyes closed. When the sun was hanging just over the mountains, they again arranged themselves on the veranda to wait. The sun sank, and Maggie telephoned the station: Yes, the train had been two hours late. They ate supper in tense silence and went back to the veranda. The moon was up and everything flooded with that weird light which made the mealie-fields lose solidity, so that there was a swaying and murmuring like a sea all around them. At last Paul shouted: 'Here he comes!' And now, when they could see the swinging hurricane lamp, that sent a dim, red flicker along the earth across the bright moonlight, they could hardly bring themselves to move. They were thinking: Well, it needn't be today, after all – perhaps we'll have this waiting tomorrow, too.

The man handed in the sack. Maggie took it, removed the bundle of letters and handed them to Alec; she could see a Government envelope. She was feeling sick, and Paul was white, the bones of his face showed too sharply. Alec dropped the letters and then clumsily picked them up. He made several attempts to open the envelope and at last ripped it across, tearing the letter itself. He straightened the paper, held it steady, and – but Maggie had averted her eyes and glanced at Paul. He was looking at her with a sickly and shamed smile.

Alec held the piece of paper loose by one corner, and he was sitting rigid, his eyes dark and blank. 'No good,' he said at last, in a difficult, jerking voice. He seemed to have shrunk, and the flesh on his face was tight. His lips were blue. He dropped the paper and sat staring. Then he muttered: 'I can't understand it, I simply can't understand it.'

Maggie whispered to Paul. He jumped up, relieved to get away, and went to the kitchen and soon returned with a tray of tea. Maggie poured out a big cup, sugared it heavily and handed it to Alec. Those blue lips worried her. He put it at his side, but she took it again and held it in front of him and he drank it off, rather impatiently. It was that impatient movement which reassured her. He was now sitting more easily and his face was flushed. 'I can't understand it,' he said again, in an aggrieved voice, and Maggie understood that the worst was over. She was aching with pity for him and for Paul, who was pretending to read. She could see how badly the disappointment had gripped him. But he was only a child she thought; he would get over it.

'Perhaps we should go to bed,' she suggested, in a small voice; but Alec said: 'That means . . .' he paused, then thought for a moment and said: 'I must have been wrong over – all this time I've been over-estimating the amount in a sample. I thought that was going ounces to the ton. And it means that my theory about the copper was . . .' He sat leaning forward, arms hanging loosely before him; then he jumped up, strode through to his office and returned with a divining wire. She saw it was one of the old ones, a plain iron rod. 'Have you anything gold about you?' he asked, impatiently.

She handed him a brooch her mother had given her. He took it and went towards the veranda. 'Alec,' she protested. 'Not tonight.' But he was already outside. Paul put down his book and smiled ruefully at her. She smiled back. She did not have to tell him to forget all the wild-goose daydreams. Life would seem flat and grey for a while, but not for long – that was what she wanted to say to him; she would have liked, too, to add a little lecture about working for what one wanted in life, and not to trust to luck; but the words stuck. 'Get yourself to bed,' she suggested; but he shook his head and handed her his cup for more tea. He was looking out at the moonlight, where a black, restless shape could be seen passing backwards and forwards.

She went quietly to a window and looked out, shielding herself with a curtain, as though she felt ashamed of this anxious supervision which Alec would most certainly resent if he knew. But he did not notice. The moon shone monotonously down; it looked like a polished silver sixpence; and Alec's shadow jerked and lengthened over the rough ground as he walked up and down with his divining rod. Sometimes he stopped and stood thinking. She went back to sit by Paul. She slipped an arm around him, and so they remained for a time, thinking of the man outside. Later she went to the window again, and this time beckoned to Paul and he stood with her, silently watching Alec.

'He's a very brave man,' she found herself saying, in a choked voice; for she found that determined figure in the moonlight unbearably pathetic. Paul felt awkward because of her emotion, and looked down when she insisted: 'Your father's a very brave man and don't you ever forget it.' His embarrassment sent him off to bed. He could not stand her emotion as well as his own.

Afterwards she understood that her pity for Alec was a false feeling – he did not need pity. It flashed through her mind, too – though she suppressed the thought – that words like brave were as false.

Until the moon slid down behind the house and the veld went dark, Alec remained pacing the patch of ground before the house. At last he came morosely to bed, but without the look of exposed and pitiful fear she had learned to dread: he was safe in the orderly inner world he had built for himself. She heard him remark from the bed on the other side of the room where he was sitting smoking in the dark: 'If that reef outside the front door is what I think it is, then I've found where I was wrong. Quite a silly little mistake, really.'

Cautiously she enquired: 'Are you going on with that shaft?'

'I'll see in the morning. I'll just check up on my new idea first.' They exchanged a few remarks of this kind; and then he crushed out his cigarette and lay down. He slept immediately; but she lay awake, thinking drearily of Paul's future.

In the morning Alec went straight off down to his shaft, while Paul forced himself to go and interview the bossboys about the farmwork. Maggie was planning a straight talk with the boy about his school, but his present mood frightened her. Several times he said, scornfully, just as if he had not himself been intoxicated: 'Father's crazy. He's got no sense left.' He laughed in an arrogant, half-ashamed way; and she controlled her anger at this youthful unfairness. She was tired, and afraid of her own irritability, which these days seemed to explode in the middle of the most trifling arguments. She did not want to

be irritable with Paul because, when this happened, he treated
her tolerantly, as a grown man would, and did not take her
seriously. She waited days before the opportunity came, and
then the discussion went badly after all.

'Why do you want me to be different, mother?' he asked,
sullenly, when she insisted he should study for a scholarship.
'You and father were just like everybody else, but I've got to
be something high and mighty.' Maggie already found herself
growing angry. She said, as her mother might have done:
'Everybody has the duty to better themselves and get on. If
you try you can be anything you like.' The boy's face was set
against her. There was something in the air of this country
which had formed him that made the other, older voice seem
like an anachronism. Maggie persisted: 'Your great-grand-
parents were small farmers. They rented their land from a lord.
But they saved enough to give your grandfather fifty pounds to
take to the city. He got his own shop by working for it. Your
father was just an ordinary clerk, but he took his opportunities
and made his way here. But you see no shame in accepting a
nobody's job, wherever someone's kind enough to offer it to
you.' He seemed embarrassed, and finally remarked: 'All that
class business doesn't mean anything out here. Besides, my
father's a small farmer, just like his grand-parents. I don't see
what's so new about that.' At this, as if his words had released
a spring marked *anger*, she snapped out: 'So, if that's what you
are, the way you look at things, it's a waste of time even . . .'
She checked herself, but it was too late. Her loss of control had
ended the contact between them. Afterwards she wondered if
perhaps he was right. In a way, the wheel had come the circle:
the difference between that old Scotsman and Alec was that
one worked his land with his own hands; he was limited only
by his own capacities; while the other worked through a large
labour-force: he was as much a slave to his ill-fed, backward,
and sullen labourers as they were to him. Well then, and if this
were true, and Paul could see it as clearly as she did, why could
he not decide to break the circle and join the men who had
power because they had knowledge: the free men, that was
how she saw them. Knowledge freed a man; and to that belief
she clung, because it was her nature; and she was to grieve all

her life because such a simple and obvious truth was not simple for Paul.

Some days later she said, tartly, to Paul: 'If you're not going back to school, then you might as well put your mind to the farmwork.' He replied that he was trying to; to her impatience he answered with an appeal: 'It's difficult, mother. Everything's in such a mess. I don't know where to start. I haven't the experience.' Maggie tried hard to control that demon of disappointment and anger in her that made her hard, unsympathetic; but her voice was dry: 'You'll get experience by working.'

And so Paul went to his father. He suggested, practically, that Alec should spend a month ('only a month, Dad, it's not so long') showing him the important things. Alec agreed, but Paul could see, as they went from plough to wagon, field to grazing land, that Alec's thoughts were not with him. He would ask a question, and Alec did not hear. And at the end of three days he gave it up. The boy was seething with frustration and misery. 'What do they expect me to do?' he kept muttering to himself, 'what do they want?' His mother was like a cold wall; she would not love him unless he became a college boy; his father was amiably uninterested. He took himself off to neighbouring farmers. They were kind, for everyone was sorry for him. But after a week or so of listening to advice, he was more dismayed than before. 'You'd better do something about your soil, lad,' they said. 'Your Dad's worked it out.' Or: 'The first thing is to plant trees, the wind'll blow what soil there is away unless you do something quickly.' Or: 'That big vlei of yours: do you know it was dry a month before the rains last year? Your father has ploughed up the catchment area; you'd better sink some wells quickly.' It meant a complete reorganization. He could do it, of course, but . . . the truth was he had not the heart to do it, when no one was interested in him. They just don't care, he said to himself; and after a few weeks of desultory work he took himself off to James, his adopted father. Part of the day he would spend on the lands, just to keep things going, and then he drifted over to the mine.

James was a big, gaunt man, with a broad and bony face. Small grey eyes looked steadily from deep sockets, his mouth was hard. He stood loosely, bending from the shoulders, and

his hands swung loose beside him so that there was something
of a gorilla-look about him. Strength – that was the impression
he gave, and that was what Paul found in him. And yet there
was also a hesitancy, a moment of indecision before he moved
or spoke, and a sardonic note in his drawl – it was strength on
the defensive, a watchful and precarious strength. He smoked
heavily, rough cigarettes he rolled for himself between yellow-
stained fingers; and regularly drank just a little too much. He
would get really drunk several times a year, but between these
indulgences kept to his three whiskies at sundown. He would
toss these back, standing, one after another, when he came in
from work; and then give the bottle a long look, a malevolent
look, and put it away where he could not see it. Then he took
his dinner, without pleasure, to feed the drink; and immediately
went to bed. Once Paul found him at a week-end lying sodden
and asleep sprawled over the table, and he was sickened; but
afterwards James was simple and kindly as always; nor did he
apologize, but took it as a matter of course that a man needed
to drink himself blind from time to time. This, oddly enough,
reassured the boy. His own father never drank, and Maggie
had a puritan horror of it; though she would offer visitors a
drink from politeness. It was a problem that had never touched
him; and now it was presented crudely to him and seemed no
problem at all.

He asked questions about James's life. James would give him
that shrewd, slow look, hesitate a little and then in a rather
tired voice, as if talking were disagreeable, answer the boy's
clumsy questions. He was always very patient with Paul; but
behind the good-natured patience was another emotion, like a
restrained cruelty; it was not a personal cruelty, directed against
Paul, but the self-punishment of fatalism, in which Paul was
included.

James's mother was Afrikaans and his father English. He
had the practicality, the humour, the good sense of his mother's
people, and the inverted and tongue-tied poetry of the English,
which expressed itself in just that angry fatalism and perhaps
also in the drink. He had been raised in a suburb of Johannesburg, and went early to the mines. He spoke of that city with a
mixture of loathing and fascination, so that to Paul it became

an epitome of all the great and glamorous cities of the world. But even while Paul was dreaming of its delights he would hear James drawl: 'I got out of it in time, I had that much sense.' And though he did not want to have his dream darkened, he had to listen: 'When you first go down, you get paid like a prince and the world's your oyster. Then you get married and tie yourself up with a houseful of furniture on the hire-purchase and a house under a mortgage. Your car's your own, and you exchange it for a new one every year. It's a hell of a life, money pouring in and money pouring out, and your wife loves you, and everything's fine, parties and a good time for one and all. And then your best friend finds his chest is giving him trouble and he goes to the doctor, and then suddenly you find he's dropped out of the crowd; he's on half the money and all the bills to pay. His wife finds it no fun and off she goes with someone else. Then you discover it's not just one of your friends, but half the men you know are in just that position, crooks at thirty and owning nothing but the car, and they soon sell that to pay alimony. You find you drink too much – there's something on your mind, as you might say. Then, if you've got sense, you walk out while the going's good. If not, you think: It can't happen to me, and you stay on.' He allowed a minute to pass while he looked at the boy to see how much had sunk in. Then he repeated, firmly: 'That's not just my story, son, take it from me. It's happened to hundreds.'

Paul thought it over and said: 'But you didn't have a wife?'

'Oh, yes, I had a wife all right,' said James, grim and humorous. 'I had a fine wife, but only while I was underground raking in the shekels. When I decided it wasn't good enough and I wanted to save my lungs, and I went on surface work at less money, she transferred to one of the can't-happen-to-me boys. She left him when the doctor told him he was fit for the scrapheap, and then she used her brains and married a man on the stock exchange.'

Paul was silent, because this bitter note against women was not confirmed by what he felt about his mother. 'Do you ever want to go back?' he asked.

'Sometimes,' conceded James, grudgingly, 'Johannesburg's a mad house, but it's got something – but when I get the hankering I remember I'm still alive and kicking when my crowd's mostly dead or put out to grass.' He was speaking of the city as men do of the sea, or travel, or of drugs; and it gripped Paul's imagination. But James looked sharply at him and said: 'Hey, sonnie, if you've got any ideas about going south to the golden city, then think again. You don't want to get any ideas about getting rich quick. If you want to mix yourself up in that racket, then you buy yourself an education and stay on the surface bossing the others, and not underground being bossed. You take it from me, son.'

And Paul took it from him, though he did not want to. The golden city was shimmering in his head like a mirage. But what was the alternative? To stay on this shabby little farm? In comparison, James's life seemed daring and wonderful and dangerous. It seemed to him that James was telling him everything but what was essential; he was leaving something out and soon he came back again for another dose of the astringent common sense that left him unfed, acknowledging it with his mind but not his imagination.

He found James sitting on a heap of shale at the shaft-head, rolling cigarettes, his back to the evening sun. Paul stepped over the long, black shadow and seated himself on the shale. It was loose and shifted under him to form a warm and comfortable hollow. He asked for a cigarette and James good-humouredly gave him one. 'Are you glad you became a small-worker?' he asked at once.

There was a shrewd look and the slow reply: 'No complaints, there's a living as long as the seam lasts – looks as if it won't last much longer at that.' Paul ignored that last remark and persisted: 'If you had your life again, how would you change it?'

James grimaced and asked: 'Who's offering me my life again?'

The boy's face was strained with disappointment. 'I want to know,' he said, stubbornly, like a child.

'Listen, sonnie,' said James, quietly, 'I'm no person to ask for advice. I've nothing much to show. All I've got to pat myself on the back for is I had the sense to pull out of the big money in time to save my lungs.' Paul let these words go past him and he looked up at the big man, who seemed so kindly and solid and sensible, and asked: 'Are you happy?' At last the question was out. James positively started: then he gave that small, humorous grimace and put back his head and laughed. It was painful. Then he slapped Paul's knee and said, tolerantly, still laughing: 'Sonnie, you're a nice kid, don't let any of them get you down.'

Paul sat there, shamefaced, trying to smile, feeling badly let down. He felt as if James, too, had rejected him. But he clung to the man, since there was no one else; he came over in the evenings to talk, while he decided to put his mind to the farm. There was nothing else to do.

Yet while he worked he was daydreaming. He imagined himself travelling south, to the Rand, and working as James had done, saving unheard-of sums of money and then leaving, a rich man, in time to save his health. Or did not leave, but was carried out on a stretcher, with his mother and James as sorrowing witnesses of this victim of the gold industry. Or he saw himself as the greatest mine expert of the continent, strolling casually among the mine-dumps and headgear of the Reef, calmly shedding his pearls of wisdom before awed financiers. Or he bought a large tobacco farm, made fifty thousand the first season and settled vast sums on James and his parents.

Then he took himself in hand, refusing himself even the relief of daydreams, and forced himself to concentrate on the work. He would come back full of hopeful enthusiasm to Maggie, telling her that he was dividing the big field for a proper rotation of crops and that soon it would show strips of colour, from the rich, dark green of maize to the blazing yellow of the sunflower. She listened kindly, but without responding as he wanted. So he ceased to tell her what he was doing – particularly as half the time he felt uneasily that it was wrong, he simply did not know. He set his teeth over his anger and went to Alec and said: 'Now listen, you've got to answer a question.' Alec, divining rod in hand, turned and said: 'What now?' 'I want to know, should I harrow the field now or wait until the rains?' Alec hesitated and said: 'What do you think?' Paul shouted: 'I want to know what *you* think – you've had the experience, haven't you?' And then Alec lost his temper and said: 'Can't you see I'm working this thing out? Go and ask – well go and ask one of the neighbours.'

Paul would not give in. He waited until Alec had finished, and then said: 'Now come on, father, you're coming with me to the field. I want to know.' Reluctantly, Alec went. Day after day, Paul fought with his father; he learned not to ask for general advice, he presented Alec with a definite problem and insisted until he got an answer. He was beginning to find his way among the complexities of the place, when Maggie appealed to him: 'Paul, I know you'll think I'm hard, but I want you to leave your father alone.'

The boy said, in amazement: 'What do you mean? I don't ask him things oftener than once or twice a day. He's got all the rest of the time to play with his toys.'

Maggie said: 'He should be left. I know you won't understand, but I'm right, Paul.' For several days she had been watching Alec; she could see that cloud of fear in his eyes that she had seen before. When he was forced to look outside him and his private world, when he was made to look at the havoc he had created by his negligence, then he could not bear it. He lay tossing at night, complaining endlessly: 'What does he want? What more can I do? He goes on and on, and he knows I'm on to the big thing. I'll have it soon, Maggie, I know I will. This new reef'll be full of gold, I am sure . . .' It made her heart ache with pity for him. She had decided, firmly, to support her husband against her son. After all, Paul was young, he'd his life in front of him. She said, quietly: 'Leave him, Paul. You don't understand. When a person's a failure, it's cruel to make them see it.'

'I'm not making him see anything,' said Paul, bitterly. 'I'm only asking for advice, that's all, that's all!' And the big boy of sixteen burst into tears of rage; and after a helpless, wild look at his mother, ran off into the bush, stumbling as he ran. He was saying to himself: I've had enough, I'm going to run away. I'm going south . . . But after a while he quietened and went back to work. He left Alec alone. But it was not so easy. Again he said to Maggie: 'He's dug a trench right across my new contour ridges; he didn't even ask me . . .' And later: 'He's put a shaft clean in the middle of the sunflowers, he's ruined half an acre – can't you talk to him, mother?' Maggie promised to talk to her husband, and when it came to the point, lost her courage. Alec was like a child, what was the use of talking?

Later still, Paul came and said: 'Do you realize what he's spent this last year on his nonsense?'

'Yes, I know,' sighed Maggie.

'Well, he can't spend so much, and that's all there is to it.'

'What are you going to do?' said Maggie. And then quickly: 'Be gentle with him, Paul. Please . . .'

Paul insisted one evening that Alec 'should listen to him for a moment'. He made his father sit at one end of the table while he placed books of accounts before him and stood over him while he looked through them. 'You can't do it, father,' said Paul, reasonably, patiently; 'you've got to cut it down a bit.'

It hurt Maggie to see them. It hurt Paul, too – it was like pensioning off his own father. For he was simply making conditions, and Alec had to accept them. He was like a petitioner, saying: 'You're not going to take it all away from me, are you? You can't do that?' His face was sagging with disappointment, and in the end it brightened pathetically at the concession that he might keep four labourers for his own use and spend fifty pounds a year. 'Not a penny more,' said Paul. 'And you've got to fill in all the abandoned diggings and shafts. You can't walk a step over the farm now without risking your neck.'

Maggie was tender with Alec afterwards, when he came to her and said: 'That young know-all, turning everything upside down, all theories and no experience!' Then he went off to fill in the trenches and shafts, and afterwards to a distant part of the farm where he had found a new reef.

But now he tended to make sarcastic remarks to Paul; and Maggie had to be careful to keep the peace between them, feeling a traitor to both, for she would agree first with one man, then with the other – Paul was a man now, and it hurt her to see it. Sixteen, thin as a plank, sunburn dark on a strained face, much too patient with her. For Paul would look at the tired old woman who was his mother and think that by rights she should still be a young one, and he shut his teeth over the reproaches he wanted to make: Why do you support him in this craziness; why do you agree to everything he says? And so he worried through that first season; and there came the time to balance the farm books; and there happened something that no one expected.

When all the figuring and accounting was over, Alec, who had apparently not even noticed the work, went into the office and spent an evening with the books. He came out with a triumphant smile and said to Paul: 'Well, you haven't done much better than I did, in spite of all your talk.'

Paul glanced at his mother, who was making urgent signals at him to keep his temper. He kept it. He was white, but he was making an effort to smile. But Alec continued: 'You go on at me, both of you, but when it comes to the point you haven't made any profit either.' It was so unfair . . . that Paul could no longer remain silent. 'You let the farm go to pieces,' he said, bitterly, 'you won't even give me advice when I ask for it, and then you accuse me . . ..'

'Paul,' said Maggie, urgently.

'And when I find a goldmine,' said Alec, magnificently, 'and it won't be long now, you'll come running to me, you'll be sorry then! You can't run a farm and you haven't got the sense to learn elementary geology from me. You've been with me all these years and you don't even know one sort of reef from another. You're too damned lazy to live.' And with this he walked out of the room.

Paul was sitting still, head dropped a little, looking at the floor. Maggie waited for him to smile with her at this child who was Alec. She was arranging the small, humorous smile on her lips that would take the sting out of the scene, when Paul slowly rose, and said quietly: 'Well, that's the end.'

'No, Paul,' cried Maggie, 'you shouldn't take any notice; you can't take it seriously . . .'

'Can't I?' said Paul, bitterly. 'I've had enough.'

'Where are you going? What are you going to do?'

'I don't know.'

'You can't leave,' Maggie found herself saying. 'You haven't got the education to . . .' She stopped herself, but not in time. Paul's face was so hurt and abandoned that she cried out to herself: What's the matter with me? Why did I say it? Paul said: 'Well, that's that.' And he went out of the room after his father.

Paul went over to the mine, found James sitting on his veranda, and said at once: 'James, can I come as a partner with you?'

James's face did not change. He looked patiently at the boy and said, 'Sit down.' Then, when Paul had sat, and was leaning forward waiting, he said: 'There isn't enough profit for a partner here, you know that. Otherwise I'd like to have you. Besides, it looks as if the reef is finished.' He waited and asked: 'What's gone wrong?'

Paul made an impatient movement, dismissing his parents, the farm, and his past, and said: 'Why is your reef finished?'

'I told you that a long time ago.'

He had, but Paul had not taken it in. 'What are you going to do?' he enquired.

'Oh, I don't know,' said James, comfortably, lighting a cigarette. 'I'll get along.'

'Yes, but . . .' Paul was very irritated. This laxness was like his father. 'You've got to do something,' he insisted.

'Well, what do you suggest?' asked James, humorously, with the intention of loosening the lad up. But Paul gripped his hands together and shouted: 'Why should I suggest anything? Why does everyone expect me to suggest things?'

'Hey, take it easy,' soothed James. 'Sorry,' said Paul. He relaxed and said: 'Give me a cigarette.' He lit it clumsily and asked: 'Yes, but if there's no reef, there's no profit, so how are you going to live?'

'Oh, I'll get a job, or find another reef or something,' said James, quite untroubled.

Paul could not help laughing. 'Do you mean to say you've known the reef was finished and you've been sitting here without a care in the world?'

'I didn't say it was finished. It's just dwindling away. I'm not losing money and I'm not making any. But I'll pull out in a week or so, I've been thinking,' said James, puffing clouds of lazy smoke.

'Going prospecting?' asked the boy, persistently.

'Why not?'

'Can I come with you?'

'What do you mean by prospecting?' temporized James. 'If you think I'm going to wander around with a pan and a hammer, romantic-like, you're wrong. I like my comfort. I'll take my time and see what I can find.'

Paul laughed again at James's idea of comfort. He glanced into the two little rooms behind the veranda, hardly furnished at all, with the kitchen behind where the slovenly and good-natured African woman cooked meat and potatoes, potatoes and boiled fowl, with an occasional plate of raw tomatoes as relish.

James said: 'I met an old pal of mine at the station last week. He found a reef half a mile from here last month. He's starting up when he can get the machinery from town. The country's lousy with gold, don't worry.'

And with this slapdash promise of a future Paul was content. But before they started prospecting James deliberately arranged a drinking session. 'About time I had a holiday,' he said, quite seriously. James went through four bottles of whisky in two days. He drank, slowly, and persistently, until he became maudlin and sentimental, a phase which embarrassed the boy. Then he became hectoring and noisy, and complained about his wife, the mine owners of the Rand, and his parents, who had taken him from school at fifteen to make his way as he could. Then, having worked that out of his system, nicely judging his condition, he took a final half-glass of neat whisky, lay comfortably down on the bed and passed out. Paul sat beside his friend and waited for him to wake, which he did, in five or six hours, quite sober and very depressed. Then the process was repeated.

Maggie was angry when Paul came home after three days' absence, saying that James had had malaria and needed a nurse. At the same time she was pleased that her son could sit up three nights with a sick man and then come walking quietly home across the veld, without any fuss or claim for attention, to demand a meal and eat it and then take himself off to bed; all very calm and sensible, like a grown person.

She wanted to ask him if he intended to run the farm, but

did not dare. She could not blame him for feeling as he did, but she could not approve his running away either. In the end it was Alec who said to Maggie, in his son's presence: 'Your precious Paul. He runs off the farm and leaves it standing while he drinks himself under the table.' He had heard that James was in a drinking bout from one of the Africans.

'Paul doesn't drink,' said Maggie finally, telling Alec with her eyes that she was not going to sit there and hear him run down his son. Alec looked away. But he said derisively to Paul: 'Been beaten by the farm already? You can't stick it more than one season?'

Paul replied, calmly: 'As you like.'

'What are you going to do now?' asked Maggie, and Paul said: 'You'll know in good time.' To his father he could not resist saying: 'You'll know soon enough for your peace of mind!'

When he had gone, Maggie sat thinking for a long time: if he was with James it meant he was going mining; he was as bad as his father, in fact. Worse, he was challenging his father. With the tired thought that she hoped at least Alec would not understand his son was challenging him, she walked down to the fields to tell her husband that he should spend a little of his time keeping the farm going. She found him at work beside his new shaft, and sat quietly on a big stone while he explained some new idea to her. She said nothing about the farm.

As for Paul, he said to James: 'Let's start prospecting.' James said: 'There's no hurry.' 'Yes, there is, there is,' insisted the boy, and with a shrug James went to find his hammer.

Together they spent some days working over the nearer parts of the bush. At this stage they did not go near the Barnes's farm, but kept on the neighbouring farm. This neighbour was friendly because he hoped that a really big reef could be found and then he could sell his land for what he chose to ask for it. Sometimes he sent a native to tell them that there was a likely reef in such and such a place, and the man and the boy went over to test it. Nothing came of these suggestions. Mostly Paul slept in James's house. Once or twice, for the sake of peace, he went home, looking defiant. But Maggie greeted him pleasantly. She had gone beyond caring. She was listless and ironic. All she feared was that Alec would find out that Paul was prospecting. Once she said, trying to joke: 'What'd you do if Paul found gold?' Alec responded, magnificently: 'Any fool can find gold. It takes intelligence to use the divining rod properly.' Maggie smiled and shrugged. Then she found another worry: that if Paul knew that his father did not think enough of him to care, he might give up the search; and she felt it better for him to be absorbed in prospecting than in running away down South, or simply drinking his time away. She thought sadly that Paul had made for himself an image of a cruel and heartless father, whereas he was more like a shadow. To fight Alec was shadow-boxing, and she remembered what she had felt over the wedding rings. He had lost her ring, she felt as if the bottom had dropped out of their marriage, and all he said was: 'Send to town for another one, what's in a ring, after all?' And what *was* in a ring? He was right. With Alec, any emotion always ended in a shrug of the shoulders.

And then, for a time, there was excitement. Alec found a reef that carried gold; not much but almost as much as the mine on the ridge. And of course he wanted to work it. Maggie would not agree. She said it was too risky; and anyway, where would they find the capital? Alec said, calmly, that money could be borrowed. Maggie said it would be hanging a millstone around their necks . . . and so on. At last experts came from town and gave a verdict: it was under the workable minimum. The experts went back again, but oddly enough, Alec seemed encouraged rather than depressed. 'There you are,' he said, 'I always said there was gold, didn't I?' Maggie soothed him, and he went off to try another reef.

Paul, who had not been home for a couple of weeks, got wind of this discovery and came striding over with a fevered look to demand: 'Is it true that father's found gold?'

'No,' said Maggie. And then, with sad irony: 'Wouldn't you be pleased for his sake if he did?' At that look he coloured, but he could not bring himself to say he would be pleased. Suddenly Maggie asked: 'Are you drinking, Paul?' He did not look well, but that was due to the intensity of his search for gold, not due to drink. James would not let him drink: 'You can do what you like when you're twenty-one,' he said, just like a father. 'But you're not drinking when you're with me till then.'

Paul did not want to tell his mother that he allowed James to order him about, and he said: 'You've got such a prejudice against drink.'

'Plenty of people'd be pleased if they'd been brought up with *that* prejudice,' she said, dryly. 'Look how many ruin themselves in this country with drink.'

He said, obstinately: 'James is all right, isn't he? There's nothing wrong with him – and he drinks off and on.'

'Can't you be "all right" without drinking off and on?' enquired Maggie, with that listless irony that upset Paul because it was not like her. He kissed her and said: 'Don't worry about me, I'm doing fine.' And back he went to James.

For now he and James spent every spare moment prospecting. It was quite different from Alec's attitude. James seemed to assume that since this was gold country, gold could be found; it was merely a question of persistence. Quite calmly, he closed down his mine, and dismissed his labour force, and set himself to find another. It had a convincing ring to Paul; it was not nearly as thrilling as with Alec, who was always on the verge of a discovery that must shake the world, no less; but it was more sensible. Perhaps, too, Paul was convinced because it was necessary; and what is necessary has its own logic.

When they had covered the neighbour's farm they hesitated before crossing the boundary on to Alec's. But one evening they straddled over the barbed fence, while Paul lagged behind, feeling unaccountably guilty. James wanted to go to the quartz reef. He glanced enquiringly back at the boy, who slowly followed him, persuading himself there was no need to feel guilty. Prospecting was legal, and he had a right to it. They slowly made their way to the reef. The trenches had been roughly filled in, and the places where the stone had been hammered and blasted were already weathering over. They worked on the reef for several days, and sometimes James said, humorously: 'When your father does a thing he does it thoroughly . . .' For there was hardly a piece of that mile-long reef which had not been examined. Soon they left it, and worked their way along the ridge. The ground was broken by jutting reefs, outcrops, boulders, but here, it seemed, Alec had not been.

'Well, sonnie,' said James, 'this looks likely, hey?'

There was no reason why it should be any more likely than any other place, but Paul was trusting to the old miner's instinct. He liked to watch him move slowly over the ground, pondering over a slant of rock, a sudden scattering of sparkling white pebbles. It seemed like a kind of magic, as ways of thinking do that have not yet been given names and classified. Yet it was based on years of experience of rock and minerals and soil; although James did not consciously know why he paused beside this outcrop and not the next; and to Paul it appeared an arbitrary process.

One morning they met Alec. At first Paul hung back; then he defiantly strode forward. Alec's face was hostile and he demanded: 'What are you two doing here?'

'It's legal to prospect, Mr Barnes,' said James.

Alec frowned and said: 'You didn't have the common decency to ask.' He was looking at Paul and not at James. Then, when Paul could not find words, he seemed to lose interest and began moving away. They were astounded to hear him remark: 'You're quite right to try here, though. It always did seem a likely spot. Might have another shot here myself one day.' Then he walked slowly off.

Paul felt bad; he had been imagining his father as an antagonist. So strong was his reaction that he almost lost interest in the thing; he might even have gone back to the farm if James had not been there to keep him to it. For James was not the sort of man to give up a job once he had started.

Now he glanced at Paul and said: 'Don't you worry, son. Your Dad's a decent chap, when all's said. He was right, we should have asked, just out of politeness.'

'It's all very well,' said Paul, hugging his old resentment. 'He sounds all right now, but you should have heard the things he said.'

'Well, well, we all lose our tempers,' said James, tolerantly.

Several days later James remarked: 'This bit of rock looks quite good, let's pan it.' They panned it, and it showed good gold. 'Doesn't prove anything,' said James. 'We'd better dig a trench or two.' A trench or two were dug, and James said, casually: 'Looks as if this might be it.' It did not immediately come home to Paul that this was James's way of announcing success. It was too unheroic. He even found himself thinking: If this is all it is, what's the point of it? *To find gold* – what a phrase it is! Impossible to hear it without a quickening of the pulse. And so through the rest: I might find gold, you could find gold; they, most certainly, always seem to find gold. But not only was it possible to drop the words, as if they were the most ordinary in the world, it did not occur to James that Paul might be disappointed. 'Yes, this is it,' he confirmed himself, some days later, and added immediately: 'Let's get some food, no point in being uncomfortable for nothing.'

So flat was the scene, just a few untidy diggings in the low greenish scrub, with the low, smoky September sky pressing down, that Paul was making the thing verbally dramatic in his mind, thus: 'We have found gold. James and I have found gold. And won't my father be cross!' But it was no use at all; and he obediently followed James back to the little shack for cold meat and potatoes. It all went on for weeks, while James surveyed the whole area, digging cross trenches, sinking a small shaft. Then he sent some rocks in to the Assay people and their assessment was confirmed. Surely this should be a moment of rejoicing, but all James said was: 'We won't get rich on this lot, but it could be worse.' It seemed as if he might even shrug the whole thing off and start again somewhere else.

Once again the experts came out, standing over the diggings making their cautious pronouncements; city men, dressed in the crisp khaki they donned for excursions into the veld. 'Yes, it was workable. Yes, it might even turn out quite prosperous, with luck.' Paul felt cheated of glory, and there was no one who would understand this feeling. Not even Maggie; he tried to catch her eye and smile ruefully, but her eye would not be caught. For she was there on her son's invitation. She walked over to see Paul's triumph without telling Alec. And all the time she watched the experts, watched Paul and James, she was thinking of Alec, who would have to be told. After all these years of work with his divining rods and his theories; after all that patient study of the marsh light, gold, it seemed too cruel that his son should casually walk over the ridge he had himself prospected so thoroughly and find a reef within a

matter of weeks. It was so cruel that she could not bring herself
to tell him. Why did it have to be there, on that same ridge?
Why not anywhere else in the thousands of acres of veld? And
she felt even more sad for Alec because she knew quite well
that the reef's being there, in that ridge, was part of Paul's
triumph. She was afraid that Alec would see that gleam of
victory in his son's eyes.

In the meantime the important piece of ground lay waiting,
guarded by the prescribed pegging notices that were like
signboards on which were tacked the printed linen notices
listing fines and penalties against any person – even Alec
himself – who came near to the still invisible gold without
permission. Then out came the businessmen and the lawyers,
and there was a long period of signing documents and drinking
toasts to everyone concerned.

Paul came over to supper one evening, and Maggie sat in
suspense, waiting for him to tell his father, waiting for the cruel
blow to fall. The boy was restless, and several times opened his
mouth to speak, fell silent, and said nothing. When Alec had
gone to his office to work out some calculations for a new reef,
Maggie said: 'Well, I suppose you're pleased with yourself.'

Paul grinned and said: 'Shouldn't I be?'

'Your poor father – can't you see how he's going to feel
about it?'

All she could get out of him was: 'All right, you tell him
then. I won't say anything.'

'I'm glad you've got some feeling for him.'

So Paul left and she was faced with the task of telling Alec.
She marvelled that he did not know already. All he had to do
was lift his eyes and look close at the ridge. There, among the
bare thinned trees of the September veld, were the trenches,
like new scars, and a small black activity of workers.

Then one day Paul came again and said – and now he
sounded apologetic: 'You'll have to tell him, you know. We're
moving the heavy machinery tomorrow. He'll see for himself.'

'I really will tell him,' she promised.

'I don't want him to feel bad, really I don't, mother.' He
sounded as insistent as a child who needs to be forgiven.

'You didn't think of it before,' she said, dryly.

He protested: 'But surely – you've never said you were glad, not once. Don't you understand? This might turn out to be a really big thing; the experts said it might. I might be a partner of a really big mine quite soon.'

'And you're not eighteen yet,' she said, smiling to soften the words. She was thinking that it was a sad falling-off from what she had hoped. What was he? A small-worker. Half-educated, without ambition, dependent on the terrible thing, luck. He might be a small-worker all his life, with James for companion, drinking at week-ends, the African woman in the kitchen – oh, yes, she knew what went on, although he seemed to think she was a fool. And if they were lucky, he would become a rich man, one of the big financiers of the sub-continent. It was possible, anything was possible – she smiled tolerantly and said nothing.

That night she lay awake, trying to arouse in herself the courage to tell Alec. She could not. At breakfast she watched his absorbed, remote face, and tried to find the words. They would not come. After the meal he went into his office, and she went quickly inside. Shading her eyes she looked across the mealie-fields to the ridge. Yes, there went the heavy wagons, laden with the black bulk of the headgear, great pipes, pulleys: Alec had only to look out of his window to see. She slowly went inside and said: 'Alec, I want to tell you something.' He did not lift his eyes. 'What is it?' he asked, impatiently.

'Come with me for a minute.' He looked at her, frowned, then shrugged and went after her. She pointed at the red dust track that showed in the scrub and said: 'Look.' Her voice sounded like a little girl's.

He glanced at the laden wagons, then slowly moved his eyes along the ridge to where the diggings showed.

'What is it?' he asked. She tried to speak and found that her lips were trembling. Inside she was crying: Poor thing; poor, poor thing! 'What is it?' he demanded again. Then, after a pause: 'Have they found something?'

'Yes,' she brought out at last.

'Any good?'

'They say it might be very good.' She dared to give him a

sideways glance. His face was thoughtful, no more, and she was encouraged to say: 'James and Paul are partners.'

'And on that ridge,' he exclaimed at last. There was no resentment in his voice. She glanced at him again. 'It seems hard, doesn't it?' he said, slowly; and at once she clutched his arm and said: 'Yes, my dear, it is, it is, I'm so very sorry . . .' And here she began to cry. She wanted to take him in her arms and comfort him. But he was still gazing over at the ridge. 'I never tried just that place,' he said, thoughtfully. She stopped crying. 'Funny, I was going to sink a trench just there, and then – I forget why I didn't.'

'Yes?' she said, in a little voice. She was understanding that it was all right. Then he remarked: 'I always said there was gold on that ridge, and there is. I always said it, didn't I?'

'Yes, my dear, you did – where are you going?' she added, for he was walking away, the divining rod swinging from his hand.

'I'll just drop over and do a bit of work around their trenches,' she heard as he went. 'If they know how the reefs lie, then I can test . . .'

He vanished into the bush, walking fast, the tails of his bush-shirt flying.

When Paul saw him coming he went forward to meet him, smiling a rather sickly smile, his heart beating with guilt, and all Alec said was: 'Your mother told me you'd struck it lucky. Mind if I use my rod around here a bit?' And then, as Paul remained motionless from surprise, he said, impatiently: 'Come on, there's a good kid, I'm in a hurry.'

And as the labourers unloaded the heavy machinery and James and Paul directed the work, Alec walked in circles and in zigzags, the rods rising and falling in his hands like a variety of trapped·insects, his face rapt with thought. He was oblivious to everything. They had to pull him aside to avoid being crushed by the machinery. When, at midday, they asked him to share their cold meat, and broke it to him that they had found a second reef, even richer than the first, with every prospect of 'going as deep as China', all he said was, and in a proud, pleased voice: 'Well, that proves it. I told you, didn't I? I always told you so.'

The Antheap

Beyond the plain rose the mountains, blue and hazy in a strong blue sky. Coming closer they were brown and grey and green, ranged heavily one beside the other, but the sky was still blue. Climbing up through the pass the plain flattened and diminished behind, and the peaks rose sharp and dark grey from lower heights of heaped granite boulders, and the sky overhead was deeply blue and clear and the heat came shimmering off in waves from every surface. 'Through the range, down the pass, and into the plain the other side – let's go quickly, there it will be cooler, the walking easier.' So thinks the traveller. So the traveller has been thinking for many centuries, walking quickly to leave the stifling mountains, to gain the cool plain where the wind moves freely. But there is no plain. Instead, the pass opens into a hollow which is closely surrounded by kopjes: the mountains clench themselves into a fist here, and the palm is a mile-wide reach of thick bush, where the heat gathers and clings, radiating from boulders, rocking off the trees, pouring down from a sky which is not blue, but thick and low and yellow, because of the smoke that rises, and has been rising so long from this mountain-imprisoned hollow. For though it is hot and close and arid half the year, and then warm and steamy and wet in the rains, there is gold here, so there are always people, and everywhere in the bush are pits and slits where the prospectors have been, or shallow holes, or even deep shafts. They say that the Bushmen were here, seeking gold, hundreds of years ago. Perhaps, it is possible. They say that trains of Arabs came from the coast, with slaves and warriors, looking for gold to enrich the courts of the Queen of Sheba. No one has proved they did not.

But it is at least certain that at the turn of the century there was a big mining company which sank half a dozen fabulously deep shafts, and found gold going ounces to the ton sometimes, but it is a capricious and chancy piece of ground, with reefs all broken and unpredictable, and so this company loaded its heavy equipment into lorries and off they went to look for gold somewhere else, and in a place where the reefs lay more evenly.

For a few years the hollow in the mountains was left silent, no smoke rose to dim the sky, except perhaps for an occasional prospector, whose fire was a single column of wavering blue smoke, as from the cigarette of a giant, rising into the blue, hot sky.

Then all at once the hollow was filled with violence and noise and activity and hundreds of people. Mr Macintosh had bought the rights to mine this gold. They told him he was foolish, that no single man, no matter how rich, could afford to take chances in this place.

But they did not reckon with the character of Mr Macintosh, who had already made a fortune and lost it, in Australia, and then made another in New Zealand, which he still had. He proposed to increase it here. Of course, he had no intention of sinking those expensive shafts which might or might not reach gold and hold the dipping, chancy reefs and seams. The right course was quite clear to Mr Macintosh, and this course he followed, though it was against every known rule of proper mining.

He simply hired hundreds of African labourers and set them to shovel up the soil in the centre of that high, enclosed hollow in the mountains, so that there was soon a deeper hollow, then a vast pit, then a gulf like an inverted mountain. Mr Macintosh was taking great swallows of the earth, like a gold-eating monster, with no fancy ideas about digging shafts or spending money on roofing tunnels. The earth was hauled, at first, up the shelving sides of the gulf in buckets, and these were suspended by ropes made of twisted bark fibre, for why spend money on steel ropes when this fibre was offered free to mankind on every tree? And if it got brittle and broke and the buckets went plunging into the pit, then they were not harmed by the fall, and there was plenty of fibre left on the trees. Later, when the gulf grew too deep, there were trucks on rails, and it was not unknown for these, too, to go sliding and plunging to the bottom, because in all Mr Macintosh's dealings there was a fine, easy good-humour, which meant he was more likely to laugh at such an accident than grow angry. And if someone's head got in the way of falling buckets or trucks, then there were plenty of black heads and hands for the hiring. And if the loose, sloping bluffs of soil fell in landslides, or if a tunnel, narrow as an antbear's hole, that was run off sideways from the main pit like a tentacle exploring for new reefs, caved in suddenly, swallowing half a dozen men – well, one can't make an omelette without breaking eggs. This was Mr Macintosh's favourite motto.

The Africans who worked this mine called it 'the pit of death', and they called Mr Macintosh 'The Gold Stomach'. Nevertheless, they came in their hundreds to work for him, thus providing free arguments for those who said: 'The native doesn't understand good treatment, he only appreciates the whip, look at Macintosh, he's never short of labour.'

Mr Macintosh's mine, raised high in the mountains, was far from the nearest police station, and he took care that there was always plenty of kaffir beer brewed in the compound, and if the police patrols came searching for criminals, these could count on Mr Macintosh facing the police for them and assuring them that such and such a native, Registration Number Y2345678, had never worked for him. Yes, of course they could see his books.

Mr Macintosh's books and records might appear to the simple-minded as casual and ineffective, but these were not the words used of his methods by those who worked for him, and so Mr Macintosh kept his books himself. He employed no book-keeper, no clerk. In fact, he employed only one white man, an engineer. For the rest, he had six overseers or bossboys whom he paid good salaries and treated like important people.

The engineer was Mr Clarke, and his house and Mr Macintosh's house were on one side of the big pit, and the compound for the Africans was on the other side. Mr Clarke earned fifty pounds a month, which was more than he would earn anywhere else. He was a silent, hardworking man, except when he got drunk, which was not often. Three or four times in the year he would be off work for a week, and then Mr Macintosh did his work for him till he recovered, when he greeted him with the good-humoured words: 'Well, laddie, got that off your chest?'

Mr Macintosh did not drink at all. His not drinking was a passionate business, for like many Scots people he ran to extremes. Never a drop of liquor could be found in his house. Also, he was religious, in a reminiscent sort of way, because of his parents, who had been very religious. He lived in a two-roomed shack, with a bare wooden table in it, three wooden chairs, a bed and a wardrobe. The cook boiled beef and carrots and potatoes three days a week, roasted beef three days, and cooked a chicken on Sundays.

Mr Macintosh was one of the richest men in the country, he was more than a millionaire. People used to say to him: But for heaven's sake, he could do anything, go anywhere, what's the point of having so much money if you live in the back of beyond with a parcel of blacks on top of a big hole in the ground?

But to Mr Macintosh it seemed quite natural to live so, and when he went for a holiday to Cape Town, where he lived in the most expensive hotel, he always came back again long before he was expected. He did not like holidays. He liked working.

He wore old, oily khaki trousers, tied at the waist with an old red tie, and he wore a red handkerchief loose around his neck over a white singlet. He was short and broad and strong, with a big square head tilted back on a thick neck. His heavy brown arms and neck sprouted thick black hair around the edges of the singlet. His eyes were small and grey and shrewd. His mouth was thin, pressed tight in the middle. He wore an old felt hat on the back of his head, and carried a stick cut from the bush, and he went strolling around the edge of the pit, slashing the stick at bushes and grass or sometimes at lazy Africans, and he shouted orders to his bossboys, and watched the swarms of workers far below him in the bottom of the pit, and then he would go to his little office and make up his books, and so he spent his day. In the evenings he sometimes asked Mr Clarke to come over and play cards.

Then Mr Clarke would say to his wife: 'Annie, he wants me,' and she nodded and told her cook to make supper early.

Mrs Clarke was the only white woman on the mine. She did not mind this, being a naturally solitary person. Also, she had been profoundly grateful to reach this haven of fifty pounds a month with a man who did not mind her husband's bouts of drinking. She was a woman of early middle age, with a thin, flat body, a thin, colourless face, and quiet blue eyes. Living here, in this destroying heat, year after year, did not make her ill, it sapped her slowly, leaving her rather numbed and silent. She spoke very little, but then she roused herself and said what was necessary.

For instance, when they first arrived at the mine it was to a two-roomed house. She walked over to Mr Macintosh and said: 'You are alone, but you have four rooms. There are two of us and the baby, and we have two rooms. There's no sense in it.' Mr Macintosh gave her a quick, hard look, his mouth tightened, and then he began to laugh. 'Well, yes, that is so,' he said, laughing, and he made the change at once, chuckling every time he remembered how the quiet Annie Clarke had put him in his place.

Similarly, about once a month Annie Clarke went to his house and said: 'Now get out of my way, I'll get things straight for you.' And when she'd finished tidying up she said: 'You're nothing but a pig, and that's the truth.' She was referring to his habit of throwing his clothes everywhere, or wearing them for weeks unwashed, and also to other matters which no one else dared to refer to, even as indirectly as this. To this he might reply, chuckling with the pleasure of teasing her: 'You're a married woman, Mrs Clarke,' and she said: 'Nothing stops you getting married that I can see.' And she walked away very straight, her cheeks burning with indignation.

She was very fond of him, and he of her. And Mr Clarke liked and admired him, and he liked Mr Clarke. And since Mr Clarke and Mrs Clarke lived amiably together in their four-roomed house, sharing bed and board without ever quarrelling, it was to be presumed they liked each other too. But they seldom spoke. What was there to say?

It was to this silence, to these understood truths, that little Tommy had to grow up and adjust himself.

Tommy Clarke was three months when he came to the mine, and day and night his ears were filled with noise, every day and every night for years, so that he did not think of it as noise, rather it was a different sort of silence. The mine-stamps thudded *gold*, gold, *gold*, gold, *gold*, gold, on and on, never changing, never stopping. So he did not hear them. But there came a day when the machinery broke, and it was when Tommy was three years old, and the silence was so terrible and so empty that he went screeching to his mother: 'It's stopped, it's stopped,' and he wept, shivering, in a corner until the thudding began again. It was as if the heart of the world had gone silent. But when it started to beat, Tommy heard it, and he knew the difference between silence and sound, and his ears acquired a new sensitivity, like a conscience. He heard the shouting and the singing from the swarms of working Africans, reckless, noisy people because of the danger they always must live with. He heard the picks ringing on stone, the softer, deeper thud of picks on thick earth. He heard the clang of the trucks, and the roar of falling earth, and the rumbling of trolleys on rails. And at night the owls hooted and the nightjars screamed, and the crickets chirped. And when it stormed it seemed the sky itself was flinging down bolts of noise against the mountains, for the thunder rolled and crashed, and the lightning darted from peak to peak around him. It was never silent, ever, save for that awful moment when the heart stopped beating. Yet later he longed for it to stop again, just for an hour, so that he might hear a true silence. That was when he was a little older, and the quietness of his parents was beginning to trouble him. There they were, always so gentle, saying so little, only: That's how things are; or: You ask so many questions; or: You'll understand when you grow up.

It was a false silence, much worse than that real silence had been.

He would play beside his mother in the kitchen, who never said anything but Yes, and No, and – with a patient, sighing voice, as if even his voice tired her: You talk so much, Tommy!

And he was carried on his father's shoulders around the big, black working machines, and they couldn't speak because of the din the machines made. And Mr Macintosh would say: Well, laddie? and give him sweets from his pocket, which he always kept there, especially for Tommy. And once he saw Mr Macintosh and his father playing cards in the evening, and they didn't talk at all, except for the words that the game needed.

So Tommy escaped to the friendly din of the compound across the great gulf and played all day with the black children, dancing in their dances, running through the bush after rabbits, or working wet clay into shapes of bird or beast. No silence there, everything noisy and cheerful, and at evening he returned to his equable, silent parents, and after the meal he lay in bed listening to the *thud*, thud, *thud*, thud, *thud*, thud, of the stamps. In the compound across the gulf they were drinking and dancing, the drums made a quick beating against the slow thud of the stamps, and the dancers around the fires yelled, a high, undulating sound like a big wind coming fast and crooked through a gap in the mountains. That was a different world, to which he belonged as much as to this one, where people said: Finish your pudding; or: It's time for bed; and very little else.

When he was five years old he got malaria and was very sick. He recovered, but in the rainy season of the next year he got it again. Both times, Mr Macintosh got into his big American car and went streaking across the thirty miles of bush to the nearest hospital for the doctor. The doctor said quinine, and be careful to screen for mosquitoes. It was easy to give quinine, but Mrs Clarke, that tired, easy-going woman, found it hard to say: Don't, and Be in by six; and Don't go near water; and so, when Tommy was seven, he got malaria again. And now Mrs Clarke was worried, because the doctor spoke severely, mentioning blackwater.

Mr Macintosh drove the doctor back to his hospital and then came home, and at once went to see Tommy, for he loved Tommy very deeply.

Mrs Clarke said: 'What do you expect, with all these holes everywhere, they're full of water all the wet season.'

'Well, lassie, I can't fill in all the holes and shafts, people have been digging up here since the Queen of Sheba.'

'Never mind about the Queen of Sheba. At least you could screen our house properly.'

'I pay your husband fifty pounds a month,' said Mr Macintosh, conscious of being in the right.

'Fifty pounds and a proper house,' said Annie Clarke.

Mr Macintosh gave her that quick, narrow look, and then laughed loudly. A week later the house was encased in fine wire mesh all around from roof-edge to veranda-edge, so that it looked like a new meat safe, and Mrs Clarke went over to Mr Macintosh's house and gave it a grand cleaning, and when she left she said: 'You're nothing but a pig, you're as rich as the Oppenheimers, why don't you buy yourself some new vests at least? And you'll be getting malaria, too, the way you go traipsing about at nights.'

She turned to Tommy, who was seated on the veranda behind the grey-glistening wire-netting, in a big deck chair. He was very thin and white after the fever. He was a long child, bony, and his eyes were big and black, and his mouth full and pouting from the petulances of the illness. He had a mass of richly-brown hair, like caramels, on his head. His mother looked at this pale child of hers, who was yet so brightly coloured and full of vitality, ad her tired will-power revived enough to determine a new régime for him. He was never to be out after six at night, when the mosquitoes were abroad. He was never to be out before the sun rose.

'You can get up,' she said, and he got up, thankfully throwing aside his covers.

'I'll go over to the compound,' he said at once.

She hesitated, and then said: 'You mustn't play there any more.'

'Why not?' he asked, already fidgeting on the steps outside the wire-netting cage.

Ah, how she hated these Whys, and Why nots! They tired her utterly. 'Because I say so,' she snapped.

But he persisted: 'I always play there.'

'You're getting too big now, and you'll be going to school soon.'

Tommy sank on to the steps and remained there, looking away over the great pit to the busy, sunlit compound. He had known this moment was coming, of course. It was a knowledge that was part of the silence. And yet he had not known it. He said: 'Why, why, why, why?' singing it out in a persistent wail.

'Because I say so.' Then, in tired desperation: 'You get sick from the Africans, too.'

At this, he switched his large black eyes from the scenery to his mother, and she flushed a little. For they were derisively scornful. Yet she half-believed it herself, or rather, must believe it, for all through the wet season the bush would lie waterlogged and festering with mosquitoes, and nothing could be done about it, and one has to put the blame on something.

She said: 'Don't argue. You're not to play with them. You're too big now to play with a lot of dirty kaffirs. When you were little it was different, but now you're a big boy.'

Tommy sat on the steps in the sweltering afternoon sun that came thick and yellow through the haze of dust and smoke over the mountains, and he said nothing. He made no attempt to go near the compound, now that his growing to manhood depended on his not playing with the black people. So he had been made to feel. Yet he did not believe a word of it, not really.

Some days later, he was kicking a football by himself around the back of the house when a group of black children called to him from the bush and he turned away as if he had not seen them. They called again, and then ran away. And Tommy wept bitterly, for now he was alone.

He went to the edge of the big pit and lay on his stomach looking down. The sun blazed through him so that his bones ached, and he shook his mass of hair forward over his eyes to shield them. Below, the great pit was so deep that the men working on the bottom of it were like ants. The trucks that climbed up the almost vertical sides were matchboxes. The system of ladders and steps cut in the earth, which the workers used to climb up and down, seemed so flimsy across the gulf that a stone might dislodge it. Indeed, falling stones often did. Tommy sprawled, gripping the earth tight with tense belly and flung limbs, and stared down. They were all like ants and flies. Mr Macintosh, too, when he went down, which he did often, for no one could say he was a coward. And his father, and Tommy himself, they were all no bigger than little insects.

It was like an enormous ant-working, as brightly tinted as a fresh antheap. The levels of earth around the mouth of the pit were reddish, then lower down grey and gravelly, and lower still, clear yellow. Heaps of the inert, heavy yellow soil, brought up from the bottom, lay all around him. He stretched out his hand and took some of it. It was unresponsive, lying lifeless and dense on his fingers, a little damp from the rain. He clenched his fist, and loosened it, and now the mass of yellow earth lay shaped on his palm, showing the marks of his fingers. A shape like – what? A bit of root? A fragment of rock rotted by water? He rolled his palms vigorously around it, and it became smooth like a water-ground stone. Then he sat up and took more earth, formed a pit, and up the sides flying ladders with bits of stick, and little kips of wetted earth for the trucks. Soon the sun dried it, and it all cracked and fell apart. Tommy gave the model a kick and went moodily back to the house. The sun was going down. It seemed that he had left a golden age of freedom behind, and now there was a new country of restrictions and time-tables.

His mother saw how he suffered, but thought: Soon he'll go to school and find companions.

But he was only just seven, and very young to go all the way to the city to boarding-school. She sent for school-books, and taught him to read. Yet this was for only two or three hours in the day, and for the rest he mooned about, as she complained, gazing away over the gulf to the compound, from where he could hear the noise of the playing children. He was stoical about it, or so it seemed, but underneath he was suffering badly from this new knowledge, which was much more vital than anything he had learned from the school-books. He knew the word loneliness, and lying at the edge of the pit he formed the yellow clay into little figures which he called Betty and Freddy and Dirk. Playmates. Dirk was the name of the boy he liked best among the children in the compound over the gulf.

One day his mother called him to the back door. There stood Dirk, and he was holding between his hands a tiny duiker, the size of a thin cat. Tommy ran forward, and was about to exclaim with Dirk over the little animal, when he remembered his new status. He stopped, stiffened himself, and said: 'How much?'

Dirk, keeping his eyes evasive, said: 'One shilling, baas.'

Tommy glanced at his mother and then said, proudly, his voice high: 'Damned cheek, too much.'

Annie Clarke flushed. She was ashamed and flustered. She came forward and said quickly: 'It's all right, Tommy. I'll give you the shilling.' She took the coin from the pocket of her apron and gave it to Tommy, who handed it at once to Dirk. Tommy took the little animal gently in his hands, and his tenderness for this frightened and lonely creature rushed up to his eyes and he turned away so that Dirk couldn't see – he would have been bitterly ashamed to show softness in front of Dirk, who was so tough and fearless.

Dirk stood back, watching, unwilling to see the last of the buck. Then he said: 'It's just born, it can die.'

Mrs Clarke said, dismissingly: 'Yes, Tommy will look after it.' Dirk walked away slowly, fingering the shilling in his pocket, but looking back at where Tommy and his mother were making a nest for the little buck in a packing-case. Mrs Clarke made a feeding-bottle with some linen stuffed into the neck of a tomato sauce bottle and filled it with milk and water and sugar. Tommy knelt by the buck and tried to drip the milk into its mouth.

It lay trembling, lifting its delicate head from the crumpled, huddled limbs, too weak to move, the big eyes dark and forlorn. Then the trembling became a spasm of weakness and the head collapsed with a soft thud against the side of the box, and then slowly, and with a trembling effort, the neck lifted the head again. Tommy tried to push the wad of linen into the soft mouth, and the milk wetted the fur and ran down over the buck's chest, and he wanted to cry.

'But it'll die, mother, it'll die,' he shouted, angrily.

'You mustn't force it,' said Annie Clarke, and she went away to her household duties. Tommy knelt there with the bottle, stroking the trembling little buck and suffering every time the thin neck collapsed with weakness, and tried again and again to interest it in the milk. But the buck wouldn't drink at all.

'Why?' shouted Tommy, in the anger of his misery. 'Why won't it drink? Why? Why?'

'But it's only just born,' said Mrs Clarke. The cord was still on the creature's navel, like a shrivelling, dark stick.

That night Tommy took the little buck into his room, and secretly in the dark lifted it, folded in a blanket, into his bed. He could feel it trembling fitfully against his chest, and he cried into the dark because he knew it was going to die.

In the morning when he woke, the buck could not lift its head at all, and it was a weak, collapsed weight on Tommy's chest, a chilly weight. The blanket in which it lay was messed with yellow stuff like a scrambled egg. Tommy washed the buck gently, and wrapped it again in new coverings, and laid it on the veranda where the sun could warm it.

Mrs Clarke gently forced the jaws open and poured down milk until the buck choked. Tommy knelt beside it all morning, suffering as he had never suffered before. The tears ran steadily down his face and he wished he could die too, and Mrs Clarke wished very much she could catch Dirk and give him a good beating, which would be unjust, but might do something to relieve her feelings. 'Besides,' she said to her husband, 'it's nothing but cruelty, taking a tiny thing like that from its mother.'

Late that afternoon the buck died, and Mr Clarke, who had not seen his son's misery over it, casually threw the dry, stiff corpse to the cookboy and told him to bury it. Tommy stood on the veranda, his face tight and angry, and watched the cookboy shovel his little buck hastily under some bushes, and return whistling.

Then he went into the room where his mother and father were sitting and said: 'Why is Dirk yellow and not dark brown like the other kaffirs?'

Silence. Mr Clarke and Annie Clarke looked at each other. Then Mr Clarke said: 'They come different colours.'

Tommy looked forcefully at his mother, who said: 'He's a half-caste.'

'What's a half-caste?'

'You'll understand when you grow up.'

Tommy looked from his father, who was filling his pipe, his

eyes lowered to the work, then at his mother, whose cheek-bones held that proud, bright flush.

'I understand now,' he said, defiantly.

'Then why do you ask?' said Mrs Clarke, with anger. Why, she was saying, do you infringe the rule of silence?

Tommy went out, and to the brink of the great pit. There he lay, wondering why he had said he understood when he did not. Though in a sense he did. He was remembering, though he had not noticed it before, that among the gang of children in the compound were two yellow children. Dirk was one, and Dirk's sister another. She was a tiny child, who came toddling on the fringe of the older children's games. But Dirk's mother was black, or rather, dark-brown like the others. And Dirk was not really yellow, but light copper colour. The colour of this earth, were it a little darker. Tommy's fingers were fiddling with the damp clay. He looked at the little figures he had made, Betty and Freddy. Idly, he smashed them. Then he picked up Dirk and flung him down. But he must have flung him down too carefully, for he did not break, and so he set the figure against the stalk of a weed. He took a lump of clay, and as his fingers experimentally pushed and kneaded it, the shape grew into the shape of a little duiker. But not a sick duiker, which had died because it had been taken from its mother. Not at all, it was a fine strong duiker, standing with one hoof raised and its head listening, ears pricked forward.

Tommy knelt on the verge of the great pit, absorbed, while the duiker grew into its proper form. He became dissatisfied it was too small. He impatiently smashed what he had done, and taking a big heap of the yellowish, dense soil, shook water on it from an old rusty railway sleeper that had collected rainwater, and made the mass soft and workable. Then he began again. The duiker would be half life-size.

And so his hands worked and his mind worried along its path of questions: Why? Why? Why? And finally: If Dirk is half black, or rather half white and half dark-brown, then who is his father?

For a long time his mind hovered on the edge of the answer, but did not finally reach it. But from time to time he looked across the gulf to where Mr Macintosh was strolling, swinging his big cudgel, and he thought: There are only two white men on this mine.

The buck was now finished, and he wetted his fingers in rusty rainwater, and smoothed down the soft clay to make it glisten like the surfaces of fur, but at once it dried and dulled, and as he knelt there he thought how the sun would crack it and it would fall to pieces, and an angry dissatisfaction filled him and he hung his head and wanted very much to cry. And just as the first tears were coming he heard a soft whistle from behind him, and he turned, and there was Dirk, kneeling behind a bush and looking out through the parted leaves.

'Is the buck all right?' asked Dirk.

Tommy said: 'It's dead,' and he kicked his foot at his model duiker so that the thick clay fell apart in lumps.

Dirk said: 'Don't do that, it's nice,' and he sprang forward and tried to fit the pieces together.

'It's no good, the sun'll crack it,' said Tommy, and he began to cry, although he was so ashamed to cry in front of Dirk. 'The buck's dead,' he wept, 'it's dead.'

'I can get you another,' said Dirk, looking at Tommy rather surprised. 'I killed its mother with a stone. It's easy.'

Dirk was seven, like Tommy. He was tall and strong, like Tommy. His eyes were dark and full, but his mouth was not full and soft, but long and narrow, clenched in the middle. His hair was very black and soft and long, falling uncut around his face, and his skin was a smooth, yellowish copper. Tommy stopped crying and looked at Dirk. He said: 'It's cruel to kill a buck's mother with a stone.' Dirk's mouth parted in surprised laughter over his big white teeth. Tommy watched him laugh, and he thought: Well, now I know who his father is.

He looked away to his home, which was two hundred yards off, exposed to the sun's glare among low bushes of hibiscus and poinsettia. He looked at Mr Macintosh's house, which was a few hundred yards farther off. Then he looked at Dirk. He was full of anger, which he did not understand, but he did understand that he was also defiant, and this was a moment of decision. After a long time he said: 'They can see us from here,' and the decision was made.

They got up, but as Dirk rose he saw the little clay figure laid against a stem, and he picked it up. 'This is me,' he said at once.. For crude as the thing was, it was unmistakably Dirk, who smiled with pleasure. 'Can I have it?' he asked, and Tommy nodded, equally proud and pleased.

They went off into the bush between the two houses, and then on for perhaps half a mile. This was the deserted part of the hollow in the mountains, no one came here, all the bustle and noise was on the other side. In front of them rose a sharp peak, and low at its foot was a high anthill, draped with Christmas fern and thick with shrub.

The two boys went inside the curtains of fern and sat down. No one could see them here. Dirk carefully put the little clay figure of himself inside a hole in the roots of a tree. Then he said: 'Make the buck again.' Tommy took his knife and knelt beside a fallen tree, and tried to carve the buck from it. The wood was soft and rotten, and was easily carved, and by night there was the clumsy shape of the buck coming out of the trunk. Dirk said: 'Now we've both got something.'

The next day the two boys made their way separately to the antheap and played there together, and so it was every day.

Then one evening Mrs Clarke said to Tommy just as he was going to bed: 'I thought I told you not to play with the kaffirs?'

Tommy stood very still. Then he lifted his head and said to her, with a strong look across at his father: 'Why shouldn't I play with Mr Macintosh's son?'

Mrs Clarke stopped breathing for a moment, and closed her eyes. She opened them in appeal at her husband. But Mr Clarke was filling his pipe. Tommy waited and then said good night and went to his room.

There he undressed slowly and climbed into the narrow iron bed and lay quietly, listening to the thud, thud, gold, gold, thud, thud, of the mine-stamps. Over in the compound they were dancing, and the tom-toms were beating fast, like the quick beat of the buck's heart that night as it lay on his chest. They were yelling like the wind coming through gaps in a mountain and through the window he could see the high, flaring light of the fires, and the black figures of the dancing people were wild and active against it.

Mrs Clarke came quickly in. She was crying. 'Tommy,' she said, sitting on the edge of his bed in the dark.

'Yes?' he said, cautiously.

'You mustn't say that again. Not ever.'

He said nothing. His mother's hand was urgently pressing his arm. 'Your father might lose his job,' said Mrs Clarke, wildly. 'We'd never get this money anywhere else. Never. You must understand, Tommy.'

'I do understand,' said Tommy, stiffly, very sorry for his mother, but hating her at the same time. 'Just don't say it, Tommy, don't ever say it.' Then she kissed him in a way that was both fond and appealing, and went out, shutting the door. To her husband she said it was time Tommy went to school, and next day she wrote to make the arrangements.

And so now Tommy made the long journey by car and train into the city four times a year, and four times a year he came back for the holidays. Mr Macintosh always drove him to the station and gave him ten shillings pocket money, and he came to fetch him in the car with his parents, and he always said: 'Well, laddie, and how's school?' And Tommy said: 'Fine, Mr Macintosh.' And Mr Macintosh said: 'We'll make a college man of you yet.'

When he said this, the flush came bright and proud on Annie Clarke's cheeks, and she looked quickly at Mr Clarke, who was smiling and embarrassed. But Mr Macintosh laid his hand on Tommy's shoulder and said: 'There's my laddie, there's my laddie,' and Tommy kept his shoulders stiff and still. Afterwards, Mrs Clarke would say, nervously: 'He's fond of you, Tommy, he'll do right by you.' And once she said: 'It's natural, he's got no children of his own.' But Tommy scowled at her and she flushed and said: 'There's things you don't understand yet, Tommy, and you'll regret it if you throw away your chances.' Tommy turned away with an impatient movement. Yet it was not clear at all, for it was almost as if he were a rich man's son, with all that pocket money, and the parcels of biscuits and sweets that Mr Macintosh sent into school during the term, and being fetched in the great rich car. And underneath it all he felt as if he were dragged along by the nose. He felt as if he were part of a conspiracy of some kind that no one ever spoke about. Silence. His real feelings were growing up slow and complicated and obstinate underneath that silence.

At school it was not at all complicated, it was the other world. There Tommy did his lessons and played with his friends and did not think of Dirk. Or rather, his thoughts of him were proper for that world. A half-caste, ignorant, living in the kaffir location – he felt ashamed that he played with Dirk in the holidays, and he told no one. Even on the train coming home he would think like that of Dirk, but the nearer he reached home the more his thoughts wavered and darkened. On the first evening at home he would speak of the school, and how he was the first in the class, and he played with this boy or that, or went to such fine houses in the city as a guest. The very first morning he would be standing on the veranda looking at the big pit and at the compound away beyond it, and his mother watched him, smiling in nervous supplication. And then he walked down the steps, away from the pit, and into the bush to the antheap. There Dirk was waiting for him. So it was every holiday. Neither of the boys spoke at first of what divided them. But, on the eve of Tommy's return to school after he had been there a year, Dirk said: 'You're getting educated, but I've nothing to learn.' Tommy said: 'I'll bring back books and teach you.' He said this in a quick voice, as if ashamed, and Dirk's eyes were accusing and angry. He gave his sarcastic laugh and said: 'That's what you say, white boy.'

It was not pleasant, but what Tommy said was not pleasant either, like a favour wrung out of a condescending person.

The two boys were sitting on the antheap under the fine lacy curtains of Christmas fern, looking at the rocky peak soaring into the smoky yellowish sky. There was the most unpleasant sort of annoyance in Tommy, and he felt ashamed of it. And on Dirk's face there was an aggressive but ashamed look. They continued to sit there, a little apart, full of dislike for each other, and knowing that the dislike came from the pressure of the outside world. 'I said I'd teach you, didn't I?' said Tommy, grandly, shying a stone at a bush so that the leaves flew off in all directions. 'You white bastard,' said Dirk, in a low voice, and he let out that sudden ugly laugh, showing his white teeth. 'What did you say?' said Tommy, going pale and jumping to his feet. 'You heard,' said Dirk, still laughing. He too got up. Then Tommy flung himself on Dirk and they overbalanced and rolled off into the bushes, kicking and scratching. They rolled apart and began fighting properly, with fists. Tommy was better-fed and more healthy. Dirk was tougher. They were a match, and they stopped when they were too tired and battered to go on. They staggered over to the antheap and sat there side by side, panting, wiping the blood off their faces. At last they lay on their backs on the rough slant of the anthill and looked up at the sky. Every trace of dislike had vanished; and they felt easy and quiet. When the sun went down they walked together through the bush to a point where they could not be seen from the houses, and there they said, as always: 'See you tomorrow.'

When Mr Macintosh gave him the usual ten shillings, he put them into his pocket thinking he would buy a football, but he did not. The ten shillings stayed unspent until it was nearly the end of term, and then he went to the shops and bought a reader and some exercise books and pencils, and an arithmetic. He hid these at the bottom of his trunk and whipped them out before his mother could see them.

He took them to the antheap next morning, but before he could reach it he saw there was a little shed built on it, and the Christmas fern had been draped like a veil across the roof of the shed. The bushes had been cut on the top of the anthill, but left on the sides, so that the shed looked as if it rose from the tops of the bushes. The shed was of unbarked poles pushed into the earth, the roof was of thatch, and the upper half of the front was left open. Inside there was a bench of poles and a table of planks on poles. There sat Dirk, waiting hungrily, and Tommy went and sat beside him, putting the books and pencils on the table.

'This shed is fine,' said Tommy, but Dirk was already looking at the books. So he began to teach Dirk how to read. And for all that holiday they were together in the shed while Dirk pored over the books. He found them more difficult than Tommy did, because they were full of words for things Dirk did not know, like curtains or carpet, and teaching Dirk to read the word carpet meant telling him all about carpets and the furnishings of a house. Often Tommy felt bored and restless and said: 'Let's play,' but Dirk said fiercely: 'No, I want to read.' Tommy grew fretful, for after all he had been working in the term and now he felt entitled to play. So there was another fight. Dirk said Tommy was a lazy white bastard, and Tommy said Dirk was a dirty half-caste. They fought as before, evenly matched and to no conclusion, and afterwards felt fine and friendly, and even made jokes about the fighting. It was arranged that they should work in the mornings only and leave the afternoons for play. When Tommy went back home that evening his mother saw the scratches on his face and the swollen nose, and said hopefully: 'Have you and Dirk been fighting?' But Tommy said no, he had hit his face on a tree.

His parents, of course, knew about the shed in the bush, but did not speak of it to Mr Macintosh. No one did. For Dirk's very existence was something to be ignored by everyone, and none of the workers, not even the overseers, would dare to mention Dirk's name. When Mr Macintosh asked Tommy what he had done to his face, he said he had slipped and fallen.

And so their eighth year and their ninth went past. Dirk could read and write and do all the sums that Tommy could do. He was always handicapped by not knowing the different way of living, and soon he said, angrily, it wasn't fair, and there was another fight about it, and then Tommy began another way of teaching. He would tell how it was to go to a cinema in the city, every detail of it, how the seats were arranged in such a way, and one paid so much, and the lights were like this, and the picture on the screen worked like that. Or he would describe how at school they ate such things for breakfast and other things for lunch. Or tell how the man had come with picture slides talking about China. The two boys got out an atlas and found China, and Tommy told Dirk every word of what the lecturer had said. Or it might be Italy or some other country. And they would argue that the lecturer should have said this or that, for Dirk was always hotly scornful of the white man's way of looking at things, so arrogant, he said. Soon Tommy saw things through Dirk; he saw the other life in town clear and brightly-coloured and a little distorted, as Dirk did.

Soon, at school, Tommy would involuntarily think: I must remember this to tell Dirk. It was impossible for him to do

anything, say anything, without being very conscious of just
how it happened, as if Dirk's black, sarcastic eye had got inside
him, Tommy, and never closed. And a feeling of unwillingness
grew in Tommy, because of the strain of fitting these two
worlds together. He found himself swearing at niggers or kaffirs
like the other boys, and more violently than they did, but
immediately afterwards he would find himself thinking: I must
remember this so as to tell Dirk. Because of all this thinking,
and seeing everything clear all the time, he was very bright at
school, and found the work easy. He was two classes ahead of
his age.

That was the tenth year, and one day Tommy went to the
shed in the bush and Dirk was not waiting for him. It was the
first day of the holidays. All the term he had been remembering
things to tell Dirk, and now Dirk was not there. A dove was
sitting on the Christmas fern, cooing lazily in the hot morning,
a sleepy, lonely sound. When Tommy came pushing through
the bushes it flew away. The mine-stamps thudded heavily,
gold, gold, and Tommy saw that the shed was empty even of
books, for the case where they were usually kept was hanging
open.

He went running to his mother: 'Where's Dirk?' he asked.

'How should I know?' said Annie Clarke, cautiously. She
really did not know.

'You do know, you do!' he cried, angrily. And then he went
racing off to the big pit. Mr Macintosh was sitting on an
upturned truck on the edge, watching the hundreds of workers
below him, moving like ants on the yellow bottom. 'Well,
laddie?' he asked, amiably, and moved over to allow Tommy
to sit by him.

'Where's Dirk?' asked Tommy, accusingly, standing in front
of him.

Mr Macintosh tipped his old felt hat even farther back and
scratched at his front hair and looked at Tommy.

'Dirk's working,' he said, at last.

'Where?'

Mr Macintosh pointed to the bottom of the pit. Then he said
again: 'Sit down, laddie, I want to talk to you.'

'I don't want to,' said Tommy, and he turned away and went

blundering over the veld to the shed. He sat on the bench and cried, and when dinner-time came he did not go home. All that day he sat in the shed, and when he had finished crying he remained on the bench, leaning his back against the poles of the shed, and stared into the bush. The doves cooed and cooed, kru-kruuuu, kru-kruuuuu, and a woodpecker tapped, and the mine-stamps thudded. Yet it was very quiet, a hand of silence gripped the bush and he could hear the borers and the ants at work in the poles of the bench he sat on. He could see that although the anthill seemed dead, a mound of hard, peaked, baked earth, it was very much alive, for there was a fresh outbreak of wet, damp earth in the floor of the shed. There was a fine crust of reddish, lacy earth over the poles of the walls. The shed would have to be built again soon, because the ants and borers would have eaten it through. But what was the use of a shed without Dirk?

All that day he stayed there, and did not return until dark, and when his mother said: 'What's the matter with you, why are you crying?' he said angrily, 'I don't know,' matching her dishonesty with his own. The next day, even before breakfast, he was off to the shed, and did not return until dark, and refused his supper although he had not eaten all day.

And the next day it was the same, but now he was bored and lonely. He took his knife from his pocket and whittled at a stick, and it became a boy, bent and straining under the weight of a heavy load, his arms clenched up to support it. He took the figure home at supper-time and ate with it on the table in front of him.

'What's that?' asked Annie Clarke, and Tommy answered: 'Dirk.'

He took it to his bedroom, and sat in the soft lamp-light, working away with his knife, and he had it in his hand the following morning when he met Mr Macintosh at the brink of the pit. 'What's that, laddie?' asked Mr Macintosh, and Tommy said: 'Dirk.'

Mr Macintosh's mouth went thin, and then he smiled and said: 'Let me have it.'

'No, it's for Dirk.'

Mr Macintosh took out his wallet and said: 'I'll pay you for it.'

'I don't want any money,' said Tommy, angrily, and Mr Macintosh, greatly disturbed, put back his wallet. Then Tommy, hesitating, said: 'Yes, I do.' Mr Macintosh, his values confirmed, was relieved, and he took out his wallet again and produced a pound note, which seemed to him very generous. 'Five pounds,' said Tommy, promptly. Mr Macintosh first scowled, then laughed. He tipped back his head and roared with laughter. 'Well, laddie, you'll make a business man yet. Five pounds for a little bit of wood!'

'Make it for yourself then, if it's just a bit of wood.'

Mr Macintosh counted out five pounds and handed them over. 'What are you going to do with that money?' he asked, as he watched Tommy buttoning them carefully into his shirt pocket. 'Give them to Dirk,' said Tommy, triumphantly, and Mr Macintosh's heavy old face went purple. He watched while Tommy walked away from him, sitting on the truck, letting the heavy cudgel swing lightly against his shoes. He solved his immediate problem by thinking: He's a good laddie, he's got a good heart.

That night Mrs Clarke came over while he was sitting over his roast beef and cabbage, and said: 'Mr Macintosh, I want a word with you.' He nodded at a chair, but she did not sit. 'Tommy's upset,' she said, delicately, 'he's been used to Dirk, and now he's got no one to play with.'

For a moment Mr Macintosh kept his eyes lowered, then he said: 'It's easily fixed, Annie, don't worry yourself.' He spoke heartily, as it was easy for him to do, speaking of a worker, who might be released at his whim for other duties.

That bright protesting flush came on to her cheeks, in spite of herself, and she looked quickly at him, with real indignation. But he ignored it and said: 'I'll fix it in the morning, Annie.'

She thanked him and went back home, suffering because she had not said those words which had always soothed her conscience in the past: You're nothing but a pig, Mr Macintosh . . .

As for Tommy, he was sitting in the shed, crying his eyes out. And then, when there were no more tears, there came such a storm of anger and pain that he would never forget it as long as he lived. What for? He did not know, and that was the worst of it. It was not simply Mr Macintosh, who loved him, and who thus so blackly betrayed his own flesh and blood, nor the silences of his parents. Something deeper, felt working in the substance of life as he could hear those ants working away with those busy jaws at the roots of the poles he sat on, to make a new material for their different forms of life. He was testing those words which were used, or not used – merely suggested – all the time, and for a ten-year-old boy it was almost too hard to bear. A child may say of a companion one day that he hates so and so, and the next: He is my friend. That is how a relationship is, shifting and changing, and children are kept safe in their hates and loves by the fabric of social life their parents make over their heads. And middle-aged people say: This is my friend, this is my enemy, including all the shifts and changes of feeling in one word, for the sake of an easy mind. In between these ages, at about twenty perhaps, there is a time when the young people test everything, and accept many hard and cruel truths about living, and that is because they do not know how hard it is to accept them finally, and for the rest of their lives. It is easy to be truthful at twenty.

But it is not easy at ten, a little boy entirely alone, looking at words like friendship. What, then, was friendship? Dirk was his friend, that he knew, but did he like Dirk? Did he love him? Sometimes not at all. He remembered how Dirk had said: 'I'll get you another baby buck. I'll kill its mother with a stone.' He remembered his feeling of revulsion at the cruelty. Dirk was cruel. But – and here Tommy unexpectedly laughed, and for the first time he understood Dirk's way of laughing. It was really funny to say that Dirk was cruel, when his very existence was a cruelty. Yet Mr Macintosh laughed in exactly the same way, and his skin was white, or rather, white browned over by the sun. Why was Mr Macintosh also entitled to laugh, with that same abrupt ugliness? Perhaps somewhere in the beginnings of the rich Mr Macintosh there had been the same cruelty, and that had worked its way through the life of Mr Macintosh until it turned into the cruelty of Dirk, the coloured boy, the half-caste? If so, it was all much deeper than differently coloured skins, and much harder to understand.

And then Tommy thought how Dirk seemed to wait always, as if he, Tommy, were bound to stand by him, as if this were a justice that was perfectly clear to Dirk; and he, Tommy, did in fact fight with Mr Macintosh for Dirk, and he could behave in no other way. Why? Because Dirk was his friend? Yet there were times when he hated Dirk, and certainly Dirk hated him, and when they fought they could have killed each other easily, and with joy.

Well, then? Well, then? What was friendship, and why were they bound so closely, and by what? Slowly the little boy, sitting alone on his antheap, came to an understanding which is proper to middle-aged people, that resignation in knowledge which is called irony. Such a person may know, for instance, that he is bound most deeply to another person, although he does not like that person, in the way the word is ordinarily used, or like the way he talks, or his politics, or anything else. And yet they are friends and will always be friends, and what happens to this bound couple affects each most deeply, even though they may be in different continents, or may never see each other again. Or after twenty years they may meet, and there is no need to say a word, everything is understood. This is one of the ways of friendship, and just as real as amiability or being alike.

Well, then? For it is a hard and difficult knowledge for any little boy to accept. But he accepted it, and knew that he and Dirk were closer than brothers and always would be so. He grew many years older in that day of painful struggle, while he listened to the mine-stamps saying gold, gold, and to the ants working away with their jaws to destroy the bench he sat on, to make food for themselves.

Next morning Dirk came to the shed, and Tommy, looking at him, knew that he, too, had grown years older in the months of working in the great pit. Ten years old – but he had been working with men and he was not a child.

Tommy took out the five pound notes and gave them to Dirk.

Dirk pushed them back. 'What for?' he asked.

'I got them from *him*,' said Tommy, and at once Dirk took them as if they were his right.

And at once, inside Tommy, came indignation, for he felt he was being taken for granted, and he said: 'Why aren't you working?'

'He said I needn't. He means, while you are having your holidays.'

'I got you free,' said Tommy, boasting.

Dirk's eyes narrowed in anger. 'He's my father,' he said, for the first time.

'But he made you work,' said Tommy, taunting him. And then: 'Why do you work? I wouldn't. I should say no.'

'So you would say no?' said Dirk in angry sarcasm.

'There's no law to make you.'

'So there's no law, white boy, no law . . .' But Tommy had sprung at him, and they were fighting again, rolling over and over, and this time they fell apart from exhaustion and lay on the ground panting for a long time.

Later Dirk said: 'Why do we fight, it's silly?'

'I don't know,' said Tommy, and he began to laugh, and Dirk laughed too. They were to fight often in the future, but never with such bitterness, because of the way they were laughing now.

It was the following holidays before they fought again. Dirk was waiting for him in the shed.

'Did he let you go?' asked Tommy at once, putting down new books on the table for Dirk.

'I just came,' said Dirk. 'I didn't ask.'

They sat together on the bench, and at once a leg gave way and they rolled off on to the floor laughing. 'We must mend it,' said Tommy. 'Let's build the shed again.'

'No,' said Dirk at once, 'don't let's waste time on the shed. You can teach me while you're here, and I can make the shed when you've gone back to school.'

Tommy slowly got up from the floor, frowning. Again he felt he was being taken for granted. 'Aren't you going to work on the mine during the term?'

'No, I'm not going to work on that mine again. I told him I wouldn't.'

'You've got to work,' said Tommy, grandly.

'So I've got to work,' said Dirk, threateningly. 'You can go to school, white boy, but I've got to work, and in the holidays I can just take time off to please you.'

They fought until they were tired, and five minutes afterwards they were seated on the anthill talking. 'What did you do with the five pounds?' asked Tommy.

'I gave them to my mother.'

'What did she do with them?'

'She bought herself a dress, and then food for us all, and bought me these trousers, and she put the rest away to keep.'

A pause. Then, deeply ashamed, Tommy asked: 'Doesn't he give her any money?'

'He doesn't come any more. Not for more than a year.'

'Oh, I thought he did still,' said Tommy casually, whistling.

'No.' Then, fiercely, in a low voice: 'There'll be some more half-castes in the compound soon.'

Dirk sat crouching, his fierce black eyes on Tommy, ready to spring on him. But Tommy was sitting with his head bowed, looking at the ground. 'It's not fair,' he said. 'It's not fair.'

'So you've discovered that, white boy?' said Dirk. It was said good-naturedly, and there was no need to fight. They went to their books and Tommy taught Dirk some new sums.

But they never spoke of what Dirk would do in the future, how he would use all this schooling. They did not dare.

That was the eleventh year.

When they were twelve, Tommy returned from school to be greeted by the words: 'Have you heard the news?'

'What news?'

They were sitting as usual on the bench. The shed was newly built, with strong thatch, and good walls, plastered this time with mud, so as to make it harder for the ants.

'They are saying you are going to be sent away.'

'Who says so?'

'Oh, everyone,' said Dirk, stirring his feet about vaguely under the table. This was because it was the first few minutes after the return from school, and he was always cautious, until he was sure Tommy had not changed towards him. And that 'everyone' was explosive. Tommy nodded, however, and asked apprehensively: 'Where to?'

'To the sea.'

'How do they know?' Tommy scarcely breathed the word *they*.

'Your cook heard your mother say so . . .' And then Dirk added with a grin, forcing the issue: 'Cheek, dirty kaffirs talking about white men.'

Tommy smiled obligingly, and asked: 'How, to the sea, what does it mean?'

'How should we know, dirty kaffirs.'

'Oh, shut up,' said Tommy, angrily. They glared at each other, their muscles tensed. But they sighed and looked away. At twelve it was not easy to fight, it was all too serious.

That night Tommy said to his parents: 'They say I'm going to sea. Is it true?'

His mother asked quickly: 'Who said so?'

'But is it true?' Then, derisively: 'Cheek, dirty kaffirs talking about *us*.'

'Please don't talk like that, Tommy, it's not right.'

'Oh, mother, please, how am I going to sea?'

'But be sensible, Tommy, it's not settled, but Mr Macintosh . . .'

'So it's Mr Macintosh!'

Mrs Clarke looked at her husband, who came forward and sat down and settled his elbows on the table. A family conference. Tommy also sat down.

'Now listen, son. Mr Macintosh has a soft spot for you. You should be grateful to him. He can do a lot for you.'

'But why should I go to sea?'

'You don't have to. He suggested it – he was in the Merchant Navy himself once.'

'So I've got to go just because he did.'

'He's offered to pay for you to go to college in England, and give you money until you're in the Navy.'

'But I don't want to be a sailor. I've never even seen the sea.'

'But you're good at your figures, and you have to be, so why not?'

'I won't,' said Tommy, angrily. 'I won't, I won't.' He glared at them through tears. 'You just want to get rid of me, that's all it is. You want me to go away from here, from . . .'

The parents looked at each other and sighed.

'Well, if you don't want to, you don't have to. But it's not every boy who has a chance like this.'

'Why doesn't he send Dirk?' asked Tommy, aggressively.

'Tommy,' cried Annie Clarke, in great distress.

'Well, why doesn't he? He's much better than me at figures.'

'Go to bed,' said Mr Clarke suddenly, in a fit of temper. 'Go to bed.'

Tommy went out of the room, slamming the door hard. He must be grown-up. His father had never spoken to him like that. He sat on the edge of the bed in stubborn rebellion, listening to the thudding of the stamps. And down in the compound they were dancing, the lights of the fires flickered red on his window-pane.

He wondered if Dirk were there, leaping around the fires with the others.

Next day he asked him: 'Do you dance with the others?' At once he knew he had blundered. When Dirk was angry, his eyes darkened and narrowed. When he was hurt, his mouth set in a way which made the flesh pinch thinly under his nose. So he looked now.

'Listen, white boy. White people don't like us half-castes. Neither do the blacks like us. No one does. And so I don't dance with them.'

'Let's do some lessons,' said Tommy, quickly. And they went to their books, dropping the subject.

Later Mr Macintosh came to the Clarkes' house and asked for Tommy. The parents watched Mr Macintosh and their son walk together along the edge of the great pit. They stood at the window and watched, but they did not speak.

Mr Macintosh was saying easily: 'Well, laddie, and so you don't want to be a sailor.'

'No, Mr Macintosh.'

'I went to sea when I was fifteen. It's hard, but you aren't afraid of that. Besides, you'd be an officer.'

Tommy said nothing.

'You don't like the idea?'

Mr Macintosh stopped and looked down into the pit. The earth at the bottom was as yellow as it had been when Tommy was seven, but now it was much deeper. Mr Macintosh did not know how deep, because he had not measured it. Far below, in this man-made valley, the workers were moving and shifting like black seeds tilted on a piece of paper.

'Your father worked on the mines and he became an engineer working at nights, did you know that?'

'Yes.'

'It was very hard for him. He was thirty before he was qualified, and then he earned twenty-five pounds a month until he came to this mine.'

'Yes.'

'You don't want to do that, do you?'

'I will if I have to,' muttered Tommy, defiantly.

Mr Macintosh's face was swelling and purpling. The veins along nose and forehead were black. Mr Macintosh was asking himself why this lad treated him like dirt, when he was offering to do him an immense favour. And yet, in spite of the look of sullen indifference which was so ugly on that young face, he could not help loving him. He was a fine boy, tall, strong, and his hair was a soft, bright brown, and his eyes clear and black. A much better man than his father, who was rough and marked by the long struggle of his youth. He said: 'Well, you don't have to be a sailor, perhaps you'd like to go to a university and be a scholar.'

'I don't know,' said Tommy, unwillingly, although his heart had moved suddenly. Pleasure – he was weakening. Then he said suddenly: 'Mr Macintosh, why do you want to send me to college?'

And Mr Macintosh fell right into the trap. 'I have no children,' he said, sentimentally. 'I feel for you like my own son.' He stopped. Tommy was looking away towards the compound, and his intention was clear.

'Very well then,' said Mr Macintosh, harshly. 'If you want to be a fool.'

Tommy stood with his eyes lowered and he knew quite well he was a fool. Yet he could not have behaved in any other way.

'Don't be hasty,' said Mr Macintosh, after a pause. 'Don't throw away your chances, laddie. You're nothing but a lad, yet. Take your time.' And with this tone, he changed all the emphasis of the conflict, and made it simply a question of waiting. Tommy did not move, so Mr Macintosh went on quickly: 'Yes, that's right, you just think it over.' He hastily slipped a pound note from his pocket and put it into the boy's hand.

'You know what I'm going to do with it?' said Tommy, laughing suddenly, and not at all pleasantly.

'Do what you like, do just as you like, it's your money,' said Mr Macintosh, turning away so as not to have to understand.

Tommy took the money to Dirk, who received it as if it were his right, a feeling in which Tommy was now an accomplice, and they sat together in the shed. 'I've got to be something,' said Tommy angrily. 'They're going to make me be something.'

'They wouldn't have to *make* me be anything,' said Dirk, sardonically. 'I know what I'd be.'

'What?' asked Tommy, enviously.

'An engineer.'

'How do you know what you've got to do?'

'That's what I want,' said Dirk, stubbornly.

After a while Tommy said: 'If you went to the city, there's a school for coloured children.'

'I wouldn't see my mother again.'

'Why not?'

'There's laws, white boy, laws. Anyone who lives with and after the fashion of the natives is a native. Therefore I'm a native, and I'm not entitled to go to school with the half-castes.'

'If you went to the town, you'd not be living with the natives so you'd be classed as a coloured.'

'But then I couldn't see my mother, because if she came to town she'd still be a native.'

There was a triumphant conclusiveness in this that made Tommy think: He intends to get what he wants another way . . . And then: Through me . . . But he had accepted that justice a long time ago, and now he looked at his own arm that lay on the rough plank of the table. The outer side was burnt dark and dry with the sun, and the hair glinted on it like fine copper. It was no darker than Dirk's brown arm, and no lighter. He turned it over. Inside, the skin was smooth, dusky white, the veins running blue and strong across the wrist. He looked at Dirk, grinning, who promptly turned his own arm over, in a challenging way. Tommy said, unhappily: 'You can't go to school properly because the inside of your arm is brown. And that's that!' Dirk's tight and bitter mouth expanded into the grin that was also his father's, and he said: 'That is so, white boy, that is so.'

'Well, it's not my fault,' said Tommy, aggressively, closing his fingers and banging the fists down again and again.

'I didn't say it was your fault,' said Dirk at once.

Tommy said, in that uneasy, aggressive tone: 'I've never even seen your mother.'

To this, Dirk merely laughed, as if to say: You have never wanted to.

Tommy said, after a pause: 'Let me come and see her now.'

Then Dirk said, in a tone which was uncomfortable, almost like compassion: 'You don't have to.'

'Yes,' insisted Tommy. 'Yes, now.' He got up, and Dirk rose too. 'She won't know what to say,' warned Dirk. 'She doesn't speak English.' He did not really want Tommy to go to the compound; Tommy did not really want to go. Yet they went.

In silence they moved along the path between the trees, in silence skirted the edge of the pit, in silence entered the trees on the other side, and moved along the paths to the compound. It was big, spread over many acres, and the huts were in all stages of growth and decay, some new, with shining thatch, some tumble-down, with dulled and sagging thatch, some in the process of being built, the peeled wands of the roof-frames gleaming like milk in the sun.

Dirk led the way to a big square hut. Tommy could see people watching him walking with the coloured boy, and turning to laugh and whisper. Dirk's face was proud and tight, and he could feel the same look on his own face. Outside the square hut sat a little girl of about ten. She was bronze, Dirk's colour. Another little girl, black, perhaps six years old, was squatted on a log, finger in mouth, watching them. A baby, still unsteady on its feet, came staggering out of the doorway and collapsed, chuckling, against Dirk's knees. Its skin was almost white. Then Dirk's mother came out of the hut after the baby, smiled when she saw Dirk, but went anxious and bashful when she saw Tommy. She made a little bobbing curtsey, and took the baby from Dirk, for the sake of something to hold in her awkward and shy hands.

'This is Baas Tommy,' said Dirk. He sounded very embarrassed.

She made another little curtsey and stood smiling.

She was a large woman, round and smooth all over, but her legs were slender, and her arms, wound around the child, thin and knotted. Her round face had a bashful curiosity, and her eyes moved quickly from Dirk to Tommy and back, while she smiled and smiled, biting her lips with strong teeth, and smiled again.

Tommy said: 'Good morning,' and she laughed and said, 'Good morning.'

Then Dirk said: 'Enough now, let's go.' He sounded very angry. Tommy said: 'Good-bye.' Dirk's mother said: 'Good-bye,' and made her little bobbing curtsey, and she moved her child from one arm to another and bit her lip anxiously over her gleaming smile.

Tommy and Dirk went away from the square mud hut where the variously-coloured children stood staring after them.

'There now,' said Dirk, angrily. 'You've seen my mother.'

'I'm sorry,' said Tommy uncomfortably, feeling as if the responsibility for the whole thing rested on him. But Dirk laughed suddenly and said: 'Oh, all right, all right, white boy, it's not your fault.'

All the same, he seemed pleased that Tommy was upset.

Later, with an affectation of indifference, Tommy asked, thinking of those new children: 'Does Mr Macintosh come to your mother again now?'

And Dirk answered 'Yes,' just one word.

In the shed Dirk studied from a geography book, while Tommy sat idle and thought bitterly that they wanted him to be a sailor. Then his idle hands protested, and he took a knife and began slashing at the edge of the table. When the gashes showed a whiteness from the core of the wood, he took a stick lying on the floor and whittled at it, and when it snapped from thinness he went out to the trees, picked up a lump of old wood from the ground, and brought it back to the shed. He worked on it with his knife, not knowing what it was he made, until a curve under his knife reminded him of Dirk's sister squatting at the hut door, and then he directed his knife with a purpose. For several days he fought with the lump of wood, while Dirk studied. Then he brought a tin of boot polish from the house, and worked the bright brown wax into the creamy white wood, and soon there was a bronze-coloured figure of the little girl, staring with big, curious eyes while she squatted on spindly legs.

Tommy put it in front of Dirk, who turned it around, grinning a little. 'It's like her,' he said at last. 'You can have it if you like,' said Tommy. Dirk's teeth flashed, he hesitated, and then reached into his pocket and took out a bundle of dirty cloth. He undid it, and Tommy saw the little clay figure he had made of Dirk years ago. It was crumbling, almost-worn to a lump of mud, but in it was still the vigorous challenge of Dirk's body. Tommy's mind signalled recognition – for he had forgotten he had ever made it – and he picked it up. 'You kept it?' he asked shyly, and Dirk smiled. They looked at each other, smiling. It was a moment of warm, close feeling, and yet in it was the pain that neither of them understood, and also the cruelty and challenge that made them fight. They lowered their eyes unhappily. 'I'll do your mother,' said Tommy, getting up and running away into the trees, in order to escape from the challenging closeness. He searched until he found a thorn tree, which is so hard it turns the edge of an axe, and then he took an axe and worked at the felling of the tree until the sun went down. A big stone near him was kept wet to sharpen the axe, and next day he worked on until the tree fell. He sharpened the worn axe again, and cut a length of tree about two feet, and split off the tough bark, and brought it back to the shed. Dirk had fitted a shelf against the logs of the wall at the back. On it he had set the tiny, crumbling figure of himself, and the new bronze shape of his little sister. There was a space left for the new statue. Tommy said, shyly: 'I'll do it as quickly as I can so that it will be done before the term starts.' Then, lowering .

his eyes, which suffered under this new contract of shared feeling, he examined the piece of wood. It was not pale and gleaming like almonds, as was the softer wood. It was a gingery brown, a close-fibred, knotted wood, and down its centre, as he knew, was a hard black spine. He turned it between his hands and thought that this was more difficult than anything he had ever done. For the first time he studied a piece of wood before starting on it, with a desired shape in his mind, trying to see how what he wanted would grow out of the dense mass of material he held.

Then he tried his knife on it and it broke. He asked Dirk for his knife. It was a long piece of metal, taken from a pile of scrap mining machinery, sharpened on stone until it was razor-fine. The handle was cloth wrapped tight around.

With this new and unwieldy tool Tommy fought with the wood for many days. When the holidays were ending, the shape was there, but the face was blank. Dirk's mother was full-bodied, with soft, heavy flesh and full, naked shoulders above a tight, sideways draped cloth. The slender legs were planted firm on naked feet, and the thin arms, knotted with work, were lifted to the weight of a child who, a small, helpless creature swaddled in cloth, looked out with large, curious eyes. But the mother's face was not yet there.

'I'll finish it next holidays,' said Tommy, and Dirk set it carefully beside the other figures on the shelf. With his back turned he asked cautiously: 'Perhaps you won't be here next holidays?'

'Yes I will,' said Tommy, after a pause. 'Yes I will.'

It was a promise, and they gave each other that small, warm, unwilling smile, and turned away, Dirk back to the compound and Tommy to the house, where his trunk was packed for school.

That night Mr Macintosh came over to the Clarkes' house and spoke with the parents in the front room. Tommy, who was asleep, woke to find Mr Macintosh beside him. He sat on the foot of the bed and said: 'I want to talk to you, laddie.' Tommy turned the wick of the oil-lamp, and now he could see in the shadowy light that Mr Macintosh had a look of uneasiness about him. He was sitting with his strong old body balanced behind the big stomach, hands laid on his knees, and his grey Scots eyes were watchful.

'I want you to think about what I said,' said Mr Macintosh, in a quick, bluff good-humour. 'Your mother says in two years' time you will have matriculated, you're doing fine at school. And after that you can go to college.'

Tommy lay on his elbow, and in the silence the drums came tapping from the compound, and he said: 'But Mr Macintosh, I'm not the only one who's good at his books.'

Mr Macintosh stirred, but said bluffly: 'Well, but I'm talking about you.'

Tommy was silent, because as usual these opponents were so much stronger than was reasonable, simply because of their ability to make words mean something else. And then, his heart painfully beating, he said: 'Why don't you send Dirk to college? You're so rich, and Dirk knows everything I know. He's better than me at figures. He's a whole book ahead of me, and he can do sums I can't.'

Mr Macintosh crossed his legs impatiently, uncrossed them, and said: 'Now why should I send Dirk to college?' For now Tommy would have to put into precise words what he meant, and this Mr Macintosh was quite sure he would not do. But to make certain, he lowered his voice and said: 'Think of your mother, laddie, she's worrying about you, and you don't want to make her worried, do you?'

Tommy looked towards the door, under it came a thick yellow streak of light: in that room his mother and father were waiting in silence for Mr Macintosh to emerge with news of Tommy's sure and wonderful future.

'You know why Dirk should go to college,' said Tommy in despair, shifting his body unhappily under the sheets, and Mr Macintosh chose not to hear it. He got up, and said quickly: 'You just think it over, laddie. There's no hurry, but by next holidays I want to know.' And he went out of the room. As he opened the door, a brightly-lit, painful scene was presented to Tommy: his father and mother sat, smiling in embarrassed entreaty at Mr Macintosh. The door shut, and Tommy turned down the light, and there was darkness.

He went to school next day. Mrs Clarke, turning out Mr

Macintosh's house as usual, said unhappily: 'I think you'll find everything in its proper place,' and slipped away, as if she were ashamed.

As for Mr Macintosh, he was in a mood which made others, besides Annie Clarke, speak to him carefully. His cookboy, who had worked for him twelve years, gave notice that month. He had been knocked down twice by that powerful, hairy fist, and he was not a slave, after all, to remain bound to a bad-tempered master. And when a load of rock slipped and crushed the skulls of two workers, and the police came out for an investigation, Mr Macintosh met them irritably, and told them to mind their own business. For the first time in that mine's history of scandalous recklessness, after many such accidents, Mr Macintosh heard the indignant words from the police officer: 'You speak as if you were above the law, Mr Macintosh. If this happens again, you'll see . . .'

Worst of all, he ordered Dirk to go back to work in the pit, and Dirk refused.

'You can't make me,' said Dirk.

'Who's the boss on this mine?' shouted Mr Macintosh.

'There's no law to make children work,' said the thirteen-year-old, who stood as tall as his father, a straight, lithe youth against the bulky strength of the old man.

The word *law* whipped the anger in Mr Macintosh to the point where he could feel his eyes go dark, and the blood pounding in that hot darkness in his head. In fact, it was the power of this anger that sobered him, for he had been very young when he had learned to fear his own temper. And above all, he was a shrewd man. He waited until his sight was clear again, and then asked, reasonably: 'Why do you want to loaf around the compound, why not work for money?'

Dirk said: 'I can read and write, and I know my figures better than Tommy – Baas Tommy,' he added, in a way which made the anger rise again in Mr Macintosh, so that he had to make a fresh effort to subdue it.

But Tommy was a point of weakness in Mr Macintosh, and it was then that he spoke the words which afterwards made him wonder if he'd gone suddenly crazy. For he said: 'Very well, when you're sixteen you can come and do my books and write the letters for the mine.'

Dirk said: 'All right,' as if this were no more than his due, and walked off, leaving Mr Macintosh impotently furious with himself. For how could anyone but himself see the books? Such a person would be his master. It was impossible, he had no intention of ever letting Dirk, or anyone else, see them. Yet he had made the promise. And so he would have to find another way of using Dirk, or – and the words came involuntarily – getting rid of him.

From a mood of settled bad temper, Mr Macintosh dropped into one of sullen thoughtfulness, which was entirely foreign to his character. Being shrewd is quite different from the process of thinking. Shrewdness, particularly the money-making shrewdness, is a kind of instinct. While Mr Macintosh had always known what he wanted to do, and how to do it, that did not mean he had known why he wanted so much money, or why he had chosen these ways of making it. Mr Macintosh felt like a cat whose nose has been rubbed into its own dirt, and for many nights he sat in the hot little house, that vibrated continually from the noise of the mine-stamps, most uncomfortably considering himself and his life. He reminded himself, for instance, that he was sixty, and presumably had not more than ten or fifteen years to live. It was not a thought that an unreflective man enjoys, particularly when he had never considered his age at all. He was so healthy, strong, tough. But he was sixty nevertheless, and what would be his monument? An enormous pit in the earth, and a million pounds' worth of property. Then how should he spend ten or fifteen years? Exactly as he had the preceding sixty, for he hated being away from this place, and this gave him a caged and useless sensation, for it had never entered his head before that he was not as free as he felt himself to be.

Well, then – and this thought gnawed most closely to Mr Macintosh's pain – why had he not married? For he considered himself a marrying sort of man, and had always intended to find himself the right sort of woman and marry her. Yet he was already sixty. The truth was that Mr Macintosh had no idea at all why he had not married and got himself sons; and in these slow, uncomfortable ponderings the thought of Dirk's mother intruded itself only to be hastily thrust away. Mr Macintosh, the sensualist, had a taste for dark-skinned women; and now it was certainly too late to admit as a permanent feature of his character something he had always considered as a sort of temporary whim, or makeshift, like someone who learns to enjoy an inferior brand of tobacco when better brands are not available.

He thought of Tommy, of whom he had been used to say: 'I've taken a fancy to the laddie.' Now it was not so much a fancy as a deep, grieving love. And Tommy was the son of his employee, and looked at him with contempt, and he, Mr Macintosh, reacted with angry shame as if he were guilty of something. Of what? It was ridiculous.

The whole situation was ridiculous, and so Mr Macintosh allowed himself to slide back into his usual frame of mind. Tommy's only a boy, he thought, and he'll see reason in a year or so. And as for Dirk, I'll find him some kind of a job when the time comes . . .

At the end of the term, when Tommy came home, Mr Macintosh asked, as usual, to see the school report, which usually filled him with pride. Instead of heading the class with approbation from the teachers and high marks in all subjects, Tommy was near the bottom, with such remarks as Slovenly, and Lazy, and Bad-mannered. The only subject in which he got any marks at all was that called Art, which Mr Macintosh did not take into account.

When Tommy was asked by his parents why he was not working, he replied, impatiently: 'I don't know,' which was quite true; and at once escaped to the anthill. Dirk was there, waiting for the books Tommy always brought for him. Tommy reached at once up to the shelf where stood the figure of Dirk's mother, lifted it down and examined the unworked space which would be the face. 'I know how to do it,' he said to Dirk, and took out some knives and chisels he had brought from the city.

This was how he spent the three weeks of that holiday, and when he met Mr Macintosh he was sullen and uncomfortable. 'You'll have to be working a bit better,' he said, before Tommy went back, to which he received no answer but an unwilling smile.

During that term Tommy distinguished himself in two ways besides being steadily at the bottom of the class he had so recently led. He made a fiery speech in the debating society on the iniquity of the colour bar, which rather pleased his teachers, since it is a well-known fact that the young must pass through these phases of rebellion before settling down to conformity. In fact, the greater the verbal rebellion, the more settled was the conformity likely to be. In secret Tommy got books from the city library such as are not usually read by boys of his age, on the history of Africa, and on comparative anthropology, and passed from there to the history of the moment – he ordered papers from the Government Stationery Office, on the laws of the country. Most particularly those affecting the relations between black and white and coloured. These he bought in order to take back to Dirk. But in addition to all this ferment, there was that subject Art, which in this school meant a drawing lesson twice a week, copying busts of Julius Caesar, or it might be Nelson, or shading in fronds of fern or leaves, or copying a large vase or a table standing diagonally to the class, thus learning what he was told were the laws of Perspective. There was no modelling, nothing approaching sculpture in this school, but this was the nearest thing to it, and that mysterious prohibition which forbade him to distinguish himself in Geometry or English, was silent when it came to using the pencil.

At the end of the term his report was very bad, but it admitted that he had An Interest in Current Events, and a Talent for Art.

And now this word Art, coming at the end of two successive terms, disturbed his parents and forced itself on Mr Macintosh. He said to Annie Clarke: 'It's a nice thing to make pictures, but the lad won't earn a living by it.' And Mrs Clarke said reproachfully to Tommy: 'It's all very well, Tommy, but you aren't going to earn a living drawing pictures.'

'I didn't say I wanted to earn a living with it,' shouted Tommy, miserably. 'Why have I got to *be* something, you're always wanting me to *be* something.'

That holidays Dirk spent studying the Acts of Parliament and the Reports of Commissions and Sub-Committees which Tommy had brought him, while Tommy attempted something new. There was a square piece of soft white wood which Dirk had pilfered from the mine, thinking Tommy might use it. And Tommy set it against the walls of the shed, and knelt before it and attempted a frieze or engraving – he did not know the words for what he was doing. He cut out a great pit, surrounded by mounds of earth and rock, with the peaks of great mountains beyond, and at the edge of the pit stood a big man carrying a stick, and over the edge of the pit wound a file of black figures, tumbling into the gulf. From the pit came flames and smoke. Tommy took green ooze from leaves and mixed clay to colour the mountains and edges of the pit, and he made the little figures black with charcoal, and he made the flames writhing up out of the pit red with the paint used for parts of the mining machinery.

'If you leave it here, the ants'll eat it,' said Dirk, looking with grim pleasure at the crude but effective picture.

To which Tommy shrugged. For while he was always solemnly intent on a piece of work in hand, afraid of anything that might mar it, or even distract his attention from it, once it was finished he cared for it not at all.

It was Dirk who had painted the shelf which held the other figures with a mixture that discouraged ants, and it was now Dirk who set the piece of square wood on a sheet of tin smeared with the same mixture, and balanced it in a way so it should not touch any part of the walls of the shed, where the ants might climb up.

And so Tommy went back to school, still in that mood of obstinate disaffection, to make more copies of Julius Caesar and vases of flowers, and Dirk remained with his books and his Acts of Parliament. They would be fourteen before they met again, and both knew that crises and decisions faced them. Yet they said no more than the usual: Well, so long, before they parted. Nor did they ever write to each other, although this term Tommy had a commission to send certain books and other Acts of Parliament for a purpose which he entirely approved.

Dirk had built himself a new hut in the compound, where he

lived alone, in the compound but not of it, affectionate to his mother, but apart from her. And to this hut at night came certain of the workers who forgot their dislike of the half-caste, that cuckoo in their nest, in their common interest in what he told them of the Acts and Reports. What he told them was what he had learnt himself in the proud loneliness of his isolation. 'Education,' he said, 'education, that's the key' – and Tommy agreed with him, although he had, or so one might suppose from the way he was behaving, abandoned all idea of getting an education for himself. All that term parcels came to 'Dirk, c/o Mr Macintosh', and Mr Macintosh delivered them to Dirk without any questions.

In the dim and smoky hut every night, half a dozen of the workers laboured with stubs of pencil and the exercise books sent by Tommy, to learn to write and do sums and understand the Laws.

One night Mr Macintosh came rather late out of that other hut, and saw the red light from a fire moving softly on the rough ground outside the door of Dirk's hut. All the others were dark. He moved cautiously among them until he stood in the shadows outside the door, and looked in. Dirk was squatting on the floor, surrounded by half a dozen men, looking at a newspaper.

Mr Macintosh walked thoughtfully home in the starlight. Dirk, had he known what Mr Macintosh was thinking, would have been very angry, for all his flaming rebellion, his words of resentment were directed against Mr Macintosh and his tyranny. Yet for the first time Mr Macintosh was thinking of Dirk with a certain rough, amused pride. Perhaps it was because he was a Scot, after all, and in every one of his nation is an instinctive respect for learning and people with the determination to 'get on'. A chip off the old block, thought Mr Macintosh, remembering how he, as a boy, had laboured to get a bit of education. And if the chip was the wrong colour – well, he would do something for Dirk. Something, he would decide when the time came. As for the others who were with Dirk, there was nothing easier than to sack a worker and engage another. Mr Macintosh went to his bed, dressed as usual in vest and pyjama trousers, unwashed and thrifty in candlelight.

In the morning he gave orders to one of the overseers that Dirk should be summoned. His heart was already soft with thinking about the generous scene which would shortly take place. He was going to suggest that Dirk should teach all the overseers to read and write – on a salary from himself, of course – in order that these same overseers should be more useful in the work. They might learn to mark pay-sheets, for instance.

The overseer said that Baas Dirk spent his days studying in Baas Tommy's hut – with the suggestion in his manner that Baas Dirk could not be disturbed while so occupied, and that this was on Tommy's account.

The man, closely studying the effect of his words, saw how Mr Macintosh's big, veiny face swelled, and he stepped back a pace. He was not one of Dirk's admirers.

Mr Macintosh, after some moments of heavy breathing, allowed his shrewdness to direct his anger. He dismissed the man, and turned away.

During that morning he left his great pit and walked off into the bush in the direction of the towering blue peak. He had heard vaguely that Tommy had some kind of hut, but imagined it as a child's thing. He was still very angry because of that calculated 'Baas Dirk'. He walked for a while along a smooth path through the trees, and came to a clearing. On the other side was an anthill, and on the anthill a well-built hut, draped with Christmas fern around the open front, like curtains. In the opening sat Dirk. He wore a clean white shirt, and long smooth trousers. His head, oiled and brushed close, was bent over books. The hand that turned the pages of the books had a brass ring on the little finger. He was the very image of an aspiring clerk: that form of humanity which Mr Macintosh despised most.

Mr Macintosh remained on the edge of the clearing for some time, vaguely waiting for something to happen, so that he might fling himself, armoured and directed by his contemptuous anger, into a crisis which would destroy Dirk for ever. But nothing did happen. Dirk continued to turn the pages of the books, so Mr Macintosh went back to his house, where he ate boiled beef and carrots for his dinner.

Afterwards he went to a certain drawer in his bedroom, and from it took an object carelessly wrapped in cloth which, exposed, showed itself as that figure of Dirk the boy Tommy had made and sold for five pounds. And Mr Macintosh turned and handled and pored over that crude wooden image of Dirk in a passion of curiosity, just as if the boy did not live on the same square mile of soil with him, fully available to his scrutiny at most hours of the day.

If one imagines a Judgment Day with the graves giving up their dead impartially, black, white, bronze, and yellow, to a happy reunion, one of the pleasures of that reunion might well be that people who have lived on the same acre or street all their lives will look at each other with incredulous recognition. 'So that is what you were like,' might be the gathering murmur around God's heaven. For the glass wall between colour and colour is not only a barrier against touch, but has become thick and distorted, so that black men, white men, see each other through it, but see – what? Mr Macintosh examined the image of Dirk as if searching for some final revelation, but the thought that came persistently to his mind was that the statue might be of himself as a lad of twelve. So after a few moments he rolled it again in the cloth and tossed it back into the corner of a drawer, out of sight, and with it the unwelcome and tormenting knowledge.

Late that afternoon he left his house again and made his way towards the hut on the antheap. It was empty, and he walked through the knee-high grass and bushes till he could climb up the hard, slippery walls of the antheap and so into the hut.

First he looked at the books in the case. The longer he looked the faster faded that picture of Dirk as an oiled and mincing clerk, which he had been clinging to ever since he threw the other image into the back of a drawer. Respect for Dirk was reborn. Complicated mathematics, much more advanced than he had ever done. Geography. History. *The Development of the Slave Trade in the Eighteenth Century*. *The Growth of Parliamentary Institutions in Great Britain*. This title made Mr Macintosh smile – the freebooting buccaneer examining a coastguard's notice perhaps. Mr Macintosh lifted down one book after another and smiled. Then, beside these books, he saw a pile of slight, blue pamphlets, and he examined them. *The Natives Employment Act. The Natives Juvenile Employment Act. The Natives Passes Act.* And Mr Macintosh flipped over the leaves and laughed, and had Dirk heard that laugh it would have been worse to him than any whip.

For as he patiently explained these laws and others like them to his bitter allies in the hut at night, it seemed to him that every word he spoke was like a stone thrown at Mr Macintosh, his father. Yet Mr Macintosh laughed, since he despised these laws, although in a different way, as much as Dirk did. When Mr Macintosh, on his rare trips to the city, happened to drive past the House of Parliament, he turned on it a tolerant and appreciative gaze. 'Well, why not?' he seemed to be saying. 'It's an occupation, like any other.'

So to Dirk's desperate act of retaliation he responded with a smile, and tossed back the books and pamphlets on the shelf. And then he turned to look at the other things in the shed, and for the first time he saw the high shelf where the statuettes were arranged. He looked, and felt his face swelling with that fatal rage. There was Dirk's mother, peering at him in bashful sensuality from over the baby's head, there the little girl, his daughter, squatting on spindly legs and staring. And there, on the edge of the shelf, a small, worn shape of clay which still held the vigorous strength of Dirk. Mr Macintosh, breathing heavily, holding down his anger, stepped back to gain a clearer view of those figures, and his heel slipped on a slanting piece of wood. He turned to look, and there was the picture Tommy had carved and coloured of his mine. Mr Macintosh saw the great pit, the black little figures tumbling and sprawling over into the flames, and saw himself, stick in hand, astride on his two legs at the edge of the pit, his hat on the back of his head.

And now Mr Macintosh was so disturbed and angry that he was driven out of the hut and into the clearing, where he walked back and forth through the grass, looking at the hut while his anger growled and moved inside him. After some time he came close to the hut again and peered in. Yes, there was Dirk's mother, peering bashfully from her shelf, as if to say: Yes, it's me, remember? And there on the floor was the square tinted piece of wood which said what Tommy thought of him and his life. Mr Macintosh took a box of matches from his pocket. He lit a match. He understood he was standing in the hut with a lit match in his hand to no purpose. He dropped the match and ground it out with his foot. Then he put a pipe in his mouth, filled it and lit it, gazing all the time at the shelf and at the square carving. The second match fell to the floor and lay spurting a small white flame. He ground his heel hard on it. Anger heaved up in him beyond all sanity, and he lit another match, pushed it into the thatch of the hut, and walked out of it and so into the clearing and away into the bush. Without looking behind him he walked back to his house where his supper of boiled beef and carrots was waiting for him. He was amazed, angry, resentful. Finally he felt aggrieved, and wanted to explain to someone what a monstrous injustice was Tommy's view of him. But there was no one to explain it to; and he slowly quietened to a steady dulled sadness, and for some days remained so, until time restored him to normal. From this condition he looked back at his behaviour and did not like it. Not that he regretted burning the hut, it seemed to him unimportant. He was angry at himself for allowing his anger to dictate his actions. Also he knew that such an act brings its own results.

So he waited, and thought mainly of the cruelty of fate in denying a son who might carry on his work – for he certainly thought of his work as something to be continued. He thought sadly of Tommy, who denied him. And so, his affection for Tommy was sprung again by thinking of him, and he waited, thinking of reproachful things to say to him.

When Tommy returned from school he went straight to the clearing and found a mound of ash on the antheap that was already sifted and swept by the wind. He found Dirk, sitting on a tree trunk in the bush waiting for him.

'What happened?' asked Tommy. And then, at once: 'Did you save your books?'

Dirk said: '*He* burnt it.'

'How do you know?'

'I know.'

Tommy nodded. 'All your books have gone,' he said, very grieved, and as guilty as if he had burnt them himself.

'Your carvings and your statues are burnt too.'

But at this Tommy shrugged, since he could not care about his things once they were finished. 'Shall we build the hut again now?' he suggested.

'My books are burnt,' said Dirk, in a low voice, and Tommy, looking at him, saw how his hands were clenched. He instinctively moved a little aside to give his friend's anger space.

'When I grow up I'll clear you all out, all of you, there won't be one white man left in Africa, not one.'

Tommy's face had a small half-scared smile on it. The hatred Dirk was directing against him was so strong he nearly went away. He sat beside Dirk on the tree trunk and said: 'I'll try and get you more books.'

'And then he'll burn them again.'

'But you've already got what was in them inside your head,' said Tommy, consolingly. Dirk said nothing, but sat like a clenched fist, and so they remained on the tree trunk in the quiet bush while the doves cooed and the mine-stamps thudded, all that hot morning. When they had to separate at midday to return to their different worlds, it was with deep sadness, knowing that their childhood was finished, and their playing, and something new was ahead.

And at that meal Tommy's mother and father had his school report on the table, and they were reproachful. Tommy was at the foot of his class, and he would not matriculate that year. Or any year if he went on like this.

'You used to be such a clever boy,' mourned his mother, 'and now what's happened to you?'

Tommy, sitting silent at the table, moved his shoulders in a hunched, irritable way, as if to say: Leave me alone. Nor did he feel himself to be stupid and lazy, as the report said he was.

In his room were drawing blocks and pencils and hammers and chisels. He had never said to himself he had exchanged one purpose for another, for he had no purpose. How could he, when he had never been offered a future he could accept? Now, at this time, in his fifteenth year, with his reproachful parents deepening their reproach, and the knowledge that Mr Macintosh would soon see that report, all he felt was a locked stubbornness, and a deep strength.

In the afternoon he went back to the clearing, and he took his chisels with him. On the old, soft, rotted tree trunk that he had sat on that morning, he sat again, waiting for Dirk. But Dirk did not come. Putting himself in his friend's place he understood that Dirk could not endure to be with a white-skinned person – a white face, even that of his oldest friend, was too much the enemy. But he waited, sitting on the tree trunk all through the afternoon, with his chisels and hammers in a little box at his feet in the grass, and he fingered the soft, warm wood he sat on, letting the shape and texture of it come into the knowledge of his fingers.

Next day, there was still no Dirk.

Tommy began walking around the fallen tree, studying it. It was very thick, and its roots twisted and slanted into the air to the height of his shoulder. He began to carve the root. It would be Dirk again.

That night Mr Macintosh came to the Clarkes' house and read the report. He went back to his own, and sat wondering why Tommy was set so bitterly against him. The next day he went to the Clarkes' house again to find Tommy, but the boy was not there.

He therefore walked through the thick bush to the antheap, and found Tommy kneeling in the grass working on the tree root.

Tommy said: 'Good morning,' and went on working, and Mr Macintosh sat on the trunk and watched.

'What are you making?' asked Mr Macintosh.

'Dirk,' said Tommy, and Mr Macintosh went purple and almost sprang up and away from the tree trunk. But Tommy was not looking at him. So Mr Macintosh remained, in silence. And then the useless vigour of Tommy's concentration on that rotting bit of root goaded him, and his mind moved naturally to a new decision.

'Would you like to be an artist?' he suggested.

Tommy allowed his chisel to rest, and looked at Mr Macintosh as if this were a trap. He shrugged, and with the appearance of anger, went on with his work.

'If you've a real gift, you can earn money by that sort of thing. I had a cousin back in Scotland who did it. He made souvenirs, you know, for travellers.' He spoke in a soothing and jolly way.

Tommy let the souvenirs slide by him, as another of these impositions on his independence. He said: 'Why did you burn Dirk's books?'

But Mr Macintosh laughed in relief. 'Why should I burn his books?' It seemed ridiculous to him, his rage had been against Tommy's work, not Dirk's.

'I know you did,' said Tommy. 'I know it. And Dirk does too.'

Mr Macintosh lit his pipe in good humour. For now things seemed much easier. Tommy did not know why he had set fire to the hut, and that was the main thing. He puffed smoke for a few moments and said: 'Why should you think I don't want Dirk to study? It's a good thing, a bit of education.'

Tommy stared disbelievingly at him.

'I asked Dirk to use his education, I asked him to teach some of the others. But he wouldn't have any of it. Is that my fault?'

Now Tommy's face was completely incredulous. Then he went scarlet, which Mr Macintosh did not understand. Why should the boy be looking so foolish? But Tommy was thinking: We were on the wrong track . . . And then he imagined what his offer must have done to Dirk's angry, rebellious pride, and he suddenly understood. His face still crimson, he laughed. It was a bitter, ironical laugh, and Mr Macintosh was upset – it was not a boy's laugh at all.

Tommy's face slowly faded from crimson, and he went back to work with his chisel. He said, after a pause: 'Why don't you send Dirk to college instead of me? He's much more clever than me. I'm not clever, look at my report.'

'Well, laddie . . .' began Mr Macintosh reproachfully – he had been going to say: 'Are you being lazy at school simply to force my hand over Dirk?' He wondered at his own impulse to say it; and slid off into the familiar obliqueness which Tommy ignored: 'But you know how things are, or you ought to by now. You talk as if you didn't understand.'

But Tommy was kneeling with his back to Mr Macintosh, working at the root, so Mr Macintosh continued to smoke. Next day he returned and sat on the tree trunk and watched.

Tommy looked at him as if he considered his presence an unwelcome gift, but he did not say anything.

Slowly, the big fanged root which rose from the trunk was taking Dirk's shape. Mr Macintosh watched with uneasy loathing. He did not like it, but he could not stop watching. Once he said: 'But if there's a veld fire, it'll get burnt. And the ants'll eat it in any case.' Tommy shrugged. It was the making of it that mattered, not what happened to it afterwards, and this attitude was so foreign to Mr Macintosh's accumulating nature that it seemed to him that Tommy was touched in the head. He said: 'Why don't you work on something that'll last? Or even if you studied like Dirk it would be better.'

Tommy said: 'I like doing it.'

'But look, the ants are already at the trunk – by the time you get back from your school next time there'll be nothing of it.'

'Or someone might set fire to it,' suggested Tommy. He looked steadily at Mr Macintosh's reddening face with triumph. Mr Macintosh found the words too near the truth. For certainly, as the days passed, he was looking at the new work with hatred and fear and dislike. It was nearly finished. Even if nothing more were done to it, it could stand as it was, complete.

Dirk's long, powerful body came writhing out of the wood like something struggling free. The head was clenched back, in the agony of the birth, eyes narrowed and desperate, the mouth – Mr Macintosh's mouth – tightened in obstinate purpose. The shoulders were free, but the hands were held; they could not pull themselves out of the dense wood, they were imprisoned. His body was free to the knees, but below them the human limbs were uncreated, the natural shapes of the wood swelled to the perfect muscled knees.

Mr Macintosh did not like it. He did not know what art was, but he knew he did not like this at all, it disturbed him deeply, so that when he looked at it he wanted to take an axe and cut it to pieces. Or burn it, perhaps . . .

As for Tommy, the uneasiness of this elderly man who watched him all day was a deep triumph. Slowly, and for the first time, he saw that perhaps this was not a sort of game that he played, it might be something else. A weapon – he watched

Mr Macintosh's reluctant face, and a new respect for himself and what he was doing grew in him.

At night, Mr Macintosh sat in his candle-lit room and he thought or rather *felt*, his way to a decision.

There was no denying the power of Tommy's gift. Therefore, it was a question of finding the way to turn it into money. He knew nothing about these matters, however, and it was Tommy himself who directed him, for towards the end of the holidays he said: 'When you're so rich you can do anything. You could send Dirk to college and not even notice it.'

Mr Macintosh, in the reasonable and persuasive voice he now always used, said, 'But you know these coloured people have nowhere to go.'

Tommy said: 'You could send him to the Cape. There are coloured people in the university there. Or Johannesburg.' And he insisted against Mr Macintosh's silence: 'You're so rich you can do anything you like.'

But Mr Macintosh, like most rich people, thought not of money as things to buy, things to do, but rather how it was tied up in buildings and land.

'It would cost thousands,' he said. 'Thousands for a coloured boy.'

But Tommy's scornful look silenced him, and he said hastily: 'I'll think about it.' But he was thinking not of Dirk, but of Tommy. Sitting alone in his room he told himself it was simply a question of paying for knowledge.

So next morning he made his preparations for a trip to town. He shaved, and over his cotton singlet he put a striped jacket, which half concealed his long, stained khaki trousers. This was as far as he ever went in concessions to the city life he despised. He got into his big American car and set off.

In the city he took the simplest route to knowledge.

He went to the Education Department, and said he wanted to see the Minister of Education. 'I'm Macintosh,' he said, with perfect confidence; and the pretty secretary who had been patronizing his clothes, went at once to the Minister and said: 'There is a Mr Macintosh to see you.' She described him as an old, fat, dirty man with a large stomach, and soon the doors opened and Mr Macintosh was with the spring of knowledge.

He emerged five minutes later with what he wanted, the name of a certain expert. He drove through the deep green avenues of the city to the house he had been told to go to, which was a large and well-kept one, and comforted Mr Macintosh in his faith that art properly used could make money. He parked his car in the road and walked in.

On the veranda, behind a table heaped with books, sat a middle-aged man with spectacles. Mr Tomlinson was essentially a scholar with working hours he respected, and he lifted his eyes to see a big, dirty man with black hair showing above the dirty whiteness of his vest, and he said sharply: 'What do you want?'

'Wait a minute, laddie,' said Mr Macintosh easily, and he held out a note from the Minister of Education, and Mr Tomlinson took it and read it, feeling reassured. It was worded in such a way that his seeing Mr Macintosh could be felt as a favour he was personally doing the Minister.

'I'll make it worth your while,' said Mr Macintosh, and at once distaste flooded Mr Tomlinson, and he went pink, and said: 'I'm afraid I haven't the time.'

'Damn it, man, it's your job, isn't it? Or so Wentworth said.'

'No,' said Mr Tomlinson, making each word clear, 'I advise on ancient monuments.'

Mr Macintosh stared, then laughed, and said: 'Wentworth said you'd do, but it doesn't matter, I'll get someone else.' And he left.

Mr Tomlinson watched this hobo go off the veranda and into a magnificent car, and his thought was: 'He must have stolen it.' Then puzzled and upset, he went to the telephone. But in a few moments he was smiling. Finally he laughed. Mr Macintosh was the Mr Macintosh, a genuine specimen of the old-timer. It was the phrase 'old-timer' that made it possible for Mr Tomlinson to relent. He therefore rang the hotel at which Mr Macintosh, as a rich man, would be bound to be staying, and he said he had made an error, he would be free the following day to accompany Mr Macintosh.

And so next morning Mr Macintosh, not at all surprised that the expert was at his service after all, with Mr Tomlinson, who preserved a tolerant smile, drove out to the mine.

They drove very fast in the powerful car, and Mr Tomlinson held himself steady while they jolted and bounced, and listened to Mr Macintosh's tales of Australia and New Zealand, and thought of him rather as he would of an ancient monument.

At last the long plain ended, and the foothills of greenish scrub heaped themselves around the car, and then high mountains piled with granite boulders, and the heat came in thick, slow waves into the car, and Mr Tomlinson thought: I'll be glad when we're through the mountains into the plain. But instead they turned into a high, enclosed place with mountains all around, and suddenly there was an enormous gulf in the ground, and on one side of it were two tiny tin-roofed houses, and on the other acres of kaffir huts. The mine-stamps thudded regularly, like a pulse of the heart, and Mr Tomlinson wondered how anybody, white or black, could bear to live in such a place.

He ate boiled beef and carrots and greasy potatoes with one of the richest men in the sub-continent, and thought how well and intelligently he would use such money if he had it – which is the only consolation left to the cultivated man of moderate income. After lunch, Mr Macintosh said: 'And now, let's get it over.'

Mr Tomlinson expressed his willingness, and smiling to himself, followed Mr Macintosh off into the bush on a kaffir path. He did not know what he was going to see. Mr Macintosh had said: 'Can you tell if a youngster has got any talent just by looking at a piece of wood he has carved?'

Mr Tomlinson said he would do his best.

Then they were beside a fallen tree trunk, and in the grass knelt a big lad, with untidy brown hair failing over his face, labouring at the wood with a large chisel.

'This is a friend of mine,' said Mr Macintosh to Tommy, who got to his feet and stood uncomfortably, wondering what was happening. 'Do you mind if Mr Tomlinson sees what you are doing?'

Tommy made a shrugging movement and felt that things were going beyond his control. He looked in awed amazement at Mr Tomlinson, who seemed to him rather like a teacher or professor, and certainly not at all what he imagined an artist to be.

'Well?' said Mr Macintosh to Mr Tomlinson, after a space of half a minute.

Mr Tomlinson laughed in a way which said: 'Now don't be in such a hurry.' He walked around the carved tree root, looking at the figure of Dirk from this angle and that.

Then he asked Tommy: 'Why do you make these carvings?'

Tommy very uncomfortably shrugged, as if to say: What a silly question; and Mr Macintosh hastily said: 'He gets high marks for Art at school.'

Mr Tomlinson smiled again and walked around to the other side of the trunk. From here he could see Dirk's face, flattened back on the neck, eyes half-closed and strained, the muscles of the neck shaped from natural veins of the wood.

'Is this someone you know?' he asked Tommy in an easy, intimate way, one artist to another.

'Yes,' said Tommy, briefly; he resented the question.

Mr Tomlinson looked at the face and then at Mr Macintosh. 'It has a look of you,' he observed dispassionately, and coloured himself as he saw Mr Macintosh grow angry. He walked well away from the group, to give Mr Macintosh space to hide his embarrassment. When he returned, he asked Tommy: 'And so you want to be a sculptor?'

'I don't know,' said Tommy, defiantly.

Mr Tomlinson shrugged rather impatiently, and with a nod at Mr Macintosh suggested it was enough. He said good-bye to Tommy, and went back to the house with Mr Macintosh.

There he was offered tea and biscuits, and Mr Macintosh asked: 'Well, what do you think?'

But by now Mr Tomlinson was certainly offended at this casual cash-on-delivery approach to art, and he said: 'Well, that rather depends, doesn't it?'

'On what?' demanded Mr Macintosh.

'He seems to have talent,' conceded Mr Tomlinson.

'That's all I want to know,' said Mr Macintosh, and suggested that now he could run Mr Tomlinson back to town.

But Mr Tomlinson did not feel it was enough, and he said:

'It's quite interesting, that statue. I suppose he's seen pictures in magazines. It has quite a modern feeling.'

'Modern?' said Mr Macintosh. 'What do you mean?'

Mr Tomlinson shrugged again, giving it up. 'Well,' he said, practically, 'what do you mean to do?'

'If you say he has talent, I'll send him to the university and he can study Art.'

After a long pause, Mr Tomlinson murmured: 'What a fortunate boy he is.' He meant to convey depths of disillusionment and irony, but Mr Macintosh said: 'I always did have a fancy for him.'

He took Mr Tomlinson back to the city, and as he dropped him on his veranda, presented him with a cheque for fifty pounds, which Mr Tomlinson most indignantly returned. 'Oh, give it to charity,' said Mr Macintosh impatiently, and went to his car, leaving Mr Tomlinson to heal his susceptibilities in any way he chose.

When Mr Macintosh reached his mine again it was midnight, and there were no lights in the Clarkes' house, and so his need to be generous must be stifled until the morning.

Then he went to Annie Clarke and told her he would send Tommy to university, where he could be an artist, and Mrs Clarke wept gratitude, and said that Mr Macintosh was much kinder than Tommy deserved, and perhaps he would learn sense yet and go back to his books.

As far as Mr Macintosh was concerned it was all settled.

He set off through the trees to find Tommy and announce his future to him.

But when he arrived at seeing distance there were two figures, Dirk and Tommy, seated on the trunk talking, and Mr Macintosh stopped among the trees, filled with such bitter anger at this fresh check to his plans that he could not trust himself to go on. So he returned to his house, and brooded angrily – he knew exactly what was going to happen when he spoke to Tommy, and now he must make up his mind, there was no escape from a decision.

And while Mr Macintosh mused bitterly in his house, Tommy and Dirk waited for him; it was now all as clear to them as it was to him.

Dirk had come out of the trees to Tommy the moment the two men left the day before. Tommy was standing by the fanged root, looking at the shape of Dirk in it, trying to understand what was going to be demanded of him. The word 'artist' was on his tongue, and he tasted it, trying to make the strangeness of it fit that powerful shape struggling out of the wood. He did not like it. He did not want – but what did he want? He felt pressure on himself, the faint beginnings of something that would one day be like a tunnel of birth from which he must fight to emerge; he felt the obligations working within himself like a goad which would one day be a whip perpetually falling behind him so that he must perpetually move onwards.

His sense of fetters and debts was confirmed when Dirk came to stand by him. First he asked: 'What did they want?'

'They want me to be an artist, they always want me to be something,' said Tommy sullenly. He began throwing stones at the tree and shying them off along the tops of the grass. Then one hit the figure of Dirk, and he stopped.

Dirk was looking at himself. 'Why do you make me like that?' he asked. The narrow, strong face expressed nothing but that familiar, sardonic antagonism, as if he said: 'You, too – just like the rest!'

'Why, what's the matter with it?' challenged Tommy at once.

Dirk walked around it, then back. 'You're just like all the rest,' he said.

'Why? Why don't you like it?' Tommy was really distressed. Also, his feeling was: What's it got to do with him? Slowly he understood that his emotion was that belief in his right to freedom which Dirk always felt immediately, and he said in a different voice: 'Tell me what's wrong with it?'

'Why do I have to come out of the wood? Why haven't I any hands or feet?'

'You have, but don't you see . . .' But Tommy looked at Dirk standing in front of him and suddenly gave an impatient movement: 'Well, it doesn't matter, it's only a statue.'

He sat on the trunk and Dirk beside him. After a while he said: 'How should you be, then?'

'If you made yourself, would you be half wood?'

Tommy made an effort to feel this, but failed. 'But it's not me, it's you.' He spoke with difficulty, and thought: But it's important, I shall have to think about it later. He almost groaned with the knowledge that here it was, the first debt, presented for payment.

Dirk said suddenly: 'Surely it needn't be wood? You could do the same thing if you put handcuffs on my wrists.' Tommy lifted his head and gave a short, astonished laugh. 'Well, what's funny?' said Dirk, aggressively. 'You can't do it the easy way, you have to make me half wood, as if I was more a tree than a human being.'

. Tommy laughed again, but unhappily. 'Oh, I'll do it again,' he acknowledged at last. 'Don't fuss about that one, it's finished. I'll do another.'

There was a silence.

Dirk said: 'What did that man say about you?'

'How do I know?'

'Does he know about art?'

'I suppose so.'

'Perhaps you'll be famous,' said Dirk at last. 'In that book you gave me, it said about painters. Perhaps you'll be like that.'

'Oh, shut up,' said Tommy, roughly. 'You're just as bad as *he* is.'

'Well, what's the matter with it?'

'Why have I got to *be* something? First it was a sailor, and then it was a scholar, and now it's an artist.'

'They wouldn't *have* to make me be anything,' said Dirk sarcastically.

'I know,' admitted Tommy grudgingly. And then, passionately: 'I shan't go to university unless he sends you too.'

'I know,' said Dirk at once, 'I know you won't.'

They smiled at each other, that small, shy, revealed smile, which was so hard for them because it pledged them to such a struggle in the future.

Then Tommy asked: 'Why didn't you come near me all this time?'

'I get sick of you,' said Dirk. 'I sometimes feel I don't want to see a white face again, not ever. I feel that I hate you all, every one.'

'I know,' said Tommy, grinning. Then they laughed, and the last strain of dislike between them vanished.

They began to talk, for the first time, of what their lives would be.

Tommy said: 'But when you've finished training to be an engineer, what will you do? They don't let coloured people be engineers.'

'Things aren't always going to be like that,' said Dirk.

'It's going to be very hard,' said Tommy, looking at him questioningly, and was at once reassured when Dirk said, sarcastically: 'Hard, it's going to be hard? Isn't it hard now, white boy?'

Later that day Mr Macintosh came towards them from his house.

He stood in front of them, that big, shrewd, rich man, with his small, clever grey eyes, and his narrow, loveless mouth; and he said aggressively to Tommy: 'Do you want to go to the university and be an artist?'

'If Dirk comes too,' said Tommy immediately.

'What do you want to study?' Mr Macintosh asked Dirk, direct.

'I want to be an engineer,' said Dirk at once.

'If I pay your way through the university then at the end of it I'm finished with you. I never want to hear from you and you are never to come back to this mine once you leave it.'

Dirk and Tommy both nodded, and the instinctive agreement between them fed Mr Macintosh's bitter unwillingness in the choice, so that he ground out viciously: 'Do you think you two can be together in the university? You don't understand. You'll be living separate, and you can't go around together just as you like.'

The boys looked at each other, and then as if some sort of pact had been made between them, simply nodded.

'You can't go to university anyway, Tommy, until you've done a bit better at school. If you go back for another year and work you can pass your matric. and go to university, but you can't go now, right at the bottom of the class.'

Tommy said: 'I'll work.' He added at once: 'Dirk'll need more books to study here till we can go.'

The anger was beginning to swell Mr Macintosh's face, but Tommy said: 'It's only fair. You burnt them, and now he hasn't any at all.'

'Well,' said Mr Macintosh heavily. 'Well, so that's how it is!'

He looked at the two boys, seated together on the tree trunk. Tommy as leaning forward, eyes lowered, a troubled but determined look on his face. Dirk was sitting erect, looking straight at his father with eyes filled with hate.

'Well,' said Mr Macintosh, with an effort at raillery which sounded harsh to them all: 'Well, I send you both to university and you don't give me so much as a thank you!'

At this, both faced towards him, with such bitter astonishment, that he flushed.

'Well, well,' he said. 'Well, well . . .' And then he turned to leave the clearing, and cried out as he went, so as to give the appearance of dominance: 'Remember, laddie, I'm not sending you unless you do well at school this year . . .'

And so he left them and went back to his house, an angry old man, defeated by something he did not begin to understand.

As for the boys, they were silent when he had gone.

The victory was entirely theirs, but now they had to begin again, in the long and difficult struggle to understand what they had won and how they would use it.

Events in the Skies

I once knew a man, a black man, who told me he had been brought up in a village so far from the nearest town he had to walk a day to reach it. Later he knew this 'town' was itself a village, having in it a post office, a shop, and a butcher. He had still to experience the white men's towns, which he had heard about. This was in the southern part of Africa. The villagers were subsistence farmers, and grew maize, millet, pumpkins, chickens. They lived as people have done for thousands of years except for one thing. Every few days a little glittering airplane appeared in the sky among the clouds and the circling hawks. He did not know what it was, where it came from, or where it went. Remote, unreachable, a marvel, it appeared over the forest where the sun rose, and disappeared where it went down. He watched for it. He thought about it. His dreams filled with shining and fragile emanences that could sit on a branch and sing or that ran from his father and the other hunting men like a duiker or a hare, but that always escaped their spears. He told me that when he remembered his childhood that airplane was in the sky. It connected not with what he was now, a sober modern man living in a large town, but with the tales and songs of his people, for it was not real, not something to be brought down to earth and touched.

When he was about nine his family went to live with relatives near a village that was larger than either the handful of huts in the bush or the 'town' where they had sometimes bought a little sugar or tea or a piece of cloth. There the black people worked in a small gold mine. He learned that twice a week an airplane landed in the bush on a strip of cleared land, unloaded parcels, mail, and sometimes a person, and then flew off. He was by now going to a mission school. He walked there with his elder brother and his younger sister every morning; leaving at six to get there at eight, then walked back in the afternoon. Later, when he measured distances not by the time it took to cover them, but by the miles, yards, and feet he learned in school, he knew he walked eight miles to school and eight back.

This school was his gateway to the life of riches and plenty enjoyed by white people. This is how he saw it. Motorcars, bicycles, the goods in the shops, clothes – all these things would be his if he did well in school. School had to come first, but on Saturdays and Sundays and holidays he went stealthily to the edge of the airstrip, sometimes with his brother and sister, and crouched there waiting for the little plane. The first time he saw a man jump down out of its high uptilted front his heart stopped, then it thundered, and he raced shouting exuberantly into the bush. He had not before understood that this apparition of the skies, like a moth but made out of some substance unknown to him, had a person in it: a young white man, like the storemen or the foremen in the mines. In the village of his early childhood he had played with grasshoppers, pretending they were airplanes. Now he made little planes out of the silver paper that came in the packets of cigarettes that were too expensive for his people to smoke.

With these infant models in his hands the airplane seemed close to him, and he crept out of the bush to reach out and touch it, but the pilot saw him, shouted at him – and so he ran away. In his mind was a region of confusion, doubt and delight mixed, and this was the distance between himself and the plane. He never said to himself, 'I could become a pilot when I grow up.' On the practical level what he dreamed of was a bicycle, but they cost so much – five pounds – that his father, who had one, would need a year to get it paid off. (His father had become a storeman in a mine shop, and that job, and the move to this new place, was to enable his children to go to school and enter the new world.) No, what that airplane meant was wonder, a dazzlement of possibilities, but they were all unclear. When he saw that airplane on the landing strip or, later, that one or another in the skies, it made him dream of how he would get on his bicycle when he had one, and race along the paths of the bush so fast that . . .

When he had finished four years at school he could have left. He already had more schooling than most of the children of his country at that time. He could read a little, write a little, and do sums rather well. With these skills he could get a job as a boss boy or perhaps working in a shop. But this is not what his father wanted. Because these children were clever, they had been invited to attend another mission school, and the fees meant the father had to work not only at the store job in the daytime, but at night as a watchman. And they, the children, did odd jobs on weekends and through holidays, running errands, selling fruit at the back doors of white houses with their mother. They all worked and worked; and, again, walking to and from the new school took the children four hours of every day. (I once knew a man from Czechoslovakia who said he walked six miles to school and six miles back in snow or heat or rain, because he was a poor boy, one of eleven children, and this is what he had to do to get an education. He became a doctor.)

This man, the African, at last finished school. He had understood the nature of the cloudy region in his mind where the airplane still lived. He had seen much larger planes. He knew now the shining creature of his childhood was nothing compared to the monsters that went to the big airports in the cities. A war had come and gone, and he had read in the newspapers of great battles in Europe and the East, and he understood what airplanes could be used for. The war had not made much difference to him and his family. Then his country, which until that point had been loosely ruled by Britain in a way that affected him personally very little (and he knew this was unlike some of the countries further south), became independent and had a black government. By now the family lived in the capital of the country. They had a two-room house in a township. This move, too, this bettering, was for the children. Now the brother took a job in a store as a clerk, and the sister was a nurse in the hospital, but he decided to go on learning. At last he became an accountant and understood the modern world and what had separated that poor black child he had been from the airplane. These days he might smile at his early imaginings, but he loved them. He still loved the little airplane. He said to himself: 'It was never possible for me to fly an airplane, it never occurred to me, because black men did not become pilots. But my son . . .'

His son, brought up in a town where airplanes came and went every day, said, 'Who wants to be a pilot? What a life!' He decided to be a lawyer, and that is what he is.

My friend, who told me all this, said, 'My son would never understand, never in his life, what that little plane meant to me and the kids in the bush.'

But I understood. On the farm where I grew up, once a week I watched a small airplane appear, coming from the direction of the city. It descended over the ridge into the bush on to the airstrip of the Mandora Mine, a Lonrho mine. I was transported with delight and longing. In those days, ordinary people did not fly. A lucky child might get taken up for a 'flip' around the sky, price five pounds. It was a lot of money, and I did not fly for years.

Last year I met a little Afghan girl, a refugee with her family in Pakistan. She had lived in a village that had water running through it from the mountains, and it had orchards and fields, and all her family and her relatives were there. Sometimes a plane crossed the sky from one of the larger cities of Afghanistan to another. She would run to the edge of the village to get nearer to that shining thing in the sky, and stand with her hands cradling her head as she stared up . . . up . . . . up . . . Or she called to her mother, 'An airplane, look!'

And then the Russians invaded, and one day the visiting airplane was a gunship. It thundered over her village, dropped its bombs, and flew off. The house she had lived in all her days was rubble, and her mother and her little brother were dead. So were several of her relatives. And as she walked across the mountains with her father, her uncle, her aunt, and her three surviving cousins, they were bombed by the helicopters and the planes, so that more people died. Now, living in exile in the refugee camp, when she thinks of the skies of her country she knows they are full of aircraft, day and night, and the little plane that flew over her village with the sunlight shining on its wings seems like something she once imagined, a childish dream.

Doris Lessing

Love, Again

'This is a grand novel, boldly hewn, more literary than it declares, and yielding the occasional swooning glimpse of beauty. An encounter with a magnificent mind and temperament in artistic maturity, capable of turning her equal gaze on George Eliot.'   CANDIA McWILLIAM, *Independent on Sunday*

Love, Again is the story of Sarah Durham, a sixty-year-old producer and founder of a leading fringe theatre, who commissions a play based on the journals of Julie Vairon, a beautiful and wayward nineteenth-century mulatto woman. The play captivates all who come into contact with it, and dramatically changes the lives of all who take part in it. For Sarah, the change is profound – she falls in love with two younger men, one after the other, causing her to relive her own stages of growing up, from immature and infantile love (the beautiful and androgynous Bill) to the mature love, Henry.

Love, Again is a fierce and compelling examination of the nature and origins of love, of its remorseless ability to overwhelm and surprise us.

'Lessing's mixture of passionate involvement and the capacity to stand back and take a long look at what was going on, or will go on, is unlike that of any novelist writing now, except perhaps Saul Bellow, and the late Anthony Burgess. It grips, maddens, depresses and excites the reader from the first page to the last.'
A.S. BYATT, *The Times*

'A wholly compelling book, as vigorous and thought-provoking as anything she has ever written.'
RUTH BRANDON, *New Statesman & Society*

Doris Lessing

The Fifth Child

Four children, a beautiful old house, the love of relatives and friends, Harriet and David Lovatt's life is a glorious hymn to domestic bliss and old-fashioned family values. But when their fifth child is born, a sickly and implacable shadow is cast over this tender idyll. Large and ugly, violent and uncontrollable, the infant Ben, 'full of cold dislike,' tears at Harriet's breast. Struggling to care for her new-born child, faced with a darkness and a strange defiance she has never known before, Harriet is deeply afraid of what, exactly, she has brought into the world . . .

'*The Fifth Child* has the intensity of a nightmare, a horror story poised somewhere between a naturalistic account of family life and an allegory that draws on science fiction. Read it and tremble.'   CLARE TOMALIN, *Independent*

'*The Fifth Child* is a book to send shivers down your spine, but one which it is impossible to put down until it is finished.'
Sunday Times

'A powerful fable. Like the story of Frankenstein or the Minotaur, it generates all sorts of uneasiness. Its strength is expressive not didactic. A disturbing vision, *The Fifth Child* offers a faithful if chilling reflection of the world we live in.'
Sunday Telegraph

Doris Lessing

Ben, in the World

'A wonderful novel, flawless as a black pearl'   *Daily Mail*

'Outstanding . . . A *tour de force* that poses stark questions about modern-day Britain and what it is to be human.'
                                                    Sunday Times

'*Ben, in the World* picks up the story of Ben Lovatt, the neanderthal anti-child who in *The Fifth Child* experiences the family as an engine of hatred, rejection and perfectionism mobilised against him. Now an adult, Ben inhabits the world of the modern freak: the world of the homeless, the unregistered, the unwanted. With the mind of a child in a giant, simian body, he is at once vulnerable and threatening, capable of violence and terribly dependent upon approval and trust . . . Lessing has a striking ability to illustrate human moral worth through such a simple lens. In this short, gripping and tragic novel, she conveys a powerful message about the limits of love and the destructive power of selfishness; and most of all about our brutal desire to live our lives unfettered by the helpless, by those who slow us down with their need for kindness.'   *Sunday Express*

'*Ben, In the World* is huge in scope, humanity and pathos. Lessing created a monster; her triumph is that he not only personifies the human yearning to belong, but that we also come to love him.'   *Daily Telegraph*

Doris Lessing

Under My Skin

Volume One of
My Autobiography, to 1949

'By reclaiming her life from fiction and polemic, Doris Lessing
has written the most impressive book of her career.'

PENELOPE MORTIMER

Under My Skin is the first volume of Doris Lessing's long-
awaited autobiography, beginning with her childhood in
Africa, taking us through her marriages, the birth of her children, involvement in communist politics, and ending on her
arrival in London in 1949 with the typescript of *The Grass is
Singing* in her suitcase.

More distinctive and challenging, more revealing of the mind
of its creator than any other autobiography of recent times,
Under My Skin tells the story of a young woman uncompro-
mising in every respect, who battles at every turn against her
upbringing and environment in Southern Rhodesia, who
fights for her individuality and self-determination at any cost.

'A wonderful book. One of the most vivid autobiographies I
have ever read: frighteningly candid and with a stinging
intelligence.'   *Daily Telegraph*

'Doris Lessing forges backwards and forwards through the
ideas and events of our times, and in everything she says or
does she remains about twice the size of most other writers.'

Independent

0 00 654825 8

Doris Lessing

The Four-Gated City

'A brilliant and disturbing book.'   *The Times*

The 'Children of Violence' series, a quintet of novels tracing
the life of Martha Quest from her childhood in Africa to a
post-nuclear Britain of AD 2000, first established Doris
Lessing as a great radical writer. In this, the fifth and final
volume, Martha, now middle-aged, leaves Africa for post-
war London. As housekeeper to the Coldridge family, she
watches the children in her care, the new 'children of
violence', grow up in a disintegrating world, a world career-
ing towards nuclear disaster.

'*The Four-Gated City* recreates the years of spying, the end of
austerity, Aldermaston and pop culture. A magnificent and
prophetic book.'   *Observer*